THE LAST BACHELOR IN TEXAS

EMILY MARCH

ACKNOWLEDGMENTS

My special thanks to Mary Dickerson for being such a great critique partner and friend.

For
Caitlin Michelle Williams
and
Stephanie Jeanne Knautz
in celebration of a special friendship

CHAPTER 1

"TOMORROW IS THE ANNIVERSARY. I simply must be in Memphis."

Tess McKinney pulled the phone handset away from her ear and glared at it. The tinny-sounding voice continued to yammer without pause. Tess kicked off her Jimmy Choo slingbacks, crossed her ankles, and gazed out her office window toward the hazy Hollywood hills. Her client, Jennifer Hart, was young, she reminded herself. Young and extremely talented. She was allowed a few quirks.

This, however, wasn't one of them.

"Well?" she heard. "What are you going to do about it? Tess? Tess!"

She dragged her attention away from the view and twisted her chair to get a sniff of the lavender-scented, peace-promising aromatherapy candle she kept burning on her credenza. "Jennifer, we discussed this conflict before you signed the movie contract. You specifically agreed to skip your annual trip to Graceland for the vigil. You will be on the set tomorrow morning if I have to haul you there by the hair."

"But I haven't missed an August sixteenth in Memphis in ten years. It's like a holy pilgrimage."

Tess rolled her eyes, but gentled her voice. "You pay me to manage your career, Jennifer, so listen to me. I know that staying away from Memphis this year is a big step for you, and I'm proud of you for it. When you find yourself weakening, remember that this film is shaping up to be an Oscar contender."

"But Elvis—"

Is dead. "You can send flowers. It'll be fine, Jennifer. You'll be there in heart, and that's what truly matters. Dedicate your scenes tomorrow to his memory and make them the very best you've ever done. It'll be your special tribute."

"A dedication—I like that. That's a nice idea, Tess."

Sensing that the crisis was behind them, Tess picked up a pencil and drew a line through Jennifer's name on her call return list. "Now, go wash away those tears and fix up your face. You don't want the paparazzi catching you with runny mascara."

"All right. You're right. I know that. Thank you. This has been so trying. I never expected the life of a film star could be so difficult."

Keeping the handset to her ear, Tess dropped forward and quietly banged her head against the cool dark wood of her mahogany desk. Her stapler snagged a strand of her shoulder-length blond hair, and she winced. "You'll get through this, Jennifer, and you'll be stronger for it."

"True." Jennifer released a dramatic sigh. *"Shimmer* magazine says that fire is the test of gold, and adversity is the test of strong women."

The girl had always had a tendency to overact. "Sounds like Seneca to me."

"Huh?"

"Nothing. Go to work, Jennifer. 'Bye."

Replacing the handset in its cradle, Tess lifted her gaze toward the ceiling. "Give me patience, Lord."

She said the prayer every day. Anyone who attempted to manage creative personalities needed patience at the top of their list of virtues. Lately, Tess had noticed her patience growing thin. She needed a vacation, a long weekend, at least. Maybe she'd take Friday off and drive up the coast, find a little bed and breakfast, and laze around for a couple days. That, or schedule a spa weekend. A full body massage sounded heavenly right now. She loved her job, but stress could eat her alive if she didn't manage it. But then, managing was Tess's job.

Tess was considered one of Harrison & Associates' top talent managers. She'd started with the firm as a receptionist twelve years ago, fresh off the bus from Texas with a high school diploma and little else. Over time, she'd worked her way both through college and up the Harrison & Associates ladder. Now she maintained her own list of clients, and for the most part, excepting a neurosis or six, she truly liked and respected the people she represented.

That's why, when her intercom buzzed, she didn't hesitate to respond. "Yes?"

"Mr. Muldoon is holding on line two."

"Thank you, Lena." Tess picked up the handset and punched line two. "Good morning, Jake."

"Hello, beautiful. Do you have a minute?"

For the Emmy-winning star of television's most popular legal drama and the only man with a law degree she truly admired? Always. "Sure. What's up? Have you made a decision?"

Jake had been offered a role in a feature film during *Line of Defense's* hiatus next summer, and for the past three days, they'd debated the pros and cons of taking it. On top of being drop-dead gorgeous and a great actor, Jake was one of the most intelligent men Tess knew. She considered it a great testimony to her skills and instincts that he continued to seek and value her opinion.

"I'm going to turn it down."

Smiling, she sat back in her chair. "Why?"

"Because you're right. That's not the role I should take at this point in my career."

"Have you told Sam?" she asked, referring to Jake's agent, who'd been pushing him to do the film.

"Yeah. He didn't take it well. Told me I should fire you."

She laughed. "That's the third time this month. He sent a new client my way yesterday."

"He thinks you're the best."

"I am."

"Yes, you are. So, is our date still on for tonight?"

"Business dinner," Tess corrected. After they made arrangements to meet at a small, family-owned Italian restaurant that Jake often frequented, Tess hung up the phone with a smile.

Business dinner or date. They argued the point every time. Tess didn't date her clients, period. That was bad business all around. Jake had been trying to get her to change her policy for over a year now, and the man was certainly persuasive. Tempting, too. Women all across America—all across the world—fantasized about Jake Muldoon. But Tess had an inviolate list of men she'd never date. Clients, actors, and lawyers occupied three out of the top five slots, and Jake, though sexy, smart, and genuinely a nice guy, was guilty on all three counts.

Darn it.

The thought saddened her. Tess loved her job, loved living in L.A., loved her friends, her house, her car, her yoga class. She lived a full, busy life. Still, though she hated to admit it, at the end of that full, busy day, Tess was often lonely. She wanted a man in her life. One who mattered. A man who could be her family.

"Oh, stop it." Restless now, she took a look at her calendar for the rest of the afternoon. She knew just how to cure blue thoughts like these. She could squeeze in half an hour. It wouldn't hurt for her next appointment to wait on her a few minutes.

Standing, she grabbed her purse from its usual space on the credenza, blew out her lavender candle, and headed for the door. "Lena, I'm going out."

Her secretary glanced up in surprise. Her gaze quickly shifted to the wall clock. "You have Mr. Holbrook scheduled for two."

"I know. I'll be back in time." It seldom took her a full thirty minutes to buy a pair of shoes. With a wave, she exited the office and headed for the elevator.

Shoes were Tess's vice. She couldn't resist them. The owner of the boutique down the block kept a generous supply in her size, and as soon as Tess walked in the door, Linda started bringing them out. Flats, heels, sandals, sneakers—Tess had them by the dozens. She'd considered seeing a shrink about her compulsive shoe shopping, but decided that as far as neuroses go, in Los Angeles, a shoe habit was too tame for therapy.

Tess loved shoes. Buying them made her feel good, so she indulged herself. She knew plenty of people in the entertainment business in L.A. who had habits much more destructive than buying shoes. "So sue me," she muttered, then promptly bit her tongue.

Since that nuisance suit a disgruntled wannabe actor had filed against her last fall—the lawsuit that put lawyers on her Do Not Date list—she'd tried to quit using that expression. No sense borrowing trouble.

Just as the elevator bell rang to signal the car's arrival, Lena rushed out of the office. "Tess, thank God I caught you. You've a phone call. It's your sister. She says it's an emergency."

Tess hesitated. Chloe's emergencies ran the gamut from split ends to broken engagements to civil disobedience arrests. Four years younger than Tess at twenty-eight, Chloe was beautiful, vain, willful, stubborn, and more than a little selfish. She went through phases as often as the moon, and each time she changed men. In the past ten years she'd been a Buddhist, a vegetarian, an evangelical Catholic, an environmentalist, a candle maker, a Southern Baptist, and a singer in a mosh band—and those were just the ones Tess knew about. But Chloe was Tess's only sister, and Tess loved her.

"Tell her I'll be right there."

Back in her office, Tess kicked off her shoes, poured herself a glass of sweet tea—that southern habit that persisted much longer than had her Texas drawl—lifted the telephone receiver, and punched the flashing light. "Hello, Chloe."

"Tess!" Chloe sobbed. "Oh, Tess, I'm in trouble."

Tess's stomach took a roll. Something in her sister's voice said it wasn't split ends this time. "What's wrong?"

"He had somewhere to go, Tess. Now, of all times. He's gone, and I'm all alone."

Hmm...a man had left Chloe instead of her leaving him? That was unusual. No wonder the histrionics. "I'm sorry, honey. It's hard when a man lets you down, but just give it a little time. It's a cliché, but true, that time heals all wounds."

"I don't have time. I have two weeks, tops. I'm alone, Tess, and I can't do this alone. You have to come help me. You have to come to Texas." She burst into sobs.

Texas? Chloe was back in Texas? What happened to Oregon and the hot-blooded tree hugger? She hadn't mentioned breaking up with him, although that shouldn't surprise Tess. Ever since she'd criticized the conservationist for getting Chloe arrested that last time, they'd avoided the topic of men in their phone conversations. "Hush, Chloe. Get hold of yourself. Come on out to L.A., and we'll work through this together. I'll buy you a ticket. You can probably get a flight out tonight. Where in Texas are you? Which airport is closest?"

"No! I can't go anywhere. You're not listening. You have to come to Brazos Bend. My OB won't let me travel, and besides, I must be here when Snake comes home!"

Oh-Bee? Oh-Bees and snakes? What had she gotten herself involved in now?

Then another possibility occurred to her, and the breath whooshed from Tess's body. Did she mean OB as in ob-gyn? As in..."Obstetrician? Chloe, did you just tell me you're pregnant?"

"Yes. Very pregnant. Very, very pregnant. I need you, Tess. Please come."

Oh, Chloe. Tess's heart pounded. She sank into her chair as questions swirled in her mind. Finally, she asked the scariest. "Who or what is Snake?"

"He's the father. We hooked up when we were riding with the Devil's Own. We've been together over a year, Tess. He's a really good Harley mechanic."

A motorcycle gang? *And I thought the commune of candle makers was bad.*

A combination of annoyance and hurt stole through Tess. Her sister had been pregnant almost nine months. She might have thought to mention it before now.

Closing her eyes, she set aside bruised feelings and cut to the chase. "Let me get this straight. You're pregnant with this Snake person's baby, and he's abandoned you in some hellhole in Texas."

"Brazos Bend is a nice town, and Snake didn't abandon me. He's delivering a car to someone back East. He does that for extra money sometimes. He wasn't supposed to be gone this long, so

I'm...well...he'll be back. I know he will. Except maybe not in time. Please come, Tess."

Chloe was her only sister. Her only living relative. What choice did she have? Tess grabbed a lighter from her desk drawer and relit her lavender aromatherapy candle." I'll be on the next plane."

CHAPTER 2

SPRAWLED on a sofa in front of the trailer's living room window, Chloe McKinney absently rubbed the huge mound of her belly as she watched Nick Sutherland's Porsche rattle its way up the rutted dirt road. Heat rose in visible waves from the black metal, and for once she didn't envy him his car. Black cars absorbed the summer heat. She wondered why he drove the Porsche today instead of his red Ferrari.

The undercarriage of the low-slung auto scraped across a rock, and she winced. He'd have been smarter to bring his truck out here rather than one of his sports cars. Chloe appreciated beautiful things, and she hated to see them damaged.

Once upon a time, she'd been beautiful. Snake once told her she was the most beautiful woman he'd ever laid. That was before he got her pregnant. Before she'd gained all this weight. Fifty-one pounds at last count. And still counting.

Emotion clogged her throat, and tears stung her eyes. She turned her face toward the oscillating fan set three feet in front of her and blinked back the tears. Never mind that she felt like one of the whales she'd seen swimming in the Pacific when she volunteered for Save the Whales. She'd be damned if she'd let Nick Sutherland catch her having a pity party.

Besides, she dared not let him see her soft side. He'd take advantage of it sure as spit. The man was a silver-tongued shark. She'd be damned if she'd let him talk her right out of her home.

The Porsche rolled to a halt, and the sweet purr of a fine engine went silent. Chloe's gaze returned to the window in time to see the driver's door swing open and the long, tall Texan unfold from the car. She sighed. She did appreciate beautiful things.

Since he often ate lunch at the same time as Chloe at the soda fountain at Harmon Lanes, she was accustomed to seeing him in everyday work clothes—jeans and a T-shirt. Nick Sutherland certainly filled out a pair of Wranglers. Today, however, his business must have included something other than remodeling work because he wore what Chloe thought of as his "Nicholas" clothes—a designer suit and all the high-dollar trimmings. Today's version included an elegant charcoal gray pin-striped suit with a pale pink shirt and tie and buffed mahogany oxfords. Now, any other man in Brazos Bend would catch hell for wearing a pink shirt. Not Nicholas Sutherland. He'd still ooze masculinity if he wore pink sneakers and socks with purple pompoms.

Tall, with dark hair and broad shoulders worthy of a Dallas Cowboy, he still caused a stir around town despite having lived here over a year. Not too many gazillionaires moved to Brazos Bend. The women in town especially went nutzo over him. He was a gorgeous, powerful, and wealthy alpha male who every so often betrayed a wounded heart. Females found that combination irresistible. Rumor had it that he'd moved here because he'd suffered some sort of personal heartache and wanted to change his life. Whatever the reason, every single woman in Brazos Bend wished for the chance to soothe his troubled soul.

Well, not every single woman, since she technically was still a single woman, and she was committed to Snake.

Now if only Snake would return the favor.

"Stop it," Chloe scolded herself. "He'll be back." Hadn't he thrown away the riding T-shirt, the one that read, "If You Can Read This— The Bitch Fell Off," because she'd asked?

She watched as Nick reached into the car and removed a large, fluffy teddy bear with a bright yellow bow wrapped around his neck. Her breath caught in delight. Oh, how cute!

Okay, so the teddy bear was clearly a bribe. But, oh, how she loved to get presents.

Nicholas crossed the yard and climbed the wooden front steps. Rapping on the screen door, he said, "Chloe? It's Nick Sutherland."

If she wasn't beached on the sofa, she'd get up and meet him at the door. She didn't want him inside the trailer. The heat was a killer. She only had one fan, and she didn't want to share. Plus, the place was cluttered. Dishes lay piled in the sink. The trash needed emptying. One of her jumbo-sized maternity bras dangled in plain sight on the knob of her bedroom door.

Oh, well. Too pregnant to worry about good impressions or good manners, Chloe remained seated and called out, "Come in."

Hinges creaked as the door swung open. "Hello, Chloe. How are you feeling?"

The kindness in his voice combined with the gentleness in his look and the teddy bear in his arms threatened her composure.

"I'm feeling divine, thank you for asking." Determined not to cry, Chloe went on the offensive. "Like they say. Feel good, look good. You must be feeling pretty fine yourself, all dressed up in your suit and tie. Did you go to court today, lawyer man? Send somebody to prison five to life?"

"Actually, I attended a funeral in Dallas for a former neighbor of mine."

"Oh, bummer." Chloe could be sensitive upon occasion. "He was a friend?"

"She was a good friend. She loved hockey, big band music, and the color pink. She died of breast cancer at age thirty-two."

"That's awful. So young. My sister is thirty-two. I can't imagine her...I'm sorry for your loss, Nick." Compassion made her reach out and twist the fan base, sharing her precious air. She motioned toward the chair opposite her. "Here. Have a seat, please, and introduce me to your companion."

He gave those stupendous shoulders a little shake as if to throw off sad thoughts, then smiled. "A gift for the baby."

"Thank you," she said, graciously accepting the plush animal. "He's darling. I think I'll name him Honeybear. However, if he's a bribe, you've wasted your time and money. I'm staying put."

"No bribe. Just a simple gift." He set the bear on the sofa beside her. "Those in the know told me you'll receive mostly practical items at your baby shower tonight, so I thought I'd give you something impractical."

"That's so nice. I've always loved impractical."

"You're welcome, and as far as time and money goes, it's mine to waste."

Chloe snorted, but she couldn't stop her hand from stroking the downy animal. "Your money or the Widow Duncan's? Don't lawyers charge people an hourly rate?"

"Let's say my practice in Brazos Bend is unusual and leave it at that." He beguiled her with his crooked smile, then changed the subject, catching her by surprise. "Have you heard from Snake?"

Her stomach took a long, nervous roll. "Why?"

"He's been gone quite a while now, hasn't he?"

"So?"

"Will he be back before the baby's born?"

Chloe ground her teeth together. She wished he'd just go. Reason reminded her Nick Sutherland wasn't at fault here, but he wasn't helping any by bringing all this up. He had no business asking those questions. Asking Mrs. Duncan's questions. Questions for which Chloe still didn't have answers.

Quietly, Nick said, "You can't stay here alone, Chloe."

"I most certainly can," she replied, forcing herself to stay calm. "It's Snake's house, and he told me I could stay here. That nasty old busybody mother of his needs to keep her nose in her own business."

"Mrs. Duncan owns this land, and thus has a legitimate interest in what is parked on it. However, all legal issues aside"—Nick gazed pointedly around the trailer—"this place isn't healthy for you and your child."

Chloe bristled. "I keep it clean. Maybe it's been a while since I've been able to get down on my hands and knees, but I can do an okay job with a mop. It's my home, and it's—"

11

"Not air-conditioned." Nicholas nodded toward the oscillating fan. "Chloe, it's August in Texas. This trailer is like an oven."

She lifted her chin. "I like the heat. And you're supposed to keep the house warm for babies."

Nick pinned her with a skeptical look.

"Okay, maybe not this warm, but I'm going to buy a new window unit next time I go to town. Snake left me some money."

Thirty-seven dollars and twenty-nine whole cents. She'd found it yesterday stuck in the pocket of an old pair of jeans he'd left behind. "Besides, pioneers didn't have air-conditioning, and they made out okay. Otherwise, we wouldn't be here now. All the babies would have died on the prairie."

"If they'd all been born inside this trailer, you're right." Sighing, Nick continued, "Okay, think about this instead. You're a long way out from town here, Chloe. A long way from the hospital. From doctors. The cops."

"Cops?" Her muscles tensed. "Why do you say cops?"

Nick waited a measured beat before saying, "You're a woman alone. Soon, a woman and child alone. What if you need help?"

"Snake will come back." She folded her arms and propped them on her stomach. "We love each other."

"He's a lucky man to have your love. Once he comes home, there is nothing to stop y'all from moving back out here."

"I am not leaving. This is where Snake wants me to be." Besides, she didn't have the money to live anywhere else.

Nicholas leaned forward and propped his elbows on his knees. "The Widow Duncan won't let you stay here, Chloe. She's adamant about it. Snake might own a half-share of this mobile home with his mother, but since she owns the land outright, Snake's share isn't enough. If you won't leave, she's determined to have you evicted."

"What sort of lady evicts a pregnant woman from a trailer house?"

"She believes she's protecting her grandchild. She's offering you a place to stay."

"With her!" Chloe scowled at him. "I'd rather live in an outhouse than live with that woman. And you! I can't believe you're siding with her. What kind of lawyer are you, anyway?"

"A retired one, last I checked," he muttered. Frustration flashed in his eyes, then he sighed. "Look, Chloe. She has the legal right to force you out of here. Help me help you. Let's figure out a way both you and Widow Duncan can be happy."

"She doesn't really want me to live with her. She's just being mean."

"You probably shouldn't have thrown Jell-O at her at the Piccadilly in front of her Sunday school class."

"She shouldn't have told everyone I'm not good enough for Snake." It was because of the weight gain. Chloe just knew it. How fair was that? "If I hear her say one more time that she only gained twelve pounds carrying Snake, I'm going to have morning sickness all over her orthopedic shoes!"

"Herbert. Mrs. Duncan always uses his real name." Nick sat back, considered her, then said, "I know of a nice place in town that would be perfect for you and the baby."

"I won't leave here, Nick. I won't. My sister's flying in from California. She'll take care of me. She always does. I won't be alone, and we'll buy an air conditioner, and everything will be okay."

Chloe watched the lawyer process this new information, and the subtle change in his expression told her he'd decided to wait and argue his case with Tess. Well, Chloe couldn't wait to see that. Nick might be a hotshot negotiator, he might be the best attorney in Texas, but Chloe would bet those last thirty-odd dollars that once her sister came to town, Nicholas Sutherland would finally meet his match.

CHAPTER 3

"BRAZOS BEND, TEXAS," Tess read aloud as she drove her rented Lexus sedan past the green and white city limit sign a little after eight that evening. Deserted streets and blinking traffic lights fulfilled her preconceived notion of the town two hours west of Fort Worth. "Welcome to Mayberry on Valium."

Chloe's directions took Tess past a charming town square where a gazebo trimmed in white mini-lights sat at the center of a park. With no traffic to interfere, Tess slowed the car and glanced around. Ornate streetlights illuminated the park area. A brick walk meandered past wrought-iron benches and beneath the spreading boughs of huge oak trees. Flowers bloomed in riots of color everywhere she looked. Tess had to give the small town credit. She couldn't remember the last time she'd seen a city park this warm and welcoming, especially at night.

More streetlights and modern spotlights added to the illumination provided by the strings of lights that outlined the buildings surrounding the park. Carved stones set above the doorways dated construction to the 1880s. Striped awnings added a festive air, even in the absence of people.

At the stop sign, Tess turned right. The bowling alley where Chloe had told her to meet her if she arrived before ten o'clock should be coming up. There it was—a red, white, and blue neon sign shaped like a bowling pin. Harmon Lanes.

"Must be thirty cars in the parking lot," she murmured. Obviously, this was the small town's hot spot on Monday night.

The tires of the Lexus crunched on the gravel parking lot. Tess parked, switched off the ignition, and climbed out of the car. Heat hit her like a fist, the nighttime temperature continuing to hover in the nineties.

She stood staring at the neon lights on the building. A strange sensation rolled through her stomach, and it took her a moment to recognize it. She was nervous. The fact that she was nervous annoyed her.

It shouldn't be this way. Chloe was her sister, the only family Tess had left. They should share more than occasional telephone conversations. They should be friends, confidantes. They should spend holidays together. They should shop for shoes together. That's what sisters did.

"That's what we'll do," she declared, punching the button on the keyless remote to lock the car. "Chloe and me and her baby."

Her baby. Wow. Maybe it'd be a girl. A little Chloe. Imagine that. "I wonder if the world is ready."

Tess slung her purse over her shoulder and started for the door. A couple exited the building as she reached it. They smiled at her and said hello, and the man stepped back to hold the door open for her. *Welcome to the South.*

The smells hit her the moment she walked in the door. Not bad odors, just a strange combination. Popcorn and perfume and...perm solution?

The sounds were more what she expected. Balls rolling down wooden alleys, the hard clatter of pin striking pin, the buzz of conversation spiced with laughter. It was a happy, relaxing sound. Her lips lifted in a little smile as she gazed around the room, looking for her sister.

"Miss McKinney?"

Tess turned toward the pleasant male voice. Her first impression placed him with the computer whizzes of Silicon Valley rather than the bowlers of Brazos Bend. Mid-twenties, she'd guess. Tall and lanky, he had a long, thin face, freckles, and auburn hair. He wore a Texas-friendly smile.

"Yes, I'm Tess McKinney."

"I thought you must be. You and Chloe share a strong family resemblance. I'm Stewart Mooney, and Chloe asked me to watch for you. I'm a friend of hers. We met at the library a few months ago. Chloe is a voracious reader, although you must know that. Has she always been a sci-fi fan? That's how we got to be friends, you see. We're both big into sci-fi."

Tess couldn't help but smile at him. So filled with enthusiasm, so eager to please, if the man had a tail he'd be wagging it right now. "She liked fantasy novels when she was a child. I thought she read mostly self-help books now."

"Self-help? Oh, no. Not that I've noticed."

"Good." That had been another one of Chloe's phases. Every week she'd had a new condition to overcome.

Tess glanced around the bowling alley, searching for her sister. "Chloe asked me to meet her here. Do you know—"

"They're having the shower back in the community room. It's a female-only event. I know in other places it's become popular for men to attend gift showers, but in Brazos Bend we're still traditional about those types of things. In fact, I probably should warn you that some folks in town were against having the baby shower. Because she's a...well...nontraditional mother."

As in unwed, Tess supposed. Welcome to small-town Texas.

"The community room is this way." Stewart motioned right.

As they walked, he explained to her about the hodgepodge that was Harmon Lanes. Established in the years following World War II, Harmon Lanes had evolved into something bigger than a simple bowling alley after a tornado leveled much of the town back in the 1960s. The storm's path took it just north of the square and destroyed many of Brazos Bend's churches and much of its commercial space. Jack Harmon, the owner of the bowling alley, responded by closing off half his bowling lanes and making the area available for meeting space.

Stewart pointed toward what first appeared to be an office with a door and a large plate glass window. "That's Profile Beauty Salon. Jack remodeled a storeroom into a beauty shop for his wife's hairdresser. Over there is our little restaurant, with the soda fountain he salvaged from the drugstore after the tornado blew through it."

Tess read the sign above another glass-fronted room: "Harmon Lanes Gift and Antique Shop."

"The gift shop came later," Stewart explained, noting her interest. "It's now one of the most successful shops in town. In fact, you might want to make a stop in there. I can't help but notice you don't have a gift. Your sister is registered at Harmon Gifts, so you can get her something she needs. They stay open late on Monday because it's bowling league night."

Well. She'd certainly received her marching orders. In the gift shop, Tess chose a cellophane-wrapped basket of diaper-changing supplies. She signed a card while the teenager running the register tied a blue-and-pink bow around the handle.

Tess was tired and stressed and anxious to see her sister. She walked with quick, determined steps toward the double doors marked "Community Room."

Smiling, she thanked Stewart for his help, then pushed open the door and stepped inside.

The room was empty. A half-eaten sheet cake, used punch cups, and cake plates were piled upon a tray. Unwrapped boxes sat stacked on a table. Baby monitors, boxes of diapers, an infant carrier, Tess noted. A crib, a cradle, and clothing. But no Chloe.

The door opened behind Tess, and she swung around. An attractive blond in her mid-thirties smiled at Tess. "Are you looking for Chloe McKinney's shower?"

"Yes."

"You must be Tess." The blond woman set down the empty punch cups she carried, then extended her hand. "I'm Kate Cooper. So nice to meet you."

Tess shook hands. "It appears I'm too late."

"Oh, no. Not at all." She ladled yellow punch into a cup. "In fact, this is great timing. Chloe has worked herself into a tizzy, and I think she needs you."

"What's wrong?"

Kate Cooper winced. "Oh, one of Brazos Bend's old busybodies said something critical about her weight, and then Snake Duncan's mother showed up with a cheap gift and an eviction notice."

"An eviction notice!"

"Yeah. I wouldn't worry too much about that. Nicholas Sutherland is a stand-up guy. He's the lawyer Mrs. Duncan talked into drawing up the papers. He'll watch out for Chloe."

Tess smiled grimly. Damned lawyers. "Where's my sister?"

"She's crying in the bathroom."

That, Tess knew from experience, was not a good sign. "Which way?"

Kate led Tess out of the community room, then down a hallway. Taking a right into another corridor, Tess halted abruptly. The half-dozen women wearing worried expressions huddled around the ladies' room door looked up when Kate Cooper announced, "Her sister's here."

She felt like Moses at the Red Sea as the crowd parted before her. As she placed her hand on the door to push it open, a woman wearing dangling grape earrings reached out and patted her shoulder. "Good luck, dear."

Oh, lovely.

The restroom smelled like vanilla potpourri, and to Tess's surprise contained a sitting area with a large lighted mirror and vanity, a small floral love seat, and two wingback chairs. No normal, slightly dingy ladies' room for a place like Harmon Lanes. Beyond the sitting room in the stall section, Tess heard the rattle of a toilet paper roll and the honk of a nose being blown. Tess set her purse and gift basket on the vanity and waited for Chloe to emerge.

If she hadn't recognized the sound of her sobs, Tess might not have recognized the woman who shuffled into the sitting room. She'd gained weight, true. A lot of weight. But the rest—from her dowdy lace-trimmed maternity dress to her ragged, untended fingernails to her—oh, my—total lack of makeup, the Chloe McKinney Tess knew and loved had gone missing. More shocking, frightening even, was her sister's choice of footwear. Maybe pregnancy had swollen Chloe's feet, and she couldn't fit into her shoes anymore. But couldn't she find a pair of sandals'? This was her baby shower. She was the star of the evening. Why in the world was she wearing house slippers?

Oh no, she's really let herself go.

"Chloe?"

Brown wounded-doe eyes shifted toward her. "Tess!"

Tears bursting anew, Chloe collapsed in her arms.

Tess grabbed hold tight, then guided her sister awkwardly toward the love seat. Chloe's tears swelled to sobs as she sank onto the seat. "Hush now," Tess said in soothing tone. "Calm down. It's all right. I'm here now."

"Thank goodness," Chloe gasped between sobbing hiccups. "Everything's falling apart. Everything is so mixed up. I'm so mixed up. I don't know what to do anymore, Tess."

She's never known what to do.

Tired from traveling, weary from worry, Tess reached inside herself for patience. She came up empty. "What are you going to do?" she repeated, plopping down beside her sister. "I would think that's obvious. You're going to have a baby, Chloe. A baby isn't a hobby or a cause. Motherhood is not a phase you can abandon or outgrow. Motherhood is for life."

"I know that!" Chloe clutched her belly protectively. She met Tess's gaze, her eyes gleaming and fearful. "I know! That's why...I can't...what if...if..."

"What, Chloe?"

"What if Snake doesn't come back for me?" she wailed.

Tess sensed that her sister seldom voiced that particular fear, and both her heart and frustration crumbled. "It'll be okay, honey. I promise. We'll figure something out."

"I have a job. I work here, at Harmon Lanes. At the beauty shop, actually. I do nails." When Tess glanced down at her sister's neglected nails, Chloe added, "I'm on maternity leave."

Tess was happy to hear the defensive note in Chloe's voice rather than the hopelessness she'd heard moments ago.

Chloe grabbed another tissue from the box on the end table and blew her nose. "I have a place to live. Sort of. It's Snake's home. He grew up in Brazos Bend."

"I met a few people on my way to the bathroom," Tess said. "Someone said something about an eviction notice?"

"It's his mother. She's giving me a terrible time. She's an awful, wicked woman." Chloe told a long, involved tale involving her boyfriend's mother and green Jell-O and mean spirits. She made Widow Duncan sound like a small-town version of Cruella DeVille.

When Chloe had completed her tale, she sniffed hard, then squared her shoulders. "Snake told me I could stay there, and I refuse to let anyone make me leave."

"That's the spirit." Tess reached out and tucked an errant strand of Chloe's dark-honey hair behind her ear. "We'll fight the old bat and her lawyer, and we'll win. Don't worry."

"I knew you'd help me. But that eviction notice...I don't know, Tess. They say Nick Sutherland is an awfully good lawyer."

"Psst." Tess dismissed him with a twist of her wrist. "I'm an awfully good manager, and I know just how to handle lawyers. Believe me. No small-town Texas shyster is going to get the best of me. Now." She rose gracefully to her feet and brushed a piece of lint from her black silk slacks. "How about we rejoin the others, I grab a piece of cake, then we wrap this party up and head to your place. You can show me all the gifts you received."

Chloe nodded, her smile revealing the natural beauty Tess was accustomed to seeing. "Did you bring me a present?"

"Ah, now you're feeling more like your old self, aren't you?" Tess handed her the gift basket, and they ooh'd and aah'd over the contents for a moment, then rejoined the baby shower. Chloe apologized prettily for her outburst, and the ladies of Brazos Bend graciously blamed it all on hormones.

Twenty minutes later, the party wound down. Since all the gifts wouldn't fit in Tess's rental car, Kate Cooper offered to drive Chloe home, as previously planned. For a moment, Tess doubted her sister could hoist herself up into Kate's SUV, but Stewart Mooney arrived just in time to provide a helping hand.

Tess actually felt hopeful and more than a little excited as she followed the truck down a narrow farm road. They were having a baby. She was going to be an aunt.

"Auntie Tess," she said aloud. Good. That's good. She wondered what names Chloe had chosen. Please not something from her hippie phase, like Amber Dawn or Twinkle Starlight, she thought.

Maybe it'd snow in Brazos Bend tomorrow, too.

The drive took longer than Tess had anticipated. Twenty minutes after leaving the community center, they passed a moonlit vineyard and a pretty Spanish-style house. Could this be Chloe's home? Tess could see why she wouldn't want to leave. When the truck in front of her passed the driveway, she murmured, "Obviously not."

Her thoughts turned to Snake's mother and her eviction notice, which in turn made Tess think about the attorney. Nicholas Sutherland. Chloe had called him Nick. Kate Cooper said he was a stand-up guy. Yeah, right. What sort of stand-up guy would help evict a pregnant woman from her home?

Kate's SUV slowed down, and her right turn signal began to blink. Tess didn't see an electric light in sight, and concern niggled at her mind. This was the middle of nowhere.

Her car bounced on the rutted dirt road, and her concern deepened to worry. When an animal dashed across the road in front of her car and she recognized the gleaming golden eyes of a coyote, her worry turned to fear. Then they arrived at Chloe's trailer.

In the privacy of her car, Tess let out a scream.

CHAPTER 4

NICK SUTHERLAND LOVED Brazos Bend mornings. He made it his habit to awaken before dawn, then take his coffee to the porch swing, where he'd sit and listen to birdsong and see the brilliant colors of dawn steal across the sky. He'd watch cottontail rabbits, make tracks in the dew-coated grass and sit silent and still as deer slipped from the woods behind his house to drink at the banks of the small creek that ran at the bottom of the hill. Following his second cup of coffee, he'd shower, pull on a T-shirt and jeans, grab a bagel and his tools, climb into his beloved old beat-up Ford F-100 pickup, and commute to work. It took him four minutes on a slow day.

Upon arriving at the eighty-three-year-old Hutton Hotel, he'd spend a few minutes anticipating the day to come. Soon he'd hear the sounds of saws and hammers, drills and workmen happy to be employed. He'd inhale the smell of sawdust and paint and the chalky scent of plaster. Then he'd wander to his own pet project, the renovation of the faded Crystal Ballroom.

While his contractors converted the rest of the hotel to a modern, first-class assisted living center for Brazos Bend's aging population, Nick labored to restore the ballroom to the majesty of its past, when the classic stars of Hollywood had dined and danced beneath the light of the same glittering chandelier that hung above him now.

Nick loved classic movies, and he got a kick from knowing that the stars of some of his favorite films had once graced this very room with their glamour. The old-timers in town told stories about the Hutton Hotel's heyday that made Nick green with envy. Imagine pouring champagne for Clark Gable and Carole Lombard as Mr. Donahue had, or checking Dorothy Lamour's fur as Kitty Taylor had back then. How cool was that?

Within the past few years, Nick had dined with movie stars, danced with performers on Broadway, and attended a Lakers game with a television actress. They were all beautiful, intriguing women, but to Nick's mind, they simply didn't have the appeal of those grande dames of Hollywood. If he'd had a chance to dance with Katharine Hepburn—well—he'd have probably made the Three Stooges look graceful.

On this particular morning, Nick went directly to work in the ballroom, resuming his repair of the carved oak molding that rimmed the ceiling and doors. Nick worked happily with his saw and sander for some time. Ten months ago, he had a difficult time imagining that someone like Ginger Rogers had ever entered this place. Today, he could all but see her taking a spin across the dance floor.

As the town church bells tolled nine A.M., he climbed a ladder to replace a section of trim above the door leading to the kitchen. Noting missing screws in the exit sign, he decided to fix that, too. Moments later, a feminine screech rose above the whine of his electric drill.

"What in the world were you people thinking, letting a pregnant woman stay alone in a place like that?"

Nick didn't recognize the voice, but he lowered his power tool and turned his head to look at the woman.

He damned near fell off his ladder.

She was every classic movie star rolled into one spectacular package. Betty Grable legs. A Greta Garbo face. Jean Harlow curves. A pinup girl in a bright yellow sundress come to life in his bedroom. *Ballroom, Sutherland. Ballroom.*

"Mr. Sutherland? Did you hear me?"

Annoyance simmered in brown eyes flecked with gold and framed by long, lush lashes. She had high cheekbones, a creamy complexion, and thick, wavy, shoulder-length blond hair. Even one of those qualities would have made her beautiful; putting them all together made her exquisite.

That's without taking the lips into account. Thick, red, moist and bow-shaped. A man looked at them and imagined where he wanted them. Dreamed of what they could do.

His personal fantasy had come to Brazos Bend.

"Well, you're the first lawyer I've ever known who has trouble speaking. You *are* Nicholas Sutherland?"

"Nick," he absently replied. "Nick Sutherland. Folks here in town shortened it, and I decided I like it."

"I'm Tess McKinney, Chloe McKinney's sister. I need to speak with you about the eviction notice you drafted."

He snapped back to attention. "Oh. Just a moment."

Climbing down from his ladder, Nick wondered if he'd heard her first question correctly over the sound of his drill. Did she *want* her sister to be evicted from Snake's trailer?

He set the drill on the floor, then wiped his dusty hand on his thigh and extended it for a handshake. "Welcome to Brazos Bend, Ms. McKinney."

"Thank you." Her firm handshake didn't disguise the softness of her skin. "I apologize for interrupting your work, but I was led me to believe this was your law office."

"I don't have an office because I don't practice law anymore. Not if I can help it, anyway. I just do favors for folks now and then."

"Oh. I see. So this—" She held up the eviction notice. "This is a favor for Mrs. Duncan?"

Nick shook his head. "I consider this eviction to be as much a favor to Chloe as to Widow Duncan. I'm not trying to be a jerk to your sister, Ms. McKinney, but that trailer is no place for a baby."

"I completely agree, and that brings me back to my first question. How can you allow this to continue for another ten days?"

Nick tugged a screwdriver from the leather tool belt tied around his hips and absently flipped it, caught it, and flipped it again as he considered her. Obviously, big sister hadn't had any better luck talking Chloe out of that trailer than he had. "I take it you'd like her to leave sooner?"

"Oh, yes." Determination flashed in those gorgeous eyes. "I intend for her to leave tonight. I just need a little help making that happen."

"She refused to go?"

It was as if he'd opened the floodgates out at Possum Kingdom Lake. "Can you explain to me what it is about that place that's making her act so unreasonable? It's a dump. An un-air-conditioned, uncomfortable, rodent-infested rat hole. Or to be accurate, I should say *possum* hole. She has possums out there. They got into the trash can last night. I didn't know you had to all but padlock the lid on to keep them out. I live in L.A. I deal with snakes on a daily basis, the two-legged kind, not possums. Which brings me to my next question. Where is this Snake person, and when is he coming back? What kind of man leaves his pregnant girlfriend so he can drive a Maserati to Philadelphia? I'm telling you, Mr. Sutherland, I'm so angry at my sister right now I could scream!"

Nick watched in fascination as Tess McKinney paced back and forth across the ballroom's Italian tile, her fingers drumming against her side. She should be wearing an evening gown instead of casual dress, he thought, slipping back into his fantasy. Sleeveless, of course, with a plunging neckline and a slit all the way up her thigh. Her long, creamy thigh.

"She cannot stay in that trailer. It's out in the middle of nowhere. She can no longer fit behind the steering wheel of the rusted old junker she drives. What is she thinking? I don't understand it. She's acted selfishly in the past, but she's never been stupid. She's acting stupid now. She's about to have a baby!"

"Yes, I have noticed that. And please, call me Nick."

"Nick. You haven't helped the situation at all. You gave her *ten days* to vacate."

"Well, yes. That's the law."

She stopped abruptly and whirled to face him. "That's unacceptable. Chloe's not spending another night in that...place. We had the biggest fight of our lives about it this morning. And to think I came to

Texas hoping Chloe and I would grow close again. I had this silly little fantasy that we'd bond over the baby and become Norman Rockwell sisters."

"Nothing at all wrong with fantasies, Ms. McKinney," Nick said as he let his gaze quickly run up and down her luscious body.

"Tess. Fantasy is all well and good in its time and place, but at this particular time Chloe and I have to deal with reality, and that trailer house is the wrong place to do it. I want your help, Nick. I want my sister out of that tornado-catcher before sundown. So, what do we need to do to get her evicted today?"

Damn, he liked her style. "Unfortunately, Chloe can't be evicted today. It's not legal."

She scowled at him. "You're a lawyer. That means you'll find a way to get around the legalities."

He folded his arms and bit back a grin. "Now that's insulting."

She paused a moment, tilting her head as she thought about it. "You're right. I apologize. I tangled with an attorney last summer, and I've allowed it to color my view of your profession. I know better."

Tangled, hmm? He glanced at her left hand, noted the bare third finger. "A divorce?"

"No. A nuisance suit. Maybe that's the tack I should take with Chloe. She's certainly being a nuisance." She gave a rueful laugh, then added, "How 'bout it, counselor? Will you file a nuisance suit against my sister for me?"

"Sorry." He slipped the screwdriver back into his tool belt, then reached behind his back to release the buckle. "Can't do that, I'm afraid. The one rule that I've managed not to break regarding my legal practice here in Brazos Bend is my refusal to accept anyone under the age of sixty-five as a client. Were I to make an exception in your case, things around here could get very ugly, very fast."

She tucked a strand of hair behind her ear. "I sense a story there."

Nodding, he draped his tool belt over one of the ladder's steps. "It's a long one, and rather than bore you with it, how about I get you a glass of iced tea, and we can put our heads together on what to do about Chloe? I have a couple of ideas."

"That sounds good."

She smiled, and Nick felt it clear through to the bones. He offered her a seat atop a large roll of carpet, then headed for the kitchen and the refrigerator he kept stocked.

My God, the woman lit his wick, he thought as he poured tea from the pitcher in the fridge. He wondered at his reaction. Sure, she was beautiful, but beauty alone had never turned him on. She certainly wasn't coming on to him. In fact, his professional credentials had clearly turned her off. No, he was getting stirred up all on his own.

Damned if it didn't feel good.

For the past few months—okay, the last year—plus some—Nick's sex drive had slowed to...well...slow. He wasn't exceedingly concerned about the problem. He figured that once he got his head back on straight, that part of his life would get back on track, too. But it was nice to feel the zing again, and it put him in a mellow, helpful mood as he carried the drinks back to the ballroom, where he took a seat next to Tess on the bolt of red velvet carpet.

Tess toed off one shoe. Her toenails, he noted, were painted a bright, sexy red. With effort, he turned his mind toward the matter at hand. "Where is Chloe now?"

"She's at her obstetrician's office. I'm to pick her up in a couple of hours from the salon where she works. She decided to get a haircut this morning, thank heavens." Tess sipped her tea. "So, you said something about ideas?"

"Yeah. I started thinking about Chloe's situation after I went by Snake's place yesterday. I'd hoped she'd listen to you and leave there on her own. I considered the eviction notice a backup plan because it does take time to execute."

Tess nodded. "She's due in two weeks, so that's cutting it too close. All right, counselor, what do we do?"

"If direct oral arguments haven't worked, and force is not an option —" He paused and glanced at Tess for confirmation.

"I've never had much luck forcing my sister to do anything."

"Then I suggest we try presenting her with an alternative right out of her dreams."

Tess sat up straighter. "You can get Snake back? What do you know about him?"

Nick stretched out his legs. "No, I don't know where he is. As far as what I know about him, after Widow Duncan pestered me into taking her case, I checked into his background. He's had minor brushes with the law—bar fights, speeding tickets, a drunk and disorderly."

"I'm not surprised. That seems to be the type my sister falls for." Tess sat pensively for a moment, then shrugged it off. "So, talk to me about this dream thing."

Now it was Nick's turn for a pensive moment. All his life he'd been a dreamer of dreams, a seeker of dreams. Over the years, dreaming had allowed him to climb in the Himalayas, to help build a hospital in Africa, and to track down the pieces of a chess set rumored to have graced the halls of Versailles for his grandmother. Dreams, not goals, had fueled his passion for life, and he'd never expected to lose them. Then, about a year and a half ago, a pair of losses had bleached the joy from his dreams, turning them to dust. He'd tried to revive them by changing his life, by trading in Armani for Wranglers and taking on this Hutton Hotel project here in Brazos Bend. Maybe it was working. Slowly. Maybe he was coming to life again. Maybe that's why Tess McKinney affected him so strongly.

He cleared his throat. "There's a reason Chloe is holding on so hard to her home."

"Stubbornness. She's been that way all her life. If somebody told her she had to stay there, she'd move within the hour." Tess took another sip of tea, then added, "Actually, I imagine she's staying because of that man. She has a history of letting men jerk her around."

"I think you're right. When the two of them were together, she'd sparkle."

Both remained silent as they considered that a moment, then Tess asked, "Is he handsome?"

"That's a helluva question to ask a red-blooded Texan." When she sighed, he responded, "I guess some of the ladies in town think so. I've heard them call him a 'bad boy.' He certainly put stars in your sister's eyes."

Nick recalled one particular instance when he stopped by Connie's Candle Shop on the town square to buy a birthday gift for one of his

Brazos Bend clients. Chloe had been there choosing a candle for her kitchen, and he'd eavesdropped on her conversation with Connie. She'd bubbled on about napkin rings and curtains and her new wall clock. She'd spent some time deciding between a vanilla-scented candle and a cinnamon one. Remembering, he observed, "He gave her a dream."

"Of what?" Tess scoffed. "Joining the ranks of trailer trash?"

"Of having a home and family."

Tess visibly winced at that, but Nick pressed on. "She's been a wanderer, hasn't she? Maybe she's ready to put down roots. Home and family is a powerful dream."

Tess set down her iced tea, shoved to her feet, and began to pace. Despite her agitation, she moved with a sophisticated grace that distracted Nick from the subject under discussion. *Bet she dances beautifully.*

Abruptly, she halted and faced him. "I understand what you're saying, but how in the world could she want to sink roots in that horrible place? It's on wheels."

He dragged his attention back to their conversation. "It's all she has."

Tess turned on him, folding her arms. "I'd make sure she has a place to live. Chloe knows that. I've done it in the past. In fact, that's part of what we fought about this morning. I wanted to find an air-conditioned place to rent in town. She wouldn't even consider it."

"Yeah. Same thing happened to me when I told her I knew of an empty rental in town. That's when I started thinking of alternatives. It's perfectly understandable why she doesn't want to live with Widow Duncan, but her refusal to consider a rental is an emotional decision, not a logical one. That's why I decided to appeal to her emotional side with my solution to this problem. I decided to give her a house."

Tess took a step backward, her arms falling to her side. "What?"

Nick couldn't help but grin. "I thought I'd give her a house. Give her a place to call her own. Think of it as Habitat for Humanity, Brazos Bend style. I think it's probably best not to give it to her outright. People usually invest more pride of ownership in something they've earned as opposed to something they've been given. I'll carry a mortgage and keep the payments well within what she can manage on a nail technician's pay."

She continued to stare at him in shock for a long moment. Then her eyes narrowed, and she frowned. "Who are you?"

"What do you mean?"

"I don't understand what's going on here. Where I come from, a person is either a lawyer or a carpenter or a philanthropist. Not all three. Especially not all at the same time. Why would you even consider doing something like this?"

Scowling, Nick got to his feet. "Maybe I have a few issues of my own."

"Oh? Like what?"

"That's personal."

"And offering to buy my sister a house isn't personal? Excuse me, but I can't help but wonder at your motives. Chloe is a beautiful woman."

Nick didn't care at all for the innuendo. He braced his hands on his hips. "You think I'm trying to take advantage of her?"

"Maybe." Her chin came up. "I don't know you. You might be a criminal, for all I know."

"Well, then. You've found me out. I'm a serial house purchaser. You, Ms. McKinney, have been in California too long."

"All right, that does it. I've now heard one too many disparaging comments about my home since I arrived in this little burg. I don't know why you people think Texas is heaven, because I know darn well it feels like hell in the summer. California is a wonderful place to live. The weather is perfect, people are friendly, and the entertainment can't be beat. I've lived in both states, Mr. Sutherland, and I'm telling you I wouldn't move back to Texas for all the shoes in Italy!"

"Whoa, now. I didn't mean to poke a sore spot. My apologies." He sighed and rubbed the back of his neck. "Look, I have no ulterior motives. I like Chloe, and I'm nuts for babies, and I'm not all that fond of Snakes. Money is not a problem for me, and I occasionally spend it quite lavishly. Last, but certainly not least, doing this will get Widow Duncan off my back."

Tess stared at him a long moment before turning away and crossing to the ballroom's tall, arched window overlooking the pool. As she stared outside, Nick couldn't help imagining her first in an Esther Williams swimsuit, and then in a thong bikini. Then a topless thong bikini. He bit back a sigh of regret when she turned to him and asked, "What if she doesn't go for this idea? There's still the Snake factor."

"True." He grabbed his tea off the floor and took a long sip. "I'm betting otherwise, though. I sent guys from my crew over to the house first thing this morning. They'll have the nursery finished by midafternoon. We're using a unicorn theme."

Tess's eyes went wide. "Unicorns? Chloe has loved unicorns since she was a little girl. How did you know?"

"Apparently, they talk about that sort of stuff at the beauty shop."

Tess resumed pacing, and Nick couldn't look away from her. He'd bet Carole Lombard hadn't looked this gorgeous when she danced in this very ballroom with Clark Gable. Tess should have champagne. An orchestra should be playing. A waltz...

"Excuse me? Hel-lo?"

Tess stood no more than three feet away from him. When had she moved so close? *Good Lord, Sutherland. You're losing it.* "I'm sorry. You were saying?"

She gave him another curious look. "I said it's a good idea, with one change. I'll carry the mortgage."

Nick nodded. "Okay. That'll work. The house is on Pecan. Number sixteen." Then, surrendering to temptation, he added, "Can I ask you a question, Tess McKinney?"

Cautiously, she said, "All right."

"Would you like to dance?"

31

CHAPTER 5

TESS WAS STILL ADDLED from her encounter with Nick Sutherland when she turned onto Pecan Street ten minutes after leaving the Hutton Hotel. The man confused and bemused her. Living in California, working in the entertainment field, she dealt with gorgeous men on a daily basis. As a rule, she found them self-absorbed, egotistical, and shallow. Nick was different.

He was certainly handsome enough to hold his own in Hollywood. Take him out of those jeans, and—Tess lingered over that mental image a moment—put him in an Italian suit, and he'd have just the right look to play the new James Bond. A call to a casting agent friend of hers might be in order. Although that slow molasses drawl of his would never do for James Bond.

Would you like to dance?

He'd caught her completely off guard.

At that point Tess had begun to wonder if those personal issues Nick Sutherland had mentioned might be mental ones. She'd said good-bye and hurried out of the hotel.

Pecan Street curved to the left, and Tess's first sight of the house swept all other thoughts aside. Number 16 was a carriage house. A darling gingerbread carriage house. What girl hadn't dreamed of living in a house like this?

A quick glance around made it clear that 16 Pecan Street had once belonged to the big Victorian up on the hill. The wraparound porch was a charming add-on. She found the waist-high wrought-iron fence and arched gate inviting, and the red geraniums blooming in pots and window boxes added a welcoming touch. Walking up the weathered brick walk after parking her car, she noted the honeysuckle perfuming the air and wondered if the place could be more perfect.

Then she stepped inside. Drop cloths protected the hardwood flooring but failed to hide the house's appeal. It was old, but updated. The new appliances in the kitchen and fixtures in the bathroom fit the Victorian decor with all the convenience of the twenty-first century. Tess had already made up her mind to call the banker Nick had suggested before she traced the sounds of a hammer pounding a nail back to the room intended as a nursery. She took one look, then reached for her cell phone.

The banker took her information, confessed he'd already spoken to Mr. Sutherland about the situation, and promised he'd have the transaction completed by the end of the day.

"The end of the day?" Tess repeated, suspicion sharpening her tone.

"An advantage to doing business with Mr. Sutherland, ma'am."

She repeated it mockingly as she returned to her car and drove the short distance to her next designation, Harmon Lanes. Gravel crunched beneath the tires of her car when she pulled into the parking lot. A glance at her watch told her she was early to pick up Chloe, and she considered that providential. She couldn't wait to hang around Profile Beauty Salon this morning.

Traditionally, the best place to track down small-town gossip was a small-town beauty shop. Tess was after dirt on Nick Sutherland, aka the Brazos Bend Santa Claus. Was he truly on the up-and-up?

She parked her car between a pickup and a daycare center van and headed for the bowling alley's front door. Inside she was greeted by the roll, crash, and clatter of balls striking pins during morning league play, and the happy shrieks of children frolicking in a net-enclosed jungle gym filled with brightly colored plastic balls.

Profile Beauty Salon buzzed with activity and conversation as she stepped inside. The room had four style stations, two shampoo bowls, and two nail centers. It was decorated from ceiling to floor in a Scottie dog motif. The owner, Elizabeth Beck, whom she'd met at the baby shower last night, looked up from shampooing a customer, her hands full of frothy suds. "Hello there, Tess."

Chloe lifted her head from the shampoo bowl and gave her sister a pouty stare. "You might as well leave and come back later. My doctor had a delivery this morning, so his office appointments all ran late."

Tess stifled a sigh. Obviously, the squabble they'd had this morning wasn't over. Her sister could out-pout a teenage movie star when she felt like it, and apparently she felt like it today. "Actually, I stopped by hoping someone might have time to give me a manicure."

"Well, how about that," Elizabeth said with a smile. "Jan had a cancellation not ten minutes ago. She's run to the ladies' room, but she'll be right back. What would you think about adding a pedicure? Tiffany can give your feet a nice massage. She's young, just out of high school, but Chloe taught her how to do it, and your sister is the best." She glanced down at Chloe, winked, and added, "We miss her terribly around here, and we can't wait for her to come back to work."

Chloe rewarded the hairdresser with a pleased smile, and knowing it would make her life easier in the long run, Tess was quick to follow the woman's lead. "Chloe always has been a good worker. She devotes herself to every job she's done."

She's just done so many of them.

"I think a pedicure sounds wonderful."

Tiffany returned, and soon Tess had both her feet and her fingers soaking in tubs of scented warm water. As she searched her mind for the best way to approach the subject of Nick Sutherland, her sister did the work for her. "So, did you see Nick? Did you tell him what he and Mrs. Duncan can do with their eviction notice?"

An elderly woman with half her head covered in pink foam rollers sniffed in a huff as every ear in the place turned toward Tess. *Thanks for the subtlety, Sis.* "We'll talk about it later."

"Oh, come on, Tess," Elizabeth Beck said. "Nick Sutherland is one of our favorite topics of conversation around here. He's the most exciting thing to happen to Brazos Bend since the Brazos Bend High Rattlers' last state football championship. His name comes up around here at least ten times a day. Don't you agree, Mrs. Gault?"

The woman with the pink rollers motioned for her stylist to pause. "Really, Elizabeth. To comment on that borders on gossip, and you know I don't countenance such."

For a moment, the entire room went silent. Then Tiffany the nail technician choked back a strangled laugh, Elizabeth Beck snorted, and Chloe met Tess's gaze and rolled her eyes. Obviously, Mrs. Gault was known to gossip.

Tess mentally filed away that little fact just in case she didn't get the information she needed here this afternoon. Addressing Elizabeth, she asked, "Why all the interest in Nick Sutherland?"

"Girl, are you blind? He's a hottie! Every female in Brazos Bend from eight to eighty thinks so. Isn't that right, Tiffany?"

"Definitely," the girl agreed. Sitting on a towel at Chloe's feet, she popped her gum and spoke at length about Nick Sutherland's looks, wealth, cars, and clothes.

Mrs. Gault gave another disapproving sniff. "Oh, hush, Tiffany. All this talk about Mr. Sutherland's appearance and financial status—you do him a disservice. All of you should be ashamed. He is a gentleman who has gone out of his way to be of assistance to senior citizens here in Brazos Bend."

"Oh?" Tess asked. "In what way?"

The woman who didn't "countenance gossip" took a deep breath and rattled off a dozen instances when Nick took care of legal problems for the seniors of Brazos Bend. "It's much more than rewriting wills. He's solved Social Security issues and problems with contracts. And I haven't even mentioned the Brazos Bend Retirement Center. We don't have an assisted living center, you see, and with so many young people moving away from town, our seniors often don't have family around to help them in their golden years. Mr. Sutherland identified the problem and decided to do something about it. The Hutton Hotel is due to open in the fall as Brazos Bend's first assisted living center, and it will be affordable to anyone who wants to live there. The man is a saint, I tell you."

"St. Nick is trying to evict me from my home!" Chloe said, accepting Elizabeth's assistance to sit up, then stand. Her hand holding a towel in place around her head, she took a seat at the hairstylist's station.

Tess thought her sister had a point.

Chloe continued, "I thought my sister—my own flesh and blood—would help me stand against him, but I guess that's asking too much."

Choosing to ignore that dig, Tess asked, "Does St. Nick have family in town?" Like a wife? Children? Parents? Maybe an elf or two? Rudolph, Dancer, or Blitzen?

Bet he has a Vixen.

"No," Chloe said as the others shook their heads. "He's a bachelor, a newcomer just like me. He moved here from Dallas eighteen months ago or so. He was a partner in a swanky law firm."

"Really? So why did he leave Dallas for Brazos Bend?"

She might as well have dropped a bottle of foul-smelling perm solution in the middle of the room. Everyone drew back and held their breath. Finally, Elizabeth addressed the question, and it was obvious she chose her words carefully. "He'll tell you he grew tired of the congestion and pollution of the city. He did have friends here. He dated Kate Cooper before she married Max. I won't say Max was entirely thrilled to have his romantic rival move to town, but since he had won the girl, he had to be gracious about it."

She launched into a tale about the courtship of Max and Kate Cooper. While the story was interesting—sex, secrets, and scandal—Tess understood all along that Elizabeth used it to steer the conversation away from Nick and his reasons for moving to Brazos Bend. While the naturally nosy person inside her wanted the entire scoop, Tess realized she'd already received the answers she truly needed. As a carpenter, lawyer, and philanthropist, Nicholas Sutherland appeared to be legitimate.

Santa Claus was alive and well and living in Brazos Bend.

~

"I KNOW I'm doing the right thing," Nick told the passenger in his truck as he turned onto the rutted, dusty road leading to Snake Duncan's trailer. "So why does it make me feel like the Grinch?"

To the tune of *The Grinch Who Stole Christmas's* theme song, Kate Cooper sang, "You're a mean one, Mr. Nick."

He shot her a sidelong snarl. "I'd worry about being snotty if I were you. Might rub off on the baby."

"I don't have any character flaws," Kate responded with a flippant toss of her head. Beaming, she rested her hand on her still-flat stomach. She and her husband, Max, had announced their big news last week at Bingo Night, and she was still basking in the thrill of it. "This will be a perfect baby."

"With Max Cooper as a father? Puh-lease."

"You're just jealous."

"Nah. I got over that when I saw you push Max in the lake at your Christmas party. You're too ornery for me. I like a woman with spirit, but you're scary."

He pulled his truck to a halt in front of Snake's trailer and shut off the engine. Kate gazed at the structure and shook her head. "Speaking of scary."

"This is the right thing to do," he repeated.

"Yes, it is."

Nick climbed out of the truck, opened the toolbox in the back, and removed the two sets of chains and locks they'd given him at the health department. The red tags hanging from the iron links made him wince. "I can't believe I'm locking a pregnant woman out of her home."

"You're not, Nicholas. The Texas Department of Public Health is doing that. You're simply helping out an overworked bureaucrat who wouldn't have been able to make it out here for another three days. Think of it as public service."

Nick glanced toward Chloe's home and sighed. "I appreciate your help with this, Kate. I want her to have her things tonight, and I wouldn't begin to know what to take and what to leave."

"No problem. I like Chloe, and I think—Nicholas? Is something wrong?"

He'd stopped mid-stride and stood staring at the trailer. The window in Chloe's kitchen was broken. Something stained the glass. "Maybe. I'm not certain. Do me a favor, Kate. Wait in the truck until I check on things."

"But, Nicholas—"

"Humor me. Please? Now?"

"All right."

Nick waited until she'd returned to the truck before moving forward, veering off toward the north end of the trailer. He probably was being paranoid. The place appeared deserted, and something as simple as a bird could have caused the broken window. Still, a little caution never hurt, especially since he had Kate along with him.

Around back, he stopped abruptly. Bright yellow sunflowers lay broken and crushed amid once tall stalks of uncut prairie grass now pressed flat against the ground. Tire tracks. Lots of them. Two-wheeled tire tracks. Motorcycles.

"Snake."

Or maybe not. The trailer's back door hung open wide. Nick muttered a curse. *No dead bodies. Please. Not again.*

Moving toward the door, his grip tight around the chains, Nick wished he'd taken up the oh-so-Texan habit of carrying a gun in his truck.

As quietly as possible, he mounted the steps to the back porch. Taking a deep, bracing breath, he sneaked a look inside.

Nick's stomach rolled.

Blood spattered the walls.

Briefly, he closed his eyes as the past threatened to come roaring back.

No trailer house, but a nice apartment. Open door. Soft lights. Scented candles burning, sandalwood and rose. "Laura? It's Nicholas Sutherland." He followed the sound of jazz on a stereo. A bedroom. A note with his name on the front taped to the bathroom door. "Laura, are you home? Laura!"

The sound of his truck horn jerked him back, and Nick muttered a vicious curse. Concern for Kate uppermost in his mind, he took the quickest route, dashing down the short hallway to the combination kitchen-living area toward the front door. His car horn continued to sound.

Nick burst outside. She'd moved the truck within leaping distance of the front stoop. The engine gunned, and she called out the driver's-side window. "Nick? Are you okay?"

Relief tugged his heart from his throat back down to his chest. Anger put an edge in his voice. "Roll up the window, lock the damned doors, and just wait there."

He scanned the area, searching for the glint of sunlight off a bike fender, but seeing nothing, he turned and reentered the trailer. He traced the blood trail to the bedroom. Nick braced himself, thought of Chloe, then looked inside. He did a double-take.

Different animals than a Snake, thank God. Possums, three of them, lay gutted on the bed.

They hadn't been dead long, and Nick gave a silent prayer of thanks for pedicures and haircuts. He shuddered at the idea of Chloe and Tess coming home to this. He refused to think that they might have been here when it happened.

He quickly searched all the rooms. Along with the defacement, somebody had tossed the trailer. Contents of every drawer, cabinet, and closet lay strewn across the floor. Someone had taken a knife to the furniture, so stuffing, some of it blood-soaked, added to the chaos.

Nick found signs of another animal kill in the bathroom, but it was the scene he found in the room Chloe intended as a nursery that attacked his soul. Signs of a knife were everywhere—slashed diapers and clothes and the teddy bear Nick had brought the day before. Boxes and baskets overturned, their contents spilled and ruined. Blood splatters on the walls and the furniture painted a picture of an animal held by the tail and swung like a lasso. Whoever did this was a sick sonofabitch.

Fury pulsed through him, hot and mean. Had the bastard been here now, Nick would have killed him with his bare hands.

Though tempted to gather up the poor animals and dispose of them humanely, he knew not to disturb a crime scene. He retraced his steps to the front door and exited the trailer. Waiting in the cab of his truck, Kate looked ready to explode.

"Talk to me," she demanded as he opened the passenger's side door.

"Somebody searched the trailer, but I don't think they found what they were looking for." He thumbed on his cell phone, hoping for a signal. Damn. No service. "They left a graphic warning."

"What kind of warning? What did they do?"

Nick pictured the massacred animals and shook his head. "It's ugly, Kate. Let it alone. Do you have your cell?"

"Yes, but it doesn't work here. I already tried to call the sheriff."

"You up for a walk to the top of the hill? We should get reception there, and I don't want to leave until we get some law out here. Besides, I saw signs of motorcycles around back. If they decide to return, I'd just as soon see them coming."

"Was it Snake, Nicholas?" she asked as she slid across the seat and climbed down from the truck cab.

"I doubt it," he replied, thinking of the crib. "More likely, some of Snake's biker buddies."

As they started up the hill behind the trailer, unwilling to leave behind the only weapon of sorts he possessed, Nicholas slung the chains over his left shoulder. Climbing, he watched the window on his cell phone and halted when it registered service. "I'll handle the sheriff, and I'd like you to call that kid's store you've been working with today. When are they due to deliver the stuff you ordered?"

Kate glanced at her watch. "They should be there any time now. Adele is going to sign for the boxes."

"Okay." Nick thought a moment. "I'll call a delivery service I've used in the past. Order more and put it in my name. Tell the stores to have it all ready for pickup in half an hour."

"What else am I ordering?"

"Everything." He punched the number for the sheriff's office and hit the connect button. Holding the cell phone to his ear, he added, "Replace all her shower gifts, anything she needs for that baby that's not already on its way to the cottage. Then call someone and order clothes and makeup and other personal stuff Chloe will need. Get her anything you intended to take from the trailer today. Everything inside is ruined."

Kate's eyes went round with shock. "Everything? What did they do in there, Nicholas?"

Nick's expression hardened. "Just buy the stuff, honey. Chloe McKinney needs a new life."

CHAPTER 6

CHLOE BROWSED the selection at the movie rental store, enjoyed the air-conditioning, and waited for her sister to finish her cell phone call. With her hair cut and styled, sporting a new manicure and pedicure, and having lunched on a delicious chicken salad at the nicest restaurant in town, Chloe felt like a new woman. Now if only she could get Tess to drop the idea of Chloe's abandoning her home.

Oh, her sister had been much more subtle about it this afternoon than she had this morning, but Chloe could see right through her. Tess hadn't changed all that much over the years. When she wanted something, she went after it, no matter what got in the way or who she left behind in the process.

Chloe was a little worried about her sister's reaction to her situation. She'd known Tess wouldn't like Snake's place, but she hadn't expected her to side with the Wicked Widow. And look at how she'd avoided answering Chloe's question about her morning visit to Nick. Her sister was up to something.

I should never have called her and asked her to come, she thought.

She should have known Tess would try to "fix" her life. Tess always tried to fix things. That's probably why she was so good bossing celebrities around—she fixed all their screw-up's.

Isn't that why you wanted her to come to Brazos Bend?

"No," she said aloud, reaching blindly for a movie. Turning the case over, she tried to read the back blurb, but found she couldn't concentrate on the plot. Probably because she had her own drama going on.

"I don't need Tess to fix anything," she whispered to herself. She didn't. She just wanted company, that's all. Every woman is a little apprehensive about the whole labor and delivery process. Nobody wants to go through that alone.

"Hi, Chloe."

She looked up. "Stewart. Hi. What are you doing in town this time of day?"

A computer tech for the junior college, he seldom lunched in town. "I'm freelancing next door at the real estate office today. Their computer system has a few bugs in it. I saw your sister's car pull up. I couldn't help but notice that she seems upset. Is something wrong?"

"Yeah, it has to do with her work. A film producer called and said Jennifer Hart has gone AWOL from the set. Tess is her manager. Anyway, it's a big deal for everyone involved, and Tess went ballistic. Bet she's made two dozen phone calls by now."

"I did hear her using less than flattering language about the cell phone service here in town as I walked by."

Chloe smirked. "She's more than a little hot under the collar. Jennifer really screwed up. I have to say, though, Tess is pretty amazing. I never would have guessed she could sound so calm when her eyes are shooting fire and she's kicking a tire."

Stewart glanced out the plate glass window toward the parking lot, where Tess paced back and forth, talking on her phone while gesturing wildly with her hands. "I'm glad I saw y'all drive up. How did your doctor's appointment go?"

Chloe swallowed hard. "How did you know I had an appointment today?"

"You told me two weeks ago that you'd be seeing Doc Fisher every Tuesday morning until the baby is born."

"I did? Oh."

He waited expectantly, like a dog begging for a treat. "So, what did he say?"

Chloe didn't want to answer. She didn't want to think about her visit to her obstetrician. She never did. Not since her first visit, when the doctor put his cold stethoscope to her flat belly to listen to the baby's heartbeat. Every time she thought about her doctor visits, she got nauseous. She'd rather not throw up in the video store. "Fine. I'm fine."

"And the baby?"

Her stomach rolled, and she closed her eyes. "Fine."

He waited, and she knew he wanted her to elaborate. She just couldn't. After a moment, he said, "Good. That's good. I'm glad."

Chloe wished Tess would take a hint as easily as Stewart, but oh, no. Not her sister. Tess had peppered her with questions from the moment they left the beauty shop. *When does he think you'll deliver? How big does he think the baby will be? How's your blood pressure? What about ankle swelling? Did he give you any suggestions for preventing your heartburn?*

Chloe had responded in one-word answers, and she'd sent up a silent prayer of thanks when Tess's phone rang and provided a distraction.

Stewart tapped the movie Chloe held. "I didn't know you liked musicals."

A musical? Is that what she'd picked up? Chloe glanced at the box in her hand. *South Pacific.* She pictured the scene of the girl on the beach washing that man right out of her hair. Quickly, she placed the box back on the shelf. "I think I'm more in the mood for a comedy."

Stewart helped her pick a movie, then glanced at his watch. "Guess I'd better get back to work. I'm glad to know you and the baby are doing well."

"Thanks, Stewart." Chloe watched him go, returning the little wave he gave her right before he crossed the street toward the real estate office. He really was a nice man. A bit silly looking, with that long skinny face and protruding Adam's apple. Still, if someone took him in hand and got him a decent haircut and showed him how to dress properly, he wouldn't be half bad.

"I'm sorry, honey," Tess said, coming up beside her. "I think I'm done for now. Are you ready to leave?"

"Sure." Chloe returned the video to the shelf.

"Don't you want to get your movie?"

"No, I don't think so."

"Are you feeling okay? Not too tired or anything?"

"I'm fine."

"Good, then why don't you show me the best place in town for a girl to buy a pair of shoes."

Chloe's brows winged up. She'd seen her sister's suitcase. She must have brought a dozen pairs of shoes with her. "What sort of shoes are you looking for?"

"Oh, I don't know. That doesn't really matter. I just like to buy—" She broke off abruptly, her eyes focusing on the man climbing into his pickup truck in the parking lot. "Boots. I want some cowboy boots. Surely there's a place in Brazos Bend to buy cowboy boots. C'mon, Chloe. We haven't shopped in ages."

Yeah, like since they were kids and went to the five-and-dime with the five dollars they'd earned taking care of their vacationing neighbors' pets. This was too weird, Chloe thought as she followed her sister to the car. The McKinney sisters on a shopping trip in Brazos Bend, Texas. Who-da-thunk-it.

Chloe directed Tess to Cavendar's Fine Footwear on the square downtown. Once inside, Chloe sat down and propped her feet on a stool and studied her ankles. Not too swollen.

"You lookin' for shoes, missy?" the store owner asked, eyeing Chloe's foam thongs with a frown. In his sixties with a bushy salt-and-pepper mustache and thick eyebrows, Mr. Cavendar was a Brazos Bend institution. He always wore a coat and tie and favored ice-cream-colored jackets. Today's was lime sherbert.

"No, sir. I just wanted to see what my feet look like. I can only see them when I'm sitting down and they're propped up. My sister, however, is interested in a pair of boots."

Mr. Cavendar narrowed his eyes, pursed his lips, and considered Tess's feet. "Size six?"

"Six B," Tess responded with an animated smile.

"Western boot or roper?"

"Western boots, definitely. The snazzier the better."

"Hmm—an exotic, then." Mr. Cavendar nodded once, then headed for the back room.

Tess hummed as she toed off first one shoe, then the other. Chloe gazed from her sister's feet, to her own, then back to her sister's again. Her feet were wider than Tess's. That wasn't right. Her feet had always been long and narrow and pretty. Tess's were wide across the instep, and in some styles, she'd needed a wide width. That always made her mad.

Now look. Chloe's feet were even wider than her sister's. Duck feet. That's what she had now. Big fat duck feet.

The sob rumbled up from inside her, and she tried to swallow it. Oh, she hated this. She hated whiny women, and now she'd become one. She cried all the time. It had to be hormones.

"Honey, you okay?"

"I'm fi-i-hiccup-ine."

Worry dimmed Tess's gaze, then she offered a hesitant smile. "Do you want some new shoes, too? My treat."

"I don't want any shoes. I want my feet back."

"Oh, Chloe." Tess patted her knee.

"I want my stomach back."

Tess dug in her purse and handed Chloe a tissue.

"I want my Snake back!" She balled up the tissue and threw it across the store.

Emerging from the back room, Mr. Cavendar started as the small white sphere sailed past his ear. He dropped a stack of boxes, and boots tumbled across the floor. Justin, Lucchese, Tony Lama. Ostrich, lizard, and buffalo. Chloe immediately felt contrite. "I'm sorry, Mr. Cavendar. I didn't see you coming."

"Not to worry, dear."

Tess jumped up to help gather up the boxes, and her gaze zeroed in on a pair of hot pink Lucchese Saddle Vamp Diego Inlays. The sudden flare of covetousness in her sister's eyes distracted Chloe from her misery. Where in the world would Tess wear hot pink cowboy boots? "You planning to go out dancin' while you're in town?"

Tess pulled on the boots, then stood. A smile played across her lips. "I haven't done the two-step in years."

She danced the steps as if she had a partner, then laughed. "I love them. I'll take them, please. And another pair just like them in red."

Glancing at Chloe, she said, "Your turn."

"I'm not buying boots. It'd be stupid. My feet won't stay this size." They'd better not.

"So get something to wear for the next two weeks. Let me splurge on you, Chloe. It's no fun to shop alone."

A foot pushed her stomach, and Chloe absently massaged her belly. She hadn't bought new shoes in ages. "If you feel that strongly about it, okay. But nothing too dowdy. I'm so tired of looking like a house frump."

"New Italian sandals have arrived that might work for you quite well, Ms. Chloe," Mr. Cavendar said. "Let me measure your foot and see what I can find."

As she stood on the metal measuring tool, Chloe kept her face averted, just like she did when she stood on the scale. Then, just like the nurse in her OB's office did every time, Mr. Cavendar announced, "Hmm....I think an eight E should do it."

"E? Is that smaller than a W?" Chloe asked hopefully.

"It is a double W."

"A double-wide." Chloe sank glumly back into her chair. "The only good double-wide is a trailer."

Chloe noticed her sister's sudden stillness and wished she'd bit her tongue rather than use the word *trailer*. Now Tess would start in again, and they'd fight, and Chloe wouldn't walk out of here with a new pair of shoes. She wanted those shoes.

"Chloe," Tess began, "about your tra—"

"Oh, would you look at those white patent-leather pumps!" Chloe exclaimed, shoving awkwardly to her feet. "I wore a pair almost exactly like that to Easter Mass the year I was Catholic. I'll never forget because the toddler in the pew in front of me must have had grape juice in his bottle, and he threw up all over my shoes."

The story momentarily distracted Tess, but that was all Chloe needed, because Mr. Cavendar returned with a high stack of shoes. Chloe realized with that wide a selection, he must have a number of size eight WW customers. Somewhat mollified, she settled down to make her choice.

Tess's cell phone rang as Chloe debated her preference between the pink thong sandals and the black double-strapped pair. At first, Chloe paid little attention to the conversation, but when Tess's gaze shifted toward her and Chloe noted the considering look in her sister's eyes, she tuned in.

"Yes," Tess said. "Mm-hm. No. No. Yes. That should work...excellent...thank you. Yes. Just one moment—" Shifting the phone away from her mouth, she smiled at Chloe and said, "Get them both, Chloe. They're both darling."

Continuing her phone conversation, Tess said, "Twenty minutes should be fine. Yes. Wonderful. See you there. Good-bye."

Chloe nodded to Mr. Cavendar that yes, she would take both pairs of shoes, and asked her sister, "See who where?"

"It's a surprise." Tess slipped her cell phone back into her purse, then pulled out her wallet and removed a credit card. "I've another gift to give you, one I think you'll like a lot." Waving at the store owner, she said, "I think we're done here, Mr. Cavendar, although it's a safe bet you'll see me again."

With the transaction completed, the women gathered up the packages and headed for the car. "Another gift? Well, you're just full of surprises today, aren't you? What gives?"

"I spent the morning with Santa Claus, and it put me in the mood."

"What?"

Tess thumbed a button on her keyless remote and unlocked the car doors. She tossed her packages in the backseat, then shut the door. "I've declared this Christmas Make-up Day. Think of all those years when we were too poor to give each other anything more than a card. Today I'm going to fill the gift backorder."

Part of Chloe simmered with excitement, while the adult in her felt uneasy. The two parts waged war within her, until the adult won out. "No, Tess, that's not right. Shoes are one thing, but I cannot accept any more. Christmas is a reciprocal gift-giving holiday. I can't give you anything in return."

In the process of opening the driver's-side door, Tess hesitated.

After a moment's thought, she said, "That's not true. You're giving me a niece or nephew. That's just about the best present ever."

Pleasure rushed through Chloe and brought a warm smile to her lips. "You think that? Really?"

"Yes, I really do." She got in the car and waited for Chloe to settle into the passenger seat. Snapping her seat belt closed, she said, "You and I by ourselves are sisters, but once we have a baby, we'll be a family. We haven't had a family in a very long time, Chloe. Not since Mama died. I've missed that."

An old ache tugged at Chloe's heart and threatened to stir up the tears that were always so close to the surface. She cleared her throat, then asked, "Do you ever hear from Dad?"

Tess shook her head. "Not since the card he sent after Mama's funeral."

"Me either. Sometime last winter the Devil's Own rode through Bastrop. I talked Snake into taking me to the old neighborhood. I saw Mrs. Norris taking groceries into her house, and we stopped and visited for a while. She said she'd heard Dad and his wife and her kids had moved to Detroit."

"Huh. I'd wondered where he ended up." Tess started the car. "Funny how little I care about where he's gone or who he's with. He's not family anymore."

"We're family. You and me."

"And the baby."

"And Snake?"

Tess drove half a block before she dodged the question by responding, "Tell me more about him, Chloe."

Chloe linked her fingers and rested her hands atop her belly. "All right. Probably the first thing you notice about Snake is how handsome he is. He has long brown hair and the greenest eyes. When I look into them, I'm reminded of the Oregon forests. His smile makes me melt, and he can sing, Tess. He has this beautiful baritone voice, and when he sings love songs to me...ahh." She closed her eyes and sighed.

"Does he make you laugh?" Tess asked.

He used to. "I'll never forget this one time in Oklahoma. It was like a Tuesday morning, and we'd slept in a rest stop on top of a wooden picnic table. The honeysuckle was blooming and the air smelled so sweet. It was just after dawn, and I was half awake, half asleep, and all of a sudden, Snake let out a yell. A little garter snake had curled up on his belly and was sound asleep. Then the snake got scared and darted into hiding, which just happened to be inside Snake's pants. He shot off that picnic table like he was on fire, then hopped and danced and tried to yank his britches down. Just when he bared his butt, the snake slithered down his leg. I laughed so hard that I cried. Once he got over being embarrassed, he did, too."

"I like a man who can laugh at himself," Tess said. Next she asked about his motorcycle, and Chloe gave her details until Tess stopped in front of the carriage house that was part of the old Wilcox estate. When the owner passed on a bit over a year back, Nick Sutherland had purchased the big old Victorian home lock, stock, and empty stable. He'd brought in horses and refinished the pool, and between the Wilcox place and the hotel remodeling, he'd employed every building professional within three counties.

A man climbed out of a gray sedan parked in the driveway. Before Chloe could open the door, her sister was out of the car and shaking hands with the fellow. He handed her a manila folder and a pen. Tess opened the folder, scanned the contents, and scribbled something. They shook hands again, and he waved at Chloe and beat a hasty retreat.

"What was all that about?" she asked Tess.

Even as she asked her question, suspicion slithered through her. Tess never could hide a guilty look.

FROM THE CARRIAGE house kitchen window, Nick tipped back a long neck and watched Tess McKinney sign the banker's papers, making him a trespasser in the house he'd formerly owned. Good. Another task accomplished.

He wondered how Chloe would take the news of Tess's gift. Maybe she'd love it, and this part would go smooth and easy. They were due. He'd just as soon not use the ace in the hole that had sent him out to

Chloe's trailer earlier, or the news of what he'd found once he'd arrived. Until the forensics guys in Fort Worth analyzed the evidence, he'd just as soon keep Chloe in the dark about the destruction at her home.

She didn't need to worry herself into labor that some of the blood might be Snake's.

Nick surmised that drugs were the object of the search. It wouldn't surprise him if Snake Duncan was up to his tattoos in the drug trade.

Outside, Tess shook the banker's hand and waved as he got into his car and drove off. When she turned to Chloe and flashed an overbright smile, Nick pursed his lips and murmured, "Damn."

That smile dashed his hopes for smooth and easy. His years in the courtroom had made him good at reading body language, and that beautiful body of Tess McKinney's was currently a bundle of nerves. She obviously expected a battle from Chloe.

Nick set down his beer, then walked out onto the front porch. Chloe spied him first, and immediately her eyes narrowed. "Well, hell."

Tess looked at her sister. "What's the matter, Chloe? Are you hurting? In your back? Oh, God. It's not back labor, is it? Here, come inside and sit down and put your feet up. Do I need to call the doctor?"

Chloe's gaze shifted between her sister and Nick as he approached. "What are we doing here? What is *he* doing here?"

Tess finally noticed Nick. "Great. Just great. Ruin my timing completely. Way to go, Mr. Sutherland."

Back to Mr. Sutherland? To hell with that. "Hi, Tess. Chloe." As he walked toward the car, he spied the bags in the back seat. "Looks like y'all have been shoe shopping."

Eyeing the storm clouds gathering on her sister's face, Tess gave an unhappy sigh. "I bought boots."

"Never mind about the boots," Chloe snapped. "Answer my questions. Although I'm pretty sure I already know the answers. I'm fat, not stupid."

"Chloe, I've never said—"

"Nick told me he had a house I could afford to rent," she interrupted. "Obviously, this is it." She folded her arms atop her enormous belly and pinned her sister with a glare. "I told him thanks, but no thanks. I'm staying at Snake's."

Tess flattened her lips in a grim smile and turned to Nick. "Our business is concluded, correct? If you'll excuse us, please? This is a family matter."

Stuffy sass. He liked that in a woman. Grinning widely, he said, "We're signed, sealed, and delivered, but I think I should stick around and offer my help."

Tess offered him a smile filled with enough saccharin to give cancer to a dozen rats. "Oh, you've provided plenty of help already."

Nick could leave and let Tess handle this herself. She'd obviously prefer it. However, he had a vested interest in the proceedings, and thus he had no intention of going anywhere. He leaned against the trunk of a nearby magnolia tree, folded his arms, and shrugged. "Thanks, but I have nothing pressing this afternoon."

Tess shot him a look of frustrated disgust, *then* turned her back, dismissing him.

"Chloe, I want you to listen to me." Tess dropped her car keys into her black leather shoulder bag and yanked its zipper closed. "I give you my word that bringing you here is not an attempt to force you from the trailer into a rental. Can you believe me when I say that?"

Chloe pursed her lips in a pout, then shrugged. "I guess. You don't often lie to me."

"I never lie to you," Tess fired back. Her grip tightened around the banker's manila file folder. "I despise liars. Lying ruins relationships and ruins lives. It destroys trust. Trust that's been damaged may be impossible to repair."

Whoa. That certainly touched a hot button. Honesty mattered big-time to Tess. Bet somebody burned her badly in the past.

"You think that's news to me, Tess?" Chloe asked. "After what Dad did?"

Tension sizzled in the air between the sisters. Nick glanced from one to the other and experienced his first glimmer of doubt. Maybe he should have left them to hash this out themselves, after all. When estrogen hung this thick in the air, any man in the vicinity risked getting burned.

Impatience simmering in her eyes, Tess said, "Now's not the time to rehash the past. Can we go inside? Please?"

Chloe flounced up the porch steps—as best as any woman that pregnant could flounce, anyway—and stepped inside the carriage house. Tess followed at her heels, completely ignoring Nick, who debated with himself for just a moment, then followed the women.

He couldn't recall the last time a pair of beautiful women had ignored him so completely. Why did it make him smile?

Once again he was struck by the air of homeyness his friend Kate had managed to create in the little house on such short notice. Working primarily with furniture and accessories from the big house, and throwing herself on the mercy of a Dallas designer with ties at the showrooms of Market Center, she'd turned the carriage house into a home. The rugs on the hardwood floor and the plush, comfy sofa and matching occasional chair looked much better here than they had up at his place. Little touches like books and quilts and even the aroma of fresh-baked ginger cookies permeating the air made the carriage house say "welcome home." He saw Chloe eye the padded bentwood rocker and matching footstool beside the fireplace. The basket of baby supplies sitting beside it was a master touch on Kate's part.

Chloe took a step toward it, then abruptly stopped. She folded her arms, lifted her chin belligerently, then threw down the verbal gauntlet. "Okay. We're inside. Start talking, Tess."

For the first time since entering the house, Tess met Nick's gaze. While he encouraged her with a nod and a smile, he wondered if Chloe observed her sister's nervousness.

Tess asked, "Remember when we were kids and Mom bought that plastic castle at a garage sale?"

That salvo obviously took Chloe in a different direction than she had anticipated. It took her a moment to respond. "The Fantasyland Playset. I remember. We lost one of the dragons that first day and never did find it. I always did think Billy Parker stole it."

"I think you're right." Tess dropped her file folder onto the oak end table beside a brass lamp. "I'm glad if he chose to steal something, it was the dragon and not one of the unicorns."

Chloe's expression softened, and though she looked toward the

53

Austin stone fireplace, Nick sensed she gazed into the past. "I loved those unicorns. I still have one of them, in fact. It's the first piece in my collection."

"I know."

The sisters shared a smile, and Nick was struck by the similarity in the two women's appearances. Since Tess's arrival in Brazos Bend, Chloe looked more like her old self—calmer, less desperate. Having her hair cut and wearing makeup made a difference, but Nick thought the changes went deeper than that. Chloe no longer wore that deer-in-the-headlights look she'd sported since Snake had left town. Tess gave her strength, something that always looked good on a woman.

Tess continued, "Everyone who knows you understands that unicorns are special to you."

"They're like a dream. A beautiful dream."

Shooting one last pray-for-me glance Nick's way, Tess reached for her sister's hand and tugged her toward the hallway. Outside the nursery door, she asked, "Will you let me give you unicorns, Chloe?"

Tess twisted the knob and the door swung open.

Chloe cupped her hands over her mouth and said a muffled, "Oh, wow."

A local artist had painted the fantasy landscape mural on the southern wall using as a guide the picture Chloe kept hanging beside her nail station at the salon. Against a backdrop of a green forest with purple mountains in the distance, a snow white unicorn nuzzled her foal beside an ice blue lake.

The theme was continued subtly throughout the rest of the room. Unicorns graced the blades on the ceiling fan, the dotted Swiss curtains, and the bedding on the white wooden crib and matching changing table. The mystical animals decorated the dresser lamp, the switch plates, and even the rag rugs on the floor.

Nick watched Chloe's face when her gaze came to rest upon each addition, and as the wonderment in her expression grew, so did his confidence. Maybe they'd just pulled this off. He wouldn't be forced to use the ace up his sleeve. Or in his jacket pocket, to be more precise. Although it was better that than the more ugly truth of the ransacking of the trailer.

"It's perfect," Chloe murmured. "It's right out of a magazine." Dazed, she approached the mural and extended her hand toward the unicorn foal.

"Careful, honey," Nick cautioned. "The paint may still be a little wet. Jen Wilson painted that, and she just finished it a couple hours ago."

Chloe's hand dropped back to her side, and she moved to the rocking chair, where she sat and folded her hands across her burgeoning belly. She didn't speak. Nick shot Tess a worried glance, but she never took her gaze off her sister.

"I'm not asking you to move into a rental," Tess said. "I haven't been a very good sister to you for the past few years, Chloe, and I'd like to change that, starting now. If I had my preference, I'd take you home with me to California, but you've made it perfectly clear that you want to stay here in Brazos Bend, and I guess I understand that. For a small town in Texas, this one is rather nice. So, because we're family and I love you and I want you to be safe, happy, and secure—" She drew a deep breath, and as she exhaled, said the rest of the words in a rush. "I bought this house. I'm giving it to you, Chloe. It's my gift to you and your baby."

For a long moment, nothing happened. Chloe didn't react. She didn't smile or squeal or clap her hands together or exhibit any sign of excitement one might expect from a person given such a gift. Neither did she show signs of anger. She simply...froze.

Tess looked ready to explode with anticipation.

Nick had opened his mouth to demand something, he wasn't sure what, when Chloe's foot began a rhythmic tap against the floor. She blinked rapidly as if fighting away tears. *Okay, that's okay. Tears are probably good.*

"You don't think Snake is coming back," she accused in a whisper.

Okay, tears are probably not so good.

"I don't know, Chloe," Tess said. "I don't know Snake. It's impossible for me to make a judgment on that."

"Ha." Chloe grabbed a tissue from one of a half dozen conveniently placed boxes in the nursery and dramatically swiped it over her eyes. "When has not knowing the man in my life ever stopped you from judging him? You're right when you say you haven't been a good sister. It's true. You've found fault with every man I've ever told you about."

Tess straightened, and her shoulders squared. "That's not true."

"Oh, yeah? Name one you didn't criticize."

Nick shifted uneasily. Maybe he should have stayed outside. Or up at the house. Hell, maybe he should have made a trip into Dallas today.

Tess tossed her purse onto the floor and rested her hands on her hips. "I never said anything bad about that banker from Saint Louis. At least not until he was—"

"Arrested. You certainly had plenty to say then."

"Chloe, the national news organizations had something to say about him. The man embezzled millions of dollars from a charitable organization. He was sent to federal prison. You're lucky you didn't end up in a jail cell yourself. If we hadn't found you a good attorney, I hate to imagine what might have happened."

"I heard that," Nick said, stepping forward to diffuse some of the tension. "You said 'good attorney.' So you admit some of us do exist."

The women paused just long enough in their argument to shoot him identical looks of scorn. Well, that certainly put me in my place, he thought.

With a push of her foot, Chloe set the rocker into motion. "Maybe I've not had the best of luck with men, but sometimes that was my fault, not theirs. I wasn't cut out to live on a Greenpeace ship. I needed land beneath my feet. My cop, now, he was a good man and he loved me. I couldn't bear the worry each night when he went off to work. I dreaded each time the phone rang. But he was a cop down to the bones, and it wouldn't have been right to ask him to choose between his work and me. I broke his heart when I left him, but I know it was the right thing to do."

Tess visibly relaxed. Quietly she said, "You never told me about that."

Chloe shrugged and allowed the pace of the rocker to slow. "I don't like to think about it." She closed her eyes and rested her head against the back of the rocker. "I'm not a bad person, Tess. Sometimes I make poor choices. With Snake, I...we're going to be parents."

She lay her hands protectively over her belly. "We'll have a settled life here in Brazos Bend. I've been thinking Snake could open a garage. I told you he's a good mechanic. We'll be happy."

"This cottage will be a good home for you and your family, Chloe."

Chloe gazed around the room. Her eyes grew misty, and when she struggled to stand, Nick moved to assist her. His forearm rested against her stomach, and he felt a little nudge. Realizing he'd felt the baby kicking, his eyes went wide. She chuckled softly, then moved to the crib, where she fingered the yellow ruffle on the unicorn bumper pad. "Yes, Tess, this cottage would make a fine home, and I thank you for the generosity of your gift. However, I cannot accept it."

"What?" Tess demanded.

"What!" Nick repeated, caught totally by surprise.

"Snake wouldn't like it, Tess. He's a proud man. He'd view it as charity." A pair of plump tears spilled from her eyes and rolled down her cheeks. "We have to live in the trailer."

With that pronouncement, she turned and headed for the front door.

For a moment, Tess simply stood there in shock. Then she snapped, "Oh, for heaven's sake. To think I almost believed she'd changed. This is vintage Chloe. Vintage drama-queen martyrdom. I'd like to wring her neck."

She marched out of the nursery and out of the cottage. Her sister had almost reached the car. "Chloe McKinney, you come back here."

Chloe turned her head away and held up her hand, signaling her sister to go back like the heroine of a silent movie melodrama. The gesture only added more starch to Tess's voice. "Chloe, don't you run away from me. We're not done here."

"I'm tired, Tess. My back hurts, and I need to lie down."

A series of emotions flashed across Tess's face. Frustration. Fear. Impatience. Anger. Love. She closed her eyes and visibly summoned her patience. Softly, she said, "Nick, please don't let me kill her."

"I'll protect you both."

She called out to Chloe. "If you need to lie down, come inside. You didn't even look at the master bedroom. There's a nice comfy queen-size bed waiting for you. Much better than that lumpy thing you've been sleeping on at Snake's."

"No, I want my own bed. I won't sleep anywhere else." She climbed into Tess's car and slammed the passenger door.

Tess turned a dazed look toward Nick. "She's totally lost her mind. She's making absolutely no sense. I do not understand her at all. Can pregnancy hormones do this? What am I going to do now?" She paced back and forth across the porch. "I can't lock her in the carriage house until she has the baby. Can I? Would somebody let me do that?"

"No, I don't think locking her up is the answer," he replied, knowing the time had come to play his ace. "Locking her out is another matter entirely. Here."

He handed an unsealed envelope to Tess. "She can't go back to the trailer."

"What? Why?" She removed the document from the envelope and scanned it. As she read, her mouth slowly fell open. "Is this...?"

"Yes. The health department authorized a padlock for the doors of Snake Duncan's trailer." Never mind that the place was now a crime scene.

Her laughter began softly, then built to an infectious giggle. "You had the place condemned?"

"Yeah."

She caught him completely by surprise when she threw herself into his arms and planted an enthusiastic kiss right on his mouth. "My hero!" she exclaimed. "Mr. Sutherland, you are downright brilliant! I might just need to change my opinion of lawyers."

Brilliant or not, he knew without a doubt what to do in situations such as this.

Yanking her against him, Nick went back for seconds.

CHAPTER 7

SPONTANEOUS KISSES HAPPENED ALL the time in Hollywood. Not a day went by that Tess didn't give or receive cheek kisses, air kisses. Friend-ship kisses. Acquaintance kisses. One client of hers, a dapper old gentleman originally from London, bestowed a kiss on her hand every time they met.

In all her years in California, in all the years of her life, no one had ever, *ever* laid a kiss on Tess like the one Nick Sutherland gave to her now.

Slanting his mouth across hers, he took control. His tongue played across her lips, coaxing, demanding she open to him. When she did, he took full advantage and thrust deeply, taking possession.

He tasted like the South, and he felt like heaven pressed against her. Tess hummed low in her throat as the scent of him filled her head. Not expensive aftershave as one might expect, but soap and sawdust, a combination new to her. She thought it the most erotic fragrance she'd ever come across.

Nick spread his legs and, with his hands on her hips, inched her closer. Hot arousal washed through her as his denim-clad thighs brushed the silk of her skirt and his groin nudged hard against her belly.

He nipped and sucked at her lips, and Tess shuddered with delight. He was big and masculine and muscular, and he made her feel tiny and feminine, but far from weak. Kissing Nick Sutherland gave her a high equal to signing three A-list actors on as clients. All in the same day. At the same lunch meeting.

My, oh my. If kissing him did this to her, imagine what going to bed with him would do.

The image flashed in her brain as he thrust his tongue into her mouth once more. Soft candlelight. Midnight blue satin sheets. Naked flesh entwined. His left hand burrowed in her unbound hair. His right, fingers splayed wide across her breast, then slowly drifting down to her waist...her hip...her—

"Excuse me? Hel-lo." Chloe's shrill voice intruded into the sensual fog clouding Tess's mind. "Does somebody want to explain just what the hell is going on here?"

Tess blinked her eyes open as Nick stepped away. He held her gaze, his eyes dark like the sheets in her fantasy, intense and mesmerizing. Her pulse pounded, and she struggled to breathe normally.

"Tess!"

The pique in her sister's tone finally enabled her to look away. Chloe marched toward them, temper flashing in her eyes. Color bloomed in her complexion. Still in a sexual stupor, Tess looked at her and said, "We should have bought you a pair of boots, too."

"Boots? You've lost your ever-loving mind! Guess he sucked it right out through your mouth, huh? Don't try to distract me. What are you doing kissing him?" She flung out her arm, gesturing at Nick. "I'm the one having a crisis here. I'm the one who needs attention. You came to Texas to take care of me, not to lock lips with Studly-Do-right here, didn't you?"

"Studly Do-right?" Nick repeated.

Tess fought back a giggle—a surprise, since she never giggled. But then, she'd never locked lips with Studly Do-right before, either. "Of course I came here to take care of you, honey," she said to Chloe, her tone conciliatory. Caretaker and diva—these were the roles she and her sister had played all their lives. Tess took comfort in the familiarity. "I was just saying thank you."

"Is there something else I can do for you?" Nick asked softly.

This time the giggle escaped, and the sound of it, the reality of it, made Chloe let out another screech. "Thank you? That was a thank you? And here I have the reputation for being the fast McKinney sister. So what did he do to earn gratitude like that? Did he buy you a plane or a Swiss chalet or a new pair of shoes?" Chloe rubbed the small of her back. "Never mind. I don't think I want to know. Let's just go now, can we? I need to rest."

"Yes, you do need to rest," Tess replied. Then, bracing herself, she added, "And you're going to do it right here, right now, in your new bedroom. You can't go back to the trailer, Chloe. The health department condemned it and padlocked the door. Like it or not, this carriage house is your new home."

Chloe froze, stared at her. In slow motion, the arm massaging her back dropped to her side. Her voice emerged in a croak. "Condemned?"

Tess nodded.

Nick stepped forward. "Upon inspection, the health department determined that your water system is inadequate and—"

"The water's bad?" She covered her belly protectively.

"Not bad," he assured her. "It's just not up to code. That was secondary, however, to the rodent problem."

"Rodent problem!" Tess and Chloe exclaimed simultaneously, then Chloe added, "I don't have mice."

"Not mice. Possums. They've chewed your wiring in at least a dozen places. It's a fire hazard."

"They get in around the plumbing hookups somehow. I told Snake he needed to do something about that." Chloe gazed toward the carriage house, her expression pensive.

"This is a good house, Chloe," Nick said, his voice kind and reassuring.

She rubbed her back and sighed heavily. "I can't believe my trailer home has been condemned." Then, stepping toward the carriage house, she added, "I wasn't *that* bad a housekeeper."

≈

EXHAUSTION SENT the McKinney sisters to bed early. The next morning, Chloe told Tess she'd slept better than she had in weeks. Tess couldn't say the same. She'd tossed and turned most of the night, thinking about The Kiss.

They spent the next morning grocery shopping and hounding the health department to release the locks on the trailer long enough to retrieve their personal belongings. They had little success.

"Something about the whole condemnation thing feels weird to me," Chloe said when they returned to the carriage house. "The health department clerk wouldn't look me in the eyes."

"She didn't answer any questions, either," Tess agreed.

"Why? I told her I didn't intend to protest the order. I'm not. I like the carriage house, love the carriage house."

And being banned from the trailer by the authorities gives her the excuse she needs to stay here, Tess thought.

Shortly before noon, Nick dropped by. To Chloe, he said, "I have some bad news. I'm afraid the contents inside your trailer are a total loss."

"I don't understand."

"Racoons weren't the only animal who invaded that trailer. Looks like a couple skunks moved in, too. The good news is that Mrs. Duncan carried a special homeowner's policy on your trailer. All you and Tess need to do is make a list of what was inside, and it will be replaced."

Chloe measured him with a long look. "Something smells about this entire scenario, I'll give you that. What are you trying to hide from me?"

"Nothing."

Tess didn't believe Nick any more than Chloe did. Something had happened at the trailer he didn't want them to know about. Tess held her breath when her sister said, "Tell me one thing. Do you have any reason at all to think that something bad might have happened to Snake?"

He looked her straight in the eye. "No."

"Okay, then. I'm not going to worry about it any longer. I'm not living with Widow Duncan, and as long as Snake's not in trouble, that's all that matters."

Unhappy to have lost the contents of her luggage, Tess debated challenging Nick, but the determination in his steady stare convinced her to follow Chloe's lead and let it go. Nothing she'd lost was irreplaceable. The bottom line was, Chloe would bring her baby home to a safe, comfortable, cool house.

That afternoon, Chloe played house. Tess spent her time on the phone, doing business and arranging to have more clothes sent from California. She was pleased to see her sister happy in the carriage house, though she wished she'd quit insisting they rearrange furniture. If Chloe asked Tess to drag that sofa around the living room one more time, she'd drag it right out of the house.

Tess's muscles wept with relief when Chloe finally declared she was headed upstairs to rearrange her changing table. The woman could fold infant sleepers to her heart's content. Checking on her ten minutes later, Tess found her sister asleep in the nursery rocking chair, a neatly folded pile of tiny T-shirts in her lap.

The doorbell rang, and Tess went back downstairs to the front door.

"The Welcome Wagon has arrived," Widow Gault said as she swept into the house like a barquentine at full sail. "My green bean casserole is still warm, and I need to set it down. Which way to the kitchen? I made it with low-fat cream of mushroom soup so it'll be all right for Chloe to eat. She's run to fat with this pregnancy, hasn't she? I'll bet Doc Fisher is giving her what-for over her weight gain."

"Oh, hush, Martha." A woman Tess recognized from the baby shower, the one who'd worn dangling grape earrings, handed Tess a gaily ribboned gift bag, but kept hold of a basket of bread. "Don't pay her any mind. She didn't have her prunes today."

"Well, I never!" Martha sniffed with disdain as she sailed forward into the kitchen.

Uncertain how to respond, Tess offered up a smile.

"I'm Adele, by the way. Adele Watkins. We all met at the baby shower, but I know it's difficult to remember names when you meet so many people at once. I'm part of Kate Cooper's family. Ms. Prune here is the Widow Gault. The Widow Mallow is the old gal in that awful yellow dress who's still outside rooting around in her trunk. Melody Mallow is the official Welcome Wagon woman in town. Martha tagged along because she's nosey. I came because I like to annoy those two. Where's Chloe? Is she resting? I hope so. The last few weeks of pregnancy are just miserable on a woman."

"Yes, Chloe is upstairs asleep."

Adele beamed a smile at Tess. Today she wore different earrings, oranges this time, and they swung back and forth in a dizzying arc as she lowered her voice and continued to talk. "Now, don't you let these old bags give you a bad impression of Brazos Bend. For the most part, the people here are just as nice as you could want. I haven't lived here all that long myself, so I can make that statement from an unclouded viewpoint."

She took a seat in the rocking chair and spoke in a normal volume. "Now, open the bag before the Widow Mallow comes in with all her refrigerator magnets. It's a little welcome gift for you."

"How nice. Thank you." Tess pulled a scented candle from the bag as Martha Gault reentered the room. Just then the doorbell sounded once more. Tess hurried to answer it. "Hello, Mrs. Mallow. Please come in."

The woman smiled, shoved a brown paper shopping bag at Tess, and launched into her spiel. "Allow me to be the first to welcome you to Brazos Bend. As a new homeowner in our fair town, you are entitled to a variety of gifts, certificates, and coupons from local merchants and businesses. I need to get a little information first for our records." She removed a steno pad from her handbag, flipped back the cover, took a seat on the sofa, then poised her pen above the page. "Let's see what I have already. You are Tess McKinney, but is there a middle name? You're from Hollywood, California? We know you have enough money to buy this house for cash in a single day. Why have you moved to Brazos Bend? We understand you're not married, but are you single, widowed, or divorced? How long have you been dating that nice TV lawyer, Jake Muldoon?"

The inquisition took Tess's breath away. "But I'm not—"

"Why don't you just ask her the last time she had sex while you're at it, Melody?" Adele drawled.

"Adele Watkins!" the Widow Gault snapped in a scandalized tone. "Really. Mrs. Mallow wouldn't ask something like that."

Adele answered with a disgusted roll of her eyes.

"I'm just trying to fill in my forms," Melody Mallow defended. "I can't leave blanks."

Adele met Tess's gaze. "Guess who made up the forms."

Ah, life in a small town, where it's everybody's business to learn everybody's business. To think she'd almost forgotten this. Falling back onto other southern small-town ways, she said, "May I offer you ladies a glass of tea and a piece of pecan pie?"

Apparently anxious to get on with the business of being nosey, everyone but Adele declined. "Plain old water will be fine for me, honey. No ice."

Tess excused herself and fled to the kitchen, filled a glass with water, and started thinking again rather than just reacting. She needed to take control of these women and this situation right now, or she'd be paying for it for as long as she remained in Brazos Bend. She managed Hollywood talent for a living. Surely she could handle the Widows of Brazos Bend.

Returning to the living room, Tess handed Adele her water, took a seat, and said, "Ladies, it's natural to be curious when a newcomer arrives in town, and I understand that. However, as someone who works with Hollywood stars on a daily basis, I also value privacy. I am willing to answer a few of your questions, but I must insist that you, in return, respect my right to privacy when I wish to assert it."

Adele Watkins sat back in her rocking chair, a satisfied smile on her face. The two widows pursed their lips into identical prune-faced frowns. "No need to be snippy," Widow Gault said. "Mrs. Mallow is simply doing her job."

Tess gave her best salesman's smile. "Let me help. My legal name is Teresa Louise McKinney, but I've gone by Tess all my life. I have not moved to Brazos Bend. I'm visiting to help my sister through these last weeks of her pregnancy, and I'll be returning to California as soon as she and her baby are settled. This is my sister's house, not mine. Let's see, what else was there? Oh, yes, I've never been married. That should do it."

"But what about Jake Muldoon?" the Widow Mallow asked.

Ignoring her, Tess reached into the paper bag the woman had given her upon arriving. "What do we have here? Why, isn't this cute. It's a little tooth."

She held up a refrigerator magnet in the shape of a molar advertising Doc Blanchard, the Gentle Dentist. "What other goodies have you brought me? Hmm...a pencil...a pen...two free games at Harmon Lanes. Oh, and look at this. A coupon for a banana split at the Harmon Lanes soda fountain. Is that as sinfully delicious as it sounds?"

Her distraction worked, and for the next fifteen minutes, her guests acted more like true Welcome Wagon ambassadors than leaders of the Spanish Inquisition. When they stood to leave, Tess experienced that familiar satisfaction of a job well done.

As Mrs. Mallow and Mrs. Gault made their way down the front walk, Adele Watkins hung behind. She gave Tess's hand a little squeeze. "Good job, girl. I had a feeling you'd know how to handle the old biddies, and I love to be proved right. I hope you enjoy your time in Brazos Bend."

"Thank you," she replied sincerely. "And thank you for the candle. I'm very glad you stopped by."

Halfway down the walk, Adele stopped, turned back, and sighed. "Tess, I have a confession to make. I'm a nosy busybody almost as bad as those two women who just left here. I watch daytime and reality TV shows and I read tabloid newspapers, and I'm simply not strong enough not to ask."

Foreboding and amusement warred within Tess, and she winced a little as she inquired, "Ask what?"

Adele took two steps closer. Lowering her voice some, but not all that much, she said, "That Jake Muldoon is the hottest man on TV. You're dating him. Is he as good in bed as he looks?"

At first, the question took her breath away. Then, her grin grew wide as the perfect response occurred to her. "Hold the thought, Adele. I'll be right back."

She laughed aloud as she strode into the house, retrieved her cell phone, then marched back outside. It took two tries and moving to different spots in the yard before the call went through, but eventually, that familiar, sexy voice rumbled, "Hello, beautiful."

"Hi, Jake."

"Jake?" Adele mouthed, her eyes going wide. "Jake Muldoon?"

The voice on the phone asked, "Are you back to civilization, I hope?"

"I'm still in Brazos Bend." Tess winked at Adele. "A friend of mine asked a question I thought you should be the one to answer. Will you talk to her?"

"For you, beautiful, anything."

"Okay. My friend's name is Adele, she's one of the leading citizens in Brazos Bend, and her question, Mr. Muldoon, is, Are you as good in bed as you look?"

There was a long pause, then he burst out laughing. "Put her on the phone."

A wicked grin tugging at her mouth, Tess handed the phone to Adele, who removed the dangling earring from her right ear and said, "Um...hello?"

Adele's eyes rounded even more as she listened intently. She staggered toward the porch and reached out to the rail for support. Her gaze flew to Tess's. "It's him," she mouthed. "It's really him."

Tess chuckled and nodded.

"Yes," Adele responded. "I did. Uh-huh. I know. Oh, heavens no. I admit to fifty-eight, but the truth is somewhere north of that."

She listened another minute, then took a seat on a porch step. "Well, it all started when Chloe, that's Tess's sister, spied a picture of you and Tess in one of the entertainment magazines at the beauty shop and showed it around. Once we realized you had a local connection, we sort of adopted you as our favorite celebrity."

Tess took a seat on the porch beside Adele and tried to pick up Jake's words. All she heard were murmurs. Then Adele's gaze flew toward Tess. "Oh, really? Yes...yes...oh my. No, I'm not going to ask that."

Tess pretended to scowl.

Adele listened, then laughed. "That's different. You're a celebrity.

Besides, you're just a voice on the phone and a pretty face on TV, but she's sitting right beside me. I have a little decorum left. Not a lot, but enough."

Tess heard Jake's laughter and smiled. The man was a born tease, plus he had a soft spot for aging women. She'd known he'd enjoy bantering with someone like Adele.

"Now, that's doable. Uh-hum. Yes. Yes." Adele chuckled. "Oh, you are wicked, Jake. Downright deliciously wicked. Yes, I'll do that. You will? Oh, I'll be the envy of Brazos Bend. That is, after Tess, here."

She rattled off her address, telephone number, and cell number, and promised to call later with news. She glanced at Tess when she said that, tipping her off to mischief ahead. Sure enough, when Adele handed Tess back her cell phone, she said, "So, that darling Jake told me he's too modest to brag about his bedroom performance, but we agreed that one of the most telling aspects of a man's capability is stamina. He said you'd vouch for his, and that you'd tell the truth."

"Okay, Muldoon," Tess murmured, staring at the phone in her hand, a smile playing on her lips. "You win."

It was an old joke between them, one that had its beginnings shortly after she'd signed him as a client and they'd run a charity 10K race together. A long distance runner, he'd finished the race having barely broken a sweat. As she crossed the finish line, sweaty, and too tired to think, she'd accused him of having the stamina of a stallion.

He'd found a way to make her pay for her choice of words ever since, the cad.

"So?" Adele prodded.

Tess sighed heavily, stood. She could attempt to explain the joke, but why bother? He probably was a stud in the bedroom. "Jake Muldoon has the stamina of a stallion."

From behind her, she heard Nick say, "Isn't it great what Viagra can do for those poor souls who need it?"

CHAPTER 8

IT WASN'T Nick's habit to eavesdrop. But then, for the past year and a half he'd abandoned many old habits and adopted plenty of new ones.

Tess turned toward him. "Nick, I didn't hear you arrive. Oh, you brought horses."

"Yeah. When I glanced down the hill and saw the Widow Gault's car, I thought you might need an escape." He also wanted to clue her in about the trouble at the trailer, and he wanted to do it privately. "There's a nice picnic spot not far from here. It's a relaxing way to greet the evening. Do you ride?"

She cast a quick, longing gaze toward the horses. "It's been a long time, and it sounds lovely, but I probably shouldn't leave Chloe. She needs to eat a healthy dinner, and—"

"I'll stay with her," Adele piped up. "I'll whip up something and see that she eats it. I need to talk to her anyway. I forgot to tell her that I've decided to accompany my new gentleman friend to Galveston in his Winnebago. We're leaving in the morning, and unless her baby comes early, I should be home in plenty of time to help when she comes home from the hospital. You are staying until the baby's born, right, Tess?"

"Yes."

"Good. Now, go with Nick. The weather's not all that hot for August, and it's hard to beat a nice horseback ride on an evening like this. I see just enough wispy clouds to give us some spectacular color at sunset."

"I saddled the palomino for you," Nick added, motioning toward the corral fence where the two horses were tied. "Her name's Ginger."

The horse was beautiful, and the gentle swish of her tail closed the deal. "Let me change. I bought some jeans today and...hmm...my new boots are dress boots. I probably shouldn't use them for riding."

"I keep extras around for guests, and I'm sure I have some that will fit you. We'll stop by the tack room and grab a pair."

They spoke little at first. Tess appeared content to watch the rabbits scamper and the cardinals flit from tree to tree. She guided her horse just off the trail to where a large wild honeysuckle grew. She plucked a blossom, tore it open, and touched the tip of her tongue to the droplet of nectar hanging from the stamen. "I haven't done that since I was a kid," she told him with delight.

As he watched her, Nick's thoughts moved in a definite adult direction.

He laughed at himself as he veered onto the side trail that would lead them through the woods down to the isolated creek that eventually flowed into Possum Kingdom Lake. Today he'd spent more time thinking about a woman, thinking about sex, than he had in the past eighteen months. Not that he'd given up sex entirely, but that was different from this. That was scratching an itch. This was...interest.

So what could he infer from this surge of libido? Was time the important factor? Had he forgotten enough? Forgiven enough? Healed enough? Or was it simply the woman?

Nick discovered he was anxious to find out.

The trail broke from the woods into a pasture. Tess pulled up beside him and asked, "Can we run the horses?"

"Be my guest. I took down the fences, so it's a clean shot all the way to the trees to the north. That road is private," he said, pointing toward a line of gravel that bisected the northern third of the pasture.

"Shouldn't be any traffic to worry about, but sometimes kids will sneak three-wheelers down this way."

"This is your land?"

He nodded.

"So you're a rancher in addition to your other occupations?"

"Shoot, no. It's not that much land. Just enough to remind me that I'm Texan. I figure if you're going to live in the country, you might as well have lots of country to live in. I own the land between my house and Bluff Creek."

She made a point of glancing back toward where they'd come, then forward in the direction of the creek, then repeated. "Not that much land?"

He grimaced. "Well, I don't run cattle. You can't call it a ranch unless you run cattle."

"That's in the rancher rule book?" she asked, a grin playing at the corners of her mouth. Had she been within reach, he'd have kissed her.

"If it's not, it should be. Now, quit giving me a hard time and let Ginger have her exercise."

Laughing, she nudged Ginger into a trot, then a run. Nick sat with his hands crossed on the saddle horn and enjoyed the sight as the two golden females flew across the pasture. Tess could ride, he observed. Good hands. Good seat.

Very nice seat.

He wondered how long she'd been involved with that actor. As a rule, Nick didn't poach other men's women. He'd always stayed completely away from married women and engaged-to-be-married women, although both continued to offer him opportunities on a regular basis. He tried to avoid women already in a relationship, but sometimes it took a date or two to figure that out. Yet as he watched Tess McKinney lean over Ginger's neck and urge her to speed, he knew he'd make a run at her no matter what. If the Hollywood star couldn't take a little competition, then he didn't deserve a woman like Tess.

Nick kicked his horse and chased after Tess. Ten minutes later, he swung from his saddle, secured his reins, then turned to help Tess dismount. She was quicker than he'd hoped, so he missed the chance to get his hands around her waist. For now.

"That was fun," Tess said, after she'd followed his example and tethered Ginger to the hitching post he'd installed a few yards away from the picnic spot. "Thank you, Nick. I hadn't realized how much I miss riding."

He tried not to let his mind follow the obvious path. "Glad you enjoyed it. Here, my picnic spot is this way."

He'd left the pathway to the bluff overgrown on purpose. This spot was Nick's retreat, and he wanted his privacy maintained. "I've cleared the path of poison ivy and poison oak," he told her as he held back the leafy branches of a cedar for her to pass. "Watch your step, though, because the path leads downhill for about fifteen feet. It's a little rocky."

Tess maneuvered the path with grace and as she approached the clearing, to Nick's surprise, he felt a little anxious. "It might not compete with a Malibu beach home for sunset watching, but it's not bad for the Texas Hill Country."

"I've always thought the Texas sky...oh, my." Tess glanced over her shoulder, her expression shocked. "This is what you call a picnic spot?"

"Yeah." Nick sauntered forward. "Isn't it great?"

At the top of a thirty-foot bluff overlooking Bluff Creek, he'd built a "picnic spot" fit for a king. Constructed of Austin stone and cedar, the architect had called the structure a modified gazebo. It reminded Nick of a three-sided bandstand. It came equipped with hot and cold running water, a bathroom, separate refrigerators for wine, beer, and real food, a great polished parquet bar rescued from the Hutton Hotel, a sound system to make Jimmy Buffett jealous, a barbeque grill to make Emeril Lagasse weep, and Nick's favorite piece of furniture ever—an old, ratty Naugahyde recliner.

"Have a seat," he said, gesturing toward a bar stool. "What can I get you to drink?"

She requested bottled water with lime, and he fixed her up, then went to work lighting the grill and seasoning the steaks. A pair of mourning doves cooed from a pecan tree on their right, so he left the sound system off and allowed nature to provide the music. He eyed the sky, checked his fire, and decided he'd timed it just about right. They should finish dinner shortly before sunset. He could put off talking about the trailer until then.

Tess sipped her water and watched the slow swirling reddish flow of the creek below. "You're wrong," she said suddenly.

"Wrong about what?"

"This spot is as nice as Malibu. It's different, certainly, and maybe the beauty is more subtle, but it's peaceful. It makes me feel like we're the only people around for miles and miles. I never feel that way in California. It's nice."

Nothing she could have said would have delighted Nick more. "I love it here."

She arched a wry brow, then shot a pointed look toward the recliner occupying the shelter's prime spot. "Obviously, or you wouldn't have furnished it with your favorite chair."

Nick grinned as he set the steaks on the grill, then paused to appreciate the resulting sizzle. "How did you guess?"

"About the chair?"

"Yeah."

Tess smirked. "You buy the best, Nick Sutherland. Everything from the appliances to the electronics to your barbecue tools are top-of-the-line, and I know because I've researched some of them for clients who do commercials. You remodeled Chloe's carriage house from top to bottom and everything in it is first class. That La-Z-Boy is an abomination. Olive green and split in two places. It doesn't fit with its surroundings, so it must fit you."

"You're pretty smart for a girl."

"That was a typically stupid remark for a lawyer."

"Ouch."

"But you're interesting, Sutherland." She swirled the ice in her glass. "That ratty old recliner makes you an interesting man."

"The fact you think so makes you an especially interesting woman, Ms. McKinney."

They shared a smile, and the mischief in her eyes made him want to show her what fun could be had in a ratty green recliner. Instead, he checked the potatoes he'd placed in the oven to bake earlier that afternoon, then pulled a pair of plates from the cabinet. Tess slid off her bar stool, washed her hands, and took over the task of setting the table. A comfortable quiet settled between them as they worked. Nick turned the steaks and decanted a bottle of Napa Valley cabernet.

He noted movement off to their left and nudged her with his elbow. Meeting her gaze, he nodded toward the trees. A doe and her fawn stood in the shadows, watching them.

"Oh, how perfect."

That sentiment pretty much summed up the evening, Nick thought as they finished dinner. They'd talked art over the salad and favorite travel spots over steak. Dessert was a cautious foray into politics. She was a typical Hollywood liberal; he, a predictable Texas conservative. The discussion was lively and intellectually stimulating, and it kept his mind off sex. For the most part. He'd have had an easier time of it had she not licked the chocolate off the strawberries before she bit into them.

The sun was beginning to sink into the hills when he took her hand and led her to a quilt spread near the edge of the bluff. Silently, they sat and watched the sky turn vibrant shades of red, orange, and gold. Nick couldn't recall the last time he'd felt this content. He didn't want to spoil it with talk of slaughtered possums. However, he'd put it off long enough.

"I need to tell you something. It's about the trailer."

She sighed softly and looked as reluctant to discuss this as he did. "It burned down, didn't it?"

"No."

"No? Since you replaced all her things, I thought something awful must have happened there."

"It did." He told her about the break-in and destruction, glossing over the bloody mess as best he could.

As he talked, Tess's complexion grew pale. "This scares me to death," she said when he'd finished. "Who would do that?"

"Don't know."

"What if she'd been there alone? What were they looking for?"

"I don't know that, either. They were definitely looking for something, but we can't be certain whether they found it or not. Due to the level of destruction, I suspect they left empty-handed. Somebody had to be seriously sick or seriously angry to do what they did."

"Maybe they were both. Nick, is Chloe in danger?"

"Honestly, I don't think so, although it's obvious good ol' Snake is right in the middle of the mess. I feel better knowing that she—and you—are at the carriage house rather than out in the middle of nowhere."

"I'd like to get my hands on Snake," Tess grumbled. "He has a lot of explaining to do."

Nick plucked a bright yellow dandelion from the grass beside the quilt and offered it to Tess. She accepted it with a smile and sat twirling it between her fingers. Lucky flower. He cleared his throat. "I've hired someone to find him."

Her brows arched in surprise.

"You said it. He has a lot of explaining to do. I'm his mother's attorney, remember, and as such it's my duty to watch out for her interests."

Pensively, Tess asked, "What do you think he's involved in?"

"Could be anything. Drugs. Car theft. My connections tell me there's a big market in Texas for stolen auto parts."

"It gives me chills to think of Chloe being involved with a man like that, having a child with a man like that. I'm afraid it's not out of character for her, though. She's always been attracted to the wild side. What do you think the chances are you'll find him?"

"Oh, we'll find him. It may take some time, but eventually we'll run him to ground."

"Hmm..." As the sun sank below the treetops, Tess stretched out her legs in front of her and tapped the toes of her boots together. "So, let me see if I have this straight. You're an attorney, a carpenter, a cowless rancher, and an accomplished chef. Now you're telling me you have 'connections'? What does that mean? Are you a private investigator? A mob boss? A government spy?"

He gave her a sidelong look. "I could prove I'm a world-class lover."

She tossed the dandelion at him. "Don't try to change the subject. What's with you, Sutherland? Why are you going out of your way to help my sister and who knows who else here in town?"

Atonement. Repentance. Guilt.

Personally, Nick would rather think about being a world-class lover.

"Brazos Bend is my home," he said, shrugging. "If I can help make it a happier, healthier place, I'm glad to do so."

Her eyes narrowed suspiciously, but he laid a finger against her lips before she could speak. "How about we forget about your sister and Snake Duncan for a while and enjoy the sunset?"

She gave him a long, considering look, then nodded, and for the next few minutes, they silently watched the sky. Fingers of vermilion and gold streaked across cerulean blue as crickets began to chirp. Nick topped off their glasses of wine, breathed deeply of the scent of burning cedar still lingering in the air, and sighed with contentment as peace stole through his soul.

Tess sipped her wine, then betrayed a terrier aspect to her character as she asked, "Tell me how you ended up in Brazos Bend."

She couldn't have picked a better subject to take the romance out of the moment. He wanted to lie back and bang his head against the ground. Instead, he opened his mouth to give her the pat response he gave everyone who asked that question, then, to his surprise, found himself telling her something—more. "I'm running away."

Tess drew back. Her eyes narrowed. "If you tell me you're secretly married with six children, I'm going to push you into that creek."

"No. No wife, no children. I was married briefly during college, but it ended before it really started." Following a moment's pause, he added in a chastising tone, "I have a lot of faults, Tess, but I'm not a cheater."

In the gathering dusk, he saw her wince. "I apologize. I'm old-fashioned and more than a little sensitive on the subject of fidelity. It's happened to me in the past, you see. I dated a man for three months who conveniently forgot to mention he had a wife and three children at home. When I learned the truth, I felt...well...I don't date married men."

"And if I were married, I wouldn't have asked you to come riding."

76

The silence that fell between them threatened to be awkward until Nick took hold of her hand and squeezed it. She smiled in response, then put the uncomfortable moment behind them while they watched the sky fade to mauve and shades of purple. When cicadas added their music to the chirp of crickets in the grass, Nick knew of no other place on earth he'd rather be at this moment.

Then, in a display of tenacity that disconcerted, but failed to surprise, him, Tess asked, "So, if not a wife, what *are* you running from?"

"I was hoping you'd forgotten about that." Nick wished he'd never opened his mouth about that. Better he talked more about the trailer trouble. How could he explain something he didn't understand himself?

He settled for telling her something he did understand. "Brazos Bend is a little like Oz."

"Complete with the Wicked Witch of the West, aka Mrs. Duncan, according to Chloe."

He smiled at her, then told her his story of how his hunt for a chess piece separated from a historical treasure during World War II had led him to discover the appeal of life in small-town Texas. He skipped the part of the story where he'd wanted to date Kate Harmon, who'd thrown him over for her old flame, Max Cooper. Some things a man didn't share.

"I needed to get away from Dallas, and it seemed a logical spot to come to. It was a good decision. I like life in Brazos Bend."

Tess gave a little shudder. "You don't miss the excitement of the city? The entertainment? The sports?"

"Hey now, Brazos Bend can be pretty exciting. As far as entertainment goes, you haven't lived until you've attended a Brazos Bend Fish Fry and Bingo Night. For sports, the high school teams put on as good a show as the Rangers or the Cowboys. There's a great golf course over at the lake, I play once a week, and the basketball court at the park suits me just fine for pickup games."

"Hmm...what about Chinese food? Can you get good Chinese in Brazos Bend?"

"Okay. I'll give you that one. But the barbecue is a decent trade-off."

She smiled, and their gazes met and held. The air between them sizzled. Nick was drawn to her like a moth to a light on a summer night, and he was tempted, oh so tempted. He had wanted her from the moment she walked into the hotel ballroom. Kissing her had only made that wanting worse. Spending time with her tonight, getting to know the woman beneath the concerned-sister-with-a-movie-star-face, took it beyond a simple sexual pull. Emotion had entered into the mix. Nick looked at Tess McKinney and wanted her in a way he hadn't wanted a woman in a very long time. In other words, not just for sex.

It scared the hell out of him.

"We should probably be getting back," he said, his gaze dropping to her mouth.

"All right."

She licked her lips, and he lost his train of thought. Would she taste like chocolate and strawberries?

"Dinner was lovely, Nick. Thank you."

"You're welcome." Welcome. Wanted. Needed. Damn. Nick rolled to his feet, and offering her a hand, helped her rise, then immediately turned her loose. She brushed off the seat of her pants. His hands itched to help. "Chloe's probably wondering what's keeping you."

"Oh. Yes. All right."

Just one little taste. That's all. He'd take just one little taste.

Yeah, right. Nick swallowed hard. "It's getting dark. The horses know the way, but we'd better go. Now. Now, before I..."

"Before you...?"

To hell with it. Nick shoved his hands into the back pockets of his jeans. He was known for his language skills in courtrooms all across the country. "Tess, I...you...we..."

"Yes?"

If asked, women in five countries, including Australia, could vouch for the smooth sophistication of his seductions. "Um...I think..."

"You think what?"

Nick was a graduate of Harvard Law. He'd dined with princesses, danced with the First Lady. He'd had an audience with the pope, for

78

heaven's sake. He always made a good impression. Always remained in control. Until now.

Obviously, he'd spent way too much time in Brazos Bend. Otherwise, when Tess asked him what he was trying to say, he never would have responded, "Tess? You wanna skip the ride back and help me plow the back forty?"

CHAPTER 9

NICK LAY SPRAWLED across his bed, caught in a crisis of self-doubt. Plow the back forty? Had he lost his ever-lovin' mind? Now that his libido had finally come roaring back—with a vengeance—had he totally lost his touch?

Needing reassurance, Nick called an old girlfriend in Milan, who cursed him in fiery, fluid Italian for waking her. An apology worthy of Casanova himself rolled smoothly off his tongue, and within fifteen minutes she'd offered to ditch her current lover, an Italian count, and meet Nick in Monaco for fun and frolic in the Mediterranean sun. He declined with believable regret and hung up marginally reassured about his seductive capabilities.

Next he dialed a Frenchwoman he'd once briefly considered marrying. Their affair had ended badly, and she'd not spoken to him since. She, too, blistered his ear for calling so late, but she, too, soon offered to take up where they'd left off. They ended the call laughing, and Nick felt more his old self.

Still, he wasn't quite back to normal. He made one more phone call, this time local, then grabbed a basketball, loaded a selection of drinks into a cooler, and left the house driving his Ferrari. He allowed himself no more than a glance at the carriage house as he drove by. Lights shone both upstairs and down. *Probably still up discussing what an idiot I am.*

He gunned the car and shot around the corner. A few minutes later, he skidded to a stop in the gravel parking lot at a neighborhood park. He grabbed the cooler and the ball and headed for the basketball court. He shot baskets for a good ten minutes before a tall figure sauntered from the shadows. "So, boy," Max Cooper said, dropping a gym bag beside the cooler. "You want to play a little one-on-one. You ready to get your ass whipped?"

"Big talk for an out-of-shape Aggie." Nick fired the ball at Max. "As I recall, I've won the last two out of three."

"Yeah, well. That's only because I was too tired after an afternoon of world-class sex with my lovely wife. You remember my wife. The beautiful woman who dumped you for me?"

Nick flipped him the bird, then the game began. It was rough and sweaty, filling the night air with the scrape of tennis shoes against cement, the clang of a ball hitting the metal hoop, and masculine grunts of exertion. It was exactly what Nick needed.

Nick won by two baskets and Max groaned with disgust. Leaning over, he braced his hands on his knees and tried to catch his breath. "I never realized how tough regular sex is on a man's basketball game. Between that and the extra slice of pound cake I ate for dessert, I'm slow on my feet tonight."

"Always have an excuse, don't you?" Nick grabbed his shirt off the picnic bench and used it to wipe the sweat rolling down his face and torso.

"Bite me."

As was their habit, they took seats atop the picnic table with the cooler between them. Nick flipped open the cooler and grabbed a bottle of water. Max chose a beer. "So, what has your panties in a wad tonight?"

"Ass," Nick responded without heat. He and Max had been rivals from the first time they met. Thus their conversations were always riddled with insults and digs. Eavesdroppers would never guess they'd become good friends. "I've been hanging around you too much, Cooper. I repeated one of your expressions at a most inopportune time."

"Yeah? What'd'ya say? To who—oh, wait. Adele told Kate. You were taking Chloe McKinney's luscious sister on a date. So, you borrowed one of my moves, hmm? Gotta be careful there, pardner. Such powerful weapons in the hands of an amateur are dangerous."

"This from the man who stored his condoms in his tackle box with his stink bait."

Max winced. "Never gonna live that one down, am I? Seriously, though, is that why you wanted to shoot hoops tonight? Looking for advice from the King of Love?"

"If so, I sure as hell wouldn't have dialed your number. No, I'm looking to learn everything I can about Snake Duncan." As Max set his beer bottle on the picnic table, Nick continued, "Did Kate tell you what we found at the trailer?"

"She said the place had been vandalized. Said you wouldn't let her in to see how bad it was, but that the sheriff told her he thought kids probably did it."

Nick polished off his water and reached for a beer. "That's what the sheriff wants to think, because otherwise he might have a problem on his hands. Somebody searched that place, Max, and got pissed off when they couldn't find what they were looking for."

"And that would be—"

"The million-dollar question. I don't believe Chloe's story that Snake took a job delivering cars across the country for a broker whose name she doesn't recall. This break-in changes everything. I want to find that jackass."

"You think he's into something shady."

"His mother's my client. I think we're better off knowing the truth. I've hired an investigator to find him. In the meantime, I looked into the local angle. Tell me everything you know about Snake Duncan, Max."

"That won't take long." Max took a pull on his beer. "He was ahead of me in school. Only contact I had with him was the night we shared a jail cell in Mineral Wells."

Nick's brows arched. "What the hell did you do?"

"Street racin'." Max smiled at the memory. "A friend of mine had an old, souped-up Charger, and we took it into the city for the races. I was the lucky guy driving against Snake Duncan's rebuilt Chavelle when the law showed up. He somehow managed to sneak a joint past the cops who arrested us. Brazen bastard smoked it right there in the city jail."

"Damn."

"His father died not long after that, and I don't remember much about him from then on. I don't even remember if he finished high school."

"The Widow Duncan told me he graduated from SMU."

Max snorted. "I'd come closer to believing Snake spent time in the Big House rather than a college classroom."

"I'm verifying facts independently."

"Good thing." Max yanked on his shoelaces, then toed off his sneakers. "You can't believe anything Widow Duncan tells you when it comes to her perfect son."

"Know where he went or what he did after he left Brazos Bend?"

"Nope. Of course, I was gone from here for a lot of years, myself. You should talk to Kate's sister. Sarah has lived in Brazos Bend all her life, and she pays attention to who is where doing what. Maybe talk to Stewart Mooney, too. He seems to know everything that goes on in this town."

"More than the widows?"

"Hard to believe, but yeah. When Snake came to Brazos Bend for his uncle's funeral a while back, I remember the two of them talked for a long time out in front of Widow Duncan's house. Struck me funny at the time, 'cause the two of 'em couldn't be more different. Stewart was tall and skinny, all spit and polish in an undertaker's suit. Snake was bulked up and dressed in full biker paraphernalia."

"Bet that made his mother happy."

Max nodded. "That was about six months before you moved to Brazos Bend, and it was the last I heard anything about him until Chloe showed up in town looking for him last spring. Nobody realized he'd been living out at that trailer for a few weeks."

Widow Duncan had told Nick that Snake and Chloe's romance had ended, and he'd moved home in an effort to avoid her continued pursuit, but the loose floozy wouldn't quit hounding him until she'd gotten herself pregnant.

Chloe told a different version. She admitted to a breakup, but claimed a reconciliation once Snake learned of her pregnancy. "Chloe says he's a good mechanic, and that he wants to open a garage in Brazos Bend. She insists that they're in love. But what kind of man wouldn't want to be around when his child is born?"

"Hmm..." Max finished his beer and tossed the empty bottle in the nearby trash can. "So you think he's run away for good?"

Nick sighed and set aside his half-empty beer. "I don't know, Max. I think he might be dead."

~

AT THE CARRIAGE HOUSE, Tess folded her arms and leaned against the bathroom door. "He didn't even kiss me," she told Chloe. "Not so much as a brush on the cheek. Here. Tell me." She blew a breath at her sister's face. "Do I have dragon breath?"

"Geeze, Tess. Don't breathe on me. What if you're sick? Getting sick would be all I'd need."

"But what about my breath?"

"It's fine." Seated on the edge of the marble tub in the master bathroom, Chloe dipped a toothbrush in scouring powder and went back to work cleaning the grout between the tiles of the backsplash.

Tess didn't know why her sister had chosen that particular project at ten-thirty P.M. The tiles and grouting looked perfectly clean to her.

"You shouldn't be worrying about it anyway. I still can't believe you went out on a date with him. What if I'd needed you?"

"Adele stayed the entire time I was gone. She'd probably be more help than me, anyway."

Chloe wrinkled her nose. "I still don't like you dating Nick Sutherland."

"Why not? Why should you care who I date?"

"I don't know. Maybe I'm a little jealous. He drives such hot cars."

84

Tess rolled her eyes. "No need to be jealous, sister dear. I'm not certain that was a date. Have they changed the dating rules in Texas since I've been gone? Have good-night kisses gone out of fashion? It wasn't like he hadn't kissed me before. Maybe it was my fault. Maybe he didn't like the way I kissed. Maybe he didn't enjoy our evening as much as I did. Maybe that's the last I'll see of Nick Sutherland."

Chloe set down her toothbrush. "Get hold of yourself, Tess. This isn't like you. You sound like you're fifteen rather than thirty."

"I know," Tess said. "I handle people for a living, and I'm good at what I do. I read people. But Nick...he's been a constant surprise. I can't figure him out at all. I'd have bet my favorite pair of heels that he was about to kiss me. Then you know what he does? He asks if I want to skip the ride home and help him plow the back forty."

Chloe covered her mouth with her hand. "Plow the back forty? That's what he asked?"

"Yes."

"Nick Sutherland?"

Was that a snort coming from her sister? Defensive now, Tess snapped, "Yes."

"And how did you answer?"

"I didn't know what to say. I didn't know what he was talking about! I made a joke of it. Said thanks, but I left my plowing shoes at home."

Chloe's snort erupted into peals of laughter. She laughed so hard that Tess grew concerned. Could she hurt the baby laughing like that?

"He asked you to have sex with him!" Chloe's laughter broke out once more, and she clutched her belly. "You've lived in the city too long, sister. He's the last bachelor in Texas I'd expect to use that euphemism, but I guess it proves that he's adapted just fine to country life."

"You are kidding me."

Chloe giggled and sputtered for another full minute until she grabbed a length of toilet paper and blew her nose. "That's the funniest thing I've heard in—oh, no." She glanced down. "I laughed so hard I must have peed my pants. I'll be so glad when I...oh. Tess?"

Fluid rushed from between Chloe's legs and slapped onto the tile floor. Tess slowly stood, her eyes on the puddle widening on the tile. "That's not—oh, Chloe. Your water just broke!"

CHAPTER 10

"SHE CAN'T DO THIS!" Tess rushed to her closet pulled out her suit-case, and flung it open on the bed. "My first Lamaze class isn't until tomorrow. She can't go into labor until I've been coached on being a coach."

She grabbed underwear from her drawer and tossed it in the bag. "Her water broke. She *is* doing this. When your water breaks, there's no going back. You're having the baby. I'm not ready for this. Labor. Ice chips."

"What are you doing?" Chloe stood in the doorway, dressed in fresh clothes. She carried a small suitcase in her left hand and rubbed her belly with her right. Serenity gleamed in her expression.

"I'm packing a suitcase. You always pack a suitcase when the baby's coming."

"Excuse me. You pack a suitcase for the *mother*. That's me." She held up the satchel in her hand. "You need to get hold of yourself, Tess. You're out of control."

Chloe was right. This wasn't like her. She managed situations. Situations didn't manage her. This situation had her frightened to her toes. "We need to call the doctor. I think I have his number—"

"I've already called him. He said I need to come on in. I realized I've probably been having mild contractions throughout the day."

"Contractions? And you didn't tell me about it?"

"I thought they were the warm-ups. They're called Braxton-Hicks contractions, and I've been having those for a while now. Get your purse and let's go."

Tess grabbed items on the way out the door. Her purse, her phone, a book, her PDA, carrot spears from the fridge. She truly was losing it.

She stowed Chloe's small suitcase in the trunk, then helped her sister into the car. Walking around to the driver's side, she glanced up the hill toward the Victorian house. This was all Nick Sutherland's fault. She wouldn't be such a basket case if he hadn't been so...so...Brazos Bend. Plow the back forty. For heaven's sake. She slid into the driver's seat, started the car, then backed down the drive. "How do I get to the hospital?"

Chloe gave her the directions, then relaxed against the headrest and closed her eyes.

Tess chewed on her bottom lip as she drove. First babies were usually late. Leave it to Chloe to have hers early. But was it *too* early? "When exactly is your due date?"

"Tomorrow, apparently."

Tess drove a few minutes more in silence before guilt prodded her to ask, "Laughing too hard can't make your water break, can it?"

"I don't think so." Chloe reached over and patted her knee. "Don't fret so, Tess. Everything will be fine."

"You're awfully calm."

"I am, aren't I?"

"We're having a total role reversal here. You do realize that?"

"Wild, isn't it? Must be the full moon."

The full moon. Of course! Emergency rooms were always crowded during a full moon. She should have expected this. A good manager would have anticipated this possibility.

"I always thought today might be the day," Chloe observed. "Full moons have powerful mojo." She paused, and her hands covered her belly. "My contractions are getting stronger."

"We're almost there. Hold on, Chloe. You can't have your baby in my car. It's a rental."

Moments later, Tess spied the red glow of Bethania Hospital's emergency room sign, and an overwhelming sense of relief washed through her. She pulled the car into the semicircular drive and threw the gearshift in park. As she reached to open the door, Chloe stayed her with a touch. "Wait. There's something I probably should tell you."

Tess recognized the note of dread in her sister's voice. Chloe sounded just like this the time she got arrested for going topless on the South Texas beach and called her for bail money. "What is it?" she asked warily.

The moment stretched out. A dozen different problems flitted through Tess's mind. *Please don't let it be something wrong with her baby.* Finally, Chloe grabbed her hand.

"Here, feel this." She pulled up her shirt and stretched her right hand across her bare belly. She moved it around a minute until she found just the right spot. "Feel that? It's a foot."

Tess felt the lump beneath her fingers and smiled.

"And here," Chloe continued, moving the hand, "here is a second foot. The third—" She stretched it way over to the side. "There, feel that? That's the third. We might not find the fourth. He likes to keep it curled toward him, but...there. There it is."

Four feet. Tess felt every one of them. "Your kid has four feet?"

"Four hands, too."

Oh. Oh, my. Her mouth dry, Tess swallowed hard. "Heads?"

"Two. Definitely two."

"And they're not connected in any way they shouldn't be connected?"

"No. They're two separate little beings."

Beings. Plural. Tess licked her lips, blew out a long breath, and said, "Twins."

"Yes, I'm having twins."

And now is the first I hear about it? Tess silently screeched. She took two deep, cleansing breaths, exhausting her knowledge of Lamaze. Okay. Doubles.

They can deal with this. She can do doubles. "Just two, though, right?"

"Just two. I don't know if they're identical or not. We won't know that until they're born. I don't even know if they're boys or girls. I wanted it to be a surprise."

Surprise. Well, she'd definitely managed a surprise. "Why didn't you tell me!"

Chloe hesitated, then spoke in a small, thready voice. "I didn't want to scare you off."

Insulted, Tess repeated, "Scare me off?"

Like turning a switch, their roles reversed, and the universe of the McKinney sisterhood righted itself. "I thought if you knew how much trouble I was in, you might not come. I needed you desperately. I couldn't risk being alone. I can't be alone in this. Promise? Promise me you won't leave me alone."

"When have I not been there for you, Chloe?"

"There's always a first time for everything." With that, Chloe launched into full whine mode. "I'm not sure I can do this. What do I know about have having babies and being a mom and being a family? I have no experience. Children need safety and security. I've never been good at that. I can barely keep myself safe. Remember when I fell out of that redwood during the logging protest? And security. If that's not a joke. What do I know about security? I'm about as secure as...as...ow, this one hurts."

Tess yanked open the car door, flew around to the passenger side, and opened Chloe's door. Her sister sat with both hands pressed against her belly. She didn't move to get out of the car.

"I'm scared, Tess. What if—"

"No. Don't think about what-if's. Think about gonna-be's. In a few hours there's gonna be two more hearts for you to love. You're good at love, Chloe. You're great at love. If you stop and think about it, love is the most important thing."

A single tear slipped from her sister's eyes and trailed down her cheek. Torment swam in her eyes as she looked up at Tess. "I'm afraid I'm not any good at that anymore. I don't...I can't...I'm afraid I don't love one of the babies, Tess."

"Now, why do you say that?"

"Because when I found out I was pregnant, I loved the baby so much. It was instant, and it was huge. It filled up everything inside me. When I found out there were two...I didn't feel it again. All I felt was fear."

While Tess tried to figure the best way to respond to that, Chloe added, "I want Snake."

"I know, honey." Tess felt a rush of anger at the absent father. "I'm sorry he's not here. You'll have to make do with me."

"I love you." Chloe's voice broke on the words.

"I love you, too. Now let's go have these babies, shall we?"

What followed were some of the longest, most harrowing hours of Tess's life. Eleven of them. Six hundred sixty minutes. Seemed like six thousand. Six hundred thousand. Chloe continued to alternate between Jekyll-and-Hyde personas. Chloe the Earth Mother declined pain meds, determined to deliver her children the natural way. Chloe the Transition Terror screamed at the top of her lungs that she'd changed her mind, she wasn't having any babies, thank you very much, and she wanted to get the hell out of this podunk little hospital in this podunk town, and give her her damned clothes back.

The labor and delivery unit had only two beds, and thankfully, the other remained unoccupied. Tess didn't think she could bear the sounds of labor in stereo. Finally, eleven hours, nine minutes, and twenty-seven seconds after they arrived at the emergency room door, Caitlin Michelle slipped squalling from her mother's womb. Stephanie Jeanne followed eighteen minutes and twenty-six seconds later.

Together, Chloe and Tess wept with joy.

KNEELING in the carriage house nursery three days after the babies' birth, Nick stared at the crib diagram and wondered how international companies went about finding such idiots to write their assembly instructions. "Forget it," he muttered, tossing the page aside and reaching for his screwdriver.

"Isn't that just like a man," Tess observed from the bedroom doorway. "They won't read instructions, won't ask for directions. Why is that?"

She wore a pink silk shirt that elegantly draped over her breasts, white hip-hugging Capris, and heeled sandals that called a man's attention to the hot pink polish on her toes. One look at her, and Nick's attention went from baby-accommodating activities to the activity that created babies.

He wanted his hands on her.

"I think it's something left over from the caveman days."

Caveman? He'd show her caveman. He'd like to grab her by that long blond hair and drag her off to bed.

"Nick, you have that rail upside down. The carvings of the forest ferns should reach toward the sky. Aren't these cribs just darling? They fit perfectly with the unicorn motif. I'm so pleased that Baby's World let me return the other one so I could get matching everything."

His sexual fantasies disappeared in the wake of baby-bed reality. Flipping the railing into its proper position, he said, "They'd have been idiots not to accommodate you, as much money as you spent in that place. Hand me that bag of eight thousand screws, would you please?"

Grinning, she tossed the small plastic bag filled with hardware toward him. It fell to the wood floor with an audible *chink*. "Not to be insulting or anything, but I thought you'd have finished this job by now. You are a professional carpenter."

"You need to be an engineer to put this blasted piece of furniture together. Honestly, I think it'd be easier to build a crib from scratch."

Her eyes sparkled with mischief. "At least the second one should go faster for you, since you will have had practice."

Nick growled at her. "Go fix dinner, woman."

"Careful there, Neanderthal." She winked and finger-waved as she turned and left the room. "Your hairy chest is showing."

"I wish," he murmured, sucking air past his teeth as he leaned over to watch those long, luscious legs stride away.

Motivated by the tempting aromas drifting from the kitchen and the prospect of Tess's company, he finished assembling both cribs in record time. Since her nieces' birth, Tess had called on him time and again, mainly to help with such manly activities as moving furniture and assembling gadgets. With Chloe and the babies due home tomorrow, she'd offered dinner tonight as a thank-you, and he'd been quick to accept. With the twins headed home, this might be his last chance to have Tess to himself for a while.

Besides, he needed to catch her up on the latest news about the break-in. To everyone's relief, forensics found only animal blood at the scene. A sheriff deputy located a witness who placed a group of four motorcyclists riding north on Highway 26 twenty minutes before Nick and Kate arrived at the trailer. As of yet, the sheriff had no leads on the perpetrators' identities.

Most interesting of all, the investigator Nick had hired to find Snake had run into some interesting walls. Information was proving harder to get than anyone had anticipated. It set Nick's trouble antenna quivering.

But right now he'd rather join Tess in the kitchen and indulge the quivering of his other antenna, so to speak. With the cribs in place and the packaging hauled out to the overflowing trash bin, he washed up, then walked into the kitchen just as Tess pulled the lasagna from the oven. "That smells great."

"In my circle, I'm famous for my red sauce," she said.

He eyed the long-legged, fair-skinned blond whose genetics screeched Scandinavia. "Ah, obviously your Italian grandmother's secret family recipe."

She laughed. "My grandmother grew up in Sundsvall, Sweden, but I only met her once, and my mother wasn't into cooking traditional family recipes. Mother wasn't into cooking much at all. When I moved to California, I rented a garage apartment from an Italian family. Mama Rose was appalled by my lack of culinary skill and took me under her wing. I do excellent manicotti, braciole, and minestrone."

"Hmm—great Italian cooking. It's possible I could be in love." He folded his arms and leaned back against the counter. "Tell me, ma'am, can you whip up a mess of chicken-fried steak?"

"A mess?" She glanced over her shoulder, her brow arched. "You know, I don't think I've heard that noun used that way since I crossed the Red River."

"How about slopping on some cream gravy with it? Frying up some potatoes and boilin' some greens? If you can do that, I reckon I might have to marry you."

"Gee, Tex," she drawled. "I'm sorry, but I guess the wedding's off. I never learned to do southern."

"Honey, I'm southern." He advanced playfully. "You can practice on me all your little heart desires. C'mon. Do me."

She hesitated, then cocked her hip and crooked her finger, motioning him closer. She reached out grabbed a handful of his shirt, then tugged his head down toward hers. Fire shot straight to his groin as she whispered in his ear. *"Nei suoi sogni!"*

He translated her Italian. *In your dreams.*

"If you only knew, darlin'. If you only knew."

Offering him the plate of antipasto, she said, "And that was as corny a come-on as I've ever seen."

Grinning, he snagged an olive and popped it into his mouth. "True, but we southern boys know how to do corny well."

Then, slanting a glance her way, he casually added, "Besides, the sentiment is completely legit."

She fumbled a piece of prosciutto on the way to her mouth. Having quick hands when required, Nick caught it waist-high. He was lifting it toward her mouth, intending to feed it to her, when the phone rang. Tess grabbed for it like a lifeline.

Nick poured them both wine from the bottle breathing on the counter and sipped from his glass, idly eavesdropping on her conversation with Kate Cooper. Apparently, Kate had just returned from visiting Chloe and the twins, and she wanted to gush. They discussed how beautiful the girls were, something Nick honestly couldn't see. They were tiny and wrinkled and bald and looking a little jaundiced to him. When the conversation took a turn toward breast feeding, he topped off his glass and beat a hasty retreat to the living room.

Tess called him to dinner a few minutes later, and he noticed right away the frown of worry creasing her brow. Kate's call was obviously bothering her. He tried to distract her by honestly praising her cooking, and though she made a decent effort, he could tell she was troubled.

"Okay," he said, giving in. "What's the matter? Do you want me to rearrange the nursery furniture? Again? Have you decided you don't like the matching pink ruffled dresses you bought to bring the twins home tomorrow? Are there not enough diapers in the house? I only counted six cases."

"Hmm..." She daintily wiped her mouth with a white linen napkin. "Come to think of it, we might need more diapers."

Nick savored a final bite of lasagna, then asked, "What's the problem, Tess?"

She sighed heavily. "I'm worried about Chloe. She's exhausted. She cries all the time. She's determined to breast-feed, and it's not going well."

More information than I needed.

"Her milk came in, and her breasts are painful and engorged."

Really more information than I needed.

"But that's probably more information than you want."

"You've come to know me so well." That managed to coax a brief smile from her. "Isn't it normal for a woman's emotions to be all over the place after childbirth? Hormones run amok?"

"Yes, and maybe this is no more than a case of the baby blues. She's probably missing Snake, that cretin. I'm sure that's part of it." Tess sipped from her water glass. "What worries me most is that I don't think she's bonding with the babies the way she should. She doesn't coo and cuddle them. Chloe has always cooed and cuddled babies. This isn't like her."

"Have you talked to her doctor about it?"

"He thinks once she gets the hang of nursing, she'll be fine. He's sending someone from La Leche League to talk with her tomorrow morning before we come home. I hope that helps. And, speaking of help, it's time to change the subject." She lifted her wineglass in salute. "A toast to you, Mr. Sutherland."

"Oh?" Smiling, Nick picked up his wineglass and waited.

"You, sir, have my everlasting gratitude and sincere thanks for all the help you've given me and my sister, especially during these last three days. As soon as we switch the changing tables with the cribs in the nursery, we'll be ready to bring home the twins tomorrow."

He almost tipped his stem. "You *do* want to rearrange furniture. I knew it!"

"Oh, quit complaining and let me finish." Tess's eyes glittered with amusement as she stood and extended her glass. "To you, Nick Sutherland. Without you my sister would be bringing her children home to a hot, marsupial-infested trailer. Without you we'd be short a crib, changing table, car seat, baby swing, etcetera, etcetera, etcetera."

He nodded, as Tess continued, "Now, a nice meal isn't enough to thank you for all of your help, although it is a start. I stand by my red sauce."

"As you well should."

She moved around the table and stopped just beyond arm's reach. Nick indulged in a quick, vivid fantasy of throwing her down on the table and having dessert. Apparently, he wasn't done with the caveman business yet.

Nor was Tess done with her little speech. "However, you deserve more than a simple dinner, and it's difficult to find something to give the man who has everything."

I don't have everything. Yet.

"But then I recalled something an artist friend of mine made a year or so ago for a client, so I called him and commissioned a special rush order. It arrived today."

Well, hell. So much for hoping for payback sex.

In the past, he'd never been one to want payback sex. As a rule he appreciated mutual enthusiasm in his romantic encounters. Now, though, with this particular woman, considering how badly he wanted her and how long it had been since he'd felt this way about anyone, he'd take whatever kind of sex he could get.

She reached beneath the table, and Nick stood as she handed him a tissue-stuffed gift bag decorated with hammers and saws. Nick couldn't help but be pleased. The people in his life seldom gave him gifts. It was always the other way around.

"You didn't need to do this," he said, beginning the dance of politeness taught from the cradle. "I was simply being neighborly."

"You went above and beyond, Nick, and you know it."

"Moving those changing tables again would be above and beyond."

"One more time. That's all. I promise."

"She promises. Right." He took his time unwrapping the tissue paper from around the gift, until Tess complained that he was too slow.

"You sound just like my mother. When everyone else had finished unwrapping their gifts on Christmas morning, I still had a stack left." He touched hard metal beneath the white paper and tested the shape, trying to guess what it could be.

"One of those types," Tess replied with a disgusted snort.

Nick glanced up, shot her a steamy look, and drawled, "Anticipation increases the pleasure, Ms. McKinney."

She blinked. "Oh."

Satisfied he'd made his point, he turned his attention to opening his gift. Delight washed through him as he fully revealed a sign artfully fashioned from wrought iron and wood. "Nick's Secret Hideout," he read aloud. He smiled as he took in the smaller print. "Girls always welcome."

"Your creekside hideaway seems the sort of place that needs a sign," Tess explained.

"I love it." He truly did. For all its adult luxury, his picnic site was an appeasement to the boy in him. He'd always wanted a Swiss Family Robinson tree house, and since trees big enough to hold one didn't exactly grow in Brazos Bend, he'd built the next best thing. No tree house—hideaway was complete without a sign, and the fact that Tess recognized that before he had figured it out touched him.

"You couldn't have chosen anything more perfect. Thank you, Tess." He grabbed her hand, pulled her toward him, and planted a kiss on her mouth. "Hmm...that is some red sauce."

"Mama Rose's recipe."

The huskiness in her voice sent heat zinging through him, and he drew her even closer and indulged them both with a long, open-mouthed kiss. Damn, but this woman felt like heaven in his arms. Tall enough that he didn't have to contort himself to taste her. Rounded in all the right places. When her arms crept up around his neck, he growled his approval low in his throat. When her teeth nipped at his bottom lip, the kiss went white-hot.

He backed her up, flattening her between his body and the kitchen wall, and plunged his tongue into her mouth. The sound of her throaty moans rumbled through him and made him shudder with need. When she twisted her hips, rubbing her belly against his raging erection, he wanted to howl.

He nipped his way across her jaw to her neck as his hand delved beneath her shirt to find the bountiful treasure of her breast. Silk. Her bra, her skin. Soft hot silk. He thumbed her nipple and knew he needed to taste her. He needed to have her. Now. And damned if he'd play the country yokel this time.

His fingers made smooth, quick work of her bra's front catch, and he spoke to her in Italian. "In my dreams? Oh, yes. I dream of a sun-kissed Tuscan vineyard. You walk beside me, a warm summer breeze stirs your hair as you pluck a plump, ripe grape from an old-wood vine. Sunshine glistens in your hair, laughter dances in your eyes as you offer me the fruit. But you're a tease, my Tess, and before my tongue reaches out to taste the red, juicy fruit, you steal it away and pop it into your mouth. I'm left to take my own satisfaction by slowly sucking the juice from your fingers one by one."

Tess shuddered. "Nick."

He smiled as he kissed his way down her throat. In French, he said, "In my dreams, you walk a Mediterranean beach in moonlight. Foamy surf laps at your bare feet as you stride across the sand. I watch you walk toward me, a confident, carefree naturist. You halt just beyond my reach and lift your arms, palms upward, back arched, face lifted toward the star-studded sky, a goddess of love bathing in Mediterranean moonlight. Seducing the man who watches and wants."

"Nick...I...oh," she sighed as his tongue laved her breast.

In a slow Texas drawl, he said, "In my dreams, woman, I lift you into my arms and carry you upstairs to your bed. In my dreams, I make love to you. Here. Tonight. Now."

She moaned low and slow as he took her breast in his mouth and tasted her, suckled her, until her knees buckled and he swept her up into his arms. "Invite me upstairs, Tess, and make my dreams come true."

She gazed up at him, her eyes soft, luminous with desire. "I want to say yes. No one has ever made me want to say yes quite this badly before."

Well, hell. That sure sounded like a no.

"Oh, Nick." She sighed breathlessly, then pulled her shirt together. "You could change my mind so easily. I can barely think as it is."

"Then why bother? Why not simply feel? We would be so good together, Tess."

"I know." She reached up and caressed his jaw. "I know. But that's what I do, Nick. I think. I don't allow my emotions to rule me. I may be from Hollywood, but I'm not that fast. I won't go blindly into an affair."

"Blindly?" He set her on her feet. "Don't tell me you've not thought about this, thought about us. We've been circling the subject since the day we met."

"Yes. That long ago. What's it been now? A whole week? No, not even that."

"I've wanted you from the moment you walked into my ballroom. I haven't felt this way about a woman in a very long time, Tess. I don't know that I've ever felt this way about a woman." But he sure as hell knew he didn't like being classified as an "affair."

She smiled wistfully. "I *know* I've never felt this way about another man. It would be so easy to climb those stairs with you, Nicholas Sutherland."

"You're killing me here, Tess."

"I'm not doing myself any favors, either. But I sense you could be very dangerous for me, Nick. I'm only a visitor in Brazos Bend. You're very settled here. What if we took this to the next step and...well..."

"Liked it?"

"Oh, I don't doubt that we'd like it. I suspect we'd like it very much, and therein lies the problem. What if we didn't want it to end? How would we manage that?"

"Why not cross that bridge when we come to it?"

Her smile turned sad. "That's not who I am, Nick. I'm a manager. I can't—I won't—go into this without having considered all the possibilities and made my peace with them."

Frustration rolled through him. "You sure know how to take the romance out of the moment."

"I know. And after you did such a grand job of putting it in there, too."

Smugly, he agreed. "I did, didn't I?"

"An Italian vineyard. The French Riviera. The language, the timbre of your voice. It was a masterful seduction, Mr. Sutherland."

"Thank you."

"However—" She cocked her head and studied him, mischief twinkling in her eyes. Nick wanted to bite her neck. "I have a sneaking suspicion that when I go to bed tonight—"

"Yes?" he prodded.

"I imagine I'll be dreaming, too."

"Whatcha gonna dream about? France? Italy?"

"Probably—" She stood on her tiptoes and whispered in his ear. "Plowing the back forty."

TESS TOOK A LONG, cold shower, then thumbed the thermostat down to extra-cool and crawled into bed. "In my dreams, Nick Sutherland," she murmured as she slipped between the soft cotton sheets. Lovely, lovely dreams.

She needed to think about this. Make a decision. She wouldn't go into an affair with the likes of Nicholas Sutherland on a hormonal high. That only asked for trouble. No, she'd weigh the pros and cons, and if she decided she wanted to do it, she'd go into the affair with her eyes wide open.

Imagine seeing Nick naked in her bed. He'd look good on midnight blue sheets. Those big hands of his would stroke across her body. Cupping her breasts, kneading them, his fingers tugging at her nipples. Stroking across her belly, her hip, while his mouth followed the path of his hand.

"Aargh!" Hot, Tess kicked off her covers. She'd better police her thoughts, or she'd need another cold shower, and she didn't want to get her hair wet again.

So, keep your thoughts on the problem, not the play.

Okay, so what was the problem? What if she did go to bed with him? Could she keep her heart out of the equation? That wasn't like her. The time or two she'd slept with a man without her heart being involved left her feeling lousy. Sexual satisfaction simply wasn't worth making herself feel...dirty.

Tess's girlfriends laughed about her old-fashioned morality, but she didn't apologize. So what if her viewpoint was the result of growing up in the middle of her parents' dysfunctional relationship? It's who she was. When she went to bed with a man, she needed emotions to be engaged. She didn't necessarily need to be in love, but she at least needed to feel like she was part of a relationship.

So, could she live with herself if she indulged in a week-long relationship with the most eligible bachelor in Texas? Could she love Nick Sutherland and leave him? She couldn't stay in this town much longer. Her clients needed her in L.A. As soon as Chloe and the girls settled in, and Adele Watkins returned from the Texas coast and assumed her nanny role, Tess needed to go home. She wanted to go home. She missed the hustle and bustle of her life in L.A. She missed her house and her friends and the hands-on aspect of her work. While life in Brazos Bend wasn't as awful as she'd originally expected, she still didn't belong here. Could never be happy here.

If she entered a relationship with Nick, what happened if she fell for him? Did she want to risk a broken heart? It wasn't beyond the realm of possibility. She liked this man. A lot. He intrigued her, amused her, and obviously, he fired her blood. If he lived in California, she wouldn't hesitate to explore the possibilities with him. She didn't need a man to be complete, but having one around certainly made life more interesting. Plus, someday she'd like to have children.

Although not two at a time, like Chloe.

And not with a motorcycle gang member who drove off into the sunset in someone else's Maserati and had friends that killed animals for kicks.

Distracted from her thoughts of Nick by worry for her sister, Tess tossed and turned and punched her pillow. She'd never seen Chloe this sad, not even when their family fell apart. Maybe Chloe just needed to be home, away from the hospital, where a nurse woke her to take vitals every time she drifted off to sleep.

Sleep. Tess had better get some sleep to be rested and ready to take on the twins. Tomorrow promised to be an extra long day.

Finally, just after midnight, Tess drifted off. She dreamed of Italian wine and French beaches and a long, tall Texan with a slow drawl and even slower hands.

She awoke smiling at two A.M. with her mind made up.

~

CHLOE AWOKE to a knife to her throat.

Disoriented, it took her a moment to grasp the reality of cold, hard steel against her neck, but in that instant, the metallic taste of fear washed through her.

"Where is he, bitch? What did that asshole do with the money?"

The figure rose above her in the deep shadows of the darkened hospital room like a monster from a nightmare.

"Don't hurt me," she whimpered as the knife point dug into her skin.

"Tell me what I want to know, or I'll slit your throat like a tomato."

Chloe couldn't think. The hulking shape above her, the stink of human sweat, and the gravelly voice overwhelmed her, and she froze, her focus entirely on the pressure at her neck. *Don't hurt me. Don't hurt me. Don't hurt me.*

"Where's Snake? What's he done with our money?" The knife bit into her neck.

Snake? This was about Snake? What money? *Oh, Snake. What have you done?*

"I don't...I don't know where he is." When the pressure at her neck increased, she added, "I haven't seen him in five weeks."

"You're lying, bitch. He came back here, didn't he?"

"No. I haven't seen him!" She wished he'd never taken that stupid job. Since Chloe moved into the trailer with him, he'd been away more than he'd been home. Before he left this last time, he'd been antsy and short of temper. He'd wanted her to leave Brazos Bend.

They'd argued about it for the three days he'd been home between trips.

A different menacing whisper came from beyond Chloe's line of sight. "Hurry up, Bubba C. One of them nurses just went in next door. Snakes bitch might be next."

Chloe's thoughts spun like a springtime tornado. Oh, Snake. How could you leave me to deal with this by myself?

The figure leaned over her and growled. "Last chance, or I start cuttin'. I want the money. Where is it?"

What money! "I have five dollars in my purse."

Pain sliced across her neck. "Try again."

"Okay...okay...okay." Terror churned inside her. She didn't know anything about any money. Snake never told her anything. He wouldn't even tell her why he'd wanted her to leave Brazos Bend. All he'd said was that he'd be more comfortable if she lived somewhere other than the trailer. What kind of reason was that?

Money. What money? What should she say? How best to protect herself? And protect the babies? The babies. Oh, God. Thank God they were in the hospital nursery. "You won't hurt me if I tell you? You won't hurt Snake or our babies?"

"Oh, I'll kill that sumbitch Snake next time I see him. You tell him that's a promise."

Chloe took a deep breath and prayed she was doing the right thing. "It's at the trailer."

"Liar. We searched the fucking trailer!"

"You did?" Well, damn. Her pulse pounded. She thought fast. "Not in the trailer itself. It's in the car. The old '72 Chevy. Did you see it? It's all but hidden in the weeds out back. The money's in the trunk."

The knife fell away from her neck, but he grabbed her by her hard, swollen breast and squeezed it like a vise. A scream rose in her throat, but she kept it to a whimper.

"I'll be back if you've lied to me, bitch, and I won't be near this nice next time. Next time you see Snake, give him a message for me." Then he muttered something about mattresses and fishes, which in her frightened state, she couldn't quite decipher.

Chloe lay still, her eyes closed, for a long minute after the men left her hospital room. She felt a bead of sweat slide across her temple. *Oh God oh God oh God. Thank God they're gone.*

What should she do now? Call the police? The FBI? Her sister? There was no money in the trunk of that car. They'd undoubtedly be back. She had to call the cops.

She couldn't call the cops. Snake was obviously involved in something shady. She couldn't get him in trouble with the law. He was the father of her children.

She had to protect her children. She had to call the cops.

"Damn you, Snake," she whispered into the dark.

This must be why he'd wanted her to leave Brazos Bend. He'd known there might be trouble. Suspected it, anyway. That's probably closer to what happened. Snake wouldn't have left her to face danger alone. Not on purpose.

And when he left, she had promised to leave the trailer and move into town with his mother. But he'd promised to be back three weeks ago.

Something awful had happened to him. She just knew it. Otherwise, he'd have been back before the babies were born. He was excited about becoming a father. He'd wanted to marry her.

They'd argued about that, too, the last time he was home. He'd wanted to marry her before the twins were born. He'd wanted to marry her even though she was fat. While she'd loved him for asking, Chloe didn't want to get married at all. Her parents had taught her how little marriage meant. The day her dad walked out on her mom, she'd sworn she'd never get married, and she'd remained consistent in that area of her life, at least. Hadn't she turned down marriage proposals from five different men?

"I should have married Snake." Maybe then he wouldn't have left her. Maybe then he wouldn't have gotten mixed up with criminals.

Wait. Maybe all this hadn't happened. Maybe she was asleep and having a nightmare.

Maybe she'd be a size six again by next week, too.

A slight squeak of door hinges sent her sitting up straight, reaching for a weapon on her bedside table, finding nothing more dangerous than a plastic bedpan. *What do I do?*

"Chloe, you're awake," said the night nurse, Sue Ayer. "That's good. We'll be bringing in the babies to nurse in just a few minutes."

She approached the bed and pulled the long beaded chain of the fluorescent light above the bed. Instinctively, Chloe ducked her head, hiding what she feared was a thin slice of red along her neck. She didn't want anyone to see it until she figured out what to do. "I'll go to the bathroom and wash."

"That's good," said Sue. "Don't work yourself up, now. I'm certain the nursing will go better this time."

Yeah. Right.

The babies. Protecting them was the most important thing. Even if she called the cops, would they be safe? Would she? They'd be more safe without her than with her.

They'd be safe with Tess.

Oh, help me, Lord. Chloe knew what she had to do.

CHAPTER 11

HOMECOMING day dawned hazy and hot, as was normal on a late August day. In Tess's bedroom at the carriage house, the clock radio switched on, and the rich, strong voice of Patsy Cline tugged Tess from a most lovely dream. She stretched sensuously against her sheets, clinging to the fading glow of a fantasy of unicorns and magical kingdoms and knights who spoke with a slow Texas drawl. Opening her eyes, she hummed along softly to "Crazy." Maybe that should be her new theme song.

Or better yet, "Foolin' 'Round."

Smiling, she sat up, laced her fingers above her head, and stretched from side to side. From the kitchen came the gurgle of the coffeepot and the aromatic perfume of her morning addiction. Tess threw back the covers and headed for the shower. Twenty minutes later, prayerfully sipping her coffee, Tess took a quick inventory of the items she needed to take with her to the hospital. Soft pink dresses and ruffled diaper panties. Itty-bitty socks. Teeny-tiny shoes. Hair bows. Car seats. Diaper bag...or diaper bags. Would having one big one or two smaller ones be better? She couldn't make up her mind.

Having finished her coffee, lighthearted and excited, she loaded her car, including two diaper bags. On the way to the hospital, she took a one-block detour to drive past the Hutton Hotel. Spying Nick's ratty old truck, she honked a hello, knowing he probably wouldn't see or hear her, but appreciating the connection nonetheless.

At the hospital, she parked, popped open her trunk, and gathered up everything but the car seats. She whistled Tanya Tucker's "Baby I'm Yours" as she sailed through Brazos Bend Hospital's central entrance and thumbed the elevator button for the second floor.

Tess couldn't stop grinning in the elevator. In her mind, today marked the official beginning of a brand-new McKinney family. No matter where she lived, where Chloe lived, or who either one of them lived with, she, her sister, and her twin nieces would always share a treasure—the bond of family.

And Tess was determined that despite the McKinney family history, they wouldn't screw it up.

The elevator stopped at the second floor, and the doors whooshed open. Tess stepped out and gave the nurse at the desk a sunny smile. The nurse winced and crossed herself.

Hmm...that's curious.

Tess turned toward the left and sauntered down the hallway toward Room 237. An orderly she passed in the hall halted abruptly, his eyes going round.

All right. That's weird.

She shifted the weight of one of the shopping bags from her right hand to her left and noticed the trio of nurses standing sentry in front of Chloe's room. To a woman, their expressions telegraphed trouble, and Tess's stomach clenched.

Something is wrong.

She dropped her shopping bags and ran to Room 237.

Inside, a pair of candy stripers sat in a pair of rocking chairs feeding bottles of formula to a pair of babies. Stephanie. Caitlin. Thank God.

"Hi, Auntie Tess," one of the volunteers said, offering a wide, though fake, smile. "Good news. The girls are just about through with their bottles, and they'll be ready for you to dress them and take them home."

107

Tess's gaze zoomed to Chloe's bed. Chloe's empty bed. Oh, God. "She's taking a shower, right? She's in the bathroom."

"Well," said the other volunteer, "not exactly."

"We don't know where she is," came the familiar voice of Chloe's obstetrician from behind her.

Tess whirled on him. "What?"

Dr. Fisher frowned gravely. "She apparently left the hospital sometime after the four A.M. feedings this morning. She left this for you."

He handed her a small stack of notepaper, three pages filled front and back and torn from a notepad advertising sleeping pills. She recognized both her sister's handwriting and the drama-queen tone of the initial sentence.

I, Chloe McKinney, do hereby state I am unable to currently fulfill the role of mother to my two female children, Caitlin Michelle and Stephanie Jeanne. I leave them in the care of my sister, Tess, who has always been the better choice between the two of us, as she well knows, because she's the one our mother chose to save from a burning car while leaving me behind to develop disfiguring scars on my breasts that are making it impossible for me to feed my poor, hungry babies.

Old guilt mixed with new anger, stirring Tess's emotions as she read. Disfiguring! Chloe had one freaking teardrop-sized scar on her right breast. The girl had used the damned thing to make Tess feel guilty for almost twenty years.

Tess, I trust you to guard my babies with your life and give them the happy, loving home we ourselves had before the accident you caused by popping your balloon—on purpose—and scaring Mom so that she drove into a tree.

Tess's heart twisted and bled.

I take after Dad, you know. Dad never forgave Mom for ruining his new car, which is why he left her for another woman. I'm leaving my girls, but I know you'll never leave them. You're the good one, the worthy one. I'm the screw-up. I'm the one not worth saving.

Tess's hands trembled so much she could barely read.

I thought my girls might save me, but it's now obvious they can't. I couldn't keep their father. I couldn't keep their home. I can't even feed them. I'm worthless. I'm leaving them in your hands, Tess. Don't try to find me. I'm going far away. That old biddy grandmother of theirs won't cause you trouble like she did with me. Take good care of them, (signed) Chloe. P.S. Please add the portable breast pump to my hospital bill. I took it with me.

The pages slipped through Tess's frozen fingers. "Is this a joke? Tell me she really is in the bathroom."

Dr. Fisher cleared his throat. "I'm afraid your sister is suffering from acute postpartum depression. It's not unheard-of for a depressed new mother to abandon her child, although the timing on this is quite...extraordinary. When you locate your sister, Miss McKinney, I recommend you see that she gets right into treatment. I admit I am worried regarding her...psyche."

"Psyche?" Tess repeated. Her stomach churned as the nurses returned the babies to the nursery bassinets. "Chloe's psyche?" Her foot began to tap. Hard. Rapidly. "Let me tell you about Chloe's psyche. She's into phases. She's had a hippie phase and an environmentalist phase and a biker-babe phase. Now she's doing martyrdom when she's supposed to be doing motherhood. But you know what? It's not going to work. I'm tired of it. I refuse to feel guilty anymore about something for which I had no responsibility. Mom didn't choose me. I was nearer to her when the fire started. That's why she reached for me first. And I didn't"—she finished at a near shout—"pop my balloon on purpose!"

At that, Caitlin and Stephanie erupted into identical newborn wails that continued for the entire time the candy stripers were helping to dress the girls in their going-home outfits. Dr. Fisher gave Tess infant-care instructions, along with the information that he'd notified the police about Chloe's disappearance. No one intended to charge her with child abandonment, but they hoped to find her for her own protection, considering the obviously precarious state of her mental health.

Tess had lots of questions about the pursuit of Chloe McKinney, but first things first. "The navel cords will fall off when?"

All too soon, it was time to leave. The babies continued to cry, her nerves to jangle. Attempting to put a positive spin on the events, one of the volunteers said, "At least you won't be dealing with pain from incision stitches."

"A joyful thought," Tess replied. She wanted to panic and screech and cry and kick something—without ruining a shoe. Basically, she wanted to run away. Just like Chloe. Instead, the responsible part of her, the manager in her, began to plan.

The immediate goal? Take the girls home from the hospital. Assets required to accomplish the goal? Babies, check. Car seats, check. Car, check. Okay, she had that covered.

Short-term goal? See the girls settled, safe, and satisfied. Requirements? Diapers, check. Cribs, check.

Formula...probably enough until tomorrow, and tomorrow she'd address it as a long-term goal. Bottles and blankets and...brownies. Thank goodness she had brownies at home. She'd definitely need chocolate to get through this.

So, she had everything she needed. "I can do this. I'll take excellent care of these babies."

Dr. Fisher nodded and handed her a card. "I suggest you display this beside your telephone at home. It's a new mother's 800 number hot line."

With that, he motioned to a nurse who waited in the doorway with a wheelchair. Tess looked at it aghast. "I don't—"

"Insurance," the nurse said. "You hold the girls and we'll get you in the car. Getting out, you're on your own."

On your own. On your own. On your own. The words echoed through Tess's head as the nurse wheeled her out of Bethania Hospital, a now-sleeping-thank-God infant cradled in each arm. *On your own. On your own. On your own.* It rang as a litany through her mind as the August heat hit hard. *On your own. On your own. On your own.* The idea made her stomach churn as she buckled Stephanie, then Caitlin into their car seats, fastened her own seat belt, and started the car.

Steph woke and began to mewl before Tess made it out of the parking lot. As she stopped at the first traffic light, Caitlin began to cry. By the time she reached the town square, both babies were screaming at an astounding volume, and Tess fought tears.

Through the watery film filling her eyes, she spied the seven-story facade of the Hutton Hotel. *On your own. On your own. On your own.* Without making a conscious decision, she steered her car toward the hotel.

Five minutes later, a crying baby in each arm, tears rolling down her own cheeks, Tess walked into the ballroom. In the process of driving a nail into a window casement, a shirtless Nick stopped his hammer mid-swing. "Tess?"

"Chloe ran off." She choked back a sob. "Chloe ran off and left me to manage, but I'm not prepared to be on my own. Adele is in Galveston, and Snake has slithered off. I need formula and more baby bottles. I can't manage. I can manage starlets and divas and egos the size of Jupiter, but I can't manage a tiny little pair of newborn babies. Not on my own, Nick. I know my limitations. I can't do it. I need another pair of hands!"

Nick set down his hammer and grabbed his T-shirt off the floor. He wiped his hands on the burnt orange cotton, then slipped it over his head as he walked toward her.

"Hush now, girls," he said in a soothing tone as he scooped up Stephanie and cuddled her against his shoulder, gently patting her back. "Everything's okay. Uncle Nick is here. Everything will be just fine. You did the right thing coming to me."

He winked at Tess and added, "It's a well-known fact I have the best hands in Texas."

~

TWO WEEKS after bringing the babies home from the hospital, Tess opened her eyes and smiled. She felt marvelous. Thanks to two women from the Brazos Bend Ladies' Benevolent Society who'd volunteered to stay the night and see to the girls' feedings, Tess had slept from dusk till dawn.

She threw off the soft cotton sheet, sat up, turned her face into the warm sunshine beaming through the windowpane, lifted her arms above her head, and stretched. "Sleep," she sighed. "Glorious, wondrous sleep."

She'd never take it for granted again.

The aroma of coffee had her reaching for her robe. She hurried downstairs, where she found four women seated at the kitchen table.

Obviously, the day shift had arrived. "Good morning, ladies," she said, her voice bright. "You wonderful, wonderful women."

Elaine Birdwell, Reverend Birdwell's wife from First Baptist, laughed. "Why, aren't you the chirpy little bird this morning? I think a good night's sleep was just the medicine you needed."

"I am ready to take on the world," Tess replied with complete sincerity as she filled a mug with steaming brew.

They discussed the babies' night over a breakfast of eggs, bacon, homemade biscuits, and cream gravy. The girls had awakened every two hours, but went right back to sleep after finishing their bottles. All in all, it had been an easy night.

After breakfast, as the night shift women prepared to leave and the day ladies began settling in, Tess tiptoed up to the nursery and peered down at the pair of angels sleeping in their cribs. How dear they were. Like lyrics from a country song, a weird combination of joy and sadness rolled through her. Chloe should be here. She shouldn't be missing these first days and weeks of her daughters' lives.

Tess's anger at Chloe had faded. She understood how their past influenced her sister's behavior, how the car accident when they were kids continued to fill her with self-doubt today, but standing here watching these precious gifts from God, falling head over heels in love with them, she also knew without a doubt that Chloe's fears were groundless.

Chloe wasn't stupid. She'd figure it out, too, just as soon as her hormones settled down. Tess was certain of it. Probably in a week or less, Chloe would come home and take up the reins. She'd be a good mother to these girls. She'd love them, protect them, provide for them. The three of them would be fine.

And Tess would go home to California.

Caitlin mewled in her sleep, and Tess reached out a hand and gave her back a series of gentle, comforting pats. California. She needed to go home. While her boss at Harrison & Associates had been understanding about her needing time off, his patience wouldn't last forever. Doing business by phone was fine up to a point, but at times personal contact was essential.

However, she'd make certain that personal contact with her nieces became a priority, too. It was nothing to hop on a plane to Texas. She could come back twice a month for a while, and when the girls got a little older, Chloe could bring them out. *I'll be here for you, girls. I won't be a stranger. I'll be part of your lives, I promise.*

Just not on a daily basis.

Stephanie cooed in her sleep, and Tess unaccountably felt tears sting her eyes. Shaking it off, she returned to the kitchen and the ladies of the Brazos Bend Benevolent Society. "I can't thank y'all enough," Tess said. "I truly feel rejuvenated. In fact, I feel so good that I'd like to take care of the babies myself today."

The four church ladies shared a concerned look. Mrs. Birdwell ventured, "Honey, there's no need. We're happy to help. Caring for one baby is difficult enough for a woman, but caring for two? Alone?"

"Just for today," Tess assured her. "Adele called from Houston yesterday. The hospital released her friend last night, and they'll be home today. She said she'll be ready to start her nanny job tomorrow."

"That's wonderful news," Mrs. Birdwell said. "We've all been concerned about Ralph. I never guessed a jellyfish sting could cause such a severe allergic reaction. It's good to hear that he's recovered."

"Adele sounded much relieved." Tess poured herself one last cup of coffee. "It's not that I don't appreciate your help—I wouldn't have survived the last few days without you. But I've had my good night's sleep, and I think it would be good for me and the girls to get to know each other a little better. I feel certain Chloe will come home soon, probably by the weekend, and I'll return to California."

Mrs. Birdwell nodded sagely. "Bonding. She's right. I've read articles about nonmaternal bonding in child care magazines. Tess needs some private time with the sweet ones in order to cement their bond to withstand the difficulties of a long-distance relationship."

The other three women looked doubtful, but Tess drew herself up, pretended she wore a red power suit rather than a bathrobe, and presented a confident front. Ten minutes later, the carriage house was empty except for her and the girls.

The phone rang just as she turned on the water for her shower. "Good morning, darlin'."

Tess smiled. "Hello, Nick."

"How was your night?"

"Glorious." She told him about the extra night help and her plans for the day.

"Do you need anything?" he asked. "I'm meeting the electrician at the hotel at ten, but I could run by the store for you after that."

She considered it a moment. "I could use a handful of things, but nothing that couldn't wait until this evening."

"Okay. Give me your list, and I'll drop it by on my way home tonight."

Stephanie woke up just as Tess hung up the phone with Nick. Before Tess could get the baby's diaper changed, Caitlin let out a cry. It took a good bit of juggling, but she managed to bathe and dress both herself and the girls, feed them, then put them down to sleep. When she closed the nursery door behind her, she dusted her hands with satisfaction.

She dusted too soon.

First, while attempting to fill bottles, she spilled a large can of formula all over the kitchen floor. No sooner had she cleaned up her mess than Stephanie awoke, her diaper half off, her sheet sopping wet. Cursing diaper tapes that didn't stay stuck, Tess ripped the crib sheet while trying to change it. She no sooner rocked Steph back to sleep than Caitlin awoke with a diaper rash.

Tess slathered cream all over the baby's bottom, wrinkling her nose at the cod-liver smell. Before she'd managed to wash all the gunk off her hands, Steph let out yet another squeal. Determined to get a load of wash going, Tess decided to take a two-minute detour to the laundry room before picking up the baby. In her rush, she knocked over a full box of laundry soap and smeared her favorite T-shirt with diaper cream.

By now, both girls were wailing.

Tess hurried back through the kitchen and into the living room and, in doing so, cut a corner close. Her foot rammed into the huge plastic tub of Legos brought over by a well-intentioned, though misguided, Brazos Bend senior whose grandchildren were now grown. Nick had spent an hour playing with them last night. The box tipped, and small red, yellow, and blue plastic blocks scattered across the room. "Ow!" she yelped as she stepped on a Lego. "Dang it, Nick. Didn't your mother teach you to pick up your toys?"

Tess lifted both girls from their cribs, walked them, rocked them, fed one, then the other. Rocked them both. Walked them both. Put them in their cribs. Picked them up again. Walked them. Rocked them. Fed them.

Finally around two, Stephanie fell asleep, and Tess put her to bed. Five minutes later, she walked toward the nursery, a slumbering Caitlin in her arms. The scent of baby powder filled the air, along with the most welcome sound of silence. Tess thought it the sweetest sound she'd ever heard.

Holding her breath, she leaned over the cradle and gently lowered her five-pound, three-ounce burden to the mattress. Gingerly, she slipped her hands from beneath the sleeping infant, her gaze never leaving those tiny, blessedly closed eyes. So far, so good.

She straightened, drew in a deep, silent breath, then slowly backed away from the cradle. *Please sleep, Caitlin. Please, you and Stephanie give me ten little minutes. Time to fix my hair and put on makeup. Time to sit at the kitchen table and have a glass of iced tea. Time for my ears to rest.*

The respite lasted eight and a half minutes. Tess wanted to cry right along with Steph.

Yet, despite the Lego bruises, spilled detergent, ruined blouses, and abbreviated self-grooming, Tess managed. She felt pretty darn proud of herself, in fact. Aunt-niece bonding was well under way.

A little after four o'clock, everything changed. Caitlin let out a long, shrill, pain-filled scream, different from anything Tess had heard from her before. Immediately, she lifted the baby, placed her against her shoulder, and patted her back in a vain attempt to comfort her. Caitlin continued to scream while Tess tried every crying-baby trick she knew. Soon Auntie Tess was as worked up as the newborn.

"Oh, no, honey, don't. It's okay. Shush. What's wrong? What could be wrong?" *Should I call the pediatrician?*

"Waaaaaaaaaaa."

Yes, she should definitely call the pediatrician.

Tess headed for the telephone handset, grateful she'd thought to program the doctor's phone number into the speed dial. No sooner had she picked up the phone than Stephanie let out a yell identical to that of her twin.

Oh, no. Maybe she should forget about calling and rush them straight to the hospital.

"Waaaaaaaaaa."

The pediatrician's nurse took her call and listened carefully as Tess described the twin's symptoms. She asked a few questions, and Tess held her breath, waiting for a diagnosis or a course of action to take.

The pediatric nurse clicked her tongue. "Oh, honey, not to worry."

In that moment, Tess knew.

"You can bring those babies into the office for the doctor to examine, but I honestly don't think it's necessary."

Stephanie and Caitlin screamed in stereo.

The nurse continued, saying aloud what Tess already suspected. Speaking the words feared by new parents across the world.

"What you've described are classic cases of colic."

UP UNTIL THIS VERY MOMENT, Nick would have considered himself an expert when it came to nipples. After all, he'd seen his fair share of them—all sizes, all shapes, all colors. All tastes. Now, though, faced with the overwhelming array displayed at the local grocery, he admitted to amateur status. Who would have guessed that nipples came in such a variety?

He didn't know what the hell to buy. When he took his turn at helping feed the girls, he hadn't paid a bit of attention to the nipples on the baby bottles Tess handed him. He barely remembered what the bottles themselves looked like.

Nick tossed four of every style of nipple into his shopping cart, then added a dozen bottles for good measure. He'd learned real fast that with those two formula-suckers in the house, it never hurt to have an extra bottle or ten ready and waiting.

"Nicholas? Nicholas!" The Widow Duncan waved at him from the end of the baby-items aisle. Her friends, the Widow Gault and the

Widow Mallow, hovered behind her like crows. "Nicholas, I need to talk with you."

Great. Just great. "Hello, ladies. Y'all out shopping this afternoon?"

"No, we're not out shopping. We've come to find you. We have an emergency situation on our hands."

Nick had too much experience dealing with The Widows to worry about her use of the word *emergency*. Calmly, he asked, "Is Mr. Jones slow about cutting his lawn again?"

"It's about That Woman," the Widow Gault said in a huff. "I want you to get to work on getting those babies away from her."

"What? Are you talking about Tess?"

"I certainly am. She's not at all a proper caretaker."

"Tess is doing an excellent job," Nick defended.

"Only because the ladies in town are helping out," said Widow Duncan. "No, I don't want that Tess woman around my granddaughters. It's clear the McKinneys have bad blood. Have you heard the latest about that child-deserting sister of hers? Chloe McKinney has been arrested for roller-skating naked through a crosswalk in downtown San Antonio."

For the first time in his life, Nick focused voluntarily on a feminine products display on the opposite shelf and gathered the ragged edges of his temper. "No, Mrs. Gault, that's not true. I heard that rumor earlier today myself, and Marlene Benson admitted she made it up."

All three women wrinkled their noses and huffed.

"I'd appreciate it if you'd help me put a halt to these vicious rumors. It's not right for Brazos Bend to treat one of their own this way. Chloe is ill. Dr. Fisher diagnosed her with severe postpartum depression. He believes her condition is temporary, and that she'll return when she's feeling better."

"Many women get the baby blues," Widow Mallow groused. "They don't run off and leave their babies behind. Still, I agree it's not neighborly to speak ill of the ill."

"Chloe's had a difficult time," Mrs. Gault agreed. "You have to admit, Melody." She nodded toward Mrs. Duncan. "Herbert isn't entirely blameless in this situation."

Herbert, Nick recalled, was Snake Duncan's given name.

The Widow Duncan swelled up like a toad. She wouldn't listen to any criticism of her son. "My Herbert has done nothing wrong. He has given me his word he is doing something good with his life—"

Yeah, right. If one considered being a drug lord a good thing.

"—which is more than anyone can say about those McKinney girls. Chloe abandons her children. That Tess works for people who call themselves Red Sex Wisdom."

"It's a band," Widow Gault added. "The female singers wear those skimpy underwear on stage. Red ones. It's disgusting."

"Sounds intriguing," Nick said, just to needle them.

The widow's eyes narrowed, then Mrs. Duncan continued. "I don't want my granddaughters exposed to that sort of people. Nicholas, you are my lawyer. I want you to take care of it."

"Take care of what?"

"Legalities must be seen to. I must protect my grandchildren. I want Chloe McKinney stripped of her parental rights, and I want custody of my granddaughters so that her sister can't take them away from Brazos Bend."

"Oh, for crying out loud," Nick began.

"Now, Mrs. Duncan, hold on." Stewart Mooney marched down the aisle holding a plastic produce bag filled with summer squash, looking like a cross between a skinny bulldog and an avenging angel. "I know you're worried. It's understandable. You love your granddaughters. However, legal action is a bit premature, don't you think?"

"Absolutely not. Why, the way things stand now, that Tess could up and take my grandchildren off to California, and I couldn't do a thing about it."

She had a point, Nick silently admitted.

"That won't happen," Stewart said. "When Chloe gets past her bout of the blues, she'll come home to her children first thing. Those babies won't leave Brazos Bend."

"Like I'd want her here," Widow Duncan said with a sniff. "She's crazy."

"Mrs. Duncan," Nick protested. "She's *ill*."

"Exactly," Stewart reiterated. "Chloe is ill, and good Christian women like yourself and Mrs. Mallow and Mrs. Gault should lead the community in demonstrating compassion toward her." He continued with a defense of Chloe so heated and enthusiastic that it took Nick aback and started him thinking.

After the widows departed and Stewart returned to the produce department, Nick threw a few dozen diapers in his shopping basket, then wandered over toward the okra. "Hey, Stewart," he casually called. "Thanks for the help with Mrs. Duncan and her cohorts."

Stewart ripped a plastic bag from the rack. "Being elderly doesn't give a person the right to be cruel."

"I agree with everything you said. You're a good friend to Chloe." Nick watched closely as he added, "I'm sure you'd help her any way you could."

"That's what friends are for." Stewart lifted an orange from a stack of fruit and deposited it in the produce bag.

Nick tried again. "The sheriff thinks someone helped Chloe get out of town. It's hard to believe she disappeared so completely on her own like that."

This time, Stewart betrayed himself with a flinch. Not much of one, but enough for Nick to press. "She called you, didn't she, Stewart? You know where she is. Is she at your house?"

"No!" Stewart grabbed three more oranges and shoved them in the sack. "Chloe isn't at my house. I don't know where she is."

Liar. "But she called you."

Stewart didn't respond.

"Chloe is seriously depressed, Mooney. She needs help."

Anger snapped in Stewart's green eyes. "She's getting it, all right? Yes, she called me, and I helped her, and now she's keeping regular appointments with a psychologist who specializes in postpartum depression."

A sense of victory mixed with relief rushed through Nick. Chloe was safe. Tess would be so relieved—and probably plenty angry. She'd phoned Stewart after bringing the girls home from the hospital that first day and questioned him. He'd denied knowing anything about Chloe's disappearance. "Where is she, Stewart?"

"I'm not exactly certain. She's gone looking for Snake."

Nick blinked. "Looking for Snake? I thought you said she's getting professional help."

"She's taking phone appointments."

"Phone appointments? From where?"

"She doesn't tell me that part."

"So she's still in touch with you?"

Stewart took a pristine handkerchief from the back pocket of his gray slacks and wiped his brow. "Yes. Occasionally."

"Dammit, man, how can you support this?"

"What else was I supposed to do? The woman was determined to find Snake Duncan. Nothing short of a chain and padlock would have stopped her, and I'm not even certain that would have done the trick."

From what he knew of Chloe, Nick couldn't disagree. Yet, he folded his arms and leveled a stern gaze on the shorter man. "Tess has been worried sick. You should have told her what you know."

"I wanted to give Chloe a good head start. Snake Duncan needs to be found, and I've reached the conclusion that Chloe is the best person for the job."

"That's bull. I've hired a professional detective to locate Snake. He'll find the man."

"Chloe will find him faster. She knows where to look for him. Time is of the essence here, and no one is more motivated to locate Snake Duncan than the mother of his newborn daughters."

"That wasn't your decision to make, Mooney," Nick snapped.

"No, it was Chloe's, and I respect that, even if you and her sister don't."

Nick shoved his hands in the pockets of his jeans and rolled back on his heels. Damn. The man had a point.

"Look, I have to get home. If you want to swing by my house, I have another letter for Tess from Chloe you can pick up."

"A letter? From where?"

"She wrote it before she left town. She asked me not to give it to Tess until someone figured out I helped her get away."

"You have all your bases covered, don't you?" Nick replied with a grudging respect.

"I'm methodical. That's one of the reasons I'm so good at what I do," Stewart said and gave an enigmatic smile, then added, "You might be surprised at just how far such skills can take a man."

Nick stood in the produce aisle and watched as Stewart got in the checkout line. Now that was a strange remark. Something about his words and the way he said them sent Nick's brows up.

Could Stewart have Chloe stashed at his house?

Maybe. Though if that were the case, why did he invite Nick to stop by to pick up a letter?

Back in his truck ten minutes later, Nick decided it wouldn't hurt to reconnoiter the Mooney abode a bit before knocking on the door.

Stewart lived in a nice, middle-class neighborhood down the street from Jack Harmon, his friend Kate's father. Nick parked his car in the Harmon drive, then made his way to the alley and hoofed it down to Stewart's house, where he skulked in the shadows of a pecan tree and focused his gaze on Mooney's back door.

He detected no sign of life during ten minutes of observation. Then, just as he made up his mind to play Peeping Tom and check out the window, the back door opened and Stewart came outside.

He carried a bottle of imported dark ale in his hand, and while he ambled toward the flower bed beside the house, he tipped it back and took a long, lusty sip. "Well well well," Nick murmured. "There's more to you than meets the eye, Stewie ole boy. I figured you more for the Dr Pepper type."

Stewart watered his pink and white begonias, drained the rest of his beer, then tossed the empty into a green plastic trash can sitting beside the back door. Never once did his movements provide any hint that someone else might await him inside. Nick figured the chances of finding Chloe holed up inside the house at slim-to-none, but what would it hurt to check for himself?

He hopped the waist-high chain link fence. "That beer sure looked good. Got an extra?"

The younger man started and whirled around, the spout of his garden hose shooting a stream of water Nick's direction. "Hey, you scared me."

"Sorry." Nick sidestepped the hose and opened the back door, saying, "Water wouldn't be bad, but I prefer the beer. Thanks."

"But...but..."

Since the beer did sound good, Nick detoured by the refrigerator. He heard the screen door bang shut behind him. "Nice place you have here."

"Um...thanks. It was my folks' house."

"Yeah?" Nick strode down the hall and, in a good imitation of the Brazos Bend Widows, peeked in each of the three bedrooms. Retracing his steps, he found Stewart standing in the living room holding a fat gray cat, scowling at Nick as he scratched the animal behind the ears. "She's not here."

"Yeah. I see."

"You could have trusted me."

"Yeah. I know."

Stewart nodded toward a bookshelf stuffed with paperback novels. On its top lay a sealed envelope, a name penned in feminine handwriting across its front:

Tess.

Nick picked up the letter and discovered it was sealed. "Hmmm....You read it?"

"Of course not. I don't read other people's mail."

Nick's thumb slid along the envelope flap. Ordinarily, he wouldn't snoop, but he felt protective of Tess right now. If Chloe had written something cruel, Tess would be better off if he ran interference and paraphrased the contents rather than handing it over. Tess had enough stress on her plate right now. She didn't need Chloe adding to it.

He tore open the envelope.

"Hey, you can't do that. That's mail tampering."

"Not technically. Letters need addresses and stamps." He unfolded the paper.

DEAR TESS,

If I die and Snake doesn't come home, please tell my babies I loved them. Love, Chloe.

"OH HELL, CHLOE," Nick murmured. That sounded suicidal. He pinned Stewart with a look. "Who's this therapist she's talking to?"

"That's private information. I'm not..."

Nick grabbed him by the shirtfront. "I want the name."

"Okay. All right." When Nick released him, Stewart backed away, smoothing the wrinkles from his shirt. "It won't do you any good, though. Therapists can't talk about their patients. Professional ethics and all."

"Name and phone number, please."

Stewart disappeared into the bedroom he used as an office and returned with a business card. Nick mentally donned his lawyer's cap and called the therapist from the phone in Stewart's kitchen. His name got him past the receptionist. It netted him nothing more than a vague assurance of protection and advocacy for at-risk patients from the doctor.

That's why Nick's first act upon returning to his truck was to call his investigator and sic him on the shrink.

During the short drive home, he debated whether to show the letter to Tess. As he pulled into the carriage house driveway, he decided that information would keep until his investigator found out a little bit more about this doctor.

It was ten minutes to six when, his arms filled with grocery bags, Nick opened the carriage house kitchen door and called, "Hello. I come bearing nipples."

The sounds of squalling babies clued him that Tess probably hadn't heard him arrive. He set the brown paper bags on the kitchen counter, then followed the trail of noise to the nursery. In the doorway, he stopped abruptly in shock. Dressed in shorts and a stained T-shirt, feet bare, hair tangled and limp, her eyes red and nose red, Tess sat slumped on the floor in a corner of the nursery, a screaming baby in an infant carrier on either side of her.

Tears poured down all three females' faces. "Damn, Tess. What happened?"

"I can't manage this," she wailed. "I don't know anything about colic. I don't know anything about newborn babies. I'm not their mother. I don't know what they want. I don't know how to help them.

I read on the Internet that this could last six weeks. Six weeks! I can't deal with this. Give me a half-dozen teenage boy bands to manage, and I'll get that job done. I can't do this! Damn Chloe. Damn her! She ran off just like she did back when we were kids and she went to a Greenpeace rally instead of helping plan Homecoming like she promised. She should be here caring for these babies. Not me. It's not my job. It's hers. Hers! It's just like always. She has the fun, but when she gets in trouble, I have to pick up the pieces. I bail her out of jail after she has too much fun at a drunken party. I send her rent money because she's spent all her money on a designer handbag. I have to nurse colicky babies, and I didn't even get to have the sex!"

Nick shook his head and clucked his tongue. "Calm down now, honey. Uncle Nick is here. I'll be happy to take care of *all* of your problems."

CHAPTER 12

AT NICK'S INSISTENCE, Tess headed for the bathtub for a soak. She'd
raided Chloe's room for one of her shower gifts, an aromatherapy
basket filled with products advertised to promote peacefulness and
calm. Attempting to tune out the babies' cries, she flipped the radio on
to the regional classical station, turned the faucet on full force, and
dumped a generous amount of bath oil into the water. Whether it was
the sandalwood-and-rose fragrance or the glass of red wine Nick
supplied or simply the respite from responsibility, she emerged from
the bathroom half an hour later shampooed, slathered in lotion,
dressed in shoes and clean clothes, and, thank heavens, emotionally
collected.

Greeted with silence, she smiled and sighed. Wistfully, she cast a
glance toward her bedroom, but duty called, and she headed for the
nursery. She almost thought she was hallucinating when she found the
twins sleeping peacefully in their cribs. Exiting the nursery quickly and
quietly, she went looking for the miracle worker named Nick. To her
surprise and delight, she found him seated with a visitor at the kitchen
table. "Adele!" she whispered, not wanting to risk waking the sleeping
girls. "I didn't expect you tonight."

"You can talk in a normal tone of voice, dear," Adele replied. "It's better that they get accustomed to sleeping with a little noise in the house. Of course, I think these little ones could sleep through a tornado tonight, as exhausted as they were. Why, it didn't take five minutes for them to drop off once I arrived."

"You put them to sleep?" Tess asked, in awe.

Nick motioned for Tess to join them at the table. "I called her cell phone, looking for advice, and she was already home. She came right over."

"I couldn't wait until morning. I was dying to see the little angels."

"She held them differently, draped each one of them over her arm and patted their backs," Nick marveled. "It was amazing. They settled right down."

"Just a trick I've picked up over the years. Doesn't always work. When a baby is colicky, it's important to remain calm and remember they'll outgrow it eventually."

Tess asked Adele half a dozen more baby-care questions, and Nick chimed in with a pair of his own. By the time the conversation turned to the older woman's trip to the Texas Gulf Coast, Tess's worry had eased.

Child-care books provided facts; Adele Watkins offered experience.

"I'm so glad you're back in Brazos Bend," she said.

"Me, too. Now, why don't you two run along to dinner? And don't rush back. After the hard day you've had, you need some time away from those girls. You'll all three be better off for it tomorrow."

Tess glanced at Nick. "Dinner?"

"Grilled salmon. Salad." Though his tone was casual, the look in his eyes was anything but. Intensity gleamed in his deep blue eyes as he added, "Stress relief."

Sex. That's what he meant.

Wow. Well. Okay. Well, she'd brought the subject up herself tonight during her semi-hysterical outburst, hadn't she?

"I thought we might go back out to my place on the creek. The clouds that rolled in this afternoon cooled things off, so it'll be nice out tonight. My boat is back from the shop, so we could cruise on out to the main body of the lake, if you'd like. We'd probably have the water all to ourselves on a weeknight this time of year."

Secluded stress relief. Yep. He was definitely talking about sex. His offer could be no plainer.

What did she want? Did she want to hold to the decision she'd made the day the babies were born? The decision she'd not had time to think about since. Did she still want to have an affair with Nick Sutherland?

Adele interrupted her reverie. "Before you go anywhere, Nick needs to give you his gift. We've made a bet. He thinks you'll like it. I think he's crazy. I couldn't believe a man with Nicholas Sutherland's taste and resources would actually give a woman like you something that corny. Me, yes, because I am the flamboyant sort. You're class, though, Tess. You won't wear thongs like those."

Tess whipped her head around toward Nick. "You bought me underwear?"

"At this stage of our relationship?" he responded, his gorgeous blue eyes gleaming with humor as he adopted an air of offense. "Really, Tess."

He rose from his seat and crossed the kitchen to the counter, where a brown paper grocery sack sat on the counter. From inside, he withdrew a pair of flip-flops, and seeing them, Tess immediately laughed.

"Oh, they're great!" Yellow plastic daisies with orange sequined centers adorned the footwear's top V-straps, while a leaf print in shades of green decorated the foam bottom. The price tag hanging from the thin plastic ring binding the shoes together read $2.99. "I love them."

"I thought you would." Nick tossed them to her, then leaned back against the counter, folded his arms, and sent Adele a smug smile. "She's a shoe slut, you know."

The older woman clucked her tongue. "I don't understand girls today. Look at her. She loves her $2.99 gift. Her $2.99 gift from a gazillionaire. Honey, they wouldn't let you in the front door at the national gold diggers convention."

Tess broke the plastic ring, kicked off her sandals, then slipped into the flip-flops. She all but giggled with delight. How perfect. The flip-flops were perfect. The man was perfect.

Of course she still wanted to have an affair with him.

She extended her legs and pointed her toes, rotating her ankles so that the sequins caught the light. "Thank you, Nick. They're marvelous. I'd wear them to dinner, except I need boots to ride—"

"No horses tonight. I left the Jeep out front and the salmon in your fridge. So, shall we go?"

Tess looked at Adele. "Are you certain...?"

"Go on with you. We'll be fine. Kate said she might stop by later, and she'll help me if I need it. She needs the practice."

A mud-splattered red Jeep awaited them in front of the house. "I've never seen you drive this," she commented as she climbed inside.

"I just bought it. I think it'll come in handy driving out to the river."

"I see." A whisper of a smile played at Tess's lips. "Just how many vehicles do you have in your garage, Nick?"

He shrugged. "Not that many. Three. Four. Okay, maybe six."

"Here in Brazos Bend." When he nodded, she continued, "So what about other towns? Rumor has it you have a beach house and a mountain cabin and a city apartment or two. Do you keep vehicles in those places, too?"

"Yeah, a few."

"So how many do you own altogether?"

"Oh, I don't know."

"Ten? Twenty? Thirty?"

"Not thirty!" he protested.

Laughing, Tess propped a flip-flop-clad shoe on the dashboard and grinned. "I may be a shoe slut, Sutherland, but you're a motorhead."

His grin flashed. "You know me well, sweet feet."

They finished the short drive to the river in companionable silence. Nick stopped the Jeep at a spot not far from where they'd left the horses on Tess's previous visit, and when he switched off the engine, quiet filled the air. Tess closed her eyes and enjoyed the moment as the lingering tension from her stress-filled afternoon drained away, leaving only the subtle hum of sexual anticipation flowing through her body.

He made a show of presenting her the "Nick's Hideout" sign now hanging from the branch of the old pecan tree guarding the entrance to his hideaway. It looked even better than she had expected, and she made a mental note to call the sculptor and relay her pleasure.

Pleasure. Bet she didn't use that word once a week. Funny how it had popped into her brain so quickly tonight.

They traveled the short path through the woods to the water's edge. Tess halted mid-step at the sight of the thirty-two-foot cabin cruiser tied to Nick's swim dock. "So you like motors that float, too?"

"Yeah. She's a great boat. I'll show you around after dinner."

They talked boats for a bit. Tess's friend Jake took her out on his often, so she was knowledgeable about the subject. She didn't mention that Jake's yacht was bigger than Nick's—she understood men and their...toys...better than that. "I'm surprised the creek is deep enough for a boat that size."

"There's twelve feet of water beneath my dock. The opposite bank is more shallow." He squirted lighter fluid onto the charcoal briquets, then reached for a book of matches, nodding toward a cabinet he'd unlocked moments ago. "Would you like to pick out a CD, or are you happy with cicadas like last time?"

Tess glanced toward the cottonwood tree hugging the opposite creek bank, where the insects' buzz competed with a mockingbird's song. "Let's go natural."

Nick froze, holding the burning match so long that it singed his finger. He cleared his throat. "I'm game."

"I figured that."

A sense of deja vu overtook Tess as she took a seat on a bar stool and watched Nick nurse his fire. What a turn life had taken since her last visit here.

She'd had only minimal control over her world since the day her sister gave birth to twins, and for a woman accustomed to managing life both personally and professionally, she found the situation all but intolerable. She wanted to change that. She wanted to take charge and grasp control.

She wanted to wrestle Nick Sutherland to the ground and have her way with him.

Warmth bloomed inside her at the tantalizing thought. "It's hotter than I expected." She hooked her finger into the neckline of her shirt and tugged the cotton away from her skin.

Nick's gaze followed the path of her finger, then dipped lower, focusing on the swell of her breast. "It's been hot for weeks."

When she dipped her chin and blew a stream of air down the front of her shirt, she heard him drop his tongs. As the fire tool clattered against a rock, that heady sense of feminine power swept through her.

There was something so sexy about seducing a powerful man.

"Is it safe to swim in Bluff Creek?" she asked, slipping from the bar stool to stand tall and proud before him.

Eyes narrowed and as hot as the charcoal, he took a step toward her. "That depends on what you'd consider dangerous."

"Alligators?"

"Not in this part of Texas."

"Snakes?"

"Shouldn't be a problem."

"What about water weasels?"

"Water weasels?" He spouted out a laugh. "Hmm. Well. Yeah, Tess. If you were to go swimmin' in Bluff Creek tonight, there's a good chance you might run into at least one water weasel."

Tess licked her lips. "Oh, Mr. Sutherland. I certainly hope so."

He blinked.

Throwing caution to the wind, she spun on her heel and whipped her shirt over her head. Her feet took the trail down to the water even as she reached around her back to unhook her hot pink lace bra.

"Damn," she heard Nick say.

Down on the dock, she slipped the button at her waistband and shucked out of her shorts. Naked but for her panties and her shoes, she paused at water's edge.

"Damnation," he said, his voice tight. "Thongs are a wondrous invention."

Brazenly, she turned to face him. Slowly, she lifted her right foot, drew her leg back, then kicked forward, flinging her flip-flop right at him. When she repeated the motion with her left foot, he reached out and caught the shoe midair.

"Quick hands, Texas."

"I can be slow when the situation warrants. Just let me know what you prefer."

"I do so admire a multitalented man."

"Give me half a chance, sweetheart, and I'll show you talent."

"I'd like to believe that," she said, inserting doubt into her voice. "Problem is, so far, you're all talk."

He let out a noise somewhere between a laugh and a growl and advanced on her, whipping off his shirt as he approached. Tess prolonged the game by taking a step back and jumping into the creek. It was cool and refreshing, and she basked in the pleasure of water caressing her bare skin. Surfacing, she found Nick stripped down to bare skin, himself.

And what bare skin it was. Tanned and toned and rippled with muscle, Nick could hold his own with any hard-body in Hollywood. Broad shoulders, sculpted abs, narrow hips. An erection big enough and bold enough to make her mouth go dry.

His gaze met hers, burned into hers, as he took one step, then two, toward the edge of the dock. There he stopped, letting her tread water and look her fill, as he said in a hardscrabble tone, "Last chance, Tess. If you don't want this, tell me now."

She swallowed hard and made herself take just a second to consider her actions. Stress relief.

It wasn't like her to treat sex so casually. This was the first time she'd begun an affair knowing it didn't stand a chance of developing into a true relationship that might have wedding bells and rose petals in its future. She wasn't going to stay in Brazos Bend, Texas, a moment longer than necessary, and Brazos Bend, Texas, fit Nicholas Sutherland like a glove.

Right now, however, she wanted to be the glove to fit Nick. "Come on in, Texas. The water's...wet."

His dive sliced the river water like a knife, and moments later, his hand closed around her ankle and he pulled her under. When she bobbed back to the surface, he was waiting. Nick pulled her into his arms and kissed her, the kick in his powerful legs keeping them afloat until he stilled, deepened the kiss, and they sank.

It was one of the most erotic moments of Tess's life. Nick's hard body entwined weightlessly with hers, the cocoon of cool water, the silence. When the need for oxygen drove them apart, Nick held her hand as together, they kicked for the surface. There, they played. They chased and splashed. They teased and tickled. They laughed.

Throughout it all, Nick took every opportunity to touch her. He caressed her with his hands, his mouth, the heat in his blue-eyed gaze. He made her tingle and shudder and moan. He stoked the fire of anticipation until finally, he captured her mouth in another soul-deep kiss, and once again, they submerged into a world in which only the two of them existed.

Abandoning herself to the moment, to the intensity of his kiss, Tess sensed that this man had the power to change her life.

~

I'M *in over my head.*

Nick kicked toward the surface, and as their heads broke the surface, he ended the kiss. His heart pounded as they treaded water, their gazes locked. What the hell was this?

Nick understood sexual attraction. He'd always liked women, and over the years, he'd enjoyed his fair share. He knew what it was like to want, to need, to ache. Yet in all the years, all the women, he'd never experienced anything like the sensation that had stolen through his bloodstream with that last kiss.

Holy hell, had he gone and fallen in love? Did it happen like that? With a kiss?

No, it damn sure didn't.

Love happened after dozens of dinner dates and months of movies. Love happened over time. A length of time. Not less than a month. Not over a baby's cries and dirty diapers and the wrong kind of bottle nipple. Not just because she proved herself to be loyal and dependable and true.

No, this wasn't love. It was souped-up, rocket-powered, hot-as-August sexual attraction. That's all. And if he didn't have her soon, he damned well might explode.

"Come to my boat, Tess," he said. "Come to my bed."

She watched him, her gaze solemn. Serious. Nick's heart skipped a beat while the seconds dragged by. Finally, she smiled. "Yes."

They swam the short distance to the *Brazos Queen*. Nick climbed onto the swim platform, then helped Tess aboard. The moment her feet found purchase, he grabbed a towel and began slowly drying her body, wielding the towel the way an Old Master might use a paint-brush, until she arched against him and all but purred. He kissed her then, and didn't stop until he'd guided her down the steps, into his cabin, and onto his bed. Kneeling above her, he stripped her of the tiny scrap of cloth that served her as panties, then pleasured himself by drinking in the sight of her. Full breasts with rosy centers, narrow waist, curvaceous hips, and legs that stretched to Sunday. "My God, Tess. You are a beautiful woman."

"You look like a movie star," she replied, her belly quivering against his hand.

Nick laughed, and his fingers flexed to stroke her soft skin. "That's what I thought about you the first time I saw you. You waltzed into my ballroom, and I thought you were Lana Turner, Marilyn Monroe, and Betty Grable all rolled into one."

"Really?" Her smile stretched wide. "They're sex goddesses. I always thought I was more Doris Day."

"Honey, you are no Doris Day."

He stretched out above her, supporting his weight on his hands and knees. She arched her back as his mouth found her breast, captured her nipple, and sucked hard, then gentled his attentions, lapping her lazily with his tongue, massaging her. Then he repeated the process all over again until she whimpered aloud and he released her, only to devote his attention to her other breast, offering the same, sweet torment.

Tess threaded her fingers through his hair, thrashing beneath him, keening sounds of need escaping from her throat. Her hands cupped his butt, and she pulled him down against her. Wrapping her legs around him, she shifted herself against his belly, seeking that most inti-mate of contact.

But Nick had promised her slow, so he shifted and evaded and counter-moved by sliding a finger into the slick, tight flesh between her thighs.

"Nick," she said on a sigh.

He stroked her, worked her. He made love to her with his hand and his mouth, probing deep within her, driving both of them wild. Just when need became a clawing, raging beast within him and he decided he'd had enough of slow, Tess rolled him on his back, reached between his legs, and took control.

Feather-light touches made him shudder. The fine pressure of her fingernail drawn down the length of him made him catch his breath. The tight clutch of her fist around him, the firm stroke up, down, up, down, made him groan.

When she dipped her head and licked him, he thought he might go blind.

For the next ten minutes—or maybe ten hours, Nick wasn't sure—Tess taught him the real meaning of slow. She teased him, tantalized him. Tortured him. Finally, his control broke.

With an animal growl deep in his throat, he grabbed a condom stowed in a drawer within reach of the bed and quickly put it on. He flipped her onto her back and thrust inside her, burying himself to the hilt. Holding still, forcing himself to wait for her tight body to adjust to him, he indulged in a deep, urgent, infinitely carnal kiss.

Tess's hands clutched his shoulders as he nipped the side of her neck and began to move within her and against her. After a few strokes, he found a rhythm that pleased them both. Soon his breath panted, his muscles quivered as he strained to hold back, to make it last. To, by God, make certain she came first.

To that end, sensing his own was almost upon him, he slipped a hand between them and thumbed her nerve center. Her inner muscles gripped him, and she gasped. He increased his pace, faster...faster...until Tess pressed upward, grinding herself against him, and let out a long, throaty groan. When the rhythmic waves of her climax stroked his erection, Nick gave himself up to the raging beast within. He pounded into her once, twice, three more times, then erupted in an hot explosion of pleasure more intense than any he could remember.

"God," she breathed as he collapsed atop her.

Heart racing, fighting to catch his breath, Nick somehow found the strength to lift his head and tease, "Yes?"

She slapped his shoulder and laughed. Smiling, Nick rolled off her and onto his back, scooting her halfway atop him to give himself room in the narrow bunk. He closed his eyes and drifted in the pleasure of the moment—a warm, satisfied, naked woman in his arms, the gentle rock of the *Brazos Queen,* the sated heaviness of his limbs, the musky scent of sex in the air.

The rumble of hunger in his stomach. Nick's eyes flew open. "Damn."

Tess lifted her head from his shoulder. "What?"

"I left the salmon sitting on the counter. I can't cook it now. It's been out too long. Might be spoiled."

She gave him a feigned look of pain. "We have no supper?"

He twisted his mouth as he thought about it. "I think I have a bag of cheese doodles here on the boat."

"You eat cheese doodles?"

"Love 'em."

"They're disgusting."

"Oh, now. Have you ever tried them with peanut butter?"

Tess sat up, providing him a nice view of her breasts, and her mouth dropped open in horror. "Cheese doodles and peanut butter?"

"That or barbecue sauce."

She blinked. "Oh, you're a sick man, Nick. Sick. Sick. Sick."

Light from the setting sun streamed through the window and gleamed off the hints of red mixed among the dozen shades of blond visible in her drying hair. The sight captivated him. Aroused him. "I'm not sick, darlin'. I'm hungry."

Her lips stretched in a slow, delighted smile. "Again?"

"Again. Feed me, Tess."

CHAPTER 13

THE MAGNETIC SIGN on the side of the minivan that pulled to a stop in front of the carriage house read "Mama's Maids, Ft. Worth, Texas." Moments later, the driver emerged from the vehicle, hidden by a forest of brooms and mops and other tools of the housekeeping trade and approached the house.

Adele Watkins responded to the doorbell. "Mama's Maids? I'm sorry, but I wasn't told to expect...oh my. Chloe, is that you?"

"Hi, Adele."

"You're back!" The older woman reached out and yanked her into her arms for a hard hug. "Thank goodness. Where in the world have you been? What have you been doing? I'm so mad at you I could just spit. We've been so worried!"

Chloe had expected the questions and prepared her answers. She'd didn't want Tess to catch even a whiff of the trouble that had followed Chloe to the hospital room. "I'm not working. I've been staying with a friend. The cleaning van is borrowed."

"Are you staying with Stewart Mooney? He told Nick you'd gone hunting for Snake."

"I'm not staying with Stewart, and as for Snake, please don't ask me

136

questions. I can't talk about it. I'm sorry I've worried you, but please, I just want to see my babies."

"All right, hon. We'll deal with all that later. But we will deal with it. To quote Ricky Ricardo, 'You have some 'splainin' to do.' "

Adele gave her one more hard hug, then stepped back and waved Chloe inside. "I knew you wouldn't stay gone for long. I told those busybody widows that very thing."

Chloe stepped into the house and shut the door. Glancing around the room, she asked, "Where are they?"

"Asleep in their cribs."

Asleep. Well, shoot.

"Tess isn't here," Adele continued, following Chloe up the stairs toward the nursery. "She on a date with Nick."

Chloe already knew the couple's whereabouts. She'd followed them to the theater, where they'd bought tickets to a movie that would last two hours and twenty-three minutes. Chloe figured with travel time figured in, she'd be safe here for two and a half hours.

Soft light from a unicorn dresser lamp cast a muted glow through the room. The scent of baby lotion perfumed the air, and the soft snuffles coming from the two cribs sounded like the sweetest of music to Chloe's ears. Tears overflowed her eyes.

"They're sweet little things," Adele said, her tone soft and gentle and just a little inquisitive.

"I'll answer your questions, Adele, but first I need to—"

"Your babies. Of course."

Standing just inside the nursery, determined to do this right, Chloe took a coin from her pocket. *Heads, Stephanie. Tails, Caitlin.* The flip showed tails, and after marking the time on her watch, Chloe crossed the room to stand beside Caitlin's crib. Her breath caught. *She's so beautiful.*

Dark hair, not a lot of it, but enough so that she wasn't bald. Pretty pink skin. A sweet little button nose and a mouth shaped like a bow. A tiny foot escaped the pink rabbit-print sacque with a drawstring bottom, and Chloe gently reached down to tuck it back inside. Her arms ached with the need to hold her, to hold them both.

Moving to Stephanie's crib, she drank in the sight of her other daughter. Same dark hair. Same pink skin and button nose and bow mouth. Same rabbit-print sacque, except in yellow. Stephanie sucked her thumb.

Adele spoke from the doorway. "Go ahead and pick her up, honey."

"Oh, I can't. She's sleeping."

"Don't be silly. Picking her up won't wake her, and even if it does, she'll go right back to sleep in your arms. Unless she's hungry, of course, and in that case she'd have awakened soon anyway."

"Are you sure?"

"Pick up your daughter, honey, and rock her. I'll go fix us both a nice glass of tea, then we can talk."

Chloe nodded, then turned back to the crib and picked up her daughter. Clutching the baby to her bosom, Chloe felt tears flooding her eyes once again.

She settled into the rocking chair next to Caitlin's bed, pulling aside the bumper pad so that she could see her while holding Stephanie. She cuddled the baby close and rocked her, the stress of the past weeks fading in the peace of the maternal moment.

She'd craved this, the weight of her child in her arms. After carrying these two around for almost nine months, she'd had trouble adjusting to the...loneliness...of her postpartum period. As tired as she'd been of being pregnant, nothing made up for the emptiness she'd felt both physically and emotionally since leaving Bethania Hospital without her babies.

A new mother shouldn't have to do this. "Damn you, Snake Duncan."

Adele entered the nursery carrying two glasses of iced tea. Setting one on the dresser within Chloe's reach, she took a seat in the second rocker. "Tess filled me in about your troubles. You know, you're not the first woman I've known to suffer postpartum depression. You must be feeling better now, though."

She could get out of bed now, anyway. For a while, she couldn't do that much. After leaving the hospital that morning, once she was safe with Stewart, she'd all but fallen apart. The meds and talking to people had helped. Her shrink actually told her the murderous rage she felt toward those men in the hospital was a good sign. "It's been a difficult time, Adele. I want to do what's best for Caitlin and Stephanie."

"I know you do, and I have every confidence that you will. It might be a little difficult at first, but I'll be here to help you. I bet we can even talk Tess into hanging around an extra few days, too, although the way her cell phone's been ringing, I know she needs to get back to California. Still, she's falling in love with those two little girls right before my eyes. I also suspect she's not in any hurry to say good-bye to Nick."

In the crib, Caitlin stirred and let out a little mewl.

"Is she waking up?" Chloe asked hopefully.

"Sure is," Adele observed, rising from her seat to head for the kitchen. "She'll be wanting her bottle in two minutes flat. Little Bit won't be far behind her."

Excitement shimmered through Chloe. When she'd decided to risk this visit, she'd hoped she'd have the opportunity to feed the girls. She watched as Caitlin's little fists came up to wave wildly in the air. When the baby opened her eyes, Chloe smiled and said, "Hello, babylove."

Within five minutes both babies were awake and nursing milk from a bottle. Chloe couldn't recall the last time she'd felt this peaceful, this content. This happy.

Then Adele had to play terrier with a bone. "Was it just awful for you, honey? The depression? Some of the things I read on the Internet scared me. Chloe, were you worried you might hurt your babies?"

"Hurt them!" Chloe bristled. "I'd never hurt them. Why would you accuse me of that?"

"I'm not accusing you of anything. It's just that for you to do something so drastic as to leave your newborns behind...well...postpartum depression can have horrible consequences. It's been on the news."

"I never worried that I might hurt my girls."

"Well, good. Some of the people in town have been—opinionated —and proper information helps me respond in your defense. This is your home, Chloe. People need to know you didn't abandon your daughters and that you weren't faking the baby blues."

"Is that what they're saying?"

Adele nodded. "Some are."

"No, I didn't abandon my daughters and I wasn't faking the blues," Chloe snapped. "I was definitely off my rocker for a while after the girls were born, but I'm better now. My hormones have settled down. Plus, I've talked to a shrink a few times. That helped." Chloe stared down at Stephanie and spoke from the heart. "However, I'm still frightened."

"Oh, hon, what has you so scared?"

It'd be easier to say what didn't scare her. Chloe brushed her thumb across her daughter's downy cheek. "I have a hard time taking care of myself. When I realized I needed to leave, the idea of taking the girls with me...it wouldn't have worked. I knew I could trust Tess to care for them. She is so confident. So competent."

"You should have seen her the first few days after the babies came home. Competent and confident aren't the words I'd use. You'd have done fine, Chloe. You'd have gotten through it, just like Tess did. Of course, the entire parenting process is easier if both parents can help." Adele shot her a sidelong look. "Any word on Snake?"

Chloe sucked her bottom lip and shook her head.

The older woman stared at her, then her eyes rounded with worry. "Oh, no. You've found out something. Is he...?"

"He's not dead," Chloe said, giving voice to her greatest fear. "I know it's clichéd to say I'd know if he were gone, but I believe it's true. He and I communicated on the same wavelength. I'd sense it if he were not still alive."

"Okay...okay...." Adele soothed both Chloe and the child in her arms who'd begun to fuss.

"He'll be back." *If not to get me, than to get what I found out at the trailer during my reconnaissance last week.*

"All right, Chloe. I believe you. I actually do think Snake will show up here one day with a bouquet of flowers and an excuse. You'll forgive him, and you'll all live happily ever after."

Chloe shut her eyes against the tears that threatened once more. "I dream about that every day."

An hour later she sat alone in the nursery, holding her two daughters, rocking them gently.

"You be good girls, you hear?" she said as she glanced at the wall clock. "I want you to mind your Auntie Tess and Adele, and to remember that your mama loves you with all her heart. I'm doing the very best I know how to do, here. Hopefully, we'll be together again soon."

When Adele returned to the nursery, Chloe said, "Neither seems ready to go back to sleep."

"Bring them to the living room and lay them on the quilt. You can stretch out beside them and play."

"That sounds lovely," Chloe said, fighting to keep her expression steady. "Maybe next time."

"Next time?"

"I need to leave now, Adele."

"Pardon me? What did you just—?"

"I didn't come home for good tonight." She kissed both daughters on the forehead, then laid them in their cribs. "This is only a visit."

"Hold on just one moment." Adele stood in the doorway, holding her palm up like a traffic cop signaling stop. "What is going on here?"

"I'm leaving." Chloe brushed past Adele as if she weren't there.

Adele followed after her. "You can't leave."

"I must."

"Why?"

The time had come to give the answers and explanations she'd concocted before coming here today—only now, her mind and heart were filled with grief over leaving her daughters, and she couldn't remember what she'd planned to say.

So instead, she said the first thing that popped into her head. "I need to be in Denver tomorrow for a Save Our Mountain Streams campaign rally."

"Save Our Mountain Streams? What about the babies?"

My babies! "I need a little more time yet, Adele. Tess will take good care of my girls until I can come home. Good-bye."

Adele stood in the doorway watching in shock and disappointment as Chloe climbed into the van and drove off. "Oh, Chloe," Adele said with a sigh. "You may have faith in Tess, but I wonder, do you realize how this could destroy her faith in you?"

～

Nick leaned against the sales counter inside Brazos Bend Sporting Goods and debated the choice between two pairs of running shoes. Were he selecting a pair for himself, he'd have gone for the Nikes on the right. Somehow, though, Tess seemed more the Adidas type to him.

He'd sent her flowers every day for a week now, but today he'd decided to do it a little differently. Today he'd intended to send her a shoe bouquet. Running shoes, high-heeled evening shoes, sandals, and a rainbow of Keds. He was still debating golf shoes. He liked to play at least once a week, but he couldn't remember if she'd mentioned enjoying the sport or not.

He settled on the Adidas, decided to skip the golf shoes, and had reached for his wallet when movement on the sidewalk in front of the store caught his attention. Tess wore baby papoose packs, one kid snuggled against her left breast, the other her right. She marched past the sporting goods store plate glass window like a soldier on a mission, her mouth set, chin jutting forward, fire blazing in her eyes.

"Uh-oh." Nick scratched his jaw and tried to recall if he'd done anything to bring out that sort of fighting mad. They'd certainly left each other on a high note last night. He'd walked her to the back door and kissed her senseless and talked her into meeting him for lunch today. "Not me," he murmured, secure in his conclusion. Somebody, though, had her wearing war paint instead of makeup.

He signed his sales receipt, grabbed the bag, and hurried out the door. He spied her just as she turned into the *Brazos Bend Times and Record News* office. The newspaper? What business does she have with the newspaper?

Bet somebody wrote something about Chloe. The Widow Mallow liked to write scathing editorials, and it would be just like her to make child abandonment an issue with only slightly veiled references to Chloe. That would certainly set Tess off.

Veering past his truck, Nick tossed in the sack of shoes—he intended to give them to her at lunch—then sauntered up the square toward the newspaper office. As he walked inside, he expected to hear either crying babies or a lecturing Auntie Tess.

Instead, she stood at the advertising desk, dictating copy.

"I want the body of the text centered under the headline," Tess said, reaching to untangle one of the twins' fingers from her hair. "It want it to say: 'I am not prepared to remain in Brazos Bend indefinitely. I have responsibilities to my professional clients, and I will not abandon them, any more than I would abandon the children your incomprehensible actions have placed in my charge. I will take Stephanie and Caitlin to California, and soon. Be prepared. Stealth visits are fixin' to get much harder.'"

The news clerk glanced up from his notepad and asked, "How do you spell Caitlin, Ms. McKinney?"

She told him, then added, "This next sentence I want bolded. 'I love you, Chloe, but the girls come first.'"

Nick walked up behind her. "Good morning, darlin'. Dare I ask what this is all about?"

She whirled on him, as best a woman can do with a pair of babies strapped to her breast. "She's here in town. She dropped by for a visit yesterday when I wasn't home. Only a visit, mind you. She was too busy to stay around and help with the two A.M. feedings."

"Chloe?"

"Oh, yes. Chloe. My dear sister, Chloe." She turned back toward the clerk and said, "And at the bottom of the ad, in bold print, I want it to say—"

"Nothing," Nick said. He grasped her arm and pulled her away from the counter, then spoke over her head to the clerk. "Cancel the ad, Joe. She's just blowing off steam."

Tess tore herself from Nick's grip. "I am not. I mean it. I want that ad run, Joe. In fact, let's make it a full page ad instead of a quarter page. I have more to say to my little sister!"

"Well, you're not going to say it in the newspaper, Tess." Nick lifted one twin from the baby carrier and cradled her against his chest. "This isn't California. In Brazos Bend we don't advertise our dirty laundry for everyone to see. Which one is this?"

"What? Oh. That's Caitlin."

"How can you tell?"

"I'm starting to see a few differences, but for quick identification, I painted her right index fingernail pink. Stephanie's is red." Tess followed Nick and Caitlin out of the newspaper office. "I recognize what you're attempting to do, Nicholas Sutherland. You're trying to manage me, but I won't be managed. I'm the manager, not the managee."

"And just what are you trying to manage by going pissed off in public?"

Her cell phone rang before she had time to respond. She spent the next ten minutes walking up and down the sidewalk discussing the pros and cons of accepting a television dog food commercial with one of her clients. She no sooner disconnected than her phone rang again with a call from a producer wanting to review a client's schedule. Nick watched her juggle a business call, her PDA, a baby who kept losing her pacifier, and a nonverbal conversation with the cop who asked her to move her car from a No Parking zone. Damn, but that woman turned him on.

Accustomed to problem-solving himself, Nick waved over the teenage son of a friend of his who was standing in line to buy movie tickets and slipped him some money to move the car. Then, holding Caitlin captive in his arms and crooking a finger toward Tess, he took off walking. She glared at him and motioned for him to stop, but eventually followed just as he'd known she would.

A few minutes later, with Tess still on the phone, Nick opened the front door of the Hutton Hotel and motioned for Tess to precede him. Deliberately, he thought, she stepped on his toe.

Inside, he led the way to the remodeled room that would serve as the retirement home's cafeteria. There, as he expected, he found the recreation planning committee holding its daily ten A.M. social hour disguised as a meeting. Committee members numbered eight Brazos Bend seniors and included Caitlin's and Stephanie's grandmother.

Nick strode across the room and handed Caitlin to Widow Duncan, who lit up like a Friday-night football scoreboard. At that, Tess abruptly ended her call. "Nick, what are you doing?"

"I promised you a tour of the building. Thought now would be a

144

good time for it since I knew we had all these built-in babysitters available."

"I can't impose like that."

"Oh, no imposition," the Widow Duncan cooed down at Caitlin. "I love spending every moment I can with my granddaughters."

At that, Tess gave a sickly little smile. Recently, she and Mrs. Duncan had established a wary truce. Mrs. Duncan didn't like Tess's sister, and Tess wanted to strangle Mrs. Duncan's son, but they both loved the girls. They vacillated between cooperation and competition, and Nick was never certain which would hold sway at any given time.

"We probably have over a hundred years' worth of child care experience in this room," Nick observed. "Mrs. Lewis has three kids and four grandchildren. Bob Norris here has four children and twelve grandchildren, as I recall. Bet you know how to hold a little one, don't you, Bob?"

"Oh, I reckon I've bounced one on my knee a time or two."

"You can't bounce babies this young," Tess protested. "Shaken baby syndrome is a...oh...you didn't mean that literally. I'm sorry, I'm just a bit"—her gaze flicked over the Widow Duncan, who held Caitlin with a proprietary air—"distracted."

Nick slipped the diaper bag off Tess's shoulder and handed it to the Widow Mallow. "Y'all won't mind watching the girls for a little while, would you?"

"We'll love to babysit," replied Mr. Norris, speaking for the group.

"But Nick, the girls will need their bottles soon, and I—"

"I'd like to hear the details of what happened after I took you home last night," he said softly.

She set her mouth grimly. "Nothing happened after I went home. All the action took place when I was with you."

"I'll say," Nick observed with grateful feeling. "Gotta love dark movie theaters."

It coaxed the first smile he'd seen from her all day and won her cooperation. She handed Stephanie to Bob Norris, took a moment to look at John Thompson's grandchildren's school pictures, then followed Nick out the door.

He grasped her hand and tugged her along toward the elevator, where he jabbed the button with his thumb, then frowned up at the light above the door indicating the car was descending from the fourth floor. Impatiently, he tapped his right boot against the tile floor.

"I should have told Mr. Norris that Stephanie needs to be burped after every ounce of formula. Caitlin belches like a beer drinker, but Steph needs help. Maybe I should go back and—"

Nick tightened his grip on her hand as the elevator *dinged* and the doors slid open. "She'll be fine." He was dragging Tess inside. "They'll both be fine."

He punched the third-floor button, waited for the doors to slide shut, then muttered, "Finally!"

She let out a little yelp of surprise as he backed her against the wall and took her mouth in a hard, demanding kiss. From the moment he'd watched her walk into his ballroom, he'd wanted her. As the days passed, that wanting had grown into a constant, clawing sexual need that Nick thought he'd sated first last week on the boat, then the following day at the carriage house, then the day after that at his house, etc.

Obviously, he'd thought wrong. Every taste he had of her only heightened his hunger.

He closed his hand over her breast. Beneath her soft cotton T-shirt and the thin satin of her bra, he felt her nipple pucker. "Nick!" she exclaimed on a breathy, laughing gasp when he released her mouth to nip at the creamy flesh of her throat. "I thought you wanted to give me a tour."

"I do." He slipped his hand beneath her shirt and stroked his hand across the silky skin of her belly. "Apartment 3C. It's our fully furnished model. It has a bed."

"That's all that matters."

What followed was, simply put, a war. Locked together in a fervent embrace, they stumbled from the elevator and up the hall to 3C. Nick fumbled in his pocket for keys, and Tess offered to help. Instead of his pocket, she went for his zipper. Seconds later, as her hand closed around him, Nick didn't care that they stood in a semipublic hallway in a partially remodeled hotel. They could be on City Hall's front steps for all he'd mind.

"Woman, you make me lose my mind."

Somehow one of them got the apartment door open, and they fought their way inside. Mouths attacked and plundered, hands pillaged and plunged. He made her come twice on the living room floor. She brought him right to the edge by capturing him between the fullness of her breasts and moving in a way that made him howl.

"The bed," he gasped. "I stashed Trojans there the other day."

"Bless you."

When they finally made it to the bedroom and the queen-size bed, they rolled and rumbled and damned near fell off. When she tried to capture him with her mouth once again, Nick surrendered.

He yanked her up, flung her onto her back, and entered her with a forceful thrust. She moaned with satisfaction, then met him stroke for stroke until they both cried out their climax.

Nick collapsed on top of her. Seconds ticked by, the only sound in the room their panting, gasping breaths. When he felt her palms press firmly against his chest, Nick worked hard to summon energy enough to roll to his back, allowing her to breathe. He lay languid and sated, one hand flung possessively over her thigh, the other dangling off the side of the narrow bed. The musky scent of sex lingered on the air.

"What just happened?" she asked, her tone filled with wonder.

"Exercise," Nick replied, knowing it was so much more than that.

Her eyes closed, her hair a tangle, her body limp, Tess said, "Beats Pilates any time."

Nick rolled to his side and up on one elbow. "You're a beautiful woman, Tess McKinney, but it's your spirit that makes you so damned sexy."

Her lashes flickered up, and surprise dawned in her tawny brown eyes.

"And your heart..." Nick reached out a finger and traced a heart on her left breast. "Your heart makes you irresistible. For a California girl, you have a heart as big as Texas."

Her eyes softened. "What a lovely thing to say."

"I want—" He broke off when the *brrring* of her cell phone sounded from the general direction of the living room.

With a groan, Tess sat up, muttering. "My shorts. My phone's in my shorts. I need to take this call. Jake Muldoon's agent is working a movie deal that could be huge for Jake." She slipped from the bed and darted from the bedroom. Seconds later, he heard her say, "Hi, Jake."

Now, call him picky, but Nick had a problem with his woman talking on the phone with another man while she was bare-ass naked. He rolled out of bed and grabbed his blue chambray work shirt off the floor, intending to help her slip it on, but as he strolled into the living room, the conversation stopped him short.

"You're right, Jake," Tess said. "Yes. Yes. No, it'll be okay. I'll bring the girls with me. Yes. Yes." She laughed softly.

Nick ground his teeth.

"That'll work. Okay. I'll see you day after tomorrow. Love you, too, Jake. Bye."

As Tess disconnected the call, Nick tossed her his shirt. "Call me picky, but when a woman's skin still glows rosy from my razor burn, I don't like hearing her telling another man she loves him."

"Nick—"

"Especially when she hasn't said those words to me yet."

CHAPTER 14

"HARDHEADED COWBOY," Tess muttered as she rinsed the soap from her body in the apartment shower. "Stubborn saw slinger. Obstinate"—distaste dripped from the word—"*lawyer.*"

His pithy comment about declarations of love had left her speechless just long enough to rile his temper even more. When she found her voice, he wouldn't listen to her. Instead, he'd grabbed his pants and flung his intention to shower down the hall over his shoulder as he left the apartment.

"What did he expect?" she grumbled as she shut off the shower and stepped from the tub. Tugging a towel from the rack, she muttered while she dried her skin. "Was I supposed to prostrate myself at his feet and declare my undying love? I've known the man a month. One lousy month!"

And you've done the deed with him every day for a week.

"An affair. It's a simple, pleasurable affair for us both to enjoy during my time in Brazos Bend."

You're lying to yourself now, Tess. That's a Chloe kinda thing to do.

Oh, no. Not that!

"Okay, so maybe it's more. Maybe I like him. Like him a lot. But falling in love? That would be a disaster."

Why?

"Because he's Brazos Bend and I'm L.A."

Does it have to be that way?

Pulling on her underwear, Tess hesitated. *Did* it have to be that way? Nick hadn't lived in Brazos Bend all that long. How deep were his roots here, anyway?

Tess mulled the question over while she finished dressing. Emerging from the bathroom, she found Nick seated at the kitchen table, his back toward her, talking on his cell phone. She took a moment to admire the way his work shirt stretched across his broad shoulders and the way his dark hair, still damp from his own shower, curled at the nape of his neck. The way his big hand curled around the slender phone made her think of how he'd held her captive by the wrists, her arms stretched above her head like a melodrama heroine, while his free hand had its lusciously wicked way with her.

"I'd appreciate the help, Alex," he said, standing and walking to the window. Pushing back the yellow gingham curtain, he added, "My experience leaves a lot to be desired when dealing with this area of the law."

He ended the call a few seconds later and stood gazing out the window. Tess wondered what the call had been about. He appeared unusually tense. When he turned around, Tess felt a shimmer of unease. She'd seen more expression on Botox patients fresh from the doctor's office. "Nick? Can we please talk?"

He gave himself a little shake. "Sorry. I didn't hear you come in."

"You were on the phone. Is something wrong?"

His gaze slid toward the cell phone. "That depends. What do you want to talk about?"

The way he looked now, the flatness in his gaze, made Tess wonder if she even needed to bring the subject up. Maybe she'd read him all wrong.

No, idiot. You hurt his feelings.

"Nick, about Jake..."

Abruptly, he stood. "Forget it. I spoke out of turn. Would you like something to drink? I have some Dr Peppers and bottled water in the fridge."

Judging by the stiffness in his stance, she'd be better off to let the subject of Jake Muldoon go for now. "Sure. Water would be nice."

Tess followed him into the kitchen and waited until he opened the refrigerator door to ask, "What were you running from when you left Dallas?"

His brows arched in surprise. "Where did that come from?"

"That day when you took me riding and we went down to your hideaway, you told me you needed to leave Dallas, but you never told me why."

"But why—?"

"You've become important to me, Nick. I know you altered your entire way of life when you moved to Brazos Bend, but I don't know why you made such a drastic change. I'd like to understand you better than I do. I think it's important."

He stared at her a long moment while he contemplated the issue. Then he returned his unopened bottle of water to the fridge and pulled out a soft drink.

"Five years ago, if you'd asked me if I come from a strong, close family, I'd have told you yes. I believed it back then. I loved my mother, adored my grandmother. My father and I had a few issues, but we got along well enough. I have two sisters who are quite a bit older than me. They both live in Europe now—one's married, the other divorced. Neither has children. Five years ago, they both lived in Dallas."

He twisted off the bottle cap, took a draw on his Dr Pepper, then continued. "Dad died in his sleep three months before we lost Mom to breast cancer. Without the folks around, with the differences in our ages and interests, the girls and I drifted apart. During that time, I grew even closer to my grandmother." He paused, and his mouth twisted in a bittersweet smile. "I recognized that she'd lost weight. I knew she'd had some health problems, but she told me she was fine, and I let myself believe it. I was busy orchestrating a hostile takeover of a Dallas-based tech firm, and I put business in front of family. I hadn't been to see her for a week. When she started hemorrhaging, she called 911, then me. It took me over a minute to take the call. She had time to say my name, just Nicholas, before she died."

151

"Oh, Nick. That must have been so difficult for you."

"I knew I had to make some changes. I picked Brazos Bend because I needed a sanctuary, and they'd always welcomed me here. I never expected I'd move here and find a family."

"But that's what happened," Tess stated, her heart aching.

"Yeah. That's exactly what happened. Brazos Bend gave me a home and a family, and I'll never take that for granted again." Nick set his Dr Pepper on the counter. "So that's my story. What's yours? Tell me about this ad you thought to take out in the newspaper."

Although Tess had more questions about the strength of his ties to Brazos Bend, his body language told her not to persist at this time, so she followed along with the change of subject. "I could wring Chloe's neck," she said. "I told you she showed up at the carriage house. Adele thought she'd come home, but oh, no. Chloe had just dropped by for a visit. Chloe has more important things to do than care for her own children. She has bigger responsibilities than her two helpless, mother-and-fatherless infants. She has to go to the mountains to save the streams!"

"She what?"

Talking about Chloe rekindled Tess's ire, and she paced the kitchen while she relayed the details of Chloe's visit. Nick picked up his soda once more when she told him how her sister beat a retreat just before Tess returned home.

"Never mind that I have a life I've put on hold to help her," Tess continued, getting more worked up the longer she talked. "Never mind that my clients pay me quite well to spend my time managing their professional lives, not to change diapers. Never mind that every day I spend with Caitlin and Stephanie will only make it harder to leave when Chloe up and decides it's time to play mommy instead of environmentalist."

"What about me?" Nick asked softly. "Will you find it easy to leave me?"

His query stopped her cold. In light of all she'd learned today, she didn't know how to respond. She needed time to think about it, to figure out what was best for her and for Nick. "That's a complicated question."

His lips twisted in a wry smile. "Actually, it's not complicated at all. All it requires is a yes or no response."

"Relationship questions can never be answered with a simple yes or no."

"Is that what we have, then? A relationship?"

Tess scowled at him. "That depends on how you define a relationship."

"I like to use adjectives."

"Adjectives? What are you talking about?"

"You tell me, Tess. Which words fit us? Temporary? Convenient? Personally, one of my favorites is 'exclusive.' Of course, I tend to use that interchangeably with 'monogamous.' In fact, if I use the word 'relationship,' I always use one of those two words. Maybe it's the lawyer in me, but I'm kinda picky about that."

"Now I get it. You're still hacked about Jake."

"No, I'm not. Well, maybe I am, damn it. Oh, hell, I don't know. You have me all stirred up. I don't know what I'm thinking except that —" A muscle worked in Nick's jaw. "You were *naked* when you talked to him."

"Excuse me, but we were on the telephone, not a video conference. He didn't know I was naked."

Nick scowled. "Don't be so sure. Guys can sense that sort of thing. We're all tuned in to naked."

She stared at him, and long seconds ticked away. "Have you lost your mind?"

He muttered a curse, shoved his hands in his pockets, and rocked back on his heels. "You're not the first person to question my choices. I could live just about anywhere on earth, and I chose to move to Brazos Bend. We have one movie theater, zero five-star restaurants, and a symphony that consists of a guitar, two spoons, and a harmonica played by three octogenarians in front of Fred's barbershop on Tuesday mornings. But it's a good place, Tess. A healing place. And as much as I don't want to say this, I can't put it off any longer. You can't leave Brazos Bend with those babies."

"Jeez, I need a road map to follow this conversation. What are you talking about now?"

"Legalities," he snapped. "Those children aren't yours. If you try to run off to California with the Widow Duncan's grandbabies, I can almost guarantee she'll file charges of some sort to stop you. Knowing her, she'll want to go for kidnapping first, and if that doesn't fly, she'll cook up some other excuse. One of the judges in town is her brother's son-in-law's second cousin. He'll grant an injunction against you first and ask questions later."

"Kidnapping!" This was not at all a turn she'd anticipated. Tess braced her hands on her hips. "That's ridiculous, Nick. Chloe left Stephanie and Caitlin in my care. I can take them wherever I care to take them. The Widow Duncan can't manipulate the law like that."

"Sure she can. This is small-town Texas, where law is enforced when it's convenient and in a way that's beneficial to those in power. Like it or not, the Widow Duncan has plenty of stroke here in town."

"Then stop her. File something on my behalf."

"I can't." Nick set his mouth in a grim smile. "I'm her attorney, not yours."

He might as well have slapped her. "Excuse me?"

"I don't drop clients because it becomes personally inconvenient to represent them."

For a long moment, Tess stood speechless, her mouth bobbing open and closed like a fish out of water. Then anger finally gave her back her voice, and when she spoke, it all but dripped venom. "Well, of course you don't. You're a man of ethics. You wouldn't sleep with a client, either, would you?"

Nick's blue eyes flashed. "Now you're pissing me off."

"Am I?" She offered up a patently false smile. "Oh, dear. We can't have that. You might file an injunction of some sort against me with Judge Roy Bean. Wait, he's dead isn't he? Tell me, counselor, does a little detail like that matter down here in the land not-quite-west of the Pecos?"

"Dammit, Tess, I'm trying to help, here. I know this town. I know these people. I know the Widow Duncan. Just give it a little more time. My man is bound to turn up something on Snake any minute now. Either that, or Chloe will come home for good or Snake will slither back into town on his own. If you'll be reasonable about this and give me a little time, a little trust, we'll avoid any small-town trouble in the offing."

"Reasonable? Oh, I'll be reasonable, and I can give you a little time. Very little time. Trust is something else entirely. But don't worry, Nick. I understand your ethics. You were Mrs. Duncan's lawyer first, so you must put her best interests ahead of mine. I'm no client. I'm just someone you screw."

"Now that's enough." He took a step toward her.

She waved him back. "If you'll give me a rain check on the rest of the hotel tour, I need to make a phone call. To my personal attorney." She lifted her cell phone from her purse and made a show of pressing only one button. "Speed dial," she smiled. "He's number one."

Nick raked a hand through his hair. "A lawyer? Oh, wonderful. That's just what this situation needs."

"It's what I need. You're the opposing counsel. I obviously need my own attorney, someone I can trust."

Nick looked as if he might bare his teeth and growl at her. Then he took a deep breath, and said, "Look. You're right. Ethically, I can't represent Mrs. Duncan anymore, so there's no need to bring any outside lawyers into the mix."

It was too little, too late. Thousands of miles away in California, Jake Muldoon answered the phone. "Hello?"

"Hi, Jake. I'd like to make a change in our plan, if you'll be so kind as to help me. I need to change our meeting location."

"All right. Just tell me when and where."

"My house in Brazos Bend. As soon as you can get here."

"Brazos Bend? You want me to come to Texas?"

"Yes, darling. I do."

Nick walked past her, his strides long and angry. He slammed the apartment door behind him.

Tess added, "And Jake? Don't forget to bring a suit or two."

"A suit? I thought Brazos Bend was a small, T-shirt-and-jeans kind of town."

"Most of the time it is. Men still wear a coat and tie to church, though. And to weddings. Funerals. Court."

There was a long pause. "You gettin' married, beautiful?"

"No."

"Somebody die?"

"Not yet."

"Oh, hell, honey. What sort of trouble are you in?"

"Your kind of trouble, Mr. Holloway," she said, referring to the character he played in *Line of Defense*. "I need a lawyer. Can I count on you for help?"

~

HOLLYWOOD ARRIVED in a helicopter that twice circled Nick's house, then set down in his front yard. The pilot cut the engine, and the *thwop thwop thwop* of the blades slowed, then rotated to a stop.

Seated in a wicker rocking chair on his front porch with his friend Max Cooper, a tin tub filled with ice and Mexican beer between them, Nick sipped from a long-necked bottle. "I'll bill that s.o.b. for damages if he leaves ruts in the lawn."

"A friend of yours?" Max asked as he reached into the tub and tugged out a beer.

"Not hardly." Nick set down his beer, stood, and grabbed one of the fishing poles from the rod holder he'd hung at the southeast corner of his house. An artificial lure stripped of its hooks dangled at the end of the line. With a flick of his wrist, Nick sent the fishing line flying toward his target—a handily placed birdbath. The lure landed with a splash, and as Nick reeled in the line and repeated the throw, he told Max the helicopter passenger's identity and gave a sketchy reason for his visit.

"Well, imagine that," Max drawled as the helicopter door swung open. "A real live TV star. Folks around here are sure to be impressed. He's the first celebrity who's come to Brazos Bend since...well...since you."

"I'm no celebrity," Nick scoffed.

"No. You're just rich. That doesn't hold a candle to being a TV star. Come to think of it, he's a very successful TV star. He might beat you out on the money angle, too."

"Don't be stupid, Cooper."

Out on the lawn, the passenger climbed out of the bird. On the porch, Max drew a bottle opener from his pocket and casually popped the top on his brew. The opener blared out an electronic rendition of the Aggie War Hymn, the song that stirred the blood of Texas A&M University alums. Nick, who had received his undergraduate degree from the University of Texas, responded to the insult by shooting Max the finger. "Now is not the time for college rivalry, Cooper. I'm being invaded by Hollywood, here."

"Sounds like a personal problem to me." Max grinned and sipped his beer. Once upon a time, he and Nick had been rivals for the same woman, but that competition had long been put to rest. The college rivalry would exist until they died.

Max settled back into his chair as Nick made a halfhearted cast toward the birdbath, and the helicopter passenger swung a garment bag over his shoulder and headed toward the carriage house. Tess came flying out the door, her arms open wide, a smile on her face as big as an oil-field dream. Nick mouthed a curse.

"You're sleeping with her?" Max observed. "I'll be damned."

"Like I'd tell your nosy ass."

Max snagged a hunk of fresh lime out of the plastic container nestled among the beer and poked it down the neck of his beer bottle. "If you wanted to keep it quiet, you should have made sure she put her shirt back on right side out after touring the retirement center with you."

Tess threw herself into the newcomer's arms, Nick muttered another invective, and Max snorted a laugh. When the visitor dropped his bag, picked Tess up, and twirled her around, Nick turned away. Scowling, he shoved his fishing pole back onto the rod holder. "Yeah, I know. I forgot to put my belt back on, too. Those widows can't hear half what's going on around them, but their eyesight doesn't miss squat. Mrs. Gault and Mrs. Mallow paid me a call last night and proposed that Mrs. Duncan sue for custody of the kids by filing a morals charge against Tess."

Max almost choked on his beer. "Based on her having had sex with you? Now that presentation would be worth a trip over to the court-house to watch." After a pause, his tone took on a more serious note. "They can't do that, can they?"

"No. Not in the real world, anyway."

"But this is Brazos Bend."

"Exactly." Nick nodded, his gaze stealing back toward the embracing couple despite his best efforts to look at something...any-thing else. "Brazos Bend justice is unique. Still, I'm not about to kiss and tell, and clothesline talk only goes so far in a court of law."

The two men observed in silence as Hollywood, aka Jake Muldoon, set Tess on her feet. Nick growled low in his throat when the TV star bent her backward over his arms for a theatrical kiss that left Tess laughing, then realized he was acting like Max during one of what his wife called his "hairy-chested man" moods and winced. What was wrong with him? He'd never acted this way with a woman before.

Tess and Jake Muldoon walked arm in arm toward the carriage house. Tess never once glanced Nick's way.

Max gave Nick a sidelong look. "So, what did you do to piss her off?"

"Nothing."

"Uh-huh."

Suddenly needing to talk about it, to defend himself, Nick declared, "She was going to leave town with the twins. I just pointed out a few reasons why that wasn't a good idea. You'd have thought I'd kicked her favorite puppy."

"You must have done a piss-poor job making your case, counselor."

"She locked up on me. Wouldn't listen one bit." Nick told Max about Chloe's visit to the carriage house, and Tess's reaction to it. "I asked her to trust me, to give me just a little leeway, but she wouldn't do it. This after we'd just set the sheets afire. What does that say about her opinion of me, anyway? I'm good enough to screw but not to trust?"

"You slut."

Nick responded to that with another hand gesture.

"Maybe I was wrong about her," Nick continued, voicing the thought that had been stewing in his brain since yesterday. "She didn't think twice about telling ol' Hollywood she'd head for the hills when he called. Maybe all she wanted was vacation sex."

Max arched a brow. "Somehow, I don't think caring for someone else's colicky twins qualifies as a vacation."

"I couldn't let her take those kids off to California."

"Why not?"

That was the million-dollar question. Why had he reacted so strongly, so uncharacteristically, so unethically, when she mentioned leaving Brazos Bend? No way would he have continued to represent the Widow Duncan against her. Not after their first date, much less the mind-blowing interlude aboard the *Brazos Queen* or any of the others that followed.

"I just couldn't." Nick grabbed a beer from the bucket, then actually used Max's opener to pop the cap.

"Da-yum," Max said as the Aggie War Hymn filled the air. "You *have* lost it. She's really done a number on you, hasn't she?"

Nick took a long sip from the bottle of beer and didn't respond to what they both knew was a rhetorical question.

Tess introduced Jake to an effervescent Adele, who asked him a dozen questions about *Line of Defense,* then requested autographs for a laundry list of people. Jake unzipped a compartment on his garment bag and pulled out a handful of publicity photos. "Tess told me to come prepared."

Adele frowned at the stack. "Hmm....That's enough for me, but I'm warning you, half the folks in Brazos Bend are going to want one of these."

"Not a problem," Tess said. "I had my office express mail two boxes yesterday. They arrived while you were at bowling league this morning."

After signing the autographs, Jake asked to see Caitlin and Stephanie. Offering Adele a sheepish smile that had her pretending to swoon, he added, "I'm a sucker for babies."

"It's true," Tess agreed. "Jake comes from a large family, and at some point during most of our meetings, he invariably pulls out pictures of nieces and nephews to show off."

Adele clicked her tongue. "A man who loves babies. Why, Jake, now I just love you even more!" She started for the staircase, waving him to follow along. "Although if you wake the sweet things up, then I'll have to kill you."

The three adults spent a few minutes in the nursery admiring the slumbering infants, then Tess showed Jake to the guest room.

"This is nice," he said as he walked to the closet and hung up his bag. "The entire house is nice, although the downstairs decor strikes me as rather froufrou for you."

"It fits my sister to a tee, however. The woman who decorated it knows Chloe." Tess walked over to the big bay window and, making a point not to glance outside, opened the drapes.

Jake didn't have the same compunction. Peering up the hill toward the big Victorian house, he asked, "Why is your neighbor fishing in a birdbath?"

"He likes to play games," Tess answered, bitterness in her voice.

Curiosity lit Jake's brilliant green eyes. "Which is the guy who beat my time in the race for your heart? The one fishing for birds or beer?"

"Jake, please. I've been up-front with you from the beginning. There was no race."

"I know, honey. I'm just teasing. So which one has you tied in knots?"

Reluctantly, Tess turned around. Gazing up the hill toward Nick's house, she saw that both he and Max Cooper stood on the front porch, fishing poles in hands. Nick cast toward the birdbath, Max toward a tin tub filled with ice and beer that now sat ten yards behind and to the right of the birdbath. "Why is it men turn everything into a contest?"

"It's written into our genetic code."

Just then Nick glanced toward the carriage house, and for a long minute, he didn't move. Though he was too far away for Tess to see his expression, she tangibly felt his stare. Jake must have felt it, too, because he draped his arm around her shoulders, smiled, and said,

"Well, I guess that answers my question. That's Nicholas Sutherland, hmm? You know what, Tess? I don't think he's happy I'm here."

With that, he raised his hand and gave a friendly wave, then reached out and snapped the drapes shut.

Tess couldn't help but laugh. "Oh, you are bad, Jake."

"I know. And it's because I'm bad that I want all the details you wouldn't go into on the phone those times we talked yesterday. What's the deal, Tess? Last I checked, America was still a free country. Do you honestly believe you need an attorney to clear the way for you to take the twins to California?"

"No. This custody battle will be fought in the court of public opinion, which makes you the perfect person to represent my interests. America may be free, but Brazos Bend is, well...think Brigadoon with a drawl. Life changes sloooooowly here. The founding families still run the town, and I've run smack up against one of them."

"The father's family."

"His mother, to be precise."

"And you want Sam Holloway, TV lawyer, to ride to the rescue."

She shrugged. "I figure your people skills might come in handy, and besides, we needed to get together anyway. This way I can needle Nick Sutherland, too. He's going to hate having you around."

Jake grinned and leaned over to press a kiss against her cheek. "That's my manager. Always multitasking."

"Now that you're here, why don't we get on with our business meeting? I spent most of the morning on the phone gathering the information you requested, and I have a stack of faxes six inches thick in my office downstairs. Based on the events of the previous two days, I have probably about an hour and a half before the babies wake up and launch into their colic mode. That'll last between two to two and a half hours."

Jake winced. "Colic? My sister's little girl suffered with that."

"Everyone suffers when a baby in the house has colic. When two babies have it—well—it's not pretty around here, Jake. If I were you, I'd plan to explore the beauty of Palo Pinto County during that time. However, this evening I can promise you a good dinner, great wine, and the down-and-dirty details about my troubles in Brazos Bend. Deal?"

"Show me your office, slave driver."

CHAPTER 15

THE SUMMER HEAT hung around late into September like a guest who wouldn't go home. In ordinary years, talk in town would have revolved around the weather, the desire for cooler days and crisp autumn evenings to accompany the resumption of the Texas Friday-night religion—high school football. This year, the topic on everyone's tongue involved a different guest, a high-profile guest. Ten days had passed since Hollywood came to town and took up residence in Chloe McKinney's carriage house.

The sonofabitch hadn't left yet.

Nick was going crazy.

Because Tess and Hollywood seldom left the carriage house, he'd spent as much time as possible away from home. That strategy had done him little good. Except for the time he spent working alone in the ballroom at the Hutton Hotel, he was bombarded by talk about the man. Gossip down at Harmon Lanes allowed that Muldoon had indicated interest in joining the fall bowling league. At the barbershop, customers claimed he'd made an appointment to get his high-dollar hairstyle maintained by a small-town barber in business for almost fifty years. Just yesterday, the Widows mailed invitations to a tea they were hosting in his honor. A tea! Nick never got any freakin' tea when he first came to town. Hell, he'd even had to buy his own cards at Bingo Night.

As Nick toweled off following his after-work shower, he tried to figure why the fellow was still hanging around. He didn't believe for a minute the rumor running rampant through the after-church crowd at Piccadilly Cafeteria that Hollywood intended to buy a vacation home at Possum Kingdom Lake. PK was a pretty lake, but it wasn't Malibu or Vail or the other places where Jake Muldoon owned property. He simply couldn't see a man like that setting down roots in a town like this.

Never mind that the same thing could be—and had been—said about him.

Nick pulled on underwear and jeans, then donned his Brazos Bend Rattlers booster club shirt. Though it came early in the season, tonight's ball game promised to be one of the most exciting matchups of the year, and he looked forward to it. The opposing quarterback was a smart, quick kid already on college recruiter radar as a sophomore, but in his construction crew's weekly betting pool, Nick had put his money on the local boys.

Checking the clock, he decided to forgo dinner and grab a hot dog from the concession at the stadium. He tugged on socks and his most comfortable pair of boots, then snatched up his keys and exited the house. A disciplined man, he kept his gaze trained straight ahead, never once veering toward the carriage house as he made his way to his garage. There, he paused and briefly debated his choice of cars, settling on the cherry red Corvette convertible. While he owned more sophisticated cars, cars more suited to himself, nothing fit a high school football game better than a Vette.

Minutes later, he roared through town, the envy of every testosterone-burdened male from eight to eighty-five. *Take that, Hollywood.*

Nick took the corner of Main and Third Street feeling better than he had in ages—or at least ten days.

Traffic slowed as he approached Memorial Stadium. Looked like the crowd might be even bigger than he'd expected. It was only after he'd parked the car and approached the gate that he realized he'd forgotten his ticket.

THE LAST BACHELOR IN TEXAS

"Not a problem," said the ticket taker at the gate. The man knew Nick, knew he owned season tickets. Just one of the perks of small-town living.

"Won't find that in California," Nick murmured, making his way into the stands.

Nick's reserved seat was with the Cooper family, so he stopped at the concessions and bought a round of soft drinks for everyone before making his way up into the stands. Shannon Cooper, Kate and Max's eight-year-old daughter, saw him coming. "Nicky. Nicky," she called, using the nickname she alone on this earth was allowed to use. "Hurry up. You'll miss all the special pregame activities."

Feigning a look of distress, he replied, "I haven't missed the baton twirlers, have I?"

"No, silly. The twirlers only perform at halftime. You have missed Sarah Parker giving Cole Norris a good-luck kiss. And Jennifer Scott and Mark Dalton had a fight, and she's gone to sit with her girlfriends." She paused, peered at the cardboard tray in his hands, and asked, "Did you bring it?"

"What do you think? Do I ever shortchange my dates?" He lowered the tray so she could see the candy bar nestled between the plastic cups, and a grin split her face.

"Oh, Nicky. I love you."

Kate Cooper watched her daughter and sighed. "I don't know whether to be proud of her for wrapping you around her finger or worried because she's so easily bought. I told her to hold out for popcorn, too."

"I promised popcorn at halftime."

"That makes me feel better."

Nick passed out the drinks, then took his seat. The Brazos Bend High School marching band struck up a rousing rendition of the theme from *Star Wars* while on the field, the two teams continued their pregame warm-ups. The stands continued to fill while Nick, Max, and Kate analyzed the leg of the opposition's kicker. Intent upon the action on the field, Nick failed to note Adele Watkins's arrival until she sat down beside him.

"Hey, stranger." She wore the home team's colors of maroon and white, athletic shoes with pom-poms attached to the end of the shoe-strings, and dangling earrings shaped like footballs.

"Evening, Adele."

"Where have you been the last week or so? We've missed seeing you around the carriage house."

"Oh?" After a slight pause, he added, "Who's 'we'?"

Adele's eyes gleamed with a knowing light. Casually, she answered, "Caitlin. Stephanie. Me."

Nick focused his gaze on the gridiron once again, but his thoughts centered on the carriage house and the frustrating woman who currently lived there.

"You handled that all wrong, you realize."

Nick knew Adele well enough to realize he need not respond. She'd offer her opinion whether he wanted her to do it or not.

"That Tess, she likes to be the one driving the bus. You never should have told her she couldn't take the girls wherever she wanted to take them. If you'd laid out the facts and let her come to that conclusion herself, she wouldn't have thrown a hissy fit. It's all in the presentation, Nick. As a lawyer, you should recognize that."

He had recognized it. He'd known the minute the words came out of his mouth that he'd screwed up, but his reaction at the time had been pure emotion. He hadn't wanted her to leave Brazos Bend. To leave him. So he'd spoken from his gut instead of his brain, and Hollywood had come to town.

"Why hasn't he left yet?" Nick blurted out as the crowd rose to cheer the home team as they returned to the locker room to prepare for the start of the game.

Adele put two fingers in her mouth and blew a loud whistle, then yelled, "Get fired up, Rattlers!"

Without glancing at Nick, she said, "You'd know if you weren't hiding out in your house."

"I'm not hiding."

She snorted, then put her hand over her heart as the band struck the first notes of "The Star-Spangled Banner." The crowd sang along with the national anthem and remained standing for the two competing schools' songs. When they'd again taken their seats, Adele leaned over and spoke in a tone only Nick could hear. "It's a big secret, but Jake has left *Line of Defense*. He's going to do a movie, a Western, and he says spending time in Brazos Bend will help him get an ear for his character's accent."

Great. Just great.

"Besides, I don't think Tess would let him go even if he wanted to. Do you know the babies haven't had a spell of colic since the first day he arrived? When that time of day rolls around, he picks them up, and we don't hear a peep out of them. Jake claims it's coincidence, but I don't believe it. That man has a magic touch with the girls."

Thankfully, the band broke into the Brazos Bend fight song, and the crowd stood up and roared as the home team burst through the butcher paper sign that read "Go Rattlers" and "Crush the Coyotes" and jogged to their side of the field. As the Rattler offense prepared to kick off the game, looking for a distraction from thoughts of Tess and Hollywood, Nick leaned over and tapped Max on the shoulder. "I'll bet you twenty bucks we score twenty points by the end of the first half."

"I hate to bet against the home team, but I've seen the Coyotes' defense," Max said. "I'll take your bet, Sutherland. I honestly doubt we'll score twenty in the entire game."

The bet served its purpose, and by the end of the first drive, Nick was wrapped up in the game. Such was his concentration that he only vaguely noted the stir that swept over the stands three minutes before the end of the first quarter. Squeals erupted from the student section. Murmurs built in the crowd among the adults.

A couple rows in front of him, Nick heard a voice say, "Look, there he is! It's Sam Holloway! From *Line of Defense!*"

"Sam Holloway," the owner of the beauty salon, Elizabeth Beck, said from her seat in the row behind her. "Oh, my stars. Sam Holloway at a Brazos Bend High football game. You know, he's the best lawyer in the business. Just like Perry Mason, he's never lost a case."

"His name's not Sam Holloway," replied her husband, Larry. "That's his TV name. His real name is Jake Muldoon."

"I know that." Elizabeth clicked her tongue. "I'm not stupid, Larry. I met him myself just day before yesterday when he stopped by Harmon Lanes and bowled a couple of frames."

"Look," Shannon Cooper piped up. "They're holding baby carriers. He and Tess brought the babies. Do you think she'll let me hold one?"

"No!" exclaimed Max and Kate in unison.

Nick watched in shock and dismay as Tess and Muldoon made slow progress through the stands. They couldn't take more than two steps without somebody stopping them, either to gander at the girls or hound ol' Hollywood for his autograph.

"What's she doing bringing the babies out in public at a venue like this one?" Max asked Kate, voicing the very question that had been running through Nick's mind.

"The pediatrician suggested it, believe it or not," Kate replied. "Between folks wanting to meet Jake and those wanting to see the twins, the phone doesn't stop ringing at the carriage house. The weather's been too hot to take them out in the daytime, so the doctor thought an hour or so here tonight would give people an opportunity to do their gawking and get it over with. I told them to come sit next to us in the Holbrooks' seats, since Jack and Dianne are in Colorado visiting their grandchildren. Hopefully after tonight, life around the carriage house will settle down."

Max nodded. "That makes sense."

Nick disagreed. The idea was just plain stupid. "It's too loud, and think of all the germs those babies will be exposed to. Everyone in town is here."

"Settle down." Adele patted his knee. "A little noise doesn't bother those two. As for germs, better they're exposed outdoors like this than have half the town traipsing through the nursery."

Nick frowned and attempted to turn his attention back to the field, where the good guys had a fine drive going. Despite his best intentions, his gaze kept returning to Tess. She looked great, he thought. Relaxed and sparkling, proud of those babies. She wore form-fitting jeans and the same T-shirt he had on. Her sneakers sported the same shoelace pom-poms as Adele's shoes, and the sight made him smile.

Then she glanced up in the stands, and their gazes met and held. All the noise, all the activity, receded as silently, Nick said, *Hi.*

Hello.

I've missed you.

I've missed you, too. A bittersweet smile stretched across her face and eased Nick's tension. He returned a smile of his own.

Then Hollywood stepped between them, breaking the connection. Nick's temper stirred.

Enough. Damned if he'd let that man get in his way anymore. Nick wanted Tess. In his bed. In his life. In his Corvette riding to a high school football game. He wanted her, and he'd damn well have her. No TV star pretty boy was going to get in his way.

It took Tess and Jake Muldoon another five minutes to make their way up into the stands to their seats, and probably would have taken longer had the Rattlers not captured the crowd's attention by scoring a touchdown. Tess introduced Hollywood first to Max, then to Nick.

"Pleased to meet you," Nick said, showing some teeth in his smile.

"Likewise," Jake responded, his gaze going narrow and hard.

Their handshake was a contest of crushing pressure Nick believed he won, and with that publicly polite exchange, the two men declared war.

They went to battle first over football. When the Rattlers returned a punt to the fifty, then lost possession on a fumble, eliciting a collective groan from the crowd, Muldoon made the tactical error of turning to Tess and asking, "What happened?"

Nick's brows winged up, and even Tess appeared surprised. She said, "We fumbled, and they got the ball."

"Oh. Okay."

Fresh meat. Nick zeroed in. "Don't follow football, Malone?"

"It's Muldoon, and no, I don't. My interest lies in more participatory sports—climbing, diving. Skydiving."

Nick glanced over his shoulder, and while he pretended to address the owner of the local sporting goods store, he spoke loud enough for the entire row to hear him. "Mr. Magoo, here, isn't a football fan."

He found the resulting collective gasp more than gratifying. Hollywood might as well have declared himself an atheist.

Muldoon fired back. "Oh Nicky is right," he said, flashing his million-dollar smile. "In fact, this is the first football game I've ever attended. It's great. I love the atmosphere. The sights, the sounds, the excitement in the air—you have opened up a whole new world to me. It's just one more reason for me to be thrilled to have discovered Brazos Bend, Texas."

The crowd around them beamed and preened. As the second quarter ticked away, Hollywood signed autographs and flirted shamelessly with everyone in a skirt from ages two to ninety-two. To impress the men and redeem himself for his lack of football knowledge, Muldoon sprinkled his conversation with the names of Hollywood beauties he'd escorted to various high-profile events.

Nick was disgusted by the way the football crowd basked in the Jake Muldoon glow. On the field, the opponents scored a tying touchdown, but did anybody notice? Barely. Except for Stewart Mooney, who'd apparently had a tiff with a couple of the widows before storming out of the stadium, all of Brazos Bend seemed to be dazzled by celebrity. It was sad. Downright pitiful. But it gave him the opportunity he'd watched for.

The baby in Muldoon's charge—Caitlin, Nick believed—signaled her restlessness by letting out a high-pitched squeal, and before Muldoon even noticed, Nick swooped her into his arms and maneuvered his way around Adele until he stood next to Tess, who visibly braced herself at his approach. *No no no, that won't do, my little spoils of war. It's time for you to deal with me.*

He met Tess's gaze and held it. "The girls have grown in the past week."

"Yes," she agreed. "They're about ready to go up a size in clothes."

"That's great." Nick asked a couple questions about their eating and sleep habits, and as Tess talked about her nieces, she relaxed. He watched her closely, and when the time felt right, he stated flat out, "I've missed them. I've missed you. Are you still mad at me?"

"Maybe." The twitch of a smile on her lips told him this frontal approach was the right choice. "You know it's difficult for two people to work out differences if they're never within shouting distance of one another."

"You're right. Let's fix it." He nudged Adele with his elbow. "Will you hold the baby and keep an eye on her sister, please? Tess and I need to have a little talk."

"Wait a minute," Tess began as Nick handed Caitlin over to the older woman.

Hollywood excused himself from his adoring fans and asked, "What's going on?"

Nick took hold of Tess's hand. "We'll be back in a few minutes. Who wants a hot dog?"

He left the stands with orders for an even dozen dogs.

"Where are you taking me?" Tess asked as he led her away from the concession.

"The north end zone bleachers."

"Why there?"

"It's the traditional stadium make-out spot."

Tess planted her heels and yanked from his grasp. "You 're crazy, Nicholas Sutherland, if you think that after everything, you can just pick up where you left off and—"

"All right. All right." He shrugged. "I'm not into public lovemaking anyway, and the north end zone bleachers are about as public a private place as you'll ever find."

She planted her hands on her hips. "Didn't you hear a word I said?"

Grinning, Nick linked his arm through hers. "I'm teasing. We're going up the hill behind the stadium. I want to show you something."

"Nick," she said in a warning tone.

"No necking involved, I promise. Although if you get the urge, I'd be happy to accommodate you." She rolled her eyes, and he chuckled. "I want to talk, Tess. Apologize. It's a good spot for that. Come with me?"

"Apologize, hmm? In that case, lead on."

The path did take them beneath the north end zone bleacher and past more than a dozen lip-locked teenage couples. One pair were going at it pretty hot and heavy, and noticing them, Tess let out a little gasp. "I know that girl. She's a checker at the grocery store after school. Nice, friendly girl."

"Friendly. Yeah. I can see that."

They exited the stadium complex through an obscure gate in a chain link fence. Nick held her hand through the flats, but when they began to climb the hill, he led the way.

Above them, a silvery moon rose to join stars twinkling in the sky like diamonds against black velvet. The summer heat had died with the setting of the sun, and the temperate evening air teased with the promise of autumn. Loose gravel crunched beneath his feet, and twice in especially rocky areas, he reached back and took Tess's hand, helping her over the difficult spots. After a ten-minute climb, they reached their destination—a large, flat rock near the top of the hill. Nick sat and brushed debris from the spot beside him. "Join me?"

Tess sat cross-legged beside him and took in the view. Below them, the stadium lights blazed, lighting up the night, while the rest of the town remained relatively dark. "It looks like everyone in town is there."

"For the most part, they are. This is what I wanted to show you, Tess. Young, old, and in between—they come out to support their own."

"That's nice."

"It's very nice. And support like that is powerful, too." Nick scooped up a handful of pebbles and started tossing them, one by one, down the hill. "It's what I moved to Brazos Bend to find."

Illuminated by starlight, she waited expectantly for him to continue.

Nick drew a deep breath and exhaled it slowly. Somewhere between leaving his seat at the game and taking a seat on this rock, he'd decided a simple apology wouldn't do. Oh, an apology might get her back in his bed, but he wanted more than that. He wanted her in his life. For that to have a prayer of happening, he knew he'd need her to understand what this town meant to him, and why.

"The last time we were together, you asked me why I left Dallas. I told you about my grandmother, but that wasn't the whole story. Can I tell you now, Tess? Will you listen to me?"

"Yes, of course."

Nick drew back his arm, then threw a grape-sized rock as hard as he could and then watched it land far down the hill. "On the day Nana died, after I made the funeral arrangements, I went back to the office. I needed to put the finishing touches on the Northrup deal, that hostile takeover I mentioned before. Heaven forbid I'd let the death of a loved one get in the way of business."

Self-disgust left a bitter taste in his mouth that he had to swallow before continuing his story. "While I was at work, the CFO of the company called and requested that I come by her place that evening to pick up one last document pertinent to the deal. Laura Northrup was the granddaughter of the company's founder. She and I had dated for a time, but I'd broken it off when she started looking toward marriage. That prior relationship made the legal work I had to do uncomfortable at times, but we'd fumbled our way through it. Or so I thought. I knew Laura was devastated at losing the family business, but I never expected..."

He side-armed another rock down the hill, then blew out a heavy sigh. "She didn't answer the door when I knocked, but she'd left it unlocked. I found her in the bathtub. She'd slit her wrists. The paper she left for me was a suicide note."

Tess put a hand over her mouth. "Oh, Nick, no. And it happened the same day your grandmother died?"

"Yeah." Nick threw the last of the small rocks in his hand all at once. "The same freakin' day."

"Oh, that must have been so awful. But Nick, you can't blame yourself for—"

"I know," he interrupted. "My grandmother was in her nineties. The doctors told me that even if I'd been with her, I couldn't have saved her. Laura, however, was different. Laura didn't have to die."

The thought never failed to depress him, and Nick brooded for a moment before continuing. "I was heartsick, disgusted with my professional life. I needed to connect with real people after that. I came here because Brazos Bend is basic. Brazos Bend is family values. Brazos Bend is real."

He took her hand and met her gaze imploringly. "I've found something here, Tess. Something special. It's—" He gestured toward the stadium. "It's Rattler Canyon. It's Harmon Lanes. It's Cavendar Shoe Shop. It's even the widows. It's a great place to live, a great place to heal. A great place to raise children. It's my home. I was wrong to tell you not to take the children and leave for the reasons I gave that day.

What I should have said was that I didn't want you to leave. I want the time and opportunity to explore what's between us. My sense is that it could be as special as...well...as special as Brazos Bend."

Tess gazed down toward the football field, where the band dressed in maroon and white finished up their show. "It's a nice little town, Nick, and now that you've shared your story, I understand why it suits you. But Brazos Bend is your sanctuary, it's not mine. I like you, Nick. A lot. I enjoy you. And yes, I agree that what we have between us could, in time, become something very special. But time isn't on our side. Nick, I'm going home in ten days. A producer is giving a party I must attend. That is my reality."

"It's *Hollywood,* Tess. It's not reality."

"Yes, it is. It's my work. My home. My accomplishments. My achievements. Very real, and very important to me."

"What about family?" Nick said softly. "What about love?"

Tess shrugged. "I can't count on family. My mom is gone, my dad is pond-sucking scum, Chloe is...Chloe. And love? I have hopes and dreams, and I like to believe that someday they might come true. But love is a risky business, and odds are against it lasting, so I won't risk what I have, what I've built for myself, on something as ephemeral as love."

"That's a sad outlook on life."

"It's realistic."

It's bull, but Nick knew better than to say that aloud. No matter how their relationship developed, Tess needed Brazos Bend just as badly as he did. She needed family and roots and Friday-night football, and deep inside, she knew it, too. Otherwise, she wouldn't have hung around waiting for Chloe this long.

Tess McKinney needed someone to show her the magic of living small. *And I'm just the man for the job.* "All right, if ten days is all we have, then ten days is what I want."

"I don't understand."

"Give me those ten days. Let's not worry about what happened last week or what might happen next month. Give me those ten days with you. With you and the girls and Brazos Bend. Will you do that, Tess?"

"Why?"

"Why not?" Nick rolled to his feet, then assisted Tess to hers. "I want to spend time with you. It need not be any more complicated than that."

"All right, as long as you understand that I'll need to work part of the time. I have some projects cooking."

Nick hoped Muldoon was one of them. Skewered on a stick. Roasting over a fire. "That's cool, although I do have one request."

"What's that?"

"For the next ten days, leave Hollywood at home, would you?"

CHLOE SAT on the fishing dock, dangling her feet in the cool, placid water of Possum Kingdom Lake. The scent of burning cedar from a campfire across the water at the state park drifted on the evening air and made her feel less alone.

But she was lonely. Empty-hearted, to-the-marrow lonely. Tonight the Brazos Bend High Rattlers were playing their archenemy, the Aledo Coyotes, and she desperately wanted to be there among the crowd. With her babies in her arms.

Tears stung her eyes, but she forcibly blinked them back. She wouldn't cry again. Not tonight. She was already over her self-allotted maximum three hours a day by at least twenty minutes.

She gave a hard kick and sent water droplets flying. "I'm so tired of this!"

"Would chocolate ice cream help?" came a voice from the top of the walkway.

Stewart. Chloe whipped her head around in surprise. Solar garden lights lining the path up to his modest cabin illuminated Stewart Mooney's tall, lanky frame. He held a half-gallon tub of ice cream in one hand, two spoons in the other. She found his sheepish smile downright endearing.

"Stewart! What are you doing here? Where's Claire?"

He winced. "The date didn't quite work out."

"Oh, Stewart."

"Don't start on me." His footsteps thudded against the walkway.

Boards squeaked, and the dock dipped slightly beneath his weight. "I told you it wouldn't work. Claire is a nice woman, but we have little in common. I couldn't think of anything to talk about."

"Then you weren't trying," she said. "You and I have little in common, and we talk all the time."

"I know," he said softly.

Chloe patted the space beside her, and Stewart took a seat. "Ice cream," she said with a sigh. "My very favorite brand, too. You spoil me, Stewart."

He handed her a spoon. She savored a rich bite of chocolate, then continued, "So, tell me about your date. What happened? It's too early for the ball game to be over. Did y'all not go?"

"We went. Our seats were up behind the Widows and that group, and about the middle of the third quarter, they started in on one of their tirades, and I got mad and left."

Picturing the old gossips at work, Chloe groaned. "What put the bee in their bonnets this time? The sound system wasn't loud enough? They didn't like the Rattlers' new uniforms? Or maybe the stadium lights were too bright?"

"Actually, they got to talking about you."

Fear clutched Chloe's stomach as he gave her a recap of the conversation. "Tess wants to leave? With my babies? She can't do that."

"Yes, she can. I warned you about this two weeks ago, Chloe. You can't expect your sister to put her life on hold indefinitely."

"But I need more time."

Impatience riddled his voice. "For what?"

Chloe glanced at him in surprise. Stewart never used that tone with her.

"Why do you need more time, Chloe? Have you been lying to me about how well you are doing? Do you still cry all the time? Are you not sleeping at night, but sleeping all day? Have you been having headaches or chest pains or heart palpitations? Can you not focus or remember or make decisions? Do you still feel worthless and guilty?"

"Who are you?" she asked glumly. "The depression police?"

"Chloe." Stewart took her hand. "You were in bad shape when you left the hospital. You couldn't have properly cared for your daughters."

"I couldn't take care of myself."

"I know that. I was there, remember?"

"I'll never forget, Stewart. Never. You saved me. Who knows what might have happened to me if you hadn't given me a safe place to stay and found me a shrink I can talk to? I owe you so much."

"You owe me nothing. I was glad to help."

"Well, someday I'll pay you back, I promise. Keep track of what you've spent on me, okay?"

"Then listen to me now. You're ready, Chloe. You can be a mother to Caitlin and Stephanie. It's what you want, isn't it?"

"Yes. I just...I'm afraid. What if I get depressed again?"

"Are you taking your medicine regularly?"

"Yes."

"Will you continue therapy?"

"Now, that depends. That Women and Children's Aid Society grant you found for me pays for four more sessions. I won't be able to afford—"

"I have another grant lined up."

"But what about Bubba C and his buddy at the hospital?"

Stewart drew a deep breath and let out a heavy sigh. "Your reasoning in allowing that threat to keep you from your children is faulty. They came looking for Snake, and they haven't been back. Maybe they found him. Have you ever thought of that?"

"Every day." A lump of emotion hung in her throat. "I think maybe they did find him. Why else would he not have come home? He loved me."

"Did he really?" Stewart snapped. "If he loved you, then why did he leave you home alone in that godforsaken trailer with little money and no emotional support mere weeks before you were due to give birth to his twins?"

"Stewart, please."

"I'm sorry, Chloe, but this is something I've wanted to say to you for weeks now. You haven't been strong enough to hear it before, but you are now. Snake Duncan isn't good enough for you. He isn't good enough to be the twins' father. You need to let him go. You need to go home and be with your girls and make a life for yourself that isn't dependent on a man who would treat you the way he has."

"I *can't* go home. What if those men didn't find him? What if they do come back? What if they threaten to hurt my girls?"

"We won't let them. I won't let them. Brazos Bend won't let them. We'll protect you, Chloe, if you give us a chance."

"How?"

"First, you need to tell the sheriff what happened at the hospital. He'll know what to do. I think we should install a security system at the carriage house and let everyone in town know to keep an eye out for strangers. We can keep you safe, Chloe, if you'll give us the chance."

"But it's a risk."

"Life is a risk. What's your alternative? Let Tess take your girls with her to California and raise them as her own? You stay in hiding the rest of your life? You can't do that, Chloe."

Chloe lifted her gaze to the sky and focused on the sliver of moon above. "I've never cared what people said about me. Unmarried and pregnant—I was a scandal in Brazos Bend. It never bothered me before. Now...well...for the first time in my life, I don't want to be a scandal anymore. I will be. In Brazos Bend, Texas, I'll always be the woman who abandoned her babies."

"You're not giving us enough credit, Chloe. I'll talk to the ministers in town. It'll be all right. I give you my word." Stewart took her hand, gave it a reassuring squeeze. "It's time. You're strong now. Go home."

Chloe leaned over and kissed Stewart on the cheek. "You're a good friend."

But was he right? Was she strong again? Could she deal with all the turmoil and trouble of life without going bonkers once again? "Let me sleep on it. It's been my habit to make rash decisions. I'm trying not to do that anymore."

"Fair enough."

"So, tell me about your date. I bet Claire wasn't happy about leaving early?"

"Not exactly. I forgot her."

"You what?"

"I left without her. I was angry, and I forgot about being on a date. I did go back for her once I remembered."

"Jeez-o'-petes, Stewart. You're hopeless."

"I know, Chloe. I'm hopelessly in love with you."

The spoon slipped from her fingers and fell with a plop into the lake. "Wha...wha...what?"

He sighed heavily and handed her his spoon. "I know. It's stupid of me, but I can't seem to help myself. I think I fell in love with you on that first visit to the library when you complained about misshelved books."

"That volunteer of yours didn't understand the Dewey Decimal System."

"Mrs. Renwick understands the system, but she doesn't see the decimals very well anymore."

"Oh." Chloe took three quick bites of ice cream.

"I *don't* ordinarily make rash decisions, but this certainly qualifies. Not my feelings, mind you," he hastened to add. "I mean telling you about them."

"Maybe I'm experiencing postpartum psychosis. Maybe I'm hallucinating this entire conversation."

"Would it make you feel better to think so?"

"Yes. No. I don't know."

"In that case, since I've already confused you, I might as well add this to the mix."

With that, Stewart Mooney, Chloe's nerd in shining armor, leaned over and claimed her mouth in a passionate kiss.

CHAPTER 16

THE BURP all but shook the rafters and startled a laugh out of Tess.

"Such a little lady, Caitlin," she said, shifting the infant from her shoulder into the cradle of her arms. Smiling down at the baby, she wondered, not for the first time, how such a big sound could come from such a little body.

She rocked the infant long after Caitlin fell asleep just for the joy of it, and as Saturday morning dawned, a profound sense of peace enveloped her. At this particular moment in time, she could think of nowhere else she'd rather be.

She smiled down at the baby and stroked a finger across her downy cheek. "I love you, Caity Cat," she murmured.

It was true. In six short weeks, she'd fallen head over heels for Caitlin and her twin. Funny how such big feelings could grow so fast.

Which, when she analyzed it, pinpointed the problem with Nick. Her feelings for him were bigger than she'd bargained for.

He didn't want her to leave Brazos Bend. His nice little speech about not worrying over yesterday or fretting about days to come was lip service. Tess could read people, and his intentions were as clear as Widow Mallow's window glass. He thought to use these next ten days to talk her into staying.

What frightened Tess was that part of her wanted to do it.

It didn't make sense. She'd worked hard for her success. She loved her job and her life in L.A. She loved her California home and her California grocery store and her California Italian shoe shop. Brazos Bend was nice for a small town, but she didn't want to live here. She wouldn't be happy living here, mothering someone else's children, falling deeper every day for a man who couldn't decide if he was a carpenter or a CEO.

Then why did the idea of leaving Brazos Bend, leaving Nick, unsettle her?

Part of the reason was Chloe. One way or another, Tess needed to settle the care-taking question. Living in limbo this way did no one any good. If she left Texas with Chloe's children, the action effectively turned this temporary commitment Tess had made to the girls into something more permanent. Though Tess did love the twins, she'd always expected to enter motherhood in a more traditional manner. No wonder she felt unnerved.

On the other hand, what if Chloe came back? What if she showed up at the door this morning ready and willing to assume her rightful role? How would Tess feel then? How would she feel flying home to California with empty arms?

The questions continued to plague her as she showered and dressed, until finally, she decided maybe Nick had it right. Maybe she shouldn't look forward. Maybe she should take life one day at a time—at least for the next ten days. Not an easy task for a manager accustomed to living and dying by her day planner, but perhaps a worthy goal to which she should aspire.

As she poured her second cup of coffee, a knock sounded on the door. She glanced at the wall clock. Ten to eight. Adele must have forgotten her key.

Instead of Adele, Tess found Kate Cooper on her doorstep. "Morning," Kate said. "If it's all right, I'm subbing for Adele. She has a last-minute dentist appointment."

"Oh, dear. I hope she's not in pain."

"No. It's purely cosmetic. She had a chance to go to the best dentist in Fort Worth and have her teeth whitened, and I jumped at the opportunity to come help with the girls." She patted her flat stomach proudly. "Mommy practice makes perfect, you know. It's been a long time for me."

Tess grinned. "You're welcome to all the practice you can stand around here. While I'm finally beginning to get a handle on child care for twins, I'm always happy to have an extra pair of hands to help. Stephanie and Caitlin are asleep right now. Would you care for a cup of herbal tea? I think I still have some of that peppermint you liked so much last time."

"Thanks, I'd love some."

Kate took a seat at the kitchen table, and the two women debated the merits of herbal teas and designer coffee while they sipped from brown earthenware mugs. Kate liked variety in her morning drinks. Tess wanted two cups of plain old Folgers each and every morning.

"You're like Max," Kate said with a smile. "His first wife got him drinking Maxwell House because of its name, and he refuses to drink anything else."

Tess knew that Max had lost his first wife to cancer when Shannon was just a baby. In the past, Kate had been open about the challenges of mothering another woman's child, and in the wake of her early-morning musings, Tess felt the urge to confide in the other woman. "Can I tell you a guilty secret of mine?"

"What self-respecting nosey woman would say no to that question?" Kate set down her cup and leaned forward. "I'm all ears."

"I never thought I could love another woman's children."

"Really?"

Tess nodded. "I've dated a couple of divorced men in the past, and while I liked their children well enough, I never connected with them. I thought I didn't have it in me to bond with a child I didn't give birth to. It's not that I don't like kids, because I do. Your Shannon is a doll. But until I came to Brazos Bend, I'd never truly loved a child."

Kate sat back. "You've fallen in love with Caitlin and Stephanie."

"Desperately."

"And...? There's obviously more to this, Tess. Spill it."

Tess stood and walked to the coffeepot on the counter, where she poured herself another cup. "Part of me doesn't want Chloe to come home. There is a part of me that grows stronger every day that wants to keep those baby girls for my own. I've already planned their nursery in my house. Not unicorns this time, but white eyelet and pink ruffles. Lots of ruffles, ribbons, and bows. I think about taking them to the beach and Disneyland and buying them shoes. I've even checked on the Internet to see if there are any Mothers of Twins clubs in my area. How sad is that? I'm awful."

Kate snorted. "You'd be awful if you *didn't* feel that way. Of course you've fallen for the girls. You're a loving woman, Tess, and if I may offer an opinion, I suspect that the reason you never bonded with children prior to now was out of self-protection. If you sensed the relationship with the father wasn't long-term, then it's only natural that you'd shield your heart from his children. It was that way with me and Shannon."

"It was?"

"Yep. I didn't want to get my heart broken, so I tried to keep some distance from her, but she was Ryan's sister and a doll, and she wormed her way into my affections pretty darn quickly. It hurt to lose her when Max and I broke up."

Tess's brows winged up. "I didn't hear that part of the story."

"You haven't?" Kate asked. Tess spied what looked suspiciously like satisfaction in Kate's eyes as she added, "Well, then. Let me tell you all about it."

Kate gave a brief synopsis of her relationship with Max from their one-night stand as teenagers until her return to Brazos Bend when their son Ryan was entering his senior year in high school. "Max had put down roots here in Brazos Bend. He wanted to raise Shannon here. Even our son wanted to stay here and get to know his relatives. Max thought we could get married and have a fantasy life in a fantasy house in a fantasy town. But I'd worked long and hard through some lousy circumstances to earn my degree and build a career, and I'd finally reached the point where I could achieve my dream—a corner office with a private bathroom."

Tess understood that desire completely.

"I faced the classic, clichéd choice—family or career. Well, I'd been doing everything for family all my life, and I decided it was time for me. I chose career, and I moved back to Dallas, and Nicholas helped me get the perfect job."

"Nick helped you? Max must have loved that."

Kate grinned. "A limited amount of jealousy expressed by her man is good for a girl's ego."

"So what happened?"

"I got a corner office and a bathroom and a bad case of the lonelies. Max offered a compromise. Up until this summer, we spent Monday through Friday in Dallas and the weekends in Brazos Bend. It took some adjustment on everyone's part, but it worked out well. I had a big-city life that fulfilled me professionally and a small-town life where my family could thrive. It took effort, and it wasn't always easy, but for a while, when I needed it, I had the best of both worlds."

"Yet you live here permanently now."

"I gave up my corner office when school let out in May. *My* choice, which made all the difference in the world. I still work two days a week from home, but I'm thinking of giving that up once the baby comes. Children grow up so fast, and then they're graduating from high school and moving off to college, then deciding that becoming a white-water rafting guide is their life's goal, and before you know it they are following the water and living in Japan. With a woman who is closer to my age than his!"

Tess cleared her throat. "Adele told me Ryan is an adventurous sort who has a lot of his father in him. I understand Max used to be a fighter pilot?"

"Jet jockey. Water rat. Thrill riders, both of them. What's the matter with the men in my family, I ask you?" She placed her hand protectively on her stomach. "Please, God. Give me a girl."

Tess heard footsteps clomping down the stairs. Wearing only athletic shorts and a scowl, Jake stumbled into the kitchen and over to the coffeepot. "My, oh my," Kate murmured, her gaze trailing over all that bare stardom.

"Mmmm..." rumbled Jake.

"Don't pay any attention to him," Tess advised. "He's not worth speaking to until he's had his caffeine fix."

Once Jake had ingested enough java to act human, he wandered into the laundry room and donned a T-shirt Adele had washed for him the day before. He was rummaging in the icebox for breakfast when the phone rang. "Sit still," he told Tess when she started to rise. Lifting the phone from the cradle, he said, "Hello. Yes, this is he."

As he listened to the voice on the other end of the phone, his posture slowly straightened. "Yes, ma'am. Yes, ma'am. Oh, yes, ma'am."

Tess and Kate shared a curious look.

"Sure. That'd be great. Yes. Yes. Thank you. I'm honored. Thank you very much."

He hung up the phone and slowly turned around. Wonder lit his eyes, and both Tess and Kate smiled at his honest excitement. "Well?" Tess asked.

"You won't believe it. That was...I just...wow."

"Jake!" Tess slapped the table. "Talk to us!"

"I just got asked to dinner."

"Okay. By who?"

"Not who. Where."

"What?"

"My dad is gonna flip. I need a tux. I didn't bring one to Brazos Bend. Who'd have thought I might need it here?" He dragged his hand down his face. "Wow. This is downright awesome."

"Jake Muldoon, if you don't tell me what 'this' is in the next five seconds, you're not going to live long enough to go to dinner anywhere."

"Not just anywhere. The White House. I just got invited to attend dinner at the White House on Tuesday night. I'll be escorting a Spanish princess."

"Oh, Jake. That's so cool." Tess rose from her seat and threw her arms around him, giving him a hard hug. "Okay, I want detailed notes. Everything. Food. The dresses. The music. Everything."

"Yeah. Okay. I can do that."

Tess laughed and gave his shoulders a friendly shove. "Go take your shower and start packing. I'll make your travel arrangements."

"Okay. Wow. The White House."

Tess grinned after him. "You know, I think this is the first time I've ever seen Jake addled."

"Oh, really?" Kate's voice sounded choked, and Tess gave her a curious look. Sure enough, when her gaze met Tess's, Kate broke out into snickers.

"What?" Tess demanded.

"Nothing. I'm just...that Nicholas. The man is certainly impressive."

"Nick? What does he have to do with anything?"

"Everything. I'll give you five-to-one odds. It's a play right out of Max's book, only Nicholas, being Nicholas, took it up a level."

"What are you talking about?"

Kate told her about the time she had a date with Nick for the Brazos Bend Bingo Night and Fish Fry, and Max decided the time had come to send Nick packing. "He called an old college buddy and had him ask Nicholas to attend a meeting that night in Dallas. Since Max's friend just happened to be the lieutenant governor of Texas, Nicholas couldn't say no. He left the fish fry, and by the end of the night, Max and I were back together. I think Nicholas followed my husband's example. "

"Are you telling me that Nick has that kind of pull..." Tess's voice trailed off.

"He does. I'll bet you he used it, too."

While Tess attempted to digest that, a halfhearted infant's cry sounded from the baby intercom. "Oh, good. Somebody's waking up. Can I go pick her up?"

"Um...sure."

Kate stood, then gave Tess's shoulder a reassuring pat. "Don't worry, hon. I think it's cool. How many girls can say that the president of the United States has taken an interest in her love life?" She paused a moment, then added, "In this administration, anyway."

NICK PLANNED his strategy like a wartime general. He had ten days to work with. Ten days to show Tess the sometimes hidden beauty of life in Brazos Bend. Ten days to get her to fall in love with him. In a surge of cockiness he hadn't felt since his courtroom days, Nick figured he'd get the job done in seven.

The first order of business had been to send ol' Hollywood packing. Second was to send Kate over to Tess's and have her plant the seed that Tess's career and a life with Nick in Brazos Bend weren't necessarily incompatible.

The next task was Nick's alone, and he approached it with keen anticipation. Romance with a capital R was the order of the day. He'd stayed up half the night planning, and he'd been on the phone at first light. Now, as he watched Hollywood toss a pair of suitcases into a rental car, give Tess and Kate a buss on the lips, then drive off, satisfaction filled his soul. His plan was progressing nicely.

Nick kept close watch on the carriage house throughout the morning. The florist's van arrived precisely at ten, just as he had arranged. At ten after, his own doorbell rang.

"Hey, Mr. Sutherland," said the teenage delivery boy when Nick opened his front door. "Ms. McKinney sent a note, like you requested."

"Good." The boy's eyes widened in delight as Nick tipped him a twenty, then shut the door. He carried Tess's note into his study, where he took a letter opener from his desk drawer and slit the envelope.

Dear Nick,

The gardenias are lovely, as was the sentiment expressed on your card. Thank you. I am pleased to accept your gracious dinner invitation and look forward to this evening.

Tess

P.S. However, I was tempted to decline just to see what you would do, since Kate assures me you have contingency plans for such an event.

Whistling, Nick sat at his desk, propped the card against the silver-framed photo of his late grandmother, and tackled the mound of paperwork that had piled up over the course of the previous week. Half an hour later, his phone rang. His private line. "Hello?"

"I can dress myself, Nicholas Sutherland."

Smiling, he leaned back in his chair and propped his feet on his desk. "I know that, Teresa McKinney. Indulge me, please?"

"I take it I'm to wear this dress tonight?"

"It's a particular fantasy of mine."

"Then I should assume you're not taking me to Dairy Delight for dinner?"

"I have Wednesday penciled in for the Dairy Delight. That's two-for-one night, you know."

"No, I wasn't aware of that," she dryly replied. "I think—oh, hold on a minute, would you, Nick? Someone's at the door, and Kate has her hands full."

"Sure."

When Tess set down the receiver, he rose, walked to the window, and peered outside. A black Lincoln waited at the curb in front of the carriage house. Must be the jewelers, he mused.

His suspicions were confirmed a few minutes later when a well-dressed, silver-haired gentleman exited the house carrying a black leather case. Before the man reached the Lincoln, Tess screeched in his ear. "Nick, what are you thinking? I can't accept this."

"Which suite did you choose? The emeralds or the sapphires?"

"Nick, I'm not letting you give me jewelry, especially not jewelry like that."

"Okay."

After a moment's pause, she said, "Well. That was easy."

Nick laughed at the petulance in her tone. "You can give them back to me if it makes you feel better, but nevertheless, I want you to wear them for me tonight. It's part of my fantasy, darlin'. Don't disappoint me."

Her sigh was long and dreamy. "That has to be the most spectacular necklace I've ever seen."

"I liked it. So, which did you pick?"

"The sapphires. They reminded me of your eyes."

Damn. "Careful, girl. You keep talking like that, and I'll be forced to come down that hill and kiss you."

She laughed. "Now that truly would be a special delivery."

"Count on it."

In the background, Nick heard a baby cry, and Tess said, "I'd better go. Kate's looking a little overwhelmed."

"Okay. Until later, then." He had started to hang up the phone when he heard her voice calling his name. "Yes?"

"I just...well...should I be watching for any other surprises this morning?"

"Hmm...what do you think?"

"Well, it's a beautiful dress and the jewelry is awesome and... well...I wondered if...oh, damn. Nick, are you sending me shoes, too?"

"The baby's crying, Tess. Talk to you later." He laughed as he hung up the phone. He had a feeling she'd pay him back in spades for the teasing, but he considered this all part of the fun of foreplay.

Nick had trouble concentrating on his work after that, and he was debating whether or not to give up when his phone rang once again. "Did you honestly think I'd forget about shoes?" he asked, expecting the call to be from Tess.

Instead, a gravelly voice replied, "Uh...Mr. Sutherland? Bryan Howell here. I wanted to let you know I'm ten minutes from Brazos Bend."

Nick glanced at his watch. "You're earlier than I expected."

"Obtaining information regarding the second subject proved relatively easy. I believe I've discovered something significant."

"What about Duncan?"

"Nothing new there, I'm afraid. Although the fact that I've been stopped by such a solid brick wall gives me an idea or two."

"I'll be interested to hear them. See you shortly."

Nick hung up the phone, then his hand continued to hover over the receiver. From the sounds of it, his investigator had turned up a solid lead on Chloe. Nick should call Tess and let her in on this meeting. That was the right thing to do.

Except he didn't want to do it.

What if Bryan Howell knew where to find Chloe? What if they

EMILY MARCH

could bring her home today? What would that do to his plans not only for tonight, but for the next ten days? He drummed his fingers on the phone, then abruptly made his decision. "Sutherland, you're an ass."

Bryan Howell arrived driving a four-door Ford and wearing khaki slacks and a golf shirt. He was of average height with average features and an average demeanor—qualities that proved to be an asset in his line of work. A former FBI agent, Bryan had worked for Nick on two previous occasions, and he'd impressed Nick with his professionalism and thoroughness.

The two men took seats at the kitchen table. "So what have you got for me?" Nick asked.

"Who do you wish to hear about first—Duncan or Ms. McKinney?"

Nick's gaze flickered to the window that looked out on the carriage house. "Tell me about Chloe."

The investigator opened his briefcase and removed a stack of papers. "Stewart Mooney owns an isolated fishing cabin at Possum Kingdom Lake. He'd had it listed for sale for over a year, but he took it off the market the last week of August."

"So she's there." Nick's felt a pang of disappointment.

"Based on the information you provided me last night, I believe it's a logical assumption."

"We could have her home by noon."

"It's possible, although I cannot be certain she's there until I have visual confirmation."

"Okay. That's a good place to start. Let's verify that she's there, first, and then we'll decide a course of action to take next."

"Very good. I'll set up surveillance of the property beginning immediately."

"Tell you what." Nick dragged a hand along his jaw. "If you do discover Chloe is at Mooney's lake house, I want you to keep watch for twenty-four...no, make that forty-eight hours. Let's see how she spends her days. See who, if anyone, visits her during that time. I'd like you to do what you can to ascertain her mental state."

"Very well."

Bryan was too professional to express curiosity regarding Nick's

190

instructions. Nevertheless, Nick felt compelled to justify himself. "I need to make certain it's safe to bring her home. Bottom line is, I want what's best for those babies."

In that, Nick spoke the truth. He might be guilty of trying to arrange the next few days to suit his own purposes, but he'd never do anything to cause innocent children harm.

"Now," he continued. "On to Snake Duncan. What do you have?"

"Suspicions, primarily. We know he left Dallas in a red Maserati and bought gas in Texarkana, dinner at a chain restaurant in Little Rock, then gas again in Texarkana two days later. That's where the paper trail ends."

"He turned around."

"Yes, it appears so."

"Do you think he's dead?"

"Could be, but if that's the case, it surprises me that the car never turned up. The search of his trailer in Brazos Bend suggests instead that someone is looking either for him or for something he possesses."

"So you think he's hiding."

Howell nodded. "I think that is a strong possibility. However, I don't believe he's doing it on his own. For Duncan to have disappeared so completely, I suspect someone is helping him."

"Who?" Nick sat up straight. "Chloe? Do you think he contacted her? That's why she ran off?"

"That's possible. However, I think it's more likely that the authorities have Duncan."

"You think he's in jail?" Nick rubbed a hand along his jaw. "We'd have already found him in that case, wouldn't we?"

"My suspicions lie in a different direction. Perhaps he's in protective custody."

"Why? What do you think he's mixed up in?"

Howell reached into his briefcase again and pulled out a folded copy of the *Fort Worth Star-Telegram*. The headline circled in ink read: *Eleven Charged With Identity Theft*. Nick scanned the one-sentence synopsis of the article printed in bold: "Prosecutors say thieves who obtained loans and bought luxury cars using the personal information of middle-aged people who had recently died are members of a new Cowboy Mafia."

"The luxury cars might be the connection to Duncan. The article is dated July 25, two days after Duncan disappeared."

Nick quickly scanned the article. Federal indictment. Charges of identity theft, false representation of a Social Security number, bank fraud. Defendants recruited additional persons, "known and unknown to the grand jury," who used counterfeit driver's licenses of recently deceased individuals to obtain auto loans. They'd buy Porsches, Mercedes, Jaguars, and Cadillacs and illegally sublease them to others. Netted $2 million in a year. "So you think Snake got caught and turned informer on these folks?"

"It's a possibility. Once he squealed, the government would have squirreled him away, thus the walls we encountered. The case comes to trial in November. I may be totally off base, but I think it's worth looking into."

Nick considered it. The idea made sense. Snake struck him as just the sort to get involved in a scheme like identity theft. "If the Feds do have him, how do we confirm it?"

"I'm working on that. I have a few calls in, and hopefully I'll have something for you in a couple of days."

"Good." He was glad Bryan wasn't expecting information today. Nick didn't want to find out anything about anybody today. With that in mind, he showed Bryan Howell to the door a short time later, saying, "I'll be out of pocket for the rest of today, but I'll call you around this time tomorrow. Any information you learn about either Chloe or Snake Duncan will keep until then."

The two men shook hands, and Nick stood on his front porch, watching him drive away. The car slowed at the end of the street to make way for a Neiman Marcus delivery truck.

Lingerie. Nick smiled.

CHAPTER 17

"Wow," Kate said as Tess descended the stairs. "I think we should start calling you Cinderella."

"Nope. Won't work." Home from the dentist and seated on the living room sofa with Stephanie stretched out on the cushion beside her, Adele fastened a disposable diaper tape, then nuzzled the baby's bare tummy. "Cinderella doesn't end the evening having sex with Prince Charming. No way does Nick Sutherland let midnight roll around without getting any."

"Adele!" Tess protested, appalled at the older woman's brazen statement, even though she privately endorsed the idea. Nick Sutherland made her blood hum.

"Well, it's true. Look at her. He sent her the dress, the jewelry, the shoes—"

"Great shoes," Kate inserted.

Adele continued, "Even the underwear. A man buys a woman underwear, he expects to get a gander at it."

"Wait a minute." At the bottom of the staircase, Tess ruined her elegant look by putting her hands on her hips and scowling at Adele. "I insist on a little clarification here so I don't sound like a hooker. I've already told him I'm not keeping the jewelry. The dress is to die for, so I'll find out how much it cost, and I'll reimburse him."

"He won't let you do that," Kate warned.

"Then I'll bury the money in his front yard or feed it to his horses. I'll make that right. The underwear I'll return to Neiman's. Even thongs show a panty line under a dress like this."

Adele clicked her tongue. "Goin' commando. Wonder how long it'll take him to figure that out?"

"Knowing Nicholas, about five seconds." Kate's admiring gaze skimmed Tess from head to toe. "What about the vintage shoes, Tess? He must have gone to a whole lot of trouble to find that particular pair. You gonna give those back?"

"Give these back?" Tess extended her foot and rotated her ankle. Rhinestones twinkled in the light. "No way. I'm keeping these babies. How many girls get to walk—literally—in Carole Lombard's shoes?"

Kate sighed with envy. *"Such* a shoe slut."

"It's my secret shame."

"It's no secret, honey." Adele lifted Stephanie and held her against her shoulder, patting her back. "Your shoe closet was the talk of the Weight Watchers meeting last week."

"How did that happen?"

"I told 'em." As a knock sounded on the kitchen door, Adele added, "That'll be Max and Shannon."

Shannon Cooper skipped into the house, wearing a pink leotard and a purple tutu. Max followed, carrying a pizza, three rental movies, and a book entitled *Babysitting for Dummies.* Noting the title, Tess winced. "Interesting reading choice, Max. I'm glad Kate will be here, too, otherwise I might be concerned."

"Nick sent it over with a note asking not to be interrupted tonight." Max set the pizza box on the counter. "Like I've never cared for a baby before. Like I wasn't a single father with an infant. It's insulting. He just wants—whoa." Max's first glimpse of Tess left him gaping like a love-struck teenager.

Tess couldn't help but feel flattered by his reaction, and she laughed when Kate rolled her eyes, nudged her husband's mouth shut with her index finger, and warned, "Get a grip, big boy."

Max puckered up for a wolf whistle. "If I were Nick, I'd have sent more than a book. I'd have a dozen backup babysitters."

Shannon clapped her hands. "Hi, Miss Tess. Do you like my tutu? I've been to ballet lessons. Can I hold the babies tonight if I'm super super careful and Mommy and Daddy help me?"

"As long as your parents help you, yes."

"Thank you. You sure look pretty."

"Thank you, Shannon."

Adele called from the living room, "A car just drove up, Tess. A stretch limousine. Gee, I don't imagine that could be your date, do you?"

Tess's stomach gave a nervous and uncharacteristic flutter. She suddenly needed to surrender to feminine vanity and check the mirror one more time. "I left my bag upstairs. Will somebody answer the door for me?"

"I will," Max said, stepping toward the door, his eyes gleaming with mischief.

As she fled upstairs, Tess wondered what pithy comment he'd make to Nick. Judging by the light in Max's eyes, she figured herself better off not knowing.

Tess took five minutes in her room, refreshing her lipstick, adding another dab of the perfume she'd found packed in the gift box with the underwear, second-guessing herself about leaving off the panties.

She gave her reflection in the dressing table mirror a critical inspection. The gown was vintage Valentino, made of sky blue silk shot with silver threads, and it flowed over her curves like a waterfall. A trio of sapphire teardrops surrounded by sparkling diamonds dangled from her ears, the design repeated in the necklace nestled in the vee of her breasts and in the bracelet hugging her wrist. Her makeup looked good. An afternoon nap had taken care of the circles beneath her eyes. To top it off, she'd actually had a good hair day, and the updo she'd managed on her own looked perfect with the dress.

Working in Hollywood, where dazzling women were the norm, she had never felt particularly pretty. Tonight she felt gorgeous.

She wondered where Nick was taking her to dinner.

Dallas, probably. She didn't think Brazos Bend had a venue appropriate for this elegant attire. This dress, this jewelry, these to-die-for shoes, would be perfect for the Academy Awards.

From downstairs came the sound of laughter. Nick's laughter. Her stomach took another dip, and she frowned. Why was she nervous? She'd dressed up and gone to dinner with handsome men before, in places much more intimidating than Brazos Bend. She'd never felt this nervous. She'd never felt this sense of anticipation. She'd never before felt like Cinderella on the way to the ball.

Maybe that was the problem. Maybe she did feel too much like Cinderella with midnight approaching. "Does it have to end?" she whispered. She *did* need to go home to California, and Nick obviously wasn't ready to leave Brazos Bend, but could they try a long-distance relationship for a while? Maybe he'd miss her so much that he'd decide to move to L.A. They could get married and...whoa. *I'm asking for heartbreak, thinking something like that.*

No, that's not right. For him to break her heart, she'd have to love him. She wasn't in love with Nick Sutherland. She hadn't known him long enough to have fallen in love. She was infatuated with him. That's all this was. Infatuation.

From downstairs, she heard Adele call, "Tess? Nick's here."

Tess picked up the evening bag that matched her shoes, opened her bedroom door, and headed for the stairs. Halfway down, she saw him.

Nick wore Armani, a classic black tux, and he had a burping cloth slung over his shoulder. He held Caitlin against him, and as Tess watched, he pressed a gentle kiss against the baby's brow.

In that moment, whether she recognized it or not, Tess fell the rest of the way in love.

NICK HAD PLANNED an evening filled with romance. Candlelight, flowers, elegant surroundings, delicious food, champagne, soft music, interesting conversation leading to slow, sensuous lovemaking on a plump mattress and satin sheets. He took one look at Tess and considered skipping straight to the sex.

"Where are you taking me?" she asked as the limo pulled away from the carriage house curb.

To bed. "We're having dinner at the Brazos Bend Retirement Center."

"Oh."

She looked surprised, which prodded him to tease. "I thought we'd play a little bingo."

"Bingo?"

"Strip bingo." Her mouth gaped, and he laughed and continued, "I've finished renovations on the Crystal Ballroom at the Hutton Hotel, and I'm hoping you'll take a step back in time with me tonight. How about dinner and dancing beneath the crystal chandelier that once lit the way for Gable and Lombard?"

"That sounds lovely. I didn't realize that the remodeling was this close to completion."

"The finish work has gone fast. I anticipate we'll have the last of the apartments ready in another two weeks. We'll have a grand opening celebration and officially rename the place then, but for now, for tonight, we'll have it all to ourselves."

"I can't wait to see it."

Personally, Nick wished he'd arranged dinner at home. They could be halfway through the meal by now, and he'd be that much closer to finding out if the lack of a detectable panty line meant what he suspected.

"You look beautiful tonight, Tess."

Her lips lifted in a smile. "Thank you. Again. That's the third time you've told me."

"It's the thirtieth time I've thought it."

They arrived at the hotel, and Nick took her hand to help her from the limousine. He didn't give it back, but tucked it around his arm as he escorted her up the steps. Wanting to avoid as much of the inevitable small-town gossip as possible, he'd imported wait staff from Fort Worth for the evening. The maitre d' opened the hotel door as they approached. "Good evening, Mr. Sutherland. Miss McKinney. Welcome to the Hutton Hotel."

"Thank you," Tess responded, offering the man a smile that caused him to stand a little taller and suck in his gut.

The doors to the ballroom were closed per Nick's instructions, two men dressed in black slacks, white shirts, and black vests waiting to open them upon his signal. Nick took hold of both of Tess's hands, turning her to face him. "The first time I saw you, I pictured you here on a night like this. Thank you for making my dream come true."

He kissed the back of her hand, one then the other, then nodded at the staff. The two wide gleaming oak doors swung slowly open, and as Nick escorted her forward, the orchestra struck up "Moonlight Serenade."

"Oh, Nick," Tess said. "It's so beautiful."

Satisfaction washed through him. The place did look great. Redone in the original colors of red, gold, and white, the Crystal Ballroom shone, from the opulent chandelier above them to the marble tile dance floor beneath their feet. Pristine white linens graced a small round table set intimately for two with fine bone china, ornate silver, and Irish crystal. He'd chosen gardenias for a centerpiece, an old-fashioned flower for a timeless night. He escorted Tess to her seat, then took his own and waited while a waiter filled their flutes with champagne, then disappeared.

Nick lifted his glass. "To you, Tess. Jean Harlow, Marlene Dietrich, and Dorothy Lamour have dined in this room. Were they here tonight, they'd pale beside your beauty."

Her eyes lit with pleasure and amusement. "Now that's a little over the top, Sutherland. Romantic, but patently untrue. If Jean Harlow sat beside me right now, you'd need a drool cup, and it wouldn't be because of me."

"Honey, you've made my mouth water since the moment I first saw you. The only reason I'm not drooling now is because I'm already dehydrated from excess salivation while imagining how you'd look in that dress. You are infinitely more droolable than Jean Harlow."

"Drink your champagne," she said, rolling her eyes and trying to smother a laugh.

Over salad, they discussed classic movies and the golden age of

Hollywood. Nick relayed stories he'd been told about the celebrities who'd visited the Hutton Hotel in its heyday.

"Clark Gable stayed here?" Tess said, setting down her fork. "Oh, wow." She glanced around the ballroom. "How about Vivien Leigh? Imagine the two of them dancing here, just like in *Gone With the Wind*. You know, I'll never forget the first time I saw that movie. I was a teenager, and they showed it at one of the old theaters downtown. I fell in love with Rhett Butler." She gave a dreamy sigh. "Clark Gable in Brazos Bend. Imagine that. Now, if that man were sitting at our table, I'd be the one drooling."

Nick arched a brow and said, "Frankly, my dear. I don't give a damn."

Tess's laughter bubbled like the champagne.

Over a main course of Chateaubriand, talk turned to the renovations and his efforts to staff the retirement center. "I want to have a mix of current Brazos Bend residents and newcomers to town. I like the idea of introducing new people and ideas to the project, but I respect the need to have those ideas tempered by folks who understand our residents' backgrounds and sensibilities."

"It's a wonderful project, Nick. Not only have you reclaimed this grand old building, but you're meeting a very real need here in Brazos Bend. You should be proud of what you're accomplishing here."

"I am." He sipped his wine, then continued, "It's fulfilling work. After my stint as a corporate legal shark, I needed a project like this. It's...redemption of a sort."

"You shouldn't be so hard on yourself."

"Sure I should. I wasted too much time and energy doing work that didn't contribute a damn thing to society."

"Oh, stop the martyrdom. As a woman who makes her living by convincing bubble-headed blonds to let Elvis rest in peace and show up at work, where they're being paid an exorbitant amount of money, I know all about questioning the validity of one's work. I work in the entertainment industry. It's big-money business, true, but let's face it, creating a hit television show is not as important as curing cancer."

"But entertainment is important," Nick defended. "A clever sitcom makes people laugh, and laughter is invaluable. Though it pains me to say it, even a show like ol' Hollywood's does some good because it allows viewers to escape from their everyday stresses for an hour every week. That has value."

"Excuse me, but you are making all of my points." Tess grinned at him over her glass of water.

The waiter arrived to clear their plates and offer a choice of dessert. Tess attempted to pass, but Nick ordered crème brûlée with two spoons.

When they were alone again, she said, "The question isn't as simple as you're attempting to make it, Nick. If your work contributes to the bottom line of a corporation, then you're helping the stockholders, right? And those stockholders probably include senior citizens, who use their dividends to help pay rent at their assisted living center."

"I helped destroy companies that in turn ruined families, Tess. That's the only bottom line that matters, and I need to make up for it somehow."

She opened her mouth to comment, then obviously had second thoughts. She dabbed her lips with her napkin. "Well, you've made a great start with this place. It's wonderful. Do you have any tenants committed to moving in yet?"

"Quite a few." Nick named some local people and few from surrounding communities. "Though most of the apartments will be ready for occupancy by the end of the month, I intend to institute staggered move-ins. A move is stressful at any time of life, but for senior citizens, it can be especially difficult. Having only a couple people moving in at a time will make it easier on everyone."

"That's a good idea."

"I didn't think of it. That was Adele's idea, not mine, and it's reinforced to me that I need a great general manager for this project, someone who is accustomed to taking charge, who recognizes potential problems before they develop, and who knows how to deal with trouble once it does come up."

In a warning tone, Tess asked, "You won't try to hire Adele away from my nieces?"

"No." Nick grinned. "She's all yours. Besides, Adele is a little too outspoken to work with the elderly. I need someone who's kind and

THE LAST BACHELOR IN TEXAS

friendly and caring. Someone who has ties to the Brazos Bend community, but who isn't an integral part of it going in. I intend to offer an extremely attractive salary, and my manager will have full authority over the day-to-day operations of the Brazos Bend Retirement Center. It'll be a great job for the right person, someone with exceptional management experience who values family and appreciates the special qualities Brazos Bend has to offer."

Tess leaned back in her chair. "Is this a job interview, Nick, or a date?"

"I'm sorry," Nick said, his smile sheepish. "I didn't intend the conversation to take this path. This is definitely a date, and I have no business bringing business to the table."

He set down his fork and casually added, "Besides, I don't need to interview you. The job is yours if you want it. Would you like to dance?"

"Nick!"

"What? You don't like to foxtrot?"

She narrowed her eyes and studied him. Nick wanted to lean over and nip her lower lip. He'd spoken the truth about not planning to bring up the job. He wanted no conflict, no questions, and no interruptions to spoil tonight. Barring a dire emergency, Kate had promised not to call about the girls, and he wouldn't mention the latest on Chloe or Snake. That could wait until tomorrow. "How about we leave the real world outside the Hutton Hotel tonight? No worries, no concerns, no past, and tomorrow can wait. Just you and me, here, now. Dance with me, Tess. Please? I need to hold you."

Her eyes softened. "You are a dangerous man, Nick Sutherland."

"Just a man. A man who wants to be with his woman."

"*His* woman?"

Nick stood and extended his hand. "Tonight you're mine."

In keeping with the theme of the evening, Nick had chosen a selection of big-band music in the style of the Hutton Hotel's heyday. At his nod, the vocalist began to sing "When Did You Leave Heaven?"

Nick held Tess close, breathed deeply of her perfume, and enjoyed the moment.

They danced to "How Deep Is the Ocean" with no verbal exchange between them, and yet their conversation never ceased. *You feel like heaven in my arms. You dance like a dream. That perfume is driving me crazy. I feel like Cinderella.*

Hearing the first line of the next song, "Cinderella, Stay in My Arms," Tess laughed with delight. Nick spun her around, once quickly, the next time slower. Then slower. He stopped.

He kissed her.

And kissed her.

And kissed her.

His hand moved slowly up her long, slender back, then down the tantalizing curve of her spine as she melted into him, pliant and open to his desires. Her fingers played in his hair, then back and forth across his shoulder. Touching her, tasting her, was as vital to Nick as air and water.

Vaguely, Nick was aware that the musicians were ending their song and departing the stage, even as the wait staff cleared the table, then the room. Soft music floated from the speaker system in the ceiling, or from his soul.

He moved his hand between them, skimmed it across the silk of her gown to capture the full, soft weight of her breast. Her own hand slipped beneath his jacket and splayed against his chest. She dragged her thumb across his nipple.

Heat ignited, shot through his entire body, and stark, demanding hunger clawed at his control. He wanted bare skin and a yielding body. He wanted to take her, to bury himself in her hot, wet core.

He knew the delight that waited him there. Her whimpers of need. The tight clench of her feminine muscles, the slick warmth of her moisture. Her frantic response to his deep, demanding strokes, again and again and again until climax exploded and took them on that free fall of pure, intense pleasure.

With effort, Nick fought the feeling back. This time was different. This time was more.

This time was love.

Slow down.

Nick broke the kiss and took a necessary step back. "You didn't have your dessert."

Tess looked up at him, a pinch of petulance spicing her tone as she muttered, "I thought we were getting around to that."

He brought her hand up to his mouth and kissed it. "Let's take it with us, shall we?"

"We're going somewhere?"

"Not far." Keeping her hand clasped firmly in his, Nick led her back to the table where he scooped up the dessert cup filled with crème brûlée, then headed for the door. In the hotel lobby, he led her toward the sweeping, red-carpeted staircase. At its base, he paused, looked at her, and said, "Clark Gable, hmm? I'll take that as a sign."

Tess's brow knotted in confusion. "What...?"

"Hold this." Nick handed her the dessert cup, then scooped her up into his arms and carried her up the stairs like *Gone With the Wind's* Rhett Butler.

The surprise in Tess's eyes softened to pleasure. "Just so you know, this is the most romantic evening I've ever had."

He glanced down at her and winked. "It's not over yet, sweetcheeks."

"Sweetcheeks?"

At the top of the staircase, he set her back on her feet. He dipped his index finger in the crème brûlée, then touched her cheekbone and moved down her face and across her bottom lip. Then he followed the path of his finger with his tongue. "Yeah, sweetcheeks."

His blue eyes burned into hers, twin flames of hunger muted with promise. Tess's heart pounded, and her entire body went hot. Desire, liquid and molten, flowed through her, then settled low and left her aching. She wanted him here, now. "Nick," she murmured softly.

"This way."

He took her down a hallway, past signs that read "The Judy Garland Suite,"

"The Jack Dempsey Suite," and "The Dorothy Lamour Suite." He stopped in front of "The Clark Gable Suite," then opened the door to a room bathed in candlelight and scented with sandalwood and rose. A saxophone wept from speakers hidden somewhere above them, and in the middle of the room, a king-size bed dressed in jewel-colored silks and satins awaited. Thank God, Tess thought as she stepped inside.

Nick set the dessert cup atop a bedside table, then slipped off his jacket and tossed it onto a chair. "I've wondered all night. Would you answer a question for me?"

"What question?" Tess's gaze strayed toward a doorway through which she spied a champagne bucket and glasses sitting at the edge of a Roman bath.

"I sent you underwear."

"You did."

Turning toward her, he deliberately tugged at his necktie. "The way the dress fits...it doesn't look like you are wearing it."

"I'm not."

"Oh." He toed off his shoes and socks. "You're wearing something of your own?"

"No."

"That's what I thought. And you said *I'm* dangerous."

She offered him a soft, inviting smile. "You are. You're tall and dark and dangerous. You make me want things that aren't good for me."

"Yeah? Like what?"

She added a touch of extra swing to her hips as she sauntered toward him, and as his gaze slid downward, she knew a rush of feminine power. It wasn't her habit to play the seductress, but tonight, under these circumstances, it felt right. Tess reached past Nick, dipped her finger in the crème brûlée, and answered his question. "Dessert."

When she sucked the sweet from her finger, he groaned aloud.

"Dammit, Tess, I'm really trying to take this slow."

She laughed, and he growled with frustration, then yanked her into his arms. Breath whooshed out of her lungs as he kissed her again, his mouth hard and hungry. His fingers found her zipper, and in seconds, she stood before him wearing vintage rhinestone sling-backs and nothing more.

She lifted a foot to kick off her shoe, and he said in a strangled tone, "No...no. Keep 'em on. And take your hair down. Please?"

"Well, if I'm going to indulge your fantasy, you need to let me have mine."

"Yeah. Sure. Whatever you want, Tess." He said it like a plea for mercy as her hair tumbled around her shoulders. "You're magnificent."

Desire hummed through her like a tune. "Nick, don't move a muscle."

Nimbly, she worked the studs on his tux shirt and slowly revealed his broad, muscled chest. "It's like opening a birthday present or unveiling a statue or tugging the cover off a high-precision race car."

"Vroom. Vroom," he said, reaching for her.

She giggled and slapped away his hands. "Stay still."

She pushed the shirt free, then reached for his belt, trailing a finger across the hard bulge of his arousal. "You know, I'll pay you back for this," he said.

"I'm counting on it." She tugged his belt away, and then stepped closer as she slipped her fingers into his waistband. Her bare breasts brushed across his bare chest, and they both held their breath. Tess felt as if the temperature in the room shot up by twenty degrees. Her fingers trembled as she slipped his trouser button and slowly teased his zipper down.

Nick cleared his throat. "Are you hot and wet for me, Tess?"

She shuddered.

"I've been hard enough to drive nails all day just from thinking about you. Imagining tonight. Planning what I want to do to you."

His pants slid down those long, muscular legs, revealing shorts and a prominent erection. At her gesture, he stepped out of his pants and stepped toward her, saying, "I pictured you lying against these satin sheets, waiting for me. Ready."

Her blood burned, and her mouth went dry, and she decided to fight fire with fire. "I've been ready for you for hours. When I was putting on my lipstick tonight, I dreamed about taking you in my mouth and tasting you."

For a long moment, Nick froze. Anticipation pulsed hot and electric through Tess as slowly his lips lifted and a wicked grin slashed across his face. He drawled, "Darlin', as far as I'm concerned, tonight is all about making dreams come true. So, you gonna let me move now?"

"Yes."

"Good, because I'm of a mind to have dessert."

Nick shucked off his shorts, then scooped her into his arms and settled her back against the bed's midnight blue satin sheets. Straddling her hips, he reached for the crème brûlée.

Like an artist creating the masterpiece of a lifetime, he painted her. Her neck, the valley between her breasts, the curve of her hip, the back of her knee. Her breasts. Her nipples.

Then, he feasted. He licked the crème away with both quick flicks and long, luscious strokes of his tongue. It was torture.

"Mmm...delicious," he murmured, his hot breath whispering over her damp nipples. The pleasure that rippled through her as he suckled was pure magic.

Then Nick raised his head. His eyes burned like twin blue flames. "I'm still hungry, Tess."

At the core of her, Tess's muscles clenched, throbbed with aching need. Instinctively, she arched her hips, lifting herself, offering. Craving. Begging.

Nick's gaze burned into hers as he dipped his finger in the luscious crème, then softly caressed her feminine folds. He took his time, his fingers playing and teasing and driving her higher. Her hands clutched his shoulders in a silent plea, and he finally pushed one finger, then two, inside her. Tess's body stretched and welcomed him, moving in time with his strokes. The ache within her built, spiraling upward, growing tighter and tighter and tighter. Her breathing quickened, and she reached toward the fire. "Nick?"

"So, so hungry." He pulled his fingers away, brought her to his mouth, and feasted.

Tess moaned and bucked against him as the climax broke over her in wave after wave of heated pleasure. And still, his tongue continued to play. "Again," he demanded when she collapsed, boneless and trembling.

She lost track of time and place as Nick took her up and over again and yet again. When finally, he settled his body over hers, his thick, pulsing head poised at her entrance, he looked down at her and said, "Somewhere along the way, I lost my dreams. Then you walked into my ballroom, into my life, and I began to find them again. I've dreamed of you this way. I've imagined you here, in this suite, this bed, beneath me, dozens of times. We are a good match, Tess." He thrust into her, filled her, then added, "We fit."

"Yes," she breathed.

Nick smiled down at her, his warm gaze holding her captive as he found a rhythm that kindled a fire within her unlike any she'd known before. Tess rose to meet him, her heart, her mind, her soul filled an intensity of feeling that could have but one name.

Taking, giving, together, they climbed to the precipice. His gaze locked onto hers, Nick once again sent her soaring, only this time, finally, he came with her.

When he collapsed upon her, his breathing harsh, his pulse pounding, Tess bore his weight with joy.

For the first time in her life, Tess had truly made love.

CHAPTER 18

THE FIRST COOL front of autumn arrived with the morning's dawn and swept into the Clark Gable Suite through a window Nick had opened sometime during the long, delightful night. Sensing the cool kiss of breeze against his bare skin, Nick reached for a sheet to throw over himself and Tess. Instead of a sheet, his fingers brushed...feathers.

Feathers? Nick wrenched open one eye and spied the pink feathered boa. Oh, yeah. The memory burst upon his brain like fireworks. Feathers.

During a conversation around two o'clock this morning, after "dessert" and a frolic in the tub and a mind-blowing indulgence in personal fantasy by Tess, aka Magic Mouth, Nick mentioned an old box of costumes they'd found in the Clark Gable Suite during renovations. Tess begged to see the vintage clothes, and Nick was more than happy to humor her—especially after she showed him new and inventive uses for a feather boa.

Wonder what she could do with that box full of magician props they'd discovered up in the attic?

Beside him, Tess stretched sinuously and sighed in her sleep. Nick eyed the length of her thigh and debated waking her for some good-morning playtime, but decided to lie still and enjoy the pleasure of having Tess McKinney sleeping beside him. No telling when he might have an opportunity like this again. No telling what revelations today might bring.

Chloe. He wondered what Bryan Howell had discovered since their conversation yesterday. I should check my messages, he thought. Though he'd just as soon hide away here for another day or ten, he knew that wasn't feasible. Besides, even if they did find Chloe and brought her home to care for the girls, Tess wouldn't leave on the next plane. Not after last night. What they had was too damned special to be thrown away, and she would recognize that. Nick didn't need to worry. Not one little bit.

Maybe it wouldn't hurt to wake her and love her one more time before the real world intruded.

Tess took the decision out of his hands when her eyes fluttered open and she stretched like a cat, then winced. *She's sore. Damn.*

Just when the idea to make love again had been growing on him, so to speak.

"Good morning," she said softly, shyly.

Nick leaned over and kissed her. "Good morning, beautiful. Would you like coffee?"

"Coffee?" She sat upright, her gaze pleading. "You have coffee?"

"I have caterers. Coffee and breakfast, if you want."

"Oh, yes. I definitely want." She kissed him hard on the mouth. "An extra-large pot of coffee, please, and—what's on the menu?"

"Anything you want."

"Mmm...bacon and eggs and orange juice and lots of coffee. You know, Nick, a girl could get used to this kind of service."

"That's the idea," he said softly as she disappeared into the bathroom with the overnight bag he'd prepared for her the previous day. His cell phone sat on the desk beside his duffle bag and Tess's evening purse. Nick pulled on a pair of gym shorts as he spoke with the caterer, and then, despite his trepidation, checked his voice mail. Three messages.

The first was left by Bryan Howell yesterday at 7:07 p.m., just about the time Nick and the limo picked up Tess. He said, "This is confirmation of Chloe McKinney's whereabouts at seven p.m. Friday. Moments ago she and Stewart Mooney departed his lake property in a green Ford Taurus. Currently, they're traveling on Farm Road 204 toward Brazos Bend."

The second message was also from the investigator. "Chloe McKinney entered the carriage house at seven thirty-nine p.m. Mooney carried a suitcase inside. He left without her at eight-ten p.m."

The final message was from Max. "You owe me big-time. I want fifty-yard-line seats when the Aggies play the 'Horns in Austin in November. Kate wanted to call Tess, but I managed to convince her to wait. Chloe's back, Nick. Looks like she's home to stay. Better warn Tess."

~

"I'M CALM," Tess said as the limo turned on the street leading to the carriage house.

"Yes, I can tell from the way you put your bagel in your lap and took a bite out of your napkin."

"Very funny," she said.

The car stopped, and moments later the passenger door swung open. Tess's gaze focused on the purple blossoms spilling around the carriage house's vine-covered fence gate. So pretty. So peaceful. These weeks here had been good ones. "As anxious as I am to see my sister, I am not looking forward to this, Nick."

"Nobody likes confrontation, Tess."

"It's not that. I'm looking forward to telling Chloe a thing or two." Pensively, she sucked her bottom lip. "It's one thing to want a situation to change and to take steps to make that happen. It's something else when change occurs when you're not looking."

"You like being in control."

"I'm a professional manager," she said, shrugging. "I'm good at my job. Excellent, in fact. But I've never been able to manage Chloe. It hasn't mattered so much in the past, but now...well...I'm not going to abandon Caitlin and Stephanie. Chloe brought me into their lives, so I am committed to them now."

Nick's brows winged up. "What do you mean? Are you going to fight her for custody, Tess?"

She didn't answer. From out of nowhere, a lump formed in her throat, and tears pooled at the back of her eyes. Fiercely, she blinked the tears away. "She's my sister, and I love her. I don't want to hurt her or cause her pain. But I'll do what I think is best for the girls, and that will depend on what Chloe has to say to me now. So I guess I'd better go on inside."

"Would you like me to come with you?"

She shook her head. "Thank you, but I think it's better that Chloe and I talk alone."

Nick climbed from the car, then took Tess's hand and helped her to her feet. "Good luck, honey. Call me later and let me know how you made out. Okay?"

"I will." After a moment's pause, she added, "Nick? Thank you. Last night was...a fantasy. It was perfect."

His slow grin caused her heart to flutter. "Yeah, it was, wasn't it? Thank *you.*" He kissed her cheek, then patted her rear. "Go get 'em, tiger."

As the limo pulled away from the curb, Tess drew a deep, bracing breath. Exhaling in a rush, she opened the front gate and started up the walk.

Adele opened the front door as Tess approached the porch. "Do you know...?"

"Chloe is here. Yes, I know. Are Kate and Max...?"

"I sent them home when I arrived this morning. Figured you might want privacy. I can stay or go, whichever your prefer."

"Where is she now?"

"Upstairs with the babies, finishing up their baths."

Tess stepped inside the house, and with her gaze fixed upon the staircase, she said, "I'd like you to stay, Adele. Please."

Adele patted her shoulder. "Don't worry, honey."

Tess smiled weakly in response and started up the stairs. Just outside the nursery door, she heard her sister's voice, and she stopped.

"That's my sweet little sunshine," Chloe cooed. "Sunshine Stephanie. Aren't you a happy girl? Look at that smile. Such a pretty, pretty smile. Sunshine Stephanie and Candylicious Cait. Mommy loves you both so, so, so very much."

Tess drew a deep breath, then stepped into the room. "I'm very happy to hear that. I was beginning to wonder."

Chloe lifted Stephanie off the changing table and tucked her against her shoulder, then turned around. Tess's eyes widened in surprise. Where had she been? A health spa?

Her sister looked great. Tanned and trim, her hair stylishly cut and professionally colored, wearing an Ann Taylor shorts set, if Tess didn't miss her guess. The health spa must have had a designer boutique.

"Hi, Tess." Her sister pasted on a big smile that might have fooled Tess if not for the nervous light in Chloe's eyes. "Adele said you were out on a date with Nick Sutherland last night. He is so fine. He never once made a smart remark about my weight gain, and that makes him just about the only man in town who didn't. At least I'm losing it now, did you notice? I'm still sixteen pounds above my prepregnancy weight, but I'll have it off before Thanksgiving."

Me. Me. Me. Nothing changes, does it, Chloe?

In her infant carrier on the floor, Caitlin let out a fussy cry, and Tess picked her up. "Chloe—"

"What do you think of my hair? I never pictured myself as a redhead—well, not since that do-it-yourself job while I was riding with the Devil's Own, and it wasn't red as much as an orangey purple. The stylist at Neiman's suggested it. Stewart took me into Fort Worth yesterday for a makeover, and Jason—he's the stylist—said short and spiky is perfect for a new mom, and that the red would make me feel perky. He wrote out specific instructions for my hair so that Elizabeth can do it here."

Sounded like she intended to stay.

"My outfit is new, too," her sister continued. "I'll have to show you the shoes. Tess. You'll love them. Little pink and yellow polka-dot sandals. You might want to try this shop next time you're in Fort Worth. They had some great vintage shoes. I think you would—"

"Stop it."

"—love this place, Tess. They're not far from the Kimball Art Museum, and you could—"

"Chloe. Stop babbling!"

"Shop and have lunch and view the art exhibits. Have you been to the Kimball before? It's a wonderful museum and...oh...oh Tess, I'm afraid of what you're going to say to me."

"Well, at least you're showing a little sense!" Tess said, trying hard to keep her voice calm so as not to disturb the girls. "Dammit, Chloe. I'm so angry with you. What the hell is going on?"

"Please don't curse in front of my daughters."

Oh-h-h-h. Taking a page from little Shannon Cooper's book of expressions, Tess bared her teeth and growled.

Chloe patted Caitlin's back rapidly. "You hate me, don't you? You think I'm an awful, horrible person. You think I'm the worst mother in the world, and you wish I'd disappeared and never come back. Well, let me tell you this, Tess. You don't feel anything I haven't already felt about myself. I abandoned my babies. I left behind a mess for you to take care of and you did. You did it wonderfully, just like I knew you would."

Tears spilled down Chloe's cheeks, and Tess hardened her heart against them. Damned if she'd let herself be manipulated that way.

"I knew I could trust you to take care of the babies for me because you always do the right thing, just like I always do the wrong thing. You are the perfect McKinney sister, and I am the screw-up, just like I've always been. But I want you to know that what I did I didn't do out of selfishness or indifference or even meanness. The reason I can stand here today and look you in eye is because I abandoned my babies for one reason alone. Believe me or not, Tess, I left my babies because I love them. There." She struck a proud martyr's pose, wiped away her tears with the back of her hand, and added. "That's my defense."

The sarcastic side of Tess wanted to clap at the performance. The angry part of her wanted to throw something breakable at Chloe. The sensible, responsible, successful career professional side of Tess's personality...well...that side deserted her.

Tess snapped. "None of that explains why you sneaked in and out of this house like a thief the week before last. The rest of it I might

213

understand. Postpartum depression is a tough illness, and I'm sorry you've been hit with it. But to wait until I'm not around to slither inside this house hiding behind a broom and a mop—that really chaps my butt, Chloe."

"I know. I knew it would upset you, and I'm sorry about that, Tess. But I had a reason for being sneaky. A good reason."

"Sure you did."

"Yes, I did, and I'm ready to tell you about it. How about we put the girls in their strollers and take them for a walk? It's a beautiful morning. We can walk down toward the creek. You can show me Nick's hideaway. I'd like to see that. We can talk."

Warily, Tess nodded. "All right."

"I'll need to fix bottles and diaper bags. Is it cool enough that they'll need sweaters, do you think?"

For some reason, being asked her opinion regarding the twins apparel smoothed Tess's feathers a bit. "I think they'll probably be fine dressed as they are, but it wouldn't hurt to bring along those little giraffe sweaters in the second drawer of their dresser."

"Okay."

"While you're doing that, I'll change my shoes and get the strollers out. Caitlin's left rear wheel needs lubricant. It squeaked horribly last time I used it."

A few minutes later, the four McKinney girls strolled across the flattened pathway leading down toward Nick's private retreat. The babies gurgled and cooed, filling the silence hovering between the older sisters. With her emotions playing pinball inside her, bouncing from anger to love to disappointment to encouragement and on and on, Tess couldn't manage small talk, and the only sounds Chloe made were heavy sighs.

Upon reaching the creek bank, Tess spread a blanket beneath the sprawling shade of an ancient live oak. Chloe lifted the girls from their strollers and settled them on their backs, and within seconds both twins had tugged off their booties and begun to play with their toes.

"Talk to me, Chloe," Tess said. "Explain it to me."

Chloe kissed the bottom of Caitlin's foot, then met her sister's gaze. "I'll try. I don't know if I can make sense of it—to myself or to you. Depression is...well...for a while after the girls were born, my world was...heavy."

For the next few minutes, Chloe gave a personal account of symptoms familiar to Tess from her reading about depression. She spoke of lethargy and insomnia and an inability to think. Hearing it all but broke Tess's heart.

"I would have helped you, Chloe. You didn't need to turn to Stewart."

"I needed you to be there for Caitlin and Stephanie. They were the most important."

"It need not have been an either/or situation," Tess protested.

"Yes, it did. You don't know the entire story. The girls wouldn't have been safe with me."

Everything inside of Tess went tense. "Not safe?"

"I never thought about hurting them, if that's what you're wondering. There's something you don't know about, Tess. I haven't told you about the men with the knife."

"What did you say?"

"In the hospital that night I left? I woke up in the middle of the night to a man holding a knife against my neck."

"What!"

"He cut me. Not bad, but enough to scare me. He was looking for Snake."

NICK PLOPPED a banana into the blender to make his usual post-run fruit smoothie. He wondered how things were going down at the carriage house. Were they coolly and calmly discussing the future? Or were they engaged in a sisterly catfight, complete with hissing and scratching?

He removed his finger from the blend button, and when the motor silenced, he heard banging on the front door, and Tess's voice calling out his name.

The moment Nick swung the door open, Tess marched inside. She carried a baby in one arm, and her free hand gripped her sister's arm just above the elbow. Chloe held the other baby and wore an expression filled with impatience.

"What's wrong?" Nick asked.

"Tell him," Tess said, giving her sister's arm a shake.

"May I have a glass of water, please?" Chloe asked. "That run up from the creek has left me positively parched."

Run? With babies in their arms? Alarm zinged through him as he led them toward the kitchen. "Tess? You want to tell me what's going on?"

"We didn't run, for one thing. My sister is being needlessly melodramatic. Funny how she'll whine about that, but keep quiet the fact somebody tried to kill her!"

The glass he'd removed from the cabinet darn near slid from Nick's hand. "What?"

"Water, please?" asked Chloe as she dropped into a seat at his kitchen table. "He didn't try to kill me, Tess. If that's what he wanted to do, he had plenty of opportunity. He wanted to threaten me, is all."

Tess's eyes were wild as she whipped her gaze around toward Nick's. "Just threaten. With a knife at her throat. No big deal. No big deal at all."

Nick set the glass of water onto the table with a bang. "From the beginning, ladies. Please."

Chloe lifted the glass and took a long sip. Impatient, Tess began to talk. "It's all because of that damned Snake Duncan. I swear, Nick, if that man walked through the door right now, I'd be hard-pressed not to wring his neck."

Nick's gaze captured Chloe's. "Why don't you tell the story, honey? I don't think your sister is altogether calm at the moment."

Chloe shifted her daughter—Nick wasn't certain which twin was which—from one shoulder to the other, then proceeded to tell a story that had Nick seriously considering adding vodka to his smoothie. "In the hospital?"

"That's why she ran off," Tess interjected. "Not because of the depression or her insecurity as a mother, like those letters she left me led us to believe."

"Now that's not true, Tess. Those were certainly part of the prob-

216

lem. Had I been thinking more clearly, I might have gone to the police right away."

"The break-in at the trailer," Nick said, putting it together. "They were looking for Snake."

"He's in some sort of trouble, Nick, and I'm terribly worried."

The infant Tess held let out a little cry, and Tess stood and nervously paced the kitchen. "Shush, Caity Cat. It's okay. Everything's okay." She glanced at Nick. "Stewart talked her into coming home."

She gave a synopsis of the arguments the computer tech had used, and Nick found himself agreeing with every point. "I'd like you to be there, Nick," Tess concluded. "You have experience with this sort of thing, and besides, I'm scared."

"Do you have any idea who these men were?" he asked Chloe.

She shook her head. "I've thought about it for weeks. Something about the man with the knife seemed familiar, but I can't put my finger on it. I do think I've probably met him somewhere, sometime."

"Here in Brazos Bend?"

"I just don't know."

"I think she should stay hidden," Tess said. "That or come with me to California right away. Like today."

No. Nick's reaction was immediate and like a kick in the gut. "Let's hold on. Take it step by step. First, we need to make certain that Chloe and the babies are safe. I'll call the security company I use, have them send a couple men. I tend to agree with Stewart's line of reasoning, but I think we'll all sleep better if we know they have protection."

"Bodyguards." Tess nodded. "That's a good idea."

"That sounds awfully expensive," Chloe said with a sigh. "One of these days, I'm going to quit living off other people. That or break into that stash of money I found."

Nick and Tess shared a look. "Stash of money?" she asked. "You didn't mention money before."

"Two hundred thirty-seven thousand dollars. I found a blue duffel bag hidden in that stack of old tires piled up north of the trailer house. I remembered that Snake sometimes used it for a hiding place as his tools, so I went by there after I left the carriage house the day I came to Brazos Bend to visit the girls. I figured it must be the money those men asked me about when they showed up at the hospital. I moved the bag but I didn't take any of it." She paused a moment, then confessed, "Okay, maybe I took a little. Three hundred dollars. That's all. It's probably dirty money, isn't it?"

Nick nodded, and Tess rolled her eyes. "Of course it's dirty money," she said. "He's a biker, for goodness sake. It's probably drug money."

"Or proceeds from identity theft," Nick mused, his mind spinning. He needed to call Bryan Howell, see if his Fed connections had gotten back to him.

Chloe scowled at her sister. "Snake isn't into drugs. He hates them. He doesn't even smoke or chew."

Ignoring Chloe, Tess addressed Nick. "Identity theft? What do you know, Nick?"

"Nothing certain."

"Is it the Widow Duncan? Does she know where Snake is? Has she known what he's been up to all this time? Have you been holding out on me?"

"You know I won't betray client/attorney privilege, Tess, but no, I don't know anything. It's all conjecture at this time. Chloe, that night in the hospital. Do you recall what the man said to you? His exact words?"

Chloe pursed her lips and absently kissed the top of Stephanie's head. "From what I remember, it was nonsensical stuff. He said something like, 'Tell Snake Bubba C said we're going to the mattress' and 'Snake doesn't know it, but he's already sleeping with the fishes.'"

Tess looked at Nick. "Are these guys for real? Is that a joke? That's a line from *The Godfather.*"

"Sonofabitch," Nick muttered. Tess was right. Bryan Howell was right. "Chloe, I hate to say it, but I think your Snake may have gotten mixed up with the new Cowboy Mafia."

CHLOE SAT WITH HER SISTER, Kate, and Adele at a work-table set up in the family room at Adele's house. Lined up neatly in rows sat spool after spool of maroon and white ribbon, and shoe boxes full of miniature cowbells, footballs, megaphones, and musical instruments. Hot glue guns at the ready, glitter paint flowing, they worked steadily to produce the ultimate expression of high school romantic adoration— the homecoming mum.

"Would you look at this," Kate said with disgust as she read the paper in her hand. "Bobby Miller has ordered a three-flower corsage for Janey Pokluda. Three flowers, four ribbon chains, six cowbells, a whole family of bears, and—what's this about a music box?"

Glitter bottle in hand, Adele glanced up from the ribbon streamer with "Go Rattlers" painted vertically in gold. "It's something new this year, a little rattle that plays the fight song. Put that order in my pile, Kate. Think I'll throw in a few extra footballs and ribbon chains. Janey's a sweetheart."

Tess looked at the order for the mum she was assembling. "Eight cowbells on this one. Imagine what it's like trying to teach over the noise of hundreds of cowbells."

"Try thousands," Chloe replied. "Remember, Adele's only handling the florist's overflow."

"Keeps me in bingo money for the entire year," Adele said. "I can't thank you girls enough for helping me."

"Excuse me." Chloe smiled at the older woman. "It's the least I can do, considering all you've done for me. Not only are you invaluable help with the babies, but Tess tells me you're my staunchest defender against the gossips."

The older woman wrinkled her nose. "Poison-tongued old busybodies. It'll help once Nick gives us the okay to talk about those criminals who attacked you in the hospital. After that, you'll be a heroine, and...oh...is that a baby I hear waking from her morning nap?"

"Let me get her." Kate stood up. "I need a break. I have paper cuts on my paper cuts."

When the second twin's cries joined her sister's, Adele set down her glue gun. "That's my cue."

Once the girls were diapered and fed, Adele and Kate stretched their mum-break by taking the girls on a walk. They'd been gone ten minutes when a rap sounded at the kitchen door. Chloe looked up from her glittering to see Stewart standing on the stoop.

"Now, why am I not surprised," murmured Tess, a teasing glint in her eyes.

"Hush." Smiling brightly, Chloe waved him inside. So what if Stewart had spent every free moment possible with her? He was her best friend, and so cute for a nerd.

"Hello, ladies. Adele told me to stop by and say hello. Do you need some help?"

"That'd be great, Stewart." Chloe patted the chair beside her. "Sit down and I'll put you to work."

Stewart asked how the girls liked the portable play mobiles he'd given them the day before. He talked about the new library's computers and how the extended summer heat had increased the electric bills now arriving in mailboxes across town. Chloe wanted to reach over and ruffle his hair.

He completed the mum Coach Wallace had ordered for the math teacher, Ms. Hargrave, and folded it carefully into the delivery box. "I guess I'd better be going. Chloe, I'm off this afternoon. Would you grab a burger at the Dairy Delight with me?"

Lunch in public with Stewart. Folks in Brazos Bend might think it was a date. Stewart might think it was a date. *I might think it is a date.* "Oh, Stewart. I don't know."

"I think it's a great idea." Tess encouraged Chloe with a smile. "The more you get out and about, honey, the faster you'll quiet the buzz."

"You mean, let them see that I'm not a lunatic. At least, not anymore."

"Chloe," Stewart said in a chastising tone, "I refuse to listen to that sort of talk." Standing, he added, "I'll be by to get you at two. Y'all have a good morning."

Chloe stared after him, slowly shaking her head. "Can you believe that? He told me what to do. He used to be so mild-mannered! I'll tell you what, Tess, sex changes everything in a relationship."

Tess dropped her glue gun. "Sex? You've had sex with Stewart Mooney?"

"No, of course not. I just had a baby. Two of them. I won't see the doctor for my postpartum checkup until next week. That's when you get an official thumbs-up to have sex again."

"So you're *planning* to have sex with Stewart Mooney?"

"No." Chloe grimaced. "I'm faithful to Snake...although I did let Stewart kiss me. It was the craziest thing, Tess. He kisses almost as good as Snake does. I couldn't believe it. I mean, he's a nerd, a geek." She sighed heavily. "But he's just so darn cute."

"I like Stewart," Tess said. "He was there for you when you needed someone. He's honest and forthright, and you can tell that he's crazy about the girls."

"I'm in love with Snake."

"Are you?"

"Yes, I am." At Tess's skeptical expression, she added, "He's the father of my children."

"He's a criminal who abandoned you, who stashed a fortune in dirty money in a pile of old tires, and who is the reason why two goons threatened you with a knife before your episiotomy stitches had healed enough to itch! How can you possibly still want to have anything to do with the man?"

"He gave me Brazos Bend, Tess. He gave me a home and a family— even if we are short one daddy these days. You told me not all that long ago that motherhood isn't a phase. Well, you are right. No more flit- ting from one cause to another, one man to another, for me. I owe it to my girls to give their father the benefit of the doubt, to be faithful to him and to put great-kissing geeks out of my mind, at least until Snake Duncan has the opportunity to explain himself to me."

"He stole two hundred thousand dollars! How can he explain that away?"

"Maybe there were mitigating circumstances."

While Tess rolled her eyes, Chloe added, "You've wanted me to change, Tess. I could use a little support here. I like Stewart very much. He's truly my knight in shining armor, and the last thing I want to do is hurt him."

"I think you're too late. I think he's in love with you."

"No." Chloe covered her mouth with both hands. "Really?"

"Really. And you know something else? I think you're a little in love with him, too."

Chloe's eyes rounded in shock. Seconds later, she groaned and banged her head against the worktable. "Oh, Tess. This is awful. I can't be in love with two men at the same time. I can't! I'm trying so hard to be a better person. What am I going to do?"

"I don't know, honey. Except, maybe, pray that Nick finds Snake Duncan fast."

CHAPTER 19

THEY'D STASHED Snake in Oklahoma City.

Nick received the call just before breakfast, and he landed in Oklahoma City around lunch. He'd pulled in dozens of markers and used nearly every connection available to him to arrange this meeting. The Feds had thrown a governmental tantrum for fear that Nick might leak information to compromise their operation—a joke, considering that the "interagency task force" running the show, an alphabet soup of agencies, had offered up the leaks that allowed Nick to find Snake in the first place.

Agent Jonathan Boles met him at the gate and escorted him to a waiting car. Neither man bothered with small talk during the drive downtown. The parameters of the upcoming meeting had already been established, and no one was entirely happy with the result. Upon their arrival at a downtown hotel, Agent Boles produced a document delineating their agreement for Nick's signature. With that done, the agent led him to the bank of elevators. He thumbed the button for the seventh floor, then, when the doors closed on the elevator, empty but for the two men, Boles said, "You caused me a helluva lot of trouble, Sutherland."

"Yeah?" Nick thought of Tess and colicky babies and Chloe with a knife to her neck. "Good."

The agent stopped in front of a door, removed a plastic card from his pocket, and keyed the electronic lock. Nick followed the Fed into a spacious suite.

The man standing at a window gazing west across the plains wore slacks, a long-sleeved dress shirt, and loafers. With his shoulder-length hair slicked back and tied neatly at his neck, his face clean-shaven, and ear-lobes absent of glittering studs or flashy hoops, he looked more like an insurance salesman than the biker warlord Nick remembered from Brazos Bend. Were the Feds trying to pull a fast one on him? "Duncan?"

After a long moment's pause, the figure at the window turned around. "Well, if it isn't Mr. Money."

Yes, this was Snake Duncan. "You're a hard man to find."

"Yeah, well, that's the idea," Snake said. He reached for a bottle of water sitting on the table next to him and tossed back a drink as if it were a shot of whiskey. Then, visibly bracing himself, he met Nick's gaze. "What are you doing here?"

He's afraid. "I understand you've landed yourself in trouble."

Snake shrugged. "I'm getting myself out of it."

"Are you?" Nick sauntered over toward the window. "Your family will be happy to hear that."

Snake's eyes flared with surprise, and he took half a step toward Nick. "Family? You mean my ma? She's okay?"

Nick's eyes narrowed. So the sonofabitch knew his family might be in danger, and he did nothing at all to protect them? "Why wouldn't your mother be okay, Herbert?"

"Her heart!" He rubbed his hand down his jaw. "When they said someone from Brazos Bend was coming, I thought it'd be her minister. I thought he'd walk in here and say she'd had a heart attack and passed. She's had chest pains. So she's really okay?"

"Widow Duncan was fine when I saw her last night at the city council meeting."

"Whoa." Snake blew out a loud, relieved sigh. "That's great. I was afraid..."

When he smiled at Nick as if he hadn't a care in the world, Nick wanted to grab him by the throat and knock him senseless. Instead, he smiled and spoke in a falsely calm tone. "You haven't asked about Chloe."

Snake massaged the back of his neck. "Chloe. Yeah. How is she doin'? Are Caitlin and Stephanie letting her get any sleep?"

"You know she had the twins?"

"On August eighteenth," he responded, nodding. "I have pictures. You want to see?" He reached into his back pocket, pulled out a wallet, and flipped it open to a plastic picture sleeve. "They're beautiful girls, aren't they?"

"How did you get these?" Nick asked, staring in shock at the traditional hospital first photos.

"Ma."

"Mrs. Duncan is in contact with you?"

"No. I haven't talked to her since I phoned and asked her to see to Chloe right before I went to the cops for help."

"Then how did you get these pictures?"

"She posted them on the Facebook. That's how I've kept track of Ma for years. She posts all kinds of personal stuff for all the world to see."

Nick glanced at Agent Boles. "You give him internet access?"

"I'm in protective custody," Snake protested. "Not jail."

"Rules are 'read only' for the internet," Boles stated.

"Y'all are big on rules around here, aren't you?" Nick observed.

Boles smirked. "The IRS is part of this task force. Oh yeah, we have a rule book."

At that, Nick decided he could like Agent Boles after all. Turning his attention back to Snake, he asked, "So your mother posts about Chloe?"

"Yeah. She talks about Chloe and the girls every day. At least, she has until the last two days, when she hasn't posted at all. That's why I thought she...oh, hell. Is this about Chloe? Is that why you're here? Is something wrong with Chloe or the girls?"

Took you long enough to ask, jerk. "No. They're fine. Now."

"What do you mean, 'now'?"

Something wasn't adding up. Nick watched Snake's expression intently as he asked, "Are you aware of Chloe's troubles?"

"Troubles?" Wariness flashed in Snake Duncan's eyes. "I know about the colic, but Ma says the babies will grow out of that. I know Ma's house is crowded with Chloe and the babies living there, but Ma says they're managing."

Ma was obviously telling lies to her online friends.

"I never expected to be gone this long, or I'd have made other arrangements," Snake continued. "Maybe you could help me with that when you go home."

"What does your mother say about you, Snake? What's her explanation for why you're not around?"

Snake shot a sheepish glance toward the agent. "Ma went a little overboard on that. All I told her was that I'm helping the government with a project. She's the one who turned me into a secret agent."

Snake Duncan, a secret agent? "I need to take a look at his mother's posts."

Boles said, "She's written nothing to compromise Mr. Duncan's safety. She can't. She doesn't know anything, and much of what she puts out there is outlandish. Anyone with knowledge of life in Brazos Bend who reads even three days' worth of postings would realize she has an active imagination."

Nick could picture the Widow Duncan lying like a rug to her online friends about her "dear Herbert." What concerned him was whether or not her tall tales could cause Chloe any grief.

"Wait a minute," Snake said. "What's goin' on here? You're makin' me nervous, Sutherland. If my ma and Chloe and the babies are okay, then why are you here?"

"Who is Bubba C?"

Like an animal sensing danger, Snake's entire body came to alert. "What about him?"

"He sent a message to you through Chloe." Nick's blood began to boil. "He put a knife to her throat. He cut her. He scared her so bad she feared for her life and the lives of her newborn children! And you brought that trouble into her life, you sonofabitch."

As Nick talked, Snake seemed to shrink.

"Chloe. That asshole went to Chloe. I never thought—"

The agent stepped forward. "Bubba C is a name you haven't given us. We're disappointed, Herbert. It's a breach of our agreement."

"No, it's not." His brow knitted, his complexion pale, Snake shook his head. "Bubba C is the guy who caused all this trouble. Bubba C is Hank Carruthers." At the government man's doubtful look, he added, "It's a handle he uses when he's in one of his crazy modes. 'C' for Corleone like in the *Godfather* movies. He claims his family is just like the mob."

"He told Chloe you'd soon be swimming with the fishes," Nick said. "That's a movie line."

"Damn. Poor Chloe." Snake sank into a chair and buried his face in his hands. "I never thought...I didn't mean...oh, crap."

Nick thought he finally had a handle on what had happened, but he wanted to hear it in Snake's own words. "She's okay now. Chloe and the girls are safe, Snake, and I'm here to make sure they stay that way. To do that, I need to understand exactly what happened, how you ended up here in this room. I've heard Agent Bole's version, but would you go over it with me?"

"You'll watch after Chloe?"

"My word on it."

Snake polished off his bottle of water, then began to talk. "It started when I found out she was having twins. Scared the shit out of me. I didn't know how the hell I'd get enough money to raise two babies. Somebody told me he could hook me up with these fellas in Fort Worth to drive cars—fine cars—from Texas to the East Coast."

"Who is 'somebody'?" Nick asked. He wondered if the agent noticed Snake's slight hesitation before he answered.

"A guy I used to ride with in the Devil's Own. Billy Joe Worrell. Anyway, I drove a Porsche from Fort Worth to Jersey and made a cool grand. In cash. I made half a dozen trips before they asked me to fill in for a guy on a trip to a bank. Hell, I didn't know what I was getting into until they handed me the fake IDs, and then it was too late."

He explained how the Fort Worth ring had targeted the dead. "Once somebody croaks, it takes a few weeks for word to make its way to the Social Security people and the credit-reporting places. They'd take advantage of that time gap—use fake driver's licenses to take out loans and buy cars and that sort of stuff."

"Who is 'they,' Snake?"

"They call it the Covenant Group. Head guys are a couple of brothers out of Tarrant County, Bob and Tag Carruthers. Supposedly the family has five brothers, and two of 'em are connected in Mexico. Bubba C. is the son of one of those guys."

"Drugs?"

"Smuggling, too. People and guns."

Which is why it's an interagency task force, Nick realized. Drugs, immigration, illegal arms, insurance fraud. Hell, could Duncan have dug this hole any deeper?

Snake shot a quick glance to the lawman. "I don't know anything about that part of it. If it's true, they kept those family businesses entirely separate. Well, all except for Bubba. He got around."

"What happened to send you to the Feds?"

Snake scowled and shook his head. "That a-hole. Bubba. That last trip they had me driving a Maserati. As I'm leaving the dealership, Bubba C shows up and wants to come along. Wouldn't tell me why, but he definitely was in a hurry to get out of town. Anyway, we're driving through Arkansas when my cell phone rings. It's Bob Carruthers, and I could tell he was majorly pissed. He'd figured out Bubba was with me, and he wanted to talk to him. Must have chewed on his ass for a good ten minutes. Anyway, after he hung up, Bubba told me to turn the car around and head for Wichita Falls."

"Back to Texas." That fit with the gas receipts Bryan Howell had uncovered.

"Yep." Snake took a deep breath, the blew it out hard. "I took Bubba to his mother's house—big place in Country Club—and he picked up a red duffel bag. It was full of bills and a bloody knife, and he was supposed to take the bag to Bob. He told me he'd killed Billy Joe. That's when I knew I was in deep shit."

Only then? Nick wondered how Chloe could have fallen for such an idiot.

"I waited until he stopped to take a piss in Bowie," Snake said, "and

I drove off without him. I contacted a lawyer I knew I could trust, and he helped me work a deal and turn myself in."

Nick thought of the money Chloe had found buried in the pile of tires. "Where's the duffel bag?"

"I turned it over to the Feds."

Minus two hundred thousand plus dollars he slipped into a blue bag, Nick said to himself.

"Sure enough, the knife was what killed poor ol' Billy Joe. They've been looking for Bubba ever since."

"What are they charging you with?"

"My testimony in the identity-theft cases and the murder case gets me a reduced sentence. I have a signed contract."

"And you didn't contact Chloe or your mother because...?"

"He's in protective custody," Agent Boles said. "We make those decisions."

"I didn't figure it hurt to keep them in the dark about this. I thought somebody might come snooping around Brazos Bend, but I didn't expect they'd hurt anybody."

"Why the hell not?" Nick exploded. "You just told me this Bubba was a killer."

"'Cause of the movie. That whole car trip, all he did was talk about *The Godfather.* He said the Carruthers are just like the Corleones. They won't go after families. I guess it's some sort of Mafia rule."

"You may be willing to trust that, but I'm not." Standing, Nick addressed the agent. "Any sign of Bubba?"

"They have him on ice. We're guessing Mexico. Regarding Ms. McKinney's safety, the task force is in agreement with Duncan. No one but us, and lately, your people, are watching Ms. McKinney."

"Y'all missed the hospital attack?"

The agent grimaced. "We didn't have a twenty-four-hour surveillance on her at that point, I'm afraid. We picked her up a few days later during one of her Fort Worth trips with Mooney."

"Mooney?" Snake asked. "Stewart Mooney?"

Nick rounded on him. "He took care of her. He did what you should have done. She was sick after she had the babies, and Stewart took care of her."

"Sick? What was wrong with her?"

"You left her alone in a trailer with no air-conditioning and no money and no support and pregnant with twins. She didn't know if you were alive or dead. She became severely depressed. She wasn't living with your mother all this time, Snake. After your friend Bubba attacked her, she ran away. She left those babies in her sister's care and disappeared. Thank God, she went to Stewart for help. He sheltered her and arranged medical help for her. If not for him, she might well be dead."

"Stewart Mooney," Snake muttered. "That sonofabitch."

Nick shot him an impatient look, then turned to Agent Boles. "This situation isn't acceptable, Agent Boles. The safety of Chloe McKinney and her children are paramount. Arrangements will have to be made."

"What kind of arrangements?" Snake asked.

Nick braced his hands on his hips and faced Jonathan Boles. "What do we do to get Mr. Duncan and his family into the Witness Protection Program?"

～

TESS HUNG up the kitchen telephone at the carriage house and sighed. Though accustomed to dealing with demanding directors, presumptive producers, and asinine actors, she'd seldom run into a situation as ridiculous as this latest brouhaha regarding her client Jennifer Hart. What kind of idiot runs off with an assistant cameraman in the middle of a film because he looks like Elvis? Tess would need to do some fast and fancy talking to save the movie, save Jennifer's career. "And I can't do it from Brazos Bend, Texas."

It was time for Tess to go home.

She didn't have ten days to steal with Nick, after all.

From the living room, Chloe called, "Tess? You ready? I told Stewart we'd meet him at the high school soccer field at seven. It's a ten-minute walk, and it's already quarter till."

Tess followed the sound of her sister's voice to find Chloe buckling Caitlin next to her sister in the double stroller. "Y'all go on," Tess said.

230

"Nick called a little while ago and said he'd be home soon. I think I'll wait for him here."

"Did he tell you where he ran off to today?"

"No. He said he'd explain it to me tonight."

Chloe licked her lips, her expression uncertain. "Do you think his trip had something to do with Snake?"

"I honestly don't know, honey."

"Maybe we should stay home, too."

Tess glanced down at the twins, appropriately bundled up for the evening air, and smiled. "No, you go on. Stewart is waiting. I imagine I'll be along before they light the bonfire at seven-thirty. Save me a place on your blanket?"

"Sure."

Tess watched from the front porch as her sister pushed the stroller down the walk, past the open gate, and onto the sidewalk that meandered through the neighborhood toward the high school. Chloe looked comfortable with the babies, she thought. She looked happy. If only Tess could trust that this phase of Chloe's would last.

Tess blew out a long, heavy sigh, then massaged the stiff muscles at the back of her neck. She sank into the white wicker porch rocker and attempted to pull her thoughts together. She had some plans to make, some decisions to contemplate.

First, she needed to convince Chloe to move to California. Tess had spent some time online today learning what she could about this new Cowboy Mafia. What she'd read had scared her. Even if Chloe and the babies were only minimally at risk from that organization, Tess still wanted her as far away from any potential danger as possible.

Next, Tess needed to have a talk with Nick. One thing she knew without a doubt; she didn't want to lose him. Hopefully, he felt the same way, too, and they could work something out.

She remained on the porch as the dusk gradually deepened, the scent of honeysuckle sweetening the temperate evening air. In the distance she heard the high school band belting out the fight song, and she frowned at the realization that she'd miss Friday's homecoming game.

The church bells rang quarter past the hour as Nick's Porsche pulled up to the curb in front of the carriage house. When he climbed from the car, Tess stifled the urge to run to him and fling herself into his arms. "Hey there, handsome," she called from the porch.

His smile beamed toward her. "Hello, darlin'. How come you're sitting there in the dark?"

"Just waiting for you to come light up my night."

He'd discarded the jacket of his charcoal gray business suit and loosened his red tie. He gave her a quick, hard kiss. As he straightened, Tess wanted to reach up and tug him back down to her. Instead, she practiced letting go.

"So, how was your day?" she asked, wincing once she realized what a wifely question that was.

"Busy. Eventful. I want to tell you about it, but I've got to have something to eat. I skipped lunch, and I'm starved. You want to go get a burger with me?"

"I have homemade chicken soup on the stove. Would you rather have that?"

"Sounds great. Thanks." Nick hesitated briefly, then nonchalantly asked, "Is Chloe around?"

Tess narrowed her eyes. "You found out something about Snake, didn't you?"

His gaze flicked toward the house. "Chloe—"

"She's taken the girls to the homecoming bonfire. I'm here alone."

"Good," he said with relief.

Judging that the fastest way to get him talking was to get him fed, Tess led the way to the kitchen, where she dished up a big bowl of soup and set out a plate of biscuits. It took effort, but she managed to wait patiently until he said, "I saw Snake Duncan today."

"What? Where?"

"Out of state. The government doesn't want me saying exactly where."

"The government?"

Nick nodded, then proceeded to tell her a story about murder, Mafia, and money that left Tess shaking in her sandals. "That's it. There can be no debate about it now. Chloe and the girls have to come with me to California tomorrow. If these people are involved in drugs and smuggling and guns and if Snake testifies against them, my family could be in danger."

"I agree we need to protect Chloe, but running off to California isn't the way to do it."

Tess shook her head. "It's the only way."

"No. I'll hire bodyguards and keep them until this thing is settled."

"Nick, you're not listening. I must go back tomorrow. One of my clients needs me in L.A."

"Tomorrow? You're leaving here tomorrow? I thought I had eight more days."

"I have to go." While Nick set down his spoon and pushed away from the table, she sank into a chair and wrapped her arms around herself. "Please be understanding about this."

"Why? I don't understand. How can you just leave?"

"I'm not 'just leaving.' I'm going home. I'm going back to work. I have responsibilities to my clients and to my sister and to myself."

"Dammit, Tess, I want you to stay."

"I've got to go."

"You can't go," he demanded. "I'm in love with you!"

I'm in love with you. His declaration echoed through her mind. Tess closed her eyes and absorbed it. Ached.

Hoped.

Licking her lips, she said, "I love you, too, Nick. Come with me."

He blinked, but didn't speak.

Encouraged, she continued, "Come to California. Let me show you my world. You might just like it. You might love it. Take a chance on me, on us."

Nick rubbed the back of his neck. "Damn, Tess. I—"

Softly, she said, "If we don't work out, you can always come back here."

Nick shoved to his feet and paced the room, his hands sunk into the pockets of his slacks. "I was supposed to have more time. Brazos Bend is a good place, Tess. It's gentle and caring and happy—a great place for us to raise our family."

Our family. He's offering me children. Tess had a vision of a little girl with her blond curls and Nick's gorgeous blue eyes. *Maybe for that, I could stay in Brazos Bend.*

Reality returned with the memory of her mother. "My mother and father dated for six years before they married, certainly long enough to know each other well. She worked for a bank in town and quit to stay home and raise children when I was born. He walked out on her when I was twelve. She had no skills, no way to support us. She finally got a job serving drinks in a bar, and before long, she consumed more than she sold."

Nick's jaw set. "You think I'm the kind of man who'd walk out on his family?"

"They grew up together, Nick. She knew him all her life, and she never saw it coming. I've known you six weeks."

"Dammit, you can't go into a marriage expecting it to fail."

"I can't go into a marriage without a realistic world-view, either." Tess paused for a moment, then said, "I've fallen in love with you, Nicholas Sutherland, and the thought of spending my life with you, raising a family with you, fills me with joy. But you're asking me to give up everything. I'm asking you to quit hiding."

His head came up. "I'm not hiding."

"Yeah, you are. You've taken a plot line right out of one of those old movies you love. You've turned Brazos Bend into your own personal Brigadoon, and you're hiding from the real world here."

"Hold on. You're fixin' to make me mad."

"I'm sorry, but it's time to take the gloves off. If we're to have a chance, then we both need to be honest. You know what? I wish I did trust in our love enough to risk everything for it. I think that would be so...big. Wonderful. So free. I dream that given time, we can get there, but we're not there now."

"Because you're not giving it a chance. It sounds to me like you're looking for a guarantee, and life doesn't come with those, Tess."

"That's right. But life isn't a fairy tale, either. You're a fairy-tale hero, Nick. You're handsome and wealthy and romantic beyond belief. You're kind to old ladies, dogs, and children. You're perfect. Too perfect."

"What, you want me to go kick a dog?"

"I want you to give me time. Give us time together." Nick's cell phone began to ring, but when he ignored it, Tess did too. She took a step toward him, her gaze imploring. "I'm not saying happily-ever-after isn't possible for us, Nick, but for me to trust in this fairy-tale romance of ours, I need to see it work. Not in Mayberry or Brigadoon or Brazos Bend, Texas, but in the real world. In my world. If this truly is true love, is that too much to ask?"

Not meeting her gaze, he chose to answer his phone rather than her question. "Hello?"

He listened without comment, but the subtle change in his body language alerted Tess to trouble. "This connection is awful. Call Tess McKinney's land line."

He thumbed the off button, and Tess asked, "Is something wrong?"

"Yeah. If Brazos Bend were Brigadoon, and I was the superpower running the place, I'd damn sure fix it so that cell phones worked."

Ring. Ring. Ring. He grabbed the receiver off the wall phone. "All right, Agent Boles. Start at the beginning."

Nick shut his mouth and listened, his expression growing darker as the seconds ticked by. Finally, after a full minute, he said, "Great. This is just effing fabulous. Can't you people do anything right?"

He banged the receiver back into its cradle, then turned to a wary Tess. "We've got trouble. I want to get to Chloe fast. Looks like Snake Duncan slithered away from his keepers."

"He what?"

"He bolted, Tess. Snake Duncan is on the loose."

FOUR FLAMING TORCHES helicoptered through the air and landed on the tall stack of wood previously soaked with jet fuel. Fire whooshed, the crowd roared, and short-skirted cheerleaders brought megaphones to their lips and chanted, "We are the Rattlers, the mighty, mighty Rattlers."

With her daughters snug in the stroller a safe distance away, Chloe gazed around the soccer field at friends and neighbors and experienced a startling revelation. She belonged.

It was true. Despite the absence of having her babies' father's wedding ring on her finger, regardless of her illness-driven actions following the twins' birth, irrespective of the less-than-glowing opinions of her held by the town's matriarchs, Brazos Bend had taken her in and made her one of them.

It was the first time since her mother lost the house after her father walked out that Chloe felt like she had a real home. "Oh, Stewart. I feel so lucky to be here."

Stewart boldly took her hand. "I'm the lucky one."

The smile on her lips dimmed fractionally, and she used the opportunity to fuss with Caitlin's pacifier to break the contact between them. Over the last few days, Stewart had become increasingly...proprietary in his manner toward her, and Chloe had just about decided that she wasn't comfortable with it. Not because of her loyalty to Snake, surprisingly enough, but because she didn't want someone else to take care of her. She wanted to take care of herself and her children. It was, for Chloe, an innovative notion.

"Chloe? Chloe!"

Hearing Tess call, she turned toward the sound. "Over here."

It surprised Chloe to see tension melt from her sister's face when their gazes met. Observing a similar reaction from Nick Sutherland when Tess pointed her out, Chloe sensed a measure of unease. "Something's wrong," she said to Stewart.

"What's going on, Nick?" he asked when they drew near.

Tess and Nick shared a look, then Tess said, "Nick has some disturbing news."

Chloe's eyes rounded. She knew. This had something to do with Snake. Forgetting her desire to stand on her own feet, she reached out and clasped Stewart's hand. "What is it?"

After escorting them away from the crowd to a spot near the tennis courts where they could speak privately, Nick told them about seeing Snake, his deal with the government, and the fact that he'd walked away from protective custody today. "He knocked out his watcher, tied him up, and stole his car. He had a good head start because the watcher wasn't found until the shift changed six hours later. I think there's a good chance he'll end up here," Nick concluded as weak knees forced Chloe to lean heavily against Stewart. "Until I told him otherwise, he thought you had moved in with his mother."

"I promised him I would," she murmured, her stomach rolling. Snake involved with murderers? Attacking federal agents? She couldn't believe it.

"Damn, Chloe. I'm sorry. This must be my fault. Something I said must have spooked him. Maybe I shouldn't have brought up the Witness Protection Program."

Courtesy lights around the tennis courts enabled Chloe to see her sister's eyes round in shock. "Witness Protection!" Tess exclaimed. "That's when they take them away from their families. I'd never see Chloe. I'd never see the girls! No." She shook her head. "No, that's not happening. Chloe, we're going to California first thing in the morning."

Witness Protection. California with Tess. *No. No. No. No. Brazos Bend is my home!*

"I've got to fix this." Turning to Nick, Chloe asked, "How do we fix this?"

Stewart spoke in a cold, hard tone she'd not heard from him before. "We keep you the hell away from Snake Duncan."

Tears stung Chloe's eyes, and fiercely, she blinked them away. "He might not care. He wouldn't have done this if he cared. If he comes to Brazos Bend at all, he might just be looking for the money."

"What money?" Stewart asked, straightening his spine. "You never said anything about any money."

"I didn't want to worry you." Chloe waved a hand. "I found a big bag of money in one of Snake's old hiding places out at the trailer. I moved it, though, so he won't know where it is when he goes looking for it. Maybe that's all he wants. He might not even try to see me."

Nick shook his head. "No, Chloe. After seeing him today, judging by his reaction when I talked about you, I think he'll definitely come to you. He loves you, and he loves those girls."

"Well, he doesn't deserve her," Stewart snapped. He took Chloe's hand and brought it to his mouth for a fervent kiss. "I love you, too, Chloe. I love all three of you. I want you to marry me and let me be a father—a good father—to Stephanie and Caitlin."

His declaration shocked Chloe; his proposal floored her. "Stew-art...this is...I didn't expect...I don't know how...oh, dear."

Nick shook his head and muttered, "Mooney, your timing is worse than mine."

Tess stepped forward. "Stewart, Texas isn't safe for my sister and nieces. They're coming with me tomorrow."

"She'll be fine here. I'll protect her." Stewart took both Chloe's hands in his and said, "Marry me, Chloe."

"Oh, Stewart," she breathed. "I can't do this now. I can't think. Please, can you ask me again later once this situation has been settled?"

"All right, but let's get it settled quickly. Where is the money, Chloe? You won't need to worry about a thing if the Carruthers get their money back."

"Hold on," Tess interrupted. "You want to give money back to drug lords and murderers? I don't think so."

Stewart pinned her with a hot look. "You want her to enter Witness Protection? You want never to see your nieces again? Giving the money back is the only viable option. It's the best way...the only way...to truly protect Chloe and the girls."

"I don't agree," Tess snapped back. "I think—"

Nick put his hand on Tess's shoulder. "Settle down, both of you. Arguing about this won't get us anywhere."

"What do you think I should do, Nick?" Chloe asked.

"Your safety is primary, of course. It's always better to keep it legal, too, if possible." Nick paused, pondered the problem, then said, "The Feds already have the carriage house under surveillance, and Snake knows that now. He won't show up there. I want to talk to him, to find out what made him bolt today. Where do you think he'll come looking for you, Chloe?"

"If he can't come to the carriage house, I don't know. The trailer, maybe? He'll go there looking for the money. He won't know I found it. Why don't we go out there and wait for him?"

Tess shook her head. "No, Chloe. Let Nick handle Snake. No telling who might be on his tail. It's better you stay completely away from him."

"He's the father of my children, Tess. I want to talk to him as much as he wants to talk to me, I'm sure." Chloe reached down and rearranged Stephanie's blanket. "But I don't want the girls anywhere around him until we've had the chance to find out what he's up to, okay?"

"I don't like it," Tess said.

"Me, either." Stewart braced his hands on his hips. "Tess is right. A murderer might be following Snake even as we speak. Chloe shouldn't be anywhere near him." He turned a pleading gaze on Chloe. "If you're bound and determined to meet with him, at least have the money handy in case something goes wrong."

Chloe pursed her lips, then shrugged. "That's no problem. The money is still out there. I just stuck it in a different place. I don't care who has the money. I just want my daughters safe." Glancing at Tess, she added, "I'd like to be able to stay in Brazos Bend."

Stewart beamed, as if that had been an acceptance to his proposal, Tess frowned, and Nick grimaced as he rubbed the back of his neck. "Let's get going, then. Snake wasn't far behind me. Stewart, will you walk Tess back to my place?"

"I'm coming with you," he declared. "I'm not abandoning the woman I love in her time of need."

"But—"

"Max is here," Tess said. "I'll ask him. Y'all go on."

Nick frowned toward the bonfire. "I'd rather stay until—"

"Go. We'll be fine." Tess wrapped her arms around Chloe and gave her a big hug. "Good luck, honey. I've a few things I want to say to ole Snake. Tell him I look forward to meeting him."

CHAPTER 20

TESS OFFERED Max a general explanation of events as they walked the quiet Brazos Bend streets toward Nick's house on the hill. Max kept a careful eye on the shadows, but neither he nor Tess expected any trouble. Nor did any appear.

Upon reaching Nick's house, Max used the house key hidden on the fishing pole rack to unlock the door, then said, "I'll stay with you until we hear from Nick."

"No, Max. You need to get back to your family. We'll be fine."

"I don't like leaving you here alone."

"Alone?" Tess nodded toward the carriage house. "The FBI, DEA, INS, and who knows who else is within shouting distance. You get on back before Shannon's dance class performs. She'll be crushed if you're not there."

"How about I send Adele back here to stay, just so you have some company?"

"Sure. That'll be fine."

Once Max left, Tess spread a blanket on Nick's living room floor, then took Stephanie and Caitlin from the stroller and laid them on their backs to play. Sitting cross-legged beside them, she'd just reached into the diaper bag and pulled out the baby wipes when the voice spoke from the shadows. "They look like their mother, don't they? Aren't they beautiful?"

Tess gasped back a scream as a man who could be none other than Snake Duncan stepped into view. At first glance, she understood what about the man had attracted her sister. Tall with broad shoulders, sculpted features, shoulder-length hair, and an earring, he might as well have had "Bad Boy" tattooed across his brow. The snake tattoos that coiled around both his arms added to his dangerous aura, but it was the unabashed love blazing from his eyes as he stared at the babies that assured Tess she had nothing to fear.

"Hello, Snake. I'm Chloe's sister, Tess."

"Hi," he said without looking away from the children. "Which one is which?"

"Stephanie is in pink. Caitlin's in the yellow."

"Oh, wow. They're so tiny. So pretty. I knew Chloe would make good-lookin' babies."

Tess cocked her head and studied him. "You sure have caused a lot of trouble."

"I know, and I hate it. I'm doing my best to get out of it."

"By running away from the law? Somehow, I don't think that's the best way to get out of trouble, Mr. Duncan."

His expression hardened and Tess felt a little ripple of unease. "Yeah, well, I have my reasons. I need to talk with your sister. It's important. Where is she?"

Tess took a moment to debate her choices, then said, "They're waiting for you out at the trailer. We expected you to attempt to retrieve the bag of money."

His brows winged up. "Chloe knows about the cash?"

"She found it and hid it somewhere different. She's going to show Nick and Stewart where it is tonight in case those men who are after you—"

"Stewart!" Snake yelped. "She's giving the money to Stewart Mooney?"

Cautiously, Tess said, "Yes."

"Holy shit." Snake turned on his boot heel and headed for the door.

Tess jumped to her feet and hurried after him. "Wait. What's wrong? What's bad about her telling Stewart where the money is?"

"Because he's the one who arranged for it to be stolen in the first place," Snake said. "He's the person who got me mixed up with this trouble to begin with. Stewart Mooney is the computer whiz for the freakin' Cowboy Mafia!"

~

Light from a near full moon bathed the rocky landscape in milky light, the deep-throated croak of a bullfrog from a stock tank nearby the only sound breaking the silence of the night. From the driver's seat of his car, Nick made a careful visual study of the run-down trailer and that land surrounding it. Though he spied no sign of life, something set his teeth on edge.

Or maybe that was a reaction to the nonsense coming from the back seat. Stewart was about to wear himself out with romantic declarations to Chloe.

Nick hoped like hell he didn't sound that desperate when talking to Tess.

Chloe tapped Nick on the shoulder. "I think I should get out of the car. I'll sit on the doorsteps."

"I think I should sit with you," Stewart said. "Snake won't mind approaching me like he might Nick, and I'll be handy to provide protection if you need it. I am licensed to carry, you'll be happy to know."

From the front passenger seat, Chloe twisted around to see Stewart. "You carry a gun?"

"Yes. A twenty-two."

"A handgun?"

"It's my legal right," he responded, a defensive note in his voice.

Nick had a sudden urge to shift the pickup into drive and take off, but before he could act on it, Chloe opened her door and stepped to the ground. "I don't like the idea of guns around my children, I'll have you know," she lectured. "Especially handguns."

Stewart grumbled, scrambling after her. "Snake used to keep a whole arsenal out here."

"Well, I didn't have children in the house then. Now I do."

As Nick climbed from the truck, Stewart grabbed Chloe's hand. "If you'll marry me, I'll get rid of all my guns. My word on it."

"Oh, Stewart," Chloe said with a sigh.

Nick rolled his eyes. How many times had he asked her now? Twenty? Thirty? "All right, you two. Go ahead and sit on the steps. I'll scout around, see if it looks like anyone has been by here today."

"What about the money?" Stewart asked. "Shouldn't we retrieve it, have it handy if we need it?"

" 'Handy' must be your middle name today," Nick observed, his instincts nudging him again so that he gave the area another good look. What bothered him? It wasn't a feeling of being watched, so he didn't think Snake had beaten them here and waited for them already. Nor was it a sense of danger, fear that a Carruthers family goon might have them in his gun-sight even now.

As Stewart led Chloe toward the trailer, his voice drifted on the shadows. "Why don't you sit down and relax as best you can. Just tell me where you hid the duffel bag, and I'll go do all the work."

"Oh, it's no work," Chloe replied. "It's in the trunk of that old rusting Chevy around back, where I told that Bubba C person I'd put it. I figured since it was sure to have been searched already, that was as good a place as any."

Stewart beamed her a smile. "Excellent."

He saw her settled on the stoop, then disappeared around back. He returned a few minutes later carrying a navy blue duffel.

Stewart Mooney sat beside Chloe and propped the money bag between his feet. Nick grabbed the flashlight from his truck and made a slow circle around the trailer, but found nothing to suggest anyone had been here anytime recently.

The cell phone on his belt began to vibrate. "Hello?"

In a half dozen seconds of choppy static before the signal faded entirely, he thought he might have heard Tess's voice. His sense of foreboding increased, and he decided to go with his instincts. He approached the stoop, slipped his hand around Chloe's arm. "This doesn't feel right. I think we should go. Now."

Chloe looked at him in surprise. "What? Leave? What about Snake?"

Stewart stood and reached for her free arm. "I'm with Nick. Let's not concern ourselves with Snake Duncan. He's not worth your time or energy, Chloe. You know, now that I've thought about it, perhaps you should go out to California with your sister for a time. We all could go. California has a lot of opportunity for those in my field. You won't need to work, you can stay home with the girls. Unless you want to work, that is. I won't stand in your way. Then, once things around here settle down, we could come back to Brazos Bend and live here."

Chloe wrenched away from them both and stalked a few steps away. "Hold on. What's the matter with the two of you? Stewart, you must stop with this marriage talk. I care for you, I truly do, but I can't make such a big decision so fast. Not anymore, anyway. I'm a mother now, and like Tess says, motherhood is not a phase. For my children's sake, I need to talk to Snake. No matter who he is or what he's done, he's still their father. I'm not leaving here until I'm certain he isn't going to show up."

Nick silently debated whether he should pick her up and move her bodily to the car when he heard the sound of wheels crunching the gravel road off the highway. Moments later, headlights pierced the shadows, and Nick realized the time for leaving had passed. As he moved to stand beside Chloe, in the seconds prior to switching off his flashlight, the light's beam illuminated Stewart Mooney's hand. He held the duffel bag in a white-knuckled grip.

Seeing it, Nick realized what had bothered him before. Stewart had asked Chloe where she hid the duffel bag. She'd never mentioned what sort of container the money was stored in. How could Stewart have known?

Maybe he guessed. A duffel bag is a logical way to carry that much money.
Maybe he's seen it before. Maybe he's in on it.
Stewart Mooney? Mr. Computer Nerd? Nah.
It's identity theft. A computer nerd would come in handy.
Handy. Damn.

Nick really wasn't in the mood to wrestle with a gun-wielding computer nerd.

A sedan that all but cried out "government issue" rolled to a stop a short distance from the trailer. Stewart moved closer to Chloe. Nick shifted closer to Stewart.

The driver's side door swung open simultaneously with the passenger door. Stewart's hand disappeared into his jacket pocket as Snake Duncan climbed from behind the wheel. Tess got out of the car, calling in a panic, "Chloe, come here."

"Snake Duncan!" Chloe said, stepping forward. "Where the hell have you been?"

Then, everyone moved at once. Nick lunged for Stewart, Stewart grabbed Chloe's arm, Snake launched himself forward toward Stewart, moonlight glinting off the knife blade in his hand, as Tess went for Chloe, who screamed, "What's happening?"

The gunshot cut through the night.

Nick's heart stopped as Tess crumpled to the ground.

"Oh, dear Lord, no," Stewart cried, dropping the gun as Chloe screamed out her sister's name. Snake hollered, "Dammit, Stewart! What the hell have you done?"

"I'm sorry. It was an accident. I didn't mean to pull the trigger."

A cold, horrible fear born of the soul seeped throughout Nick's body as he dropped to the ground beside the woman he loved. Blood pulsed from the wound high in her chest. "Hold on, baby. It'll be okay. You'll be okay. Okay. Okay."

Chloe continued to scream as Nick's mind processed the emergency in crisp and crystalline thoughts. No phone. No ambulance. In the car now. Pressure on the wound. He slipped his arms beneath her and swiftly stood. "Somebody drive."

"Me," said Snake. "I'm good."

A second car roared up as Nick climbed into the sedan's back seat with Tess. With Snake behind the wheel, the car lurched forward even as four lawmen spilled from the other vehicle.

The next minutes were the most harrowing of Nick's life. Tess lost consciousness shortly after the car gained the highway, but her chest continued to rise and fall with shallow, beautiful breaths. Snake drove like a NASCAR winner.

"Hold on, baby," Nick murmured, shuddering at the warm, sticky feel of Tess's blood coating his hands, the coppery scent of it making him nauseous. *Please, God. Please God.*

"Almost there," said Snake moments later.

Nick glanced up to see Bethania Hospital's red neon Emergency sign. "You're strong, Tess. Fight. Fight for me. Fight for us."

The car screeched to a stop, the door swung open immediately and in a flurry of activity, Tess was taken from Nick. The sense of loss all but drove him to his knees.

CHAPTER 21

CHLOE HAD NEVER FELT this afraid. Her sister was literally fighting for her life, and the thought of losing her was more than Chloe could bear.

Tess had always been the one constant in Chloe's life. No matter where Chloe was, what she was doing, who she was with, or what sort of trouble she was in, Chloe had always known that her problems could be solved with one simple phone call to Tess. Tess was the only person in Chloe's life who loved her unconditionally, and Chloe had taken advantage of it over and over. Look where that had gotten them.

Chloe lifted her head and gazed at the others in the waiting room.

Nick, pale and shaken and bloodstained, a telephone receiver glued to his ear as he called medical specialists all over the country, trying to control a situation over which he had none by ensuring that Tess received the best medical care possible.

Snake Duncan, the father of her daughters, standing slouched against the wall in one corner of the room, his arms crossed, sending pleading looks at her.

Stewart sat in the center of the small waiting room, a Palo Pinto county sheriff on one side, a government guy named Boles on the other. His elbows rested on his knees, his head hung down. The bandage on his arm covered a knife wound that had required twenty-seven stitches. Every so often Chloe heard him sniff as a shudder shook him.

The lawmen had wanted to interview and arrest and throw around their weight when they arrived, but Nick laid down his own law in a cold steel voice. Nobody talked, nobody left the room until the doctors provided news on Tess's condition.

The sheriff, being a Brazos Bend man, understood. The government guy about went crazy. One thing he demanded, and Nick had agreed, was to keep other visitors out of the waiting room. Knowing Brazos Bend, word had spread, and friends and acquaintances even now congregated somewhere in the hospital. Chloe was pretty sure she'd heard Kate Cooper's voice in the hallway outside a little while ago.

She glanced at her wrist. Seven minutes had passed since she last checked her watch, only it felt more like seven hours.

Please, God. Let my sister be okay. Chloe's eyes once again filled with tears. *Let her be okay, and I swear, I'll never do anything she needs to save me from again.*

Chloe had no sooner finished her prayer than the operating room doors opened. The doctor smiled. "Good news. Barring an unforeseen complication, I expect her to recover completely."

He gave a complex explanation of bullet trajectory and blood loss and damage to body parts Chloe had never heard of, but she didn't pay much attention beyond the words "recover completely." Nick asked a lot of questions, and even Snake put in his two cents. Stewart started rocking back and forth in his seat.

The doctor left the waiting room after telling Nick he could see Tess in recovery in approximately half an hour. After the door swung shut behind the surgeon, Nick collapsed into the chair across from Chloe. He dragged a hand down his face, his expression a combination of exhaustion and elation as he murmured, "This is not how I wanted to get the rest of my ten days."

The sheriff gave them a moment, then stepped forward. "That's great news about your sister, Chloe. Tess is well liked in town. Everyone will be thrilled to hear she's going to be okay. Now, though, I reckon it's time we heard how this terrible thing happened."

Stewart looked up. Ragged emotion etched deep creases across his face. "It's my fault. All of it."

The government agent scowled. "Let's hear it from the beginning."

Stewart closed his eyes, nodded, and appeared to be summoning his strength. When he opened his eyes and started speaking, he looked straight at Chloe. "I was a teaching assistant at a junior college in Fort Worth when Bob Carruthers hired me to tutor his son for his computer science class. I ended up helping him design a network for a new project of his. He called it the Covenant Group."

Agent Boles said, "That's the identity theft ring. You set it up?"

Stewart nodded. "At first I didn't know what I was getting into. Once I figured that out, I didn't know how to get out."

Snake piped up. "So he just dragged other people into the mire with him."

Stewart looked Snake in the eye for the first time since Tess was hurt. "You didn't care what you did as long as you made money."

"I had two babies on the way. Doctor bills and no insurance. It costs money to have babies these days."

Stewart glanced at Nick. "He had Chloe living in that ratty old trailer. I thought she deserved better."

Boles said, "So you told him about the car theft ring."

"Yes. I thought he'd move her to a nicer place."

"I would have," Snake said. "If I'd had time. I only made three runs before it all went south." To Boles, he said, "I told you about that."

"You didn't tell me everything," the agent replied. "You neglected to mention Mr. Mooney."

Snake fired a glare toward Stewart. "He was just the computer hack. I was trying to protect him because he promised to look out for Chloe. I didn't know at the time he intended to steal her from me. He lied to me the whole time I've been a guest of the government. Stewart posted stuff on the Net for me to read, too, not just my mother. It was all his idea. I didn't want to leave town without Chloe, but he convinced me it was best. He convinced me she'd be safe. When Sutherland tracked me down, I found out just how bad a liar he was." Snake took a threatening step toward Stewart. "You just wanted the money, didn't you? I told him I'd skimmed some off the top before I turned the bag over to the Feds. He's been after the money and my woman ever since."

"No!" A wild-eyed Stewart gazed at Chloe. "I didn't care about the money, honest. I wanted to find it and give it back to the Carruthers. That's true. I thought it was the best way to make you safe. If you gave back the money Snake stole, they wouldn't hold his crime against you."

"Maybe," Nick said softly, speaking for the first time. "But that's not the only way to keep her safe, is it?"

Snake sat beside Chloe and took her hand. "Witness Protection. With me."

"But Stewart knew another way. A better way, only he considered it too risky. Didn't you, Mooney?"

"What are you talking about?" Snake asked.

"Records. Names. Stewart knows, or has access to, everybody in the organization. He built the database. Right?"

Closing his eyes, Stewart nodded.

"If he gives up the information, the Feds have a chance to get them all. With the entire organization behind bars, who's going to go after Chloe? Who's going to go after Snake, for that matter? He could come back here. Back to her. They could stay here in Brazos Bend where she wants to live and raise her children."

Stewart looked at Chloe with the saddest eyes she'd ever seen. "I made poor choices because I fell in love with her. I wanted her for myself. I didn't want her to know what I'd done. If I'd known how it would turn out...I'm so sorry."

Snake tightened his grip on her hand. "You damned well ought to be sorry. You pulled a gun. You're lucky Chloe's sister wasn't killed. You're not good enough to say Chloe's name, much less talk to her about love."

"And you are?" Stewart snapped back. "You put your own wants and desires, your own welfare, above that of Chloe and the children. Be honest, Snake. You didn't want the money as much as you wanted the chance to drive ninety-thousand-dollar cars across country."

"You're a damned liar."

"Well, you're a sorry excuse for a man. You were more concerned about protecting your butt than helping Chloe when she was ill. If you hadn't run out on her, we wouldn't be sitting here right now."

"I didn't know she was sick. You didn't bother to mention it when you were lying to me about the details of her life. And the reason we're sitting here is because you decided to come after me with a gun."

"I was trying to protect Chloe. She needed—"

"Stop it!" Chloe shoved to her feet. "Just stop it, the both of you. I'm tired of this. Tired of you both. You want to know the true reason we're sitting here? It's because of me. Because I called her to come bail me out of my problems one more time. Because I've never, not in my entire life, taken responsibility for myself. I've allowed Tess to take care of me, to support me. To save me. That's what she was trying to do tonight. Save me. Well, guess what? No more. I'm done. From this moment forward, I'm standing on my own two feet. *I'm* responsible for myself and for my daughters. Not Tess. And not either one of you."

Snake reached toward her. "Now, honey, you're not thinkin' straight."

"Sure I am. I'm thinking straight for the first time in my life. I'm pretty sure that I'm a strong woman. I'm almost positive that I can be a good mother for my daughters. Both of you claim to love me, and at times, I believed I loved each of you in return. But you know what? Neither one of you knows what true love is. You lied to me. You deceived me. You used me. Frankly, I deserve better than that. Now, if you'll excuse me, I'm going home. I need to check on my daughters. Nick, will you call me if there's any change in Tess's condition?"

"I will."

Giving her head a dramatic toss, she whirled around and flounced toward the door. As her hand reached for the knob, Agent Boles spoke up. "Miss McKinney, one thing. If you'll turn over that duffel bag of cash, your part in tonight's events will be over."

"I don't have the money."

Agent Boles winced. "You don't?"

"My sister was shot. Bleeding. Maybe dying. I didn't think about any stupid money. I left the bag lying on the ground."

"But—" Agent Boles raked his fingers through his hair. "We went back out. My men didn't find it. The bag isn't there."

Chloe shrugged. Not her problem, not her responsibility. "Could be the possums dragged it off. They'll eat just about anything, you know."

THE PAIN WAS like nothing she'd known before. Centered high in her chest and radiating out to every cell in her body, it wrenched her back to consciousness. *No. No. Make it go away.* She willed herself to sink into the oblivion once more, but failed. Instead, she opened her eyes.

Nick. Asleep in a chair beside her. His hand resting on the bed beside hers. He looked awful. Exhausted. Was that blood on his shirt?

Hers. Yes, she remembered now. A crushing blow. The wild, savage light in Nick's eyes. He'd moved her, hurt her, pain so sharp that it stole her breath away. He'd pressed against her chest. She'd been shot. He'd saved her. She wet her lips and struggled to say, "My hero."

His eyes flew open. Panic, then...tears? His voice rough and gravelly. "Tess. Oh, God, Tess. You're awake."

"I'm alive."

"You're gonna be fine. The doctors promised. Not just the surgeon here, either. I brought in a couple guys—well, actually, they're both women—the best at Parkland Hospital in Dallas. They've lots of experience. Lots of gunshots at Parkland." His voice roughened. He cleared his throat. "They said you're gonna be fine."

"You...too."

Time passed in a blur, how much of it, she hadn't a clue. Days, certainly. Each time she awoke to fierce pain and the soothing sight of Nick Sutherland seated beside her bed. As far as she could tell, he never let go of her hand.

The first time she awoke clear-headed, Nick was gone. Chloe occupied his chair. She was...knitting?

"The Widow Duncan is teaching me, can you believe it? I think Snake convinced her to be nice to me in hopes of getting back in my good graces."

Chloe relayed the details of what had transpired in the hours following the shooting. "The government has both Snake and Stewart stashed away while they round up the Carruthers Cowboys. That's what the *Times and Record News* is calling them because the mafia references might tick off the Italian-American Anti-Defamation League. Anyway, they've arrested forty-two people at last count."

"I can't believe Stewart was part of all that."

"I know." Sighing, Chloe set down her knitting needles. "He feels awful about hurting you, Tess. I know if he could turn back the clock, he would. I'm so angry at both of them, Stewart and Snake. Money truly can be the root of all evil."

"What are you going to do about them?"

"I don't know. They've both written me from wherever the Feds have them stashed away. They both say they love me and want my forgiveness. I'm working on that, but right now, I don't want anything to do with either one of them. As far as love goes, I can't begin to think about that now."

Chloe leaned forward in her chair and clasped Tess's hand in both of hers. "Tess, I can't tell you enough how sorry I am for bringing this mess down upon you. If it's possible to find a silver lining in a cloud this dark, I want you to know that I've learned a lesson from it. An important lesson."

"It wasn't your fault."

"Not entirely, no, but I do share some responsibility. I haven't been fair to you all these years, but that's going to change. I'm giving you my word that from here on out, if my life needs fixing, I'll be the one to do it. I'm letting go."

"But...I don't mind helping you."

"I know, but you shouldn't have to mother me, should you? I've finally figured that out. Not that I won't ever ask for your help, because I will. The difference is that now I'll expect you to ask me for help, too. That's what sisters do."

"Sisters," Tess murmured, smiling. Tired, she drifted toward sleep, thinking of the newfound confidence and strength evident in her Chloe's manner. "I think I might like having a sister."

She woke the next time to a room filled with yellow roses and Nick's familiar face. Smiling, Tess said, "Thanks for the flowers. They're beautiful."

Pleasure lit his gorgeous blue eyes. "You're awake."

"Thinking straight, too," she replied.

"How do you feel?"

"Pain meds are one of God's great gifts to the world."

His eyes darkened, and he finger-brushed her hair off her face, comforting them both. Gently, he cupped her face in his hands, then bent down and touched his mouth to hers. "Never in my life have I been so afraid as when I saw you fall to the ground. That ride into town, those next few hours, they're a nightmare I never want to relive again. I thought I'd lost you, Tess. I thought I'd lost you."

She lifted her hand and with a finger, tried to smooth away the worry lines at his temples and brows. "It's over. I'm fine. Everything's okay."

His mouth twisted in a rueful smile. "I hate it when reality intrudes into Brigadoon."

He spent the rest of his visit catching her up on town gossip, and when she grew tired, he stood to go. "Now that you're better, I'll be scarce around here for a while. I have some business I need to attend to."

He didn't kiss her when he left. The omission left Tess feeling sad and bereft and a little uneasy. Something didn't feel right, but she couldn't think well enough to figure out what.

The hospital moved Tess out of intensive care into a private room that afternoon, and Adele arrived first, fussed over Tess for a time, then assumed the role of vetting the visitors who descended in mass. The Coopers came by, as did everyone from Profile Beauty Salon. Mr. Cavendar from the shoe store dropped by with a gift of plush house slippers, and the Widows descended with well-wishes and gift baskets that left Tess a little overwhelmed. Why were they treating her so nicely?

She put the question to Adele, who responded, "You're family, dear."

Rather than argue, Tess shut her eyes and attempted to sleep. In her mind's eye, she recalled Nick on her first visit to his hideaway. *They took me in and made me family.*

This was what Nick came to Brazos Bend looking for, what he stayed here for, what he didn't want to leave.

He'd told the truth about being scarce around the hospital, and Tess tried not to mind. Two long days passed when she didn't hear word one from him. Not even a phone call. When he did visit, he invariably arrived with someone else. They never once had time alone.

Tess's doctor told her on Wednesday morning that barring unforeseen complications, he'd sign her release on Friday. She called Nick's cell phone and told him her good news. After a pregnant pause, he answered, "Great. That's great news, honey."

"Funny," she muttered as she slammed the phone down. "He doesn't sound like he thinks it's very great."

Tess nursed her anger the entire day, and late that evening just before visiting hours ended, when she heard heavy, male-sounding footsteps approach down the hall, then pause outside her door, she prepared to let Nick Sutherland have it.

But the man who entered her room wasn't Nick. "Jake?"

"Hey, beautiful. You look better than I expected. Need to lose those shadows under your eyes, get some color in your cheeks, and gain a few pounds, but all in all, you're a keeper."

"What in the world are you doing here?"

Rubbing the back of his neck, he tried a grin. It was the worst bit of acting she'd seen out of him in ages. "Your boyfriend called me, asking for a favor."

"Nick? Nick called you?"

"Yeah."

"What's the favor?"

"He asked me to take you home tomorrow."

Home. "The carriage house."

Jake cleared his throat. "No. California. He asked me to take you home to L.A."

"What?"

"He said he's tied up with out-of-town business and can't be here to help. He didn't think it would be good for you to try to make the trip by yourself."

"Well, now," she said, her voice low and tight. "Wasn't that thoughtful of him."

"Tess...," Jake began.

"I guess he didn't even consider that I might have changed my mind about staying in Brazos Bend?"

Jake blinked. "Have you?"

She didn't even hesitate. "No. Have your helicopter warmed up and ready for me. I'll be ready to fly the minute they cut me loose from here."

Jake nodded, then hung around for a time, making small talk. When he finally left, Tess breathed a sigh of relief, then allowed the pain to come.

It erupted from deep inside her, worse than anything created by the gunshot. It threatened to overpower her.

For five long minutes, she ruthlessly fought it back. Then, when she finally had herself under control, she calmly lifted the bedside telephone and dialed Nick's home number. When the answering machine switched on, she disconnected without leaving a message.

Next she dialed his cell. It took her straight to voice mail. "Just calling to tell you I'm headed back to Hollywood." Then, in a really poor Humphrey Bogart imitation, she added, "So, here's looking at you, jerk."

CHAPTER 22

AFTER A WEEK AT HOME, Tess returned to work. She spent the morning dealing with phone calls, tackling the mess Jennifer Hart had made of her career during the days Tess lay unconscious in the hospital. By eleven a.m. she'd made significant headway, so when her secretary brought in a hand-delivered engraved invitation from the shoe store down the street, inviting her to a special showing of their winter collection set to start in twenty minutes, she couldn't say no. After all, hadn't her doctors emphasized the importance of therapeutic activities?

"Lena, I'm taking an early lunch. If anything critical comes up, you can reach me on my cell."

"Reach you on your cell," repeated the older woman. "Those words are truly music to my ears."

Halfway out the door, she paused. Turning around, she added, "If Nick Sutherland phones, I want to know immediately."

Lena smiled, and Tess did her best to ignore the sympathy in her eyes. "Sure thing, Tess."

Exiting the building, she lifted her face to the sunny sky and basked in the warmth and joy of perfect weather. Not too hot, not too cold. Perfect. California perfect.

When Chloe called last night, she had said the first true cold front of the season had blown through. The temperature in Brazos Bend last night had reached thirty-nine degrees. Tess had worn shorts and gone barefoot on her walk along the beach last night. Her solitary walk. In her solitary life. "Oh, stop with the pity party," she muttered to herself.

Her life might be solitary at the moment, but it was still a good, fulfilling life. She didn't need a man to complete it. She certainly didn't need a man who would give her up so easily.

Tess simply didn't know what to think about Nick. Once she'd gotten past the knee-jerk hurt of basically being dumped by proxy, she'd recognized that such behavior was out of character for the man she'd grown to love. But then, his behavior had changed in the wake of the shooting. He'd run to Brazos Bend after his former girlfriend's suicide. Maybe having his current girlfriend shot right in front of him had triggered the flight response once again.

"Well, no sense fretting about it now," she murmured, noting a sidewalk sign in front of the shoe store. She had serious business to attend to. She had to shop for shoes.

Drawing closer to the store, she read the sign: CAVENDAR SHOE SHOP. WEST COAST BRANCH. PRIVATE SHOWING BY INVITATION ONLY.

What! Tess's heart began to pound. Approaching the door, she extended a shaking hand to push it open. Above her, a door chime tinkled. Tess stepped inside.

This was not her ordinary shoe store, not any longer. Flickering candles provided light while a rainbow of dozens of different flowers supplied the fragrance. Soft, sexy jazz drifted from speakers hidden in the ceiling.

Then there were the shoes. Dozens of them—hundreds, even. Everything from boots to heels to flip-flops. They sat lined up on circular displays that surrounded a plump upholstered chaise.

Tess gnawed on her lips. Nick. This had to be Nick's doing.

The curtain at the back of the shoe shop fluttered. She reached out and picked up the nearest shoe at hand, a brown leather hiking boot. A man walked out of the back of the shop.

Mr. Cavendar. In Los Angeles. In her personal shoe store.

Mr. Cavendar, not Nick.

"If you'll have a seat, Miss Tess, I have a new style for you to try."

Maybe she was dreaming, she thought as she sat in the chair Mr. Cavendar indicated and extended her foot. Maybe she'd fallen asleep at her desk, and this was nothing more than a vivid dream. He slipped on a Jimmy Choo evening shoe in printed silk and an ankle strap. It pinched her toes.

A very vivid dream.

"How do you like it?" the shoe salesman asked.

"It's wonderful."

He slipped on the second shoe and asked her to stand. "Comfortable?"

"I never thought comfort mattered in a shoe as great as this."

"Excellent. Then, if you'll excuse me." Mr. Cavendar shot his cuffs and walked out the door.

She didn't see the curtain move again or hear the door open, but slowly she realized she was no longer alone. Eyes hotly gleaming, dressed in an Armani suit, Nick Sutherland watched her from the shadows. No dream, then. Just a long, tall, Texas heartbreaker.

Tess slipped off one of the Jimmy Choos and threw it at him.

"Jeez, woman! Be careful. That shoe retails for seven hundred dollars....Owww!" The other shoe hit him in the shoulder.

"What." She threw a Prada ballerina slipper at him. "Do." A Gucci pump went flying. "You." Next, a Lucchese roper. "Think." The second boot in the pair. "You're." A bedroom slipper with a pig head on the front. "Doing?"

"Could ya cease fire long enough for me to tell you?"

Breathing heavily, her heart fluttering wildly, Tess allowed her hand to hesitate over a particularly cute pair of Vera Wang sandals. "Make it fast."

Nick shrugged off his suit jacket and tossed it onto a chair before reaching up to loosen his tie. "All right. I'll make it short and sweet. I love you."

It was a good start. "Perhaps a little elaboration would be useful."

"All right. I love you, and I want to marry you."

Oh, wow. Tess sank onto the nearest seat, which just happened to be the edge of the chaise. "This isn't something you could have mentioned in Brazos Bend? Before you sent me away? With a man you totally despise?"

"Muldoon isn't so bad. He's dating someone he met at the White House, did you know that?"

"Nick," she warned.

"I needed to do this on my own, Tess, to prove it to you and prove it to myself."

"What are you trying to prove by commandeering a shoe store and importing Mr. Cavendar to be my personal shoe salesman?"

"Mr. and Mrs. Cavendar were happy to make the trip. Did you know their favorite granddaughter lives not three miles from here?"

"No, I didn't know that." Her emotions in a flux, Tess massaged the bridge of her nose. "Help me out, here, Nick. I don't understand."

"Everything you said that horrible night was true. I *was* hiding in Brazos Bend. After my grandmother's death and Laura's suicide, I'd crawled into a safe place to lick my wounds. Nurse my guilt. I hid from work, from life, from love. Then you strutted into my life and tempted me."

"I didn't strut. I never strut. I glide confidently."

A grin teased the corners of Nick's mouth. "I fell in love with you, but I was still afraid, still guilty. I wanted you to join me in my world. I wanted you with me, living our safe, secure lives in safe, secure Brazos Bend."

"The same safe Brazos Bend that spawned Snake Duncan and Stewart Mooney."

"Stupid, wasn't it? I don't do stupid often, but when I do, I do it with flair. After the shooting, when the dust settled, I knew I had to make a choice."

"Me or Brazos Bend?"

"No. Holding on or letting go. I love Brazos Bend, and I want it to always be a part of my life, but that is easily done. You, Tess, *are* my life. There's no choice there."

He said it so simply, so honestly, that her heart melted.

"I needed to let go of the fear and the guilt that had ruled me for the past couple years," Nick continued. "The only way to do that was to rejoin the world. That's what I've done. I've rented office space, hired an assistant. I'm already licensed to practice in California. Did that back when I worked with the Rangers organization."

"Here? You're opening a law practice here?"

"Not corporate. I liked helping the Brazos Bend seniors, so that's what I'll do here."

"You're moving to California," she stated, needing to hear it said flat-out.

"Yes. I don't have a house yet. I'm hoping you'll have a suggestion in that regard."

"You did it," she said, wonder melting through her. "You did what I was afraid to do. You trusted in our love enough to risk everything for it."

He took a step toward her, reached for her hand. "That's where you're wrong. It's the one thing you had wrong that night. Whether it's conducted in Brazos Bend, Texas, or Los Angeles, California, love is a risky business. I'll give you the time you asked for, Tess, and I'll do everything I can to prove that our—how did you put it? Our fairy-tale romance? I'll do everything I can to prove that our fairy-tale romance will work in the real world. But take it from someone who knows. Life can't always be safe. Love will never be safe. I'm willing to risk my heart on you. Will you give me the same promise?"

This was, she thought, like a scene out of a movie. A very romantic movie. A grand gesture by a larger-than-life hero. A fantasy come to life.

The predictable ending would be for her to melt into his arms and pledge her undying love. But would that be a satisfying ending? Would it be the *right* ending?

She could all but hear Adele Watkin's voice echoing through her mind. "*Lord love a duck, girl. Turn down Nick Sutherland? What, are you too stupid to live?*"

No. She was a smart, successful talent manager who knew a good script when she saw it. This script was not only good, it was Oscar-worthy. Except, the ending was just a little off.

"Um...Tess? There's a question on the table."

She took his hands in hers. "Yes, and it's the wrong question. Your heart is safe with me, Nick Sutherland. It's the most precious gift I've ever been given, and I will treasure it all my life. As far as *my* heart goes —" She shrugged. "It's not at risk because you already own it. You take care of what's yours. That's who you are."

He brought her hands up to his mouth and kissed them.

"However," she continued, staring deep into his eyes. "You're in Hollywood now. You may be a movie buff, but I know the industry. I'm not signing up for a remake of *Risky Business*. I want *From Here to Eternity*."

He angled his head and studied her, then his lips twisted in a slow, sexy smile. "Hmm...*From Here to Eternity*. That beach scene."

"I have a house on the beach."

"Oh, yeah?" He pulled her against him, dipped his head, and nuzzled her neck. "Maybe we should go rehearse. I feel an Academy Award performance coming on."

Heat rushed through her as she mentally blocked the scene. Salt air. Warm sand. A frothy surf lapping at their naked bodies, entwined. Sunlight glinting from the wedding bands on their fingers.

It was, she thought, the perfect ending.

EPILOGUE

THE FIRST ANONYMOUS donation arrived at the office of the Brazos Bend Ladies' Benevolent Society. The second appeared in the mailbox of Bethania Hospital's outpatient hospice program. Over the course of the following week, every church in town, every charitable organization, from the Girl Scouts to the Veterans of Foreign Wars to the Men's Glee Club, received a substantial financial gift from an unidentified source.

The following August, on the eve of the McKinney twins' first birthday, Chloe and the girls met Kate Cooper and her son, Kyle, for their daily stroll through the neighborhood. Passing the Widow Duncan's house, they watched as a dog chased a cat, knocking over the widow's trash can. The women paused to clean up the mess, which included, they saw, a blue duffel bag.

Resuming their walk, Chloe observed, "Makes me think of that old country saying about money being a lot like manure."

Kate adjusted the stroller's sun shield, keeping her son's face comfortably in the shadows. "I know that one. Piled up in one place, it stinks something fierce."

Together, the two women said, "But spread around, it does a lot of good."

The End

ALSO BY EMILY MARCH

The Brazos Bend Contemporary Romance Series
MY BIG OLD TEXAS HEARTACHE
THE LAST BACHELOR IN TEXAS
The Callahan Brothers Trilogy
LUKE—The Callahan Brothers
MATT—The Callahan Brothers
MARK—The Callahan Brothers
A CALLAHAN CAROL

The Eternity Springs Contemporary Romance Series
ANGEL'S REST
HUMMINGBIRD LAKE
HEARTACHE FALLS
MISTLETOE MINE
LOVER'S LEAP
NIGHTINGALE WAY
REFLECTION POINT
MIRACLE ROAD
DREAMWEAVER TRAIL
TEARDROP LANE

HEARTSONG COTTAGE
REUNION PASS
CHRISTMAS IN ETERNITY SPRINGS
A STARDANCE SUMMER
THE FIRST KISS OF SPRING
THE CHRISTMAS WISHING TREE

And, SEASON OF SISTERS, a stand alone women's fiction novel.

The Bad Luck Wedding Historical Romance Series
THE BAD LUCK WEDDING DRESS
THE BAD LUCK WEDDING CAKE
Bad Luck Abroad Trilogy
SIMMER ALL NIGHT
SIZZLE ALL DAY
THE BAD LUCK WEDDING NIGHT
Bad Luck Brides Quartet
HER BODYGUARD
HER SCOUNDREL
HER OUTLAW
THE LONER
Stand Alone Historical Romances
THE TEXAN'S BRIDE
CAPTURE THE NIGHT
THE SCOUNDREL'S BRIDE
THE WEDDING RANSOM
THE COWBOY'S RUNAWAY BRIDE

ABOUT THE AUTHOR

Emily March is the *New York Times, Publishers Weekly*, and *USA Today* bestselling author of over thirty novels, including the critically acclaimed Eternity Springs series. Publishers Weekly calls March a "master of delightful banter," and her heartwarming, emotionally charged stories have been named to Best of the Year lists by *Publishers Weekly, Library Journal,* and Romance Writers of America. A graduate of Texas A&M University, Emily is an avid fan of Aggie sports and her recipe for jalapeño relish has made her a tailgating legend.

Fort more information

www.emilymarch.com

emily@emilymarch.com

Made in the USA
Middletown, DE
18 July 2020